THE ROAD TO
CATHAY

KHAN-BHALIC
(PEKIN)

PE LU

MOUNTAINS

KINSAI
(HANGCHOW)

YANG-TSE RIVER

TROPIC OF CANCER

90°

100°

110°

120°

130°

The Black Rose

BOOKS BY

THOMAS B. COSTAIN

The Black Rose

Ride with Me

For My Great Folly

Joshua: A Study in Leadership
(*in collaboration with Rogers MacVeagh*)

THOMAS B. COSTAIN

The Black Rose

DOUBLEDAY & COMPANY, INC.

Garden City, New York

1946

To

DORA

Contents

		PAGE
INTRODUCTION	. . . .	ix

Book One

CHAPTER

I	OXFORD	. . . .	1
II	GURNIE	. . . .	34
III	BULAIRE	. . . .	54
IV	LONDON	. . . .	90

Book Two

V	ANTIOCH	. . . .	106
VI	MARAGHA	. . . . . .	126
VII	THE SNOWY MOUNTAINS	. . .	161
VIII	THE PE LU	. . . . . .	193
IX	THE YANG–TSE	. . . .	215
X	KINSAI	. . . .	224
XI	THE ABODE OF EVERLASTING FELICITY	. . . . .	256

Book Three

XII	ENGLAND	. . . .	288
XIII	KONKAN (*Bombay*)	. . . . . .	317

vii

CHAPTER		PAGE
XIV	LITTLE TAMITT	321
XV	VENICE	344
XVI	SCAUNDER CLOUGH	353
XVII	MARSEILLES	373
XVIII	LEEDS CASTLE	379
XIX	THE SIGN OF THE MERRYTOTTER	394

Introduction

My previous books have been built around historical characters, men who had accomplished rather remarkable things but had been almost completely forgotten. I started *The Black Rose* with three great men in mind. One was a king of England, the greatest of English kings in my humble opinion, Edward the First, sometimes called the Lawgiver. His determination to conquer Scotland cast a shadow on his memory, but in spite of that he was a man of serious and noble purpose and the real father of parliamentary rule. The second was a Mongolian general briefly mentioned in histories as Bayan of the Hundred Eyes, who conquered China for Kublai Khan in a series of brilliant campaigns. Time has draped thick cobwebs over this page of history, and only the bare outline of Bayan's aggressive warmaking can be seen, but I have a very strong conviction that, if military historians were in a position to study his operations, they would rank him high on the roster of generalship. The third was Roger Bacon. Interest in this extraordinary friar has grown with the years until today it amounts almost to a cult, and so it is not necessary to say anything about him save to register my personal belief that he was potentially the greatest scientist the world has produced.

That these remarkable men adorned one span of years in what otherwise was a dark page of the Dark Ages was a chance not to be overlooked, and so I set myself the task of inventing a tale in which all three would figure prominently. However, the story which grew out of my efforts refused to be subordinated to the narration of history. It took the bit in its teeth and left me no chance to do more than introduce my three enthusiasms at rare intervals; but in spite of the fact that none of the illustrious trio appears except in brief scenes, their accomplishments dictate the direction of the story.

The story itself grows out of a legend, a most beguiling and romantic legend which is found in a very few old English histories. As I have endeavored to retain an element of surprise to the very end of the book, it would be highly inexpedient to relate here, before the story begins, just what this legend was. All I can afford to say, therefore, is that it concerns an English crusader, who later became the father of Thomas à Becket, and an Eastern girl who knew just two words of English. It is pure legend, of course, but it has always seemed to me too engaging a tale to be buried away between the covers of forgotten histories; and so I have borrowed it and adapted it to my needs.

It should be mentioned also that the incident of the imprisonment of the children in Bulaire Castle is based on a story from Scottish history which is mentioned briefly in Sir Walter Scott's *Tales of a Grandfather.*

To forestall possible criticism I wish to say that I have not been "riving a bow beyond my reach" in the incident of the building of the ship in the Arsenal at Venice. Authentic records show that the urgent needs of the war with Turkey drove the Venetians to the construction of ships in a single day and that, moreover, they had conceived the idea of the assembly line, although they did not call it that. They were splendid ships that they built, great wooden biremes with towering superstructures and an imposing spread of sail. Speed, it is clear, is not an invention of the present day.

In addition to an almost endless labor of research, I have kept many books in front of me all through the arduous work which has gone into the writing of this story: Three volumes by Harold Lamb, *Genghis Khan, The March of the Barbarians, The Crusades,* several versions of Marco Polo, Agnes Strickland's sketch of Queen Eleanor from her *Lives of the Queens of England,* a number of Chinese histories, Pearl S. Buck's remarkable translation of *All Men Are Brothers,* by Shui Hu Chuan. Without these, and others too numerous to mention, the task of presenting this rather detailed picture of a colorful time would have been an impossible one.

THOMAS B. COSTAIN

The Black Rose

Book One

CHAPTER I

Oxford

IT WAS GROWING LATE, and still there was no sign of Engaine. Could Ninian have been mistaken? A roke had settled in early that afternoon, and the rain dripped from the roofs of Oxford with a dismal insistence. Walter had placed himself under the entrance at St. Martin's, but the fear that he might miss her led him to venture out constantly around all the points of the Quadrivium. He was wet to the skin.

Church bells began to toll. Ordinarily they had a profound effect on him, particularly at the close of day in Oxford, for there was something in the atmosphere of the gray old town which lent an additional solemnity to the tolling and fitted the sound to every mood. They could ring loud and resonant like a call to battle; they could be gay and exciting, giving a lift to the heart as well as the heels; they could be slow and sad with a warning of the futility of this earthly life; but mostly they were as sweet and ravishing as the swish of a swift's wings, bringing a lump of happiness to the throat.

But today Walter felt only impatience as he counted the strokes. Four o'clock! Was Engaine really riding up from London with her father, or had it been another of Ninian's stupid jokes? He began to suspect the latter, but he dared not give up his vigil. He had not seen Engaine for nearly two years, and Ninian had been hinting that she was soon to wed. It would be two more years before he returned home from the university; if he did not catch a glimpse of her now, he might never see her again.

A beggar with wet bare legs and a face blue from the damp and cold came up the steps of the church. As a matter of habit he began his usual quaver of, "Alms, fair sir!", holding out his wooden clackdish. Then he slanted a look at the wet student lurking in the stone entrance, and a scornful laugh took the place of the professional whine.

"Gown!" he exclaimed, with a thumb at his splayed nose. "I'm of a mind to rob my own buskin and flip ye a coin, ye starved kestril!"

Another hour passed. Walter shivered with the cold, very nearly convinced now that there would be no party riding through to Tressling. He should have been sensible, he said to himself, and spent the time at his studies. He still had so much to learn! But still he lingered, nursing the dregs of hope. Not a single pedestrian had crossed the Quadrivium in the last half hour. No sound was to be heard but the drip, drip of the rain.

Then his heart gave a bound. A clatter of hoofs sounded from the direction of the east, and a dozen or more riders on horseback came clomping over the cobbles. His doubts were resolved when he saw a mud-splattered whirlicote creaking along in the rear of the procession. Engaine's mother was an invalid and did all her traveling on wheels.

It was not his purpose to be seen, so he hugged close to one of the pillars. The squire in the lead spied him, nevertheless, and reined in his horse, calling out in a peremptory voice: "You, fellow! Which turn d'we take for the Chelt'am Road?"

Walter was giving hurried instructions, without leaving his secluded post, when another rider drew level with the squire. Under a heavy fur hood he saw the green of a *couvre-chef,* and under that again the sparkle of the loveliest blue eyes in all the world. It was Engaine!

"Walter of Gurnie!" she cried. As usual there was more than a hint of mockery in her voice. "What do you here, good Walter? Have you lingered overlong at your orisons? Surely you should be back at your books."

"I heard you were to ride through from London," he answered.

"And you waited in this rain to see me?" Clearly she was much pleased. She raised a glove to brush back the encroaching scarf and smiled at him. "I am very much flattered. But such devotion would more become one who strives to fit himself for the vows of knighthood, Sir Clerk."

Her father reined in beside her and scowled at Walter. The lord of Tressling was always in his cups, and there was an unsteadiness now to the hand with which he wiped his brow.

"The whelp of Gurnie!" he said. Then he threw back his head and indulged in a loud roar of laughter. "Well met! You may take a message to your grandfather. Tell the old nip-cheese he has been wasting his time." Then he turned to his daughter. "How often, child, must I tell you not to demean yourself in this way? This baseborn fellow is beneath your notice."

Walter's pride got the better of his discretion. He walked down the steps to the street level. "The Gurnie strain is a nobler one than Tressling, my lord," he said. "We have held our land for more than five centuries."

The lord of Tressling laughed again. "You crow loudly, my young cockerel, for one who can't claim an honest share of that noble blood," he said. "Come, girl, on with you! We must make Tressling if we ride all night."

"But Mother is ill," protested Engaine. "She can't travel much farther tonight."

"It's that lumbering coach which has held us back!" said her father. "I'll have no more of this endless packing and unpacking, this mewling over sheets and blankets, and running for hot possets and espicier's pills! We ride straight through, I tell you." He turned for a final besotted word with Walter. "Count yourself lucky I don't have my man Gullen here beat a proper respect into you, fellow. Stand back!"

Walter could no longer restrain himself. "I have no fear of Black Gullen nor of you, thief of Tressling!" he said.

The master of the train could not have heard him, for he turned and rode off. But Engaine stiffened in her saddle and tossed her head. Her furred boot tapped the flank of her horse angrily.

"Farewell, Toftman!" she cried.

Toftman! It was the supreme insult in Walter's ears. The fact that no more than a few beggarly tofts of land were left to Gurnie galled him as much as the cloud on his birth. He was stammering to find an answer when Engaine turned with one of her unpredictable shifts of mood.

"You are wet through, Walter," she said. "That cloak is too thin for such weather. You must change into dry clothes at once."

He did not move until the whirlicote, its complaining wheels grinding and sloshing, had passed him. By this time Engaine had vanished from sight on one of the roads which fanned out from the Quadrivium. Then he walked back up the steps, without conscious purpose, and entered the church.

There were lights at the altar, and the verger was pottering about at the far end of the nave. Walter sat down on the nearest bench in a mood of such overwhelming dejection that he lost all consciousness of time.

He had always known that his devotion to Engaine was hopeless. His grandfather had taken up arms with Simon de Montfort in the struggle against Old King Henry to enforce observance of the Great Charter. After the lost battle of Evesham, where great Earl Simon was killed, most of the lands of Gurnie were confiscated and given as a reward to the lord of Tressling who had fought (not too boldly, it was whispered) on the royal side. More than eight years had passed since then, eight years of poverty for his grandfather's household and of great prosperity for Tressling. The hatred between the two families had grown with the years. Walter's love for the heiress of the other house had, necessarily, been a matter that he tried to keep to himself. He had taken long walks to places where a glimpse might be had of her, particularly to Tressling church, where he would feast hungrily on her profile. Sometimes she would ride by with hawk on wrist and would draw in for a few moments and a few bantering words; ecstatic moments for him, to be treasured and conned over and worn on his heart as knights flaunted favors on their lances. Once he had smuggled a note to her by a servant in whom he could put trust; a note of adolescent passion, filled with his hopes and his dreams, and vowing his eternal devotion. It had been a blow to hear, on the next occasion when they met, that she had been able to read no more than half of it. That she blamed this on his handwriting and not on her own lack of scholarship had not seemed quite fair, for even then he had wielded a pen with clerkly precision.

He was now more convinced than ever of the hopelessness of it, and yet with the blind optimism of youth, which will grasp at straws after conceding a fact, he took some comfort from her last words. She had always liked him, in a careless and superior way, and she had given fresh proof of this by her concern over his condition. If only things had been different! If only the domain of Gurnie still stretched as nobly as before the Norman Conquest! If——

What was it her father had said? "Tell the old nip-cheese he has been wasting his time." This could have one meaning only. At the prompting of Old Harry's son, since crowned Edward the First though absent at the last of the Crusades, many of the confiscated estates had been returned to their former owners. Walter's grandfather had been besieging the royal ministers with petitions for a reconsideration of his case, and the hope had never been abandoned that the rolling acres of Gurnie would be restored. Engaine's father must have received assurances that this would not be done. Perhaps his journey to London had been for this very purpose.

Walter wondered if he should write his grandfather, but decided, reluctantly, that he dare not break the rule which prohibited him from addressing the old man directly.

The fervor which possessed every mind in these days of intense religious feeling caused him to slip forward to his knees. He began to pray in an undertone. "Gracious Father in Heaven, and good St. Aidan, in whom I have so often confided, grant me the opportunity to prove my devotion. Even if the bars between us may never be raised, permit me to stand better in her eyes."

2

Night had settled down blackly over the dripping eaves of Oxford when he left the church. He turned and ran in haste through the maze of crooked lanes lying back of St. Martin's, an instinctive fear lending speed to his heels.

The strangest thing about life at the university was that the clerkly body professed no fear of the night. At home it was far different. They lived in the shadow of many fears at Gurnie, but the one which weighed most on all minds was the certainty that the hours of darkness belonged to the devil. Walter had often watched with tightening breath the descent of the sun behind the jagged frame of oak at Algitha Scaur, half expecting to see the tips of Satan's horns above the horizon. The plowfolk came running from the fields when daylight was gone as though a covin of witches screeched at their heels. Good Father Clement pulled lustily on the bells when a storm threatened with the passing of day; nay, he was often seen issuing forth with holy water to exorcise the demons which came with the blackness and on the scud of the wind. No one breathed easily until the shutters at Gurnie were bolted to the mullions and Agnes Malkinsmaiden had brought in supper and the ale which put new courage in unsteady stomachs.

Walter knew no sound more welcome than the crow of the first cock in the morning. The old house revived to confidence then. One could hear whistling and snatches of song as the servants and the plowfolk tied up their points and sloshed cold water over their heads at the well near the kitchen midden. God's turn had come again and all was well in the world.

But here at Oxford life took on a stronger beat with the fall of darkness. The students issued forth then with surcotes gathered close around their waists to conceal the sharp blades they wore at their belts in place of ink-cases. They were filled with the prospect of adventure; a tryst with a tavern wench, perhaps, or a brush with the citizens of the town. There was zest in their voices as they shouted, "A clerk! A clerk!" to other groups passing in the narrow streets. Sometimes this deepened into a note of urgency when there was trouble with the watch; and then, at the rallying cry of *Surgite! Surgite!* the students came tumbling out of tavern and hospitium and dark garret to aid their hard-pressed brethren. The men of Oxford seemed to love the dark, but this was not because they had lost all their fear of the devil. They went to confession as apprehensive and shamefaced as the most nervous of sinners. Rather it was because the mantle of night made it easier for them to forget their youth and to strut like the bold rufflers they fancied themselves to be.

For two reasons Walter seldom went out with his fellows. The first was his desire to get on with his studies. He could hardly wait for the day when his knowledge of Latin and Greek, and the smattering of Arabic and Hebrew he was so painfully acquiring, could be put to practical use. Since the Crusades the eyes of men who needed to mend their fortunes had turned to the East. He wanted to hear the jingle of tower pounds in his pockets. He hoped a time would come when Engaine could no longer look at him with her green-blue eyes and say, "Toftman!" with so much scorn.

The second reason was his intense sensitivity on the score of his birth. His fellow clerks at Butterbump Hall (so called because they used a bittern for their house sign) had come to consider him a very prickly sort of fellow. He regretted his unpopularity but seemed unable to do anything about it. When cloaks were being donned for a nightly foray into the streets, he would want to say, "Wait for me, my masters of arts; I'm not a bad fellow, after all." But he would stifle the impulse, saying to himself: "They don't want you. Surely they've made that clear enough. Where's your pride, you fool!"

His love of Oxford was almost fanatical; but he was not happy there.

When he reached the hospitium, he found that his long wait had cost him his supper, but his regret was tempered by the odor seeping through the screens at the entrance which told him that Giles had served fish again. In all probability it had not been fresh. Would any of the clerks smuggle battles (the term they used for food consumed after hours) to their room upstairs later in the evening? If they did, he reflected ruefully, they would not invite him to share.

He had intended to settle down with St. Anselm's *Monologium* but the solar bedroom was filled with the sound of voices reading aloud. He wondered if he would dare say what was in his mind, that in France and all other really learned countries it was considered a lack of scholarship not to be able to read to yourself. Then he noticed that Ninian was reaching down his fur-lined hood from the wall. Ninian was privileged to wear this distinguishing mark of the nobility because his father was a warden on the Welsh border. Walter's father was an earl, but he himself was compelled nevertheless to wear a plain hood.

Ninian stalked over to where Walter was standing. "Bastard," he said, "I must have a talk with you, and I don't want these louts to hear. Come out with me."

Everything about him irked Walter: his assumption of superiority, his way of mumbling his words, the slackness of his lower jaw, and above all else his standing with Engaine.

"I've just come in and I'm wet now, as you must see. The candles will be snuffed in another hour, and I need every minute of the time."

"I'll let you have my quintus," grumbled Ninian. "It's a new one, and you'll have to be damnably careful of it." Then he frowned in his superior way. "Your manners will bear mending, Bastard."

"My manners are my own. I am quite content with them."

The warden's son found it hard to accept this disregard of his wishes. He rubbed his jaw and continued to frown. "You make me as angry as a kibed heel. But, after all, you are of noble degree and that makes a difference. If you'll come," he added, in a more amiable tone, "I will speak to Giles and have him get us some battles."

This put a different face on the matter. Walter realized that he was very hungry. "A cut of cold beef?" he asked.

Ninian nodded and clinked the coins in his purse. "Beef or mutton, whichever he can get. Perhaps I'll pay for a nook of pastry as well." He lowered his voice. "I want to talk to you about Engaine."

Walter threw his own wet surcote into a corner and donned the proffered quintus. He had never possessed one of these new and highly fashionable cloaks, and he strutted unconsciously when the fur collar had been fastened at the neck.

"I sorely begrudge you your inches," said Ninian, looking up at him enviously. "And why should you have both a Norman arch to your nose and that yellow hair? If I had some share of your looks, Engaine might think better of me."

They began to descend the inside staircase (a matter of great pride with the inmates of Butterbump Hall, for most of the houses in Oxford had stairs on the outside), and Ninian proceeded to tell his troubles.

"I have to confess that I'm disturbed about something I have just heard. Engaine and I are first cousins, but it has always been understood in the two families that we would marry. Naturally I favor the match. She will come into all the holdings of Tressling, and then, of course, she is quite handsome and a gamesome little wench. I won't be able to match her in lands, but I shall have the manors of Barlay from my mother's side and a goodish stretch of timber on the border. I am not a beggar exactly. And now," an aggrieved note had crept into his voice, "I hear her drunken old father has other plans. A fatter fish is dangling on the line. What would you do in my case, Bastard? You have a shrewd head on your shoulders even if you are such a cross-grained bandog, and of course you have no love for Tressling. I value your opinion. Would you go straight to the old wine sot and demand your rights?"

Walter felt a deeper concern over this unexpected revelation than the mincing Ninian. "Who is this other suitor?" he asked.

"I am not sure. They are being very sly about it at Tressling. But," with an attempt at bluster, "I have my suspicions, and I have no intention of stepping aside."

They had reached the front door when the agitated patter of Master Matthias Hornpepper's feet sounded behind them. The principilator of the Hall was a tubby little man with a long sullen nose and a constant sense of grievance. His duties kept him in such a state of turmoil that he was seldom seen, no matter what the season or the time, without perspiration on his brow.

The principilator cleared his throat nervously. "Ah, hum! Good Master Ninian!" he called after them. "A word with you, young gentleman."

Ninian muttered, "Now what does that greasy old jolthead want?" He faced about. "I am going out. I have no time to talk to you now, Master Hornpepper. You are a mangy nuisance, Master Hornpepper, and I think we must be getting ourselves a new principilator."

Master Hornpepper said in a humble voice, "I have had a serious complaint about you."

"What is wrong with this unreasonable knave?" demanded Ninian. "I pay him ten pence a week though I know he collects no more than eight from anyone else. Isn't it enough that he robs me without making my head ring with his eternal complaints?"

"It is about—well, it is about a girl. And it comes from an esquire bedel of the university."

It was apparent that Ninian was startled. A defensive gleam showed in his weak gray eyes.

"It appears," said Master Hornpepper, "that you have been most imprudent, if I may make so bold as to comment on your conduct. The girl has been foolish enough to—ahem—to get herself with child."

Ninian looked still more startled for a moment. Then a self-conscious smile spread over his long, sallow countenance. It was clear that he was pleased.

"By St. Frideswide, that is worth hearing!" he said. "My father will be proud of me. I have often heard him say a man is not a man until he has brought six bastards into the world."

"It will be a scandal, a very great scandal!" protested the principilator. "Poor Thomas Tavener's face was as white as wax when he spoke to me about it. He has always doted on his daughter, and he is quite broken over the shame you have brought her."

"Shame?" exclaimed Ninian. "Don't you see it is the best possible luck for her? There will be noble blood in her child. A settlement will be made, of course; my father will see to that. Enough to keep her, and the little bastard as well when he arrives."

Walter was having the greatest difficulty in keeping his hands from his companion's throat. Men used the word "bastard" as casually as "Good morrow" or "God rest you," but he had never become reconciled to it. Every time it was applied to him, he would think of his mother's pale face and the sorry circumstances under which she lived at Gurnie, and an inner rage would take possession of him.

They became aware at this point that they had an audience. A loud laugh sounded from the Squint in the oak screens, and the voice of Humphrey Armstraung from the west country said, "So, our highborn Ninian has been drabbing!" He appeared from behind the screens, a broad grin under the round hat he wore as a full bachelor of arts. Armstraung, generally known as the Utterly Masterful Hump, was the acknowledged leader of the Hall. Several others followed him, Rob Wynter from the Fens and Ludar Fitzberg from Ireland, among them.

The principilator clucked with dismay. "Young sirs, young sirs," he cried. "I did not know we had witnesses! No whisper of this must get out. We must think of the good name of the Hall."

"We'll keep mum," grumbled Armstraung. "Though, to my mind, it would add something to our good name if it got out."

The others nodded their assent. Walter could tell, from the way they were looking at Ninian, that the prospective father had risen mightily in their regard.

"By St. Christopher!" cried the Utterly Masterful Hump, slapping him on the back approvingly. "Here he is, a hawk among the little dab-chicks, and none of us suspected it."

"If it's a boy, you can turn him over to the king," suggested the Irishman, looking slyly at Walter. "That seems to be the right way with bas-tard sons, though some fathers prefer not to claim them."

As a mark of their change of sentiment toward the erring Ninian, they all decided to go along, and there was a rush to find cloaks. The roke had dwindled when they issued forth, seven in all, and the only discomfort they felt was underfoot.

"Where to, my wag?" demanded Hump, slapping Ninian on the back a second time. "You have the right tonight to call the tune. And pay the piper, of course."

Ninian was brimming over with gratification. "To Timothy-Two-Tunes!" he cried, recklessly. "Timothy will sing for us, and we'll have a pinch of fennel in our ale."

The tavern of Timothy-Two-Tunes was crowded when they arrived, mostly with university men of the more prosperous stripe. There were clerks from Peckwater's Inn and St. Mary's Entry and Leadenporch Hall and the Saracen's Head. At first glance Walter thought they were all Artists and, therefore, devoted to the Trivium, which consisted of grammar, rhetoric, and logic as well as Latin. He finally saw one Legist, a moist sort of fellow whose tongue was wagging about pollgreat taxes and the other dull matters which would concern him when he became a full-fledged lawyer. A priest was seated in front of the fire with the skirt of his soutane tucked up over his knees. He could be set down for a chantry priest at a glance, being fat and unconcerned of mien. The chantry brethren had no duties but to say prayers for the souls of departed patrons.

"The heaven-beck is soaking up all the heat," grumbled Hump. It was the habit of the moment at Oxford to affect irreverence. "There's no decency about a back as broad as that. Think of all the good mutton and ale needed to keep such a carcass alive! Why isn't he where he belongs, saying his *aves* for the poor soul who depends on him to escape from frying in purgatory?"

Ninian called to Timothy-Two-Tunes: "Landlord, ale for seven. And, mind you, a drop of fennel in each."

Timothy, who was singing at the other end of the room, paid no at-

tention. He pressed the wheel of his rote against the strings and went on
with his song. It was a new melody and the words of the refrain had a
curious catch to them:

"Away to Cathay.
Away! Away!"

His daughter Dervagilla came to wait on them instead. She was a
dumpling-breasted trollop who kept herself free of unwelcome attentions
by boasting so openly of her lustiness that no one dared make an advance. Settling her hands on her broad hips, she looked at Ninian scornfully and said: "Ale, is it, and fennel? Ye'll be more polite, if ye please,
or it's a pinch of mugwort and not fennel ye'll be getting." Turning to
the rest of them, she said in a whisper out of one corner of her mouth,
"If I ever got him in bed with me, I would break his back, the milting
little hinny!"

The Legist was prating now of young King Edward and what he
would do when he returned from the Crusades. "We are going to have
a real king at last. He'll put fleas under the tails of the proud barons!
Their power will be taken away from them, and we'll have peace and
order in the land again."

Peace and order in the land, with the king's power as absolute as
when wicked John tried to set all rights at naught! The fellow was mad,
Walter said to himself, to talk such nonsense.

"If there's peace and order in the land, how will lawyers make a
living?" he asked.

Hump Armstraung said to the Legist, "Pay no heed to the Bastard; he
always has a bullbeggar riding his back."

Walter made no answer. He got to his feet and walked to the other
side of the room, where he found a seat on a wooden bench. He would
have no part in such talk. The new ruler had all the kingly qualities of
the Plantagenets, that much he acknowledged—the courage and the
bitter pride as well as the tall frame, the kindling eye, and the golden
hair. They were handsome men, the Plantagenet kings. But Edward had
killed Simon de Montfort at Evesham, great Earl Simon who had fought
for the rights of the people, and his father, Old King Harry, had taken
away the lands of Gurnie. Edward the First would have no fealty from
him!

He tried to catch Ninian's eye in the hope that the latter would now
join him for their talk. What was this ominous story he had heard
about Engaine? A fatter fish dangling on the line! This could mean only

that the lord of Tressling was planning an early marriage for his daughter and heiress.

He had never been much concerned over Ninian's pretensions. But who was this more worthy suitor now in the offing? The thought of Engaine married was like a dagger thrust to the heart.

Ninian continued to snigger over his ale and never once looked in his direction. What was the matter with the fellow? Had he forgotten their reason for coming out?

The Legist finished his tiresome talk. The chantry priest hove around on his stool and winked at the company. "The uneasy soul of my deceased patron is skipping briskly," he said. "I must get back to my devotions on his behalf. I live well enough on the gold he left, and so it behooves me to keep him from roasting too long."

Walter sat up suddenly on the hard bench. A loud uproar had risen in the streets. Above the clamor of angry voices came the signal to which all clerks responded wherever they were:

"*Surgite! Surgite!*"

Walter found himself on his feet, his hand tugging with nervous haste at the knife in his belt. Armstraung sprang up with such violence that he upset the chantry priest, who rolled on the floor on his fat backsides, his legs waving in the air like those of an overturned bug. Ninian was protesting, "It's no concern of ours," but no one was paying any attention to him. They were out in the street in a trice, shouting eagerly, "A clerk! A clerk!"

3

The riot which ensued on that damp evening in the year of our Lord 1273 would be remembered as long as there were students at Oxford to recall the excitements of the past. To Walter it would always be memorable as the occasion of his meeting Tristram.

He had played a part in many pleasant little melees with the town watch, but he saw at once that this was going to be different. The students raced down Queen Street until they came to the meeting of the five ways at the Quadrivium. There they encountered the watch in full force. Two of their fellows had been taken prisoner. Their arms had been trussed behind them, and meal sacks had been pulled down over their heads. The unlucky pair were still struggling frantically, but to no purpose at all.

There was a grim air about the men of the watch. They were armed to the teeth, for one thing, with heavy épaulières on their shoulders and iron morions on their heads. Their eyes mocked the new arrivals from behind a solid hedge of brown-bills, and even the ring of their clout-nails on the cobblestones had a new note of resolution about it. Some of the townspeople had taken possession of the tower of St. Martin's and were pelting the clerks with stones and loud abuse.

The Legist said, "They've got Jack Punshon and Rick Standlack."

"Stout fellows, both of them," answered Hump Armstraung, who had assumed command of the party. "And sophisters, too. What were they doing?"

"I hear there was an argument at the Blue Baldric," said the Legist. "Over the price of a roast goose. They swallowed their share before confessing that their pockets were empty. The landlord swore he would take it out of their hides, but Jack got hold of the spit on which Tib-o'-the-Buttery had been roasted and broke his head with it. I hear," and there was a note of envy in his voice, "that it was a grand fight while it lasted."

"What are they going to do with Jack and Rick?"

"Take them to Greenditch."

"To hang them?" cried Hump, aghast. "We're not subject to town authority. That has been established time and again."

"They know it too well," agreed the Legist, sourly. "So they are not going to wait for due processes of law this time. They're going to see to it that Jack and Rick dance on thin air, and then argue the point later. What's more, there doesn't seem to be anything we can do about it."

Hump looked at the glittering ring of brown-bills which held the students back. He shook his head. *"Ad impossibile nemo tenetur,"* he said. "They would spit us like herrings if we tried to rush them."

More clerks were pouring onto the Quadrivium. Walter was sure they could force a rescue by sheer weight of numbers. He shouted in Hump's ear: "I for one am not content to stand by and do nothing. By St. Aidan, get our fellows together! One rush will break their line open."

"And will you lead the charge?"

"I am willing. But we must lose no time."

Hump frowned and said in an apologetic tone: "You've never known me to run away from a fight, Bastard. But will it help Jack and Rick if we all get our bellies ripped open on the points of their pikes?"

Ninian had come along after all, looking very unhappy over the situation. He asked in a bitter tone, "Why didn't they get to St. Giles in time and claim sanctuary?"

"They were given no chance," said Walter. "And so now we must do what we can. You, Hump, are looking forward to your trial flights as an aspirant knight. What better chance could you seek?"

Ninian quavered, "It would be sure death."

Hump nodded in glum agreement. "It would not be an honorable venture. What do you know of the laws of chivalry, Bastard?"

"Cowards!" Walter shouted at them.

Men of the town were now arriving in force, and it was evident they were in as determined mood as the watch. The usual battle between Town and Gown was developing, with clubs and quarter-staves as the weapons. Walter realized that while the townspeople fought it out with the students, the watch would march their prisoners off. They were moving down one of the side streets and were already so far along that the captain's, " 'Way there, for the King's justice!" could barely be heard.

Walter followed them, becoming aware after a moment that someone had fallen into step with him. It was a student, he was sure, and one so tall that his own chin could do no better than hobnob with the newcomer's shoulder. This irked him, for he was proud of his inches.

"You are Walter of Gurnie, I think," said the stranger.

"Yes. What's your name?"

"Tristram Griffen. I hail from your part of the country. You have never heard of me, but my father is the fletcher of Cencaster."

It was too dark to see with any clearness, but Walter decided that he liked the voice. It was respectful enough, as befitted a fletcher's son, and yet there was a resolute note in it as well. If he belonged to the student body, he must be a chamber-deacon; one of the despised clerks who lacked the means to lodge in any of the hospitia and so had to find quarters in the garrets of the town.

"I have watched Nat Griffen at the butts. There is no better bowman in all England," Walter said.

"He has never made such a claim. But—well, I think there was a time when he could draw a better bow than any man living. He's getting old, and he hasn't the strength in his arms now."

Walter looked at his companion. "I warrant you can draw a shrewd bow yourself, Tristram Griffen."

"I am good enough. But I never expect to see the day when I will be my sire's equal."

"Modestly spoken," thought Walter. Aloud, he asked, "Why haven't I seen you before?"

"I am a chamber-deacon and I lodge over a bookbinder's shop in Sheydyard Street. You have seen me, but of course you would not remember me." This was said without any bitterness—or humility, for that matter. The tone was completely matter-of-fact.

They were passing a house whose owner had come out on the steps with a torch to watch the excitement. By the light thus provided it could be seen that Tristram Griffen was magnificently built and with the broadest of shoulders. He had a thatch of stiff blond hair and a pleasant gray eye. He smiled, in a hesitant way, as though not sure how Walter would take such familiarity on his part.

Walter smiled back. He had always been slow to make friends, but he knew on the instant that he liked the fletcher's son in spite of the wide difference in their stations in life. There was forthrightness and good nature in his companion and the promise of a real staunchness of spirit.

The chamber-deacon was clearly very poor. His dagged surcote was of the roughest cloth known as falding, and his legs were bare from the knee down. His heavy boots were painted black, the distinguishing sign of low degree. "What of it?" thought Walter, "I like him better than any of them at the Hall."

"We can rescue them if we take the risk," said Tristram, nodding at the procession ahead. "I would rather have air through my ribs than stand by and see these two poor fellows taken away to be hanged."

"I feel the same way," responded Walter. "Can we count on any help? The rest seem content with making a lot of noise."

"There will be plenty to follow if we lead the way."

Tristram stopped and proceeded to take off his outer garment. Folding it carefully, he carried it to the side and laid it on the mounting-post in front of a darkened house. Then he found a loose paving stone and placed it on top.

"It's the only one I have," he explained with an apologetic smile. "I can afford a broken bone or two but not the loss of my warm jupon."

The crowd had grown denser, and the watch was moving more slowly as a result, the captain brandishing a short sword at intervals and declaiming in an indignant voice, "Keep clear o' the law, ye joltheads!"

The tall chamber-deacon rolled up his sleeves and asked, "Ready, Walter of Gurnie?"

"Ready." Walter's heart seemed to tighten in his chest. This would be a heady adventure, and he knew he might not come out of it alive.

"Wrap your cloak around your arm," advised the bowman's son. "It will serve as a shield. There is no sense in getting a pike point in your midriff."

"*You* have no cloak!" exclaimed Walter.

His companion had already gone into action. Moving with speed and an amazing energy, he lunged forward and buffeted the captain so vigorously that the head of the surprised officer snapped back in its iron morion. One large paw seized the limp watch leader by the neck while the other grasped him by the knee. With little effort the chamber-deacon raised the body on a level with his head and then catapulted it into the line. Two of the watch were bowled over, leaving a gap into which Tristram plunged with such force that in a very few moments he had disrupted their formation.

Walter followed his lead. Without knowing it, he was shouting the battle cry of the Crusades, "God wills it!" He had forgotten to wrap his cloak around his arm, but it made little difference at such close quarters. There was no chance to see if any of the other students had joined in, for he found himself immediately at grips with one of the watch, a mettlesome fellow who fought like a wildcat.

It proved a brief but sultry affair. The clerks in that vicinity had charged as soon as the gap opened in the line. They surged in with such fighting gusto, and in such numbers, that they soon filled the whole space inside the ring of bills. The ranks of the watch broke. The constables were hemmed in so closely that they could make no use of their pikes.

Walter was so busy with his stubborn antagonist that he did not realize the fight had been won until Tristram came to his assistance. Taking the fellow from behind by the neck, the chamber-deacon booted him exuberantly to the side of the road.

"Jack and Rick are free!" Tristram had to shout to make himself heard. Blood was streaming down his face, but he did not seem aware that he had been hurt. He grinned at Walter happily. "They're on their way to the chancellor now. That will be safer for them than sitting on the frith-stool at St. Giles."

Hump Armstraung had arrived on the scene and had already managed to reassert his leadership. Most of the students formed into line behind him, shouting the order to disengage and get away. They began to parade triumphantly down the street, singing in chorus the great marching song of the Crusades, "The Old Man of the Mountain."

"And now Hump will take all the credit for this," said Walter bitterly.

Receiving no reply, he turned and saw that his companion had halted a few paces back. He was looking down at the mounting-post where he had left his surcote. The paving stone was still there, but the coat was gone.

"Stolen!" Tristram exclaimed. His face looked almost gray.

The garment had been of the shoddiest kind, and it seemed impossible that its loss could mean so much. Walter said, lightly, "Tenpence will buy you another, Tristram."

"Tenpence? I have exactly that much in my pocket. But it must keep me until the end of the year."

Walter's expression changed immediately to one of concern. "You mean," he asked, "that you must live on as little as that?"

"Yes. It won't be easy, but I will manage it somehow. Many of us here in Oxford live on as little as a penny a week. Didn't you know?"

"I knew that most of the chamber-deacons had to work in their spare time."

"To earn the penny." Tristram nodded. "There is no call to look so disturbed about it. None of us starve." He looked at Walter with a cheerful grin. "It's a little harder for me because I have two to feed. I keep a pet. A badger."

"A badger! A curious kind of pet."

"I got her at a badger-draw. The dogs had dragged her out of the box three times, and I could see that once more would finish her. Her front paws were broken, and blood was running from her mouth. She was a game one, but—well, I imagined it, of course, but it seemed to me that she looked at me and begged for help. It's a cruel sport, and I couldn't stand there and see her killed. I stepped up and told them to call off their dogs. There was an uproar, naturally, but I knocked the draw-master down, and in the end I got her away from them." He smiled again. "I call her Boadicea. Because she was such a grand little fighting lady."

"But where do you keep her?"

"In my corner of the garret. She can't get around much on account of her legs. I have to take all her food to her, any scraps I can spare. She drags herself around after me when I'm there, and she always sleeps on the edge of my straw."

Walter's purse was empty, and he would have no more until his next visit to Father Francis, who kept the Chest at St. Frideswide's and paid him his two shillings at the first of each month. "You're tenpence richer than I am at the moment." he confessed.

"I was not asking for help! I can get along without a new jupon."

"But," protested Walter, "you lost it in the common cause. In all fairness we must take up a collection to replace it."

"No, no, I will get along." Tristram shook his head vigorously. Then he smiled again. "It may be a mild winter."

The main body of the students had marched off down the street by this time, and Walter sensed a new danger. The townspeople were eyeing the pair of them in a way that promised trouble.

"They will pay off the score on any of us they can catch," he whispered. "We must get away at once."

They made off without any delay. The fletcher's son had fallen into a thoughtful mood. "That fellow Townley, the captain of the watch, is a brother-in-law of the bookbinder I live with. They're a surly pair. I'm afraid they will make things hot for me."

"Then you can't risk going back there tonight." Walter frowned uneasily. This was a dilemma. He knew that he would not dare take a chamber-deacon to the Hall; the line there was drawn too closely for that. With some hesitation, he added: "I can't take you home with me. What's to be done?"

"I have couched a hogshead before this and I can do it again," said Tristram in an unconcerned tone.

"It will be a new experience for me."

They were in front of a tavern, and some light poured into the street through its partially opened door. Tristram squinted down into his companion's face to see if he meant it.

"By the Rood," he said, "that is a generous thought. But there is no need for it. I can fend for myself. You must get along now to your Hall and your own bed."

"We are in this together," said Walter. "If I can't take you through the sacred portals of Butterbump Hall, I can at least share a night in the open with you. That is settled, Tristram Griffen."

They finally found a dry spot under the outside stair of a house on the edge of the Jewry. Here the wind had deposited a soft bed of new-fallen leaves. Walter detached the warm quintus, and they huddled up together beneath it.

He began to find some amusement in the situation. "All these houses have glass in the windows," he whispered. "The Hall backs on the Jewry, and it's a favorite evening pastime with some of our fellows to watch the girls through the glass without their plackerds on. The owner of this cloak takes a special pleasure in it. I hope he's looking out and sees what a good use we are making of his finery."

Something moved in the leaves near Walter's feet, and he drew them up hurriedly. It was not going to be easy to sleep.

"I suppose," said Tristram, after a time, "you wonder what the son of a fletcher is doing in Oxford. It must seem presumptuous to you. You may not have known it, but there are many sons of common men here."

The thought had been at the back of Walter's mind since the moment they met. "I cannot see how you expect to profit by an education," he said. "Clearly you want to better your condition, but learning is not necessary for entrance to a trade guild or mistery; and what else is open to you? Do you intend to take Holy Orders?"

Tristram shook his head. "No, not that. What a waste of inches and brawn it would be to put this frame of mine into a brown frock and cowl! I belong on the land, but there will never be any land for me. I have set my mind on being a shipbuilder, and so I am on the matricula of Friar Roger Bacon."

"Roger Bacon!" Walter sat up and whistled with surprise.

He had good reason. It was said of Roger Bacon that he had a great reputation abroad for wisdom and learning, but in Oxford he was both scoffed at and feared. It was firmly believed by many that he had sold his soul to a vicar of the devil and that in return all the secrets of black magic had been revealed to him. When he walked the streets of the town, mothers dragged their children indoors and closed the shutters, that his shadow might not fall on them. Many other things were held against him in university circles. He sometimes lectured in English instead of in Latin, and that was a most grievous departure from sacred practice.

"It's generally believed," said Walter, after a moment, "that all who listen to what he teaches will end up at crossroads with stakes driven through their hearts."

"Friar Bacon," said Tristram earnestly, "is teaching me the truth about this world we live in. I am learning about navigation and the winds and the tides and the stars; how to make things, how to cast metal, how to figure accurately. Oh, I know it's said arithmetic should be left to Jews and couletiers, and that astronomy is only for magicians. But I need this knowledge if I am to build sound ships."

Walter was both puzzled and disturbed. "I have never given this matter much thought," he said. "I have always been taught to believe the so-called sciences vague and full of theory, too lacking in reality. There is no logic in science."

"I am not a scholar," answered Tristram. "I am sure you know now more than I can ever hope to learn. You have a fine reputation as a scholar all over Oxford, Walter of Gurnie. But I know one thing. The sciences are not vague. On the contrary they are exact. They are based on fact, proven fact."

"Do you imply that logic, on which all our teaching is based, is not built on fact?"

"I have never studied logic, but it seems to consist of finespun reasoning, all of which goes back to the dreams of dead philosophers."

"My teachers would call that illimitable heresy," declared Walter, employing the word which at the moment was so much on Oxford tongues that it threatened to become threadbare at its seat of use. "I have been taught to believe that reality belongs only in the realm of abstract thought. Man changes, but humanity does not change. Material things, being of the moment, have no importance. In days to come it may not be necessary to travel, and so it is unimportant to learn how to build sound ships. We need only to learn the established, ageless realities, the truths about humanity, bequeathed to us by the inspired thinkers of the past."

"Will you be angry if I say that seems to me nothing but illimitable nonsense?"

The wind had changed and was now blowing under the stair and dampening their faces with an occasional flurry of rain. Walter tried to protect his head by drawing up the fur-trimmed quintus, but discovered this left his legs completely exposed. He was finding it hard not to shiver openly. And yet, in spite of his growing discomfort, the debate was proving both disconcerting and stimulating.

"This has been a strange night," he said. "I find that I like you very much, Tristram Griffen. It never seemed possible before that anything in the way of mutual liking and intimacy could exist between men of different stations in life."

"We were born as far apart as heaven and hell," declared the fletcher's son. "And there must be just as much difference in what we think and believe. It puzzles me as much as it does you that you are ready to talk to me as though we were equals."

Walter began to laugh. "You will forgive me then if I say that never before did it seem possible that a common man could have opinions that were worth listening to. In fact, I think I was sure they were not mentally capable of having opinions. Now I am all turned around in my mind. By St. Aidan, I am even beginning to suspect you are learning more at Oxford than I am!"

"Strange as it may seem, God gave minds to common men and chamber-deacons."

They were both sitting up now, with the cloak wrapped around their knees. Walter realized that his hair was damp from the rain, which dripped down on them from the flimsy stair.

Tristram went on. "There is something I wish you would do. I will not dare show myself tomorrow, but you can do so safely enough, I think. Friar Bacon has a class at the hour of prime. Take my place there. Listen to what he has to say. It may open your mind still further."

After a moment's consideration, Walter nodded his head. "I came to Oxford to learn," he said. "Perhaps I owe it to myself to listen once to this mysterious friar. I will do as you suggest. Provided, of course," with a shiver he could not repress, "that I manage to live through the night."

4

Most classes were held in the churches of the town, but some of the masters had to find quarters elsewhere, in inns and even in private homes. Following the instructions he had received, Walter arrived at the Sign of the Ruffled Grouse, a tall house of stone and plaster in the east parish. The ground floor consisted of one large room and, when he entered, it was already filled almost to overflowing. Students sat on the reed-strewn floor, with knees hunched up to provide a resting place for ink and quill and parchment. There was no suggestion of fire in the reredos and, finding a place in a far corner, Walter wrapped his cloak about his legs to keep warm.

He had time to observe that the students were, almost without exception, poorly dressed. Certainly there was not a fur-lined hood in the room. All about him were close-cropped polls and serious faces. No one paid any attention to him.

Because of his position he could not see much of Roger Bacon when the latter entered the room; no more, in fact, than a single glimpse of a tonsured head above the brown cowl. He was conscious, nevertheless, of a sense of mounting excitement. The students about him had straightened up instantly like dogs on leash or horses set for a tilting. All he heard was the rustle of straw and rushes and the soft fall of the master's bare feet, and yet he felt as though a shout had gone up, the reverberations of which still filled the room.

"Today I shall speak the common tongue," began Friar Bacon. His voice was full and musical. "It is wise to do so because I propose to deal with the sciences and with certain wonderful things I have seen from afar much as you glimpse a star, half believing it within the reach of your hands and yet knowing full well that it lies an endless distance away across the great paths of heaven. When you speak of the sciences, even though they concern matters that can be demonstrated as truth, it is well to do so in the plainest of words lest the sense be fouled in the telling. Therefore I shall recite you my tales of wonder in the tongue we use when we tread the roads with our fellows and when we sit down to meat.

"Nevertheless, I must begin with a Latin phrase you have often heard." His voice was beginning to take on volume. "They say to you, *Credo ergo cognosco*—I believe therefore I know. It is said as though it came direct from the Word of God and must on that account be accepted without question. I question it, my young friends. Nay, I cast it out as being utterly false. I say to you instead, *Cognosco ergo credo*—I know therefore I believe!"

His voice fell off for a moment. By craning his neck around the shoulders of the man in front, Walter was able to get a clearer view of this daring friar. Roger Bacon, he saw, had a long and rather solemn face, with a hooked nose and a firm jaw. He would have seemed little different from any other Franciscan if it had not been for his eyes. They were deep-set, as brown as the robe he wore and vibrant with the bold and venturesome spirit of the man himself.

"He has none of the look of a dabbler in magic," thought Walter.

"If we are to learn," went on the monk, "we must clear our minds of the cobwebs of old teaching and the dust of dogma. It is so simple a matter to reach the truth when that has been done. It lies all about us: in the air we breathe, in the life which pulses around us, in the natural laws which govern our simplest actions. The laws of nature are not hidden away in forgotten or forbidden books. We do not reach an understanding of them by the mumbling of spells and incantations. We can reach them only by watching and by winnowing the truth and the reason from what we see.

"Consider as simple a matter as the use of a bow," he said, after a pause. "You release the arrow, and it soars into the air. The power that sends the arrow to its mark is in the arm of the bowman. Do any of you doubt that? But has it occurred to you that the source of that power remains in the arm while yet the arrow continues its flight? *It is a power, then, that can be transferred.* Is it not equally certain that the power is manifested in degrees? Yes, you may say, because some arms are stronger than others. It is conceivable that an arm might be strong enough to launch an arrow so far that it would pass out of sight. Is it not conceivable also that the power might be created in other ways than by the bend of a human arm? Ergo, some other power might be developed of such potency that by means of it a cart could be picked up from the earth—yea, even with men in it, wearing armor on their backs and pikes in their hands—and set to soaring like an arrow through the sky."

This was sheer sorcery. Walter should have been listening with the scorn reserved for talk of the kind, but instead he found himself seething with excitement. Could it be sorcery, he asked himself, when it was so reasonable? He had heard of great machines which battered down the walls of cities with stones of enormous size. He found himself thinking: "This is not black magic. Some day we may find these sources of new power, and then indeed carts will soar through the air. If only I could live long enough to see that day, and even to be one of those who rode in them!"

He was sure that his sudden change of mind was not due to the persuasive effect of necromancy. Roger Bacon was taking him to a new world; a place of great wonders and of strange winds and of lights, unbearably strong, where the secrets of time and space were known and miracles were wrought.

The teacher was speaking now of glass and the uses to which it could be put. Curious things resulted when two surfaces, one concave and one convex, were held together. "Some day," he declared, "it may be possible to see all the way across the water from Dover to Calais, and to see trees on the shore and men walking under the trees, and even the sands that the men walk on." The talk was being steered carefully to the point he desired to make, the need for continuous experiment. "We must never believe a thing until we have seen it performed before our own eyes. Not once but twice, thrice, a score of times. Nor must we build one belief on another until we are sure that the first is true beyond any possible dispute."

As an example he began to tell of a startling experiment on which he was engaged. Dealing with certain substances, he had stumbled on a result he could hardly yet accept. It had been reached only after much elimination of materials and a continuous substitution of method. When he came to this point, Roger Bacon paused and looked about him, the light in his eyes kindling until they seemed like sparks of fire. "Seven parts of salt-petre," he announced. "It must be pure and not the crude nitrum which is so often used instead. Add to it three parts of sulphur and five of charred young hazel-wood. Then set the mass alight."

Walter stirred uneasily. What strange secret was to be revealed to them through the medium of these everyday words?

"It blazes up," cried Roger Bacon, "like the rending of the world on the Day of Wrath. It shakes everything close at hand like an earthquake. And when the smoke has blown away, and the last echo has died down, there is nothing left, not even enough powder to fill the eye of a needle!"

A silence had fallen on the room. Walter could tell by the quick breathing of those around him that they had been carried away by the announcement, even as he had himself.

"To what uses can this strange law of nature be put? I wish most devoutly that I knew! I wish the scales could be lifted from my eyes so I could see far into the future, when this powder I have discovered will be put to many uses. By that time wiser men than I am will have found means of controlling and utilizing its great force. I think it will be employed to break down walls and to tear out the sides of hills for the makers of roads. Of one thing I am certain: it will be used in the waging of war." He paused, as though reluctant to go on. "I fear that means will be found to confine the shock of it and to direct it in one course so that all who stand in the path of it will be rent like the wicked at the last reckoning. I think sometimes I should destroy my notes and force from my mind all memory of the means by which it is unleashed. Perhaps I would do mankind a service if I did so; for I fear the uses to which it will be put, and I foresee much misery for mankind because of it."

Walter was so bemused with what he had heard that he missed much of what followed. He was indulging in dreams of great instruments of war which lifted black muzzles as sinister as the heads of dragons over rims of bastioned stone and belched forth the death-dealing mixture which Roger Bacon had discovered. Not for a single moment did he doubt the truth of what he had heard. When he was able to concentrate again on what was being said, the teacher had gone on to quite different matters.

He was speaking now of that far-away country known as Cathay. It lay far to the east, Walter knew, even beyond the kingdom of Prester John, and it was of a fabulous wealth. He pricked up his ears at once.

"I wish that my legs were young enough to carry me over the sands of the desert and across the tall mountains which lie between, and that my spirit were equal to the venture," Bacon was saying. "It is an old land and steeped in the knowledge of many ages. I think it may very well be that all the new things of which I have spoken are already in use there. It may be they have carriages that fly and mirrors that bring the mountains to the sea and the islands to the shore. Perhaps they discovered long ago the powder that explodes. And, if they know these things, they know much more that we have never yet dreamt. And, of course, it is a fabulously rich land. They drive their elephants with goads of gold, and they hang out loops of pearls in front of their shops." He sighed deeply and shook his head. "How maddening it is to live in darkness and yet to know that on the other side of the wall is the light ye seek!"

A class was pouring out from the Priory of St. Frideswide's when Walter passed on his way home. They gave him a friendly hail; one of them shouted across to him, "You played up well last night, Bastard!" It was the first time since coming to Oxford that he had received such friendly notice, and a grateful glow took possession of him.

One of them ran over and spoke to Walter in urgent tones. "It's said the chancellor is wroth over what happened, and that you are one chosen for punishment. You and the chamber-deacon. It might be well if both of you left Oxford for a time."

This should have been disturbing news. At the end of the year he was going up for his *determination,* which would elevate him to the ranks of the sophisters, the immediate goal of his ambitions. Ordinarily he would have felt much cast down. But even the possibility of losing this chance could make no impression on his exalted mood.

"I think you are right," he said. "We must go away. But it won't matter. Perhaps there are better things to do than to mumble over dry books." A purpose which clearly had been in his mind as he listened to Roger Bacon, although he had not suspected it until now, suddenly blazed out into words. "We can go to Cathay!"

He hurried on his way to Butterbump Hall. "I don't want to live in darkness either," he was saying to himself. "I want to see what is on the other side of the wall!"

Giles the manciple met him at the entrance to the Hall with a most solemn face. "It is bad news," he said, shaking his head. "It is very sad indeed. I hope it doesn't mean ye'll be leaving us, good Master Wat. But he says to me——"

"Who has been speaking to you?"

Giles motioned over his shoulder with a thumb in the direction of the refectory. "I put him in there. Master Hornpepper would be sore angry if he knew 'cause he wur mud to his knees. I made him scrub it off. He said he had been on the way all night."

A countryman was waiting in the refectory with the patience of his class. Turning as Walter came in, he displayed to view an iron collar around his neck, marked with the name of his master. On his arm was the gules crosslet of Bulaire.

"Are ye Walter of Gurnie?" he asked, in a mumbling tone.

"Yes." A premonition of some great loss had taken possession of Walter. He waited impatiently for the man to go on.

"I wur sent by Simeon Bautrie. Ye're to come with me at once. The good Earl of Lessford, your father and my master, is dead at Bulaire."

5

He stumbled twice in climbing the stairs to gather up his few belongings. The solar bedroom was empty when he reached it, and sitting down on the nearest bed, he let his head rest in his hands. His father was dead! It should have meant little because he had seen his father very seldom and he had been taught to hold him in scorn and hate. He began to think of the times they had met, realizing with a dull sense of wonder that he could still remember every word which had passed between them.

He had been quite young the first time, no more than five or six years old. Gurnie was then a broad and fruitful domain, and his grandfather, although of the purest Saxon stock, was a powerful figure in their part of the country. A servant had taken him in to Cencaster, riding him on the pommel of his saddle. It was the longest journey he had yet been permitted to make, and he had been very much excited. The servant went into a tavern for a drink of ale, leaving him on a corner of the mounting-stone in front. He was kicking his heels against the side and wondering how long it would be before his legs would touch the ground when a group of horsemen came galloping down the road with a great jingling of spurs and creaking of leather. The rider in the van sat so straight in his saddle and was so handsome that the boy watched him with eyes rounded in wonder, thinking he must be one of the Saxon heroes of old that the servants at home told stories about. He had golden hair hanging to his shoulders in long ringlets, and his eyes were a bright blue and as bold as those of a hawk.

Cantering up to the mounting-post, the stranger reined in and looked down at the small figure there with so much interest that Walter kept his head lowered and clutched the dagged edge of his blue tunic with nervous fingers.

"The spreading red oak of Gurnie," said the stranger, looking at the felt sewed on the boy's arm. "My lad, what is your name?"

"Walter of Gurnie, my lord."

There was a pause. The stranger was studying Walter with a smile. "So you are Walter of Gurnie," he said finally. "You are large for your age, Walter. But that, after all, is what might be expected. I think you are inclined to favor—— But, come, I must say no more about that. You look a pleasant enough boy, Walter of Gurnie."

Walter was so abashed by all this attention that he continued to keep his head down. All that he could see, as a result, were the boots of the resplendent horseman. They were high and handsome, made of fine black leather and with toes that curled up into a point. The most interesting thing about them was that they were divided into a pattern with the figure of a yellow leopard in each square of the frets. It was a lively leopard, snarling angrily and with a paw raised to strike. Walter made up his mind he would have a pair exactly like them when he grew up.

"Would you care to ride with me?" the stranger asked suddenly.

The boy looked up at that. The rider was smiling and patting the pommel in front of him invitingly. Shy as he was, Walter knew that a ride on such a fine horse was a chance not to be missed. He nodded his head. The horseman leaned down from his saddle and drew the boy up with one arm, and with a sweep which left Walter almost breathless.

They cantered off down the road, Walter thinking, "He is very strong. Can it be King Arthur, coming back to sweep the Normans into the sea?" He had been told this would surely happen some fine day.

"Do you have a horse of your own, my boy?"

"No, my lord. But I have been promised one as soon as I am old enough. Wilderkin says I shall."

"Wilderkin? Oh yes, your grandfather's seneschal." There was a long pause. "Is your mother well?"

"Sometimes she is well, my lord. But often she is quite ill and I am not allowed to see her for days."

"That makes sorry hearing, Walter." There was quite a long pause then. The tall man was deep in thought, and when he spoke again it seemed for the sole purpose of filling in the silence. "Have you dogs?"

"Yes, my lord." This was a subject on which the boy had much to say. "There are many fine dogs at Gurnie. *Hundreds* of dogs. I have one of my own. He is quite old now. Once he was called Bede, but I did not think that a very good name. I call him Slub."

"And does he answer to that name?"

"Of course, my lord. I would beat him with a stick if he didn't. He is a very obedient dog."

"Do you play games like Grimshanks-found and Crumpy-go-down?"

"No, my lord. I have no other boys to play with."

Other questions followed. Did he say his prayers? Did he have lessons to learn? Finally the stranger asked, Was he happy? Walter replied that he was, but that he would be much happier if his grandfather would speak to him. The arm holding the reins drew in so suddenly at this moment that the horse reared up. The boy would have been thrown off if the rider's other arm had not clasped him tightly. It was a full minute before their talk was resumed.

"He is a very stern man, your grandfather. He does not speak to me, Walter."

That seemed very strange. "Why does he not speak to you, my lord?"

"He feels I did him a great wrong. And—well, I am afraid he has justice on his side."

Walter was thinking, "He cannot be King Arthur, for the good king never did any man a wrong." Aloud he said: "He never speaks to my mother. The servants say he took an oath never to speak to her or to me. They say he is sorry now that he did, but of course he cannot break an oath. It makes me glad to think he would like to speak to me sometimes. I would like to talk to my grandfather about the horse I am to have. And I want a new bow."

When the stranger spoke again, it was in a low tone which suggested that he was unhappy. "I had heard he was not on speaking terms with your mother, but I hoped it wasn't true. I am very sorry to hear, Walter, that it is true, after all." He sighed. "Well, I see that your man has finished his pot of ale and is staring after us as though he thinks I plan to steal you. I think I *would* like to steal you; but instead we must ride back now."

Walter was beginning to feel quite at home with him and was sorry when they reached the mounting-post. The stranger lowered him carefully and then smiled down at him.

"Good-by, my boy," he said.

"Good-by, my lord." Walter did not want him to go until he had learned something about those handsome boots. "You have very fine boots, my lord. They *are* leopards, are they not?"

"Yes, Walter. These boots came all the way from Spain. Where the queen of our good Prince Edward lived."

"When I grow up, I am going to have a pair exactly like them."

"When you grow up and are big enough for boots like these," said the horseman in a repressed tone, "I will send you a pair, Walter. With my love."

It was several years later when Walter saw him for the second time. It was on June the fifteenth and the boy had been soundly beaten by Wilderkin on his grandfather's orders. He had done nothing wrong, but it was the general custom for boys to be whipped on certain days to impress things on their memories. June the fifteenth was the day when the Great Charter was agreed to, and so at nine o'clock Wilderkin always took him out behind the kitchen midden and gave him fifteen strokes with a hawthorn stick.

Generally he did it lightly, not believing that boys should be whipped for no fault, but this time he had laid it on heavily, saying: "After all, Master Walter, you *did* steal the simnel bun from the bakehouse. And who put the fenny snake in Old Will's bed a week agone?"

Walter had run away in a rebellious frame of mind. In his anger he paid no attention to boundaries and, before he realized it, he was a full mile within the domain of Bulaire. What he was feeling must have shown in his face, for when he met his father—he knew by that time who the handsome stranger was, for there was always a lot of sly talk among the servants at Gurnie—the latter stopped and asked, "What's wrong, Wat?"

"Nothing, my lord," he answered stiffly.

The blazing blue eyes smiled at him understandingly. "Nothing? Come, Wat, do you expect me to believe you always wear such an angry face? Who has offended you?"

"No one has offended me, my lord." He knew enough of the story by this time to feel the deepest bitterness toward his father, and he allowed it to show in his face.

The lord of Bulaire understood at once. His eyebrows raised, and his lips widened in a wry smile.

"It is clear you know the story of my iniquities," he said. "No doubt you are being taught to think hardly of me. Well, it is no more than fair. I have done a great wrong, and I must take the consequences. But

I am sorry we cannot be friends, Wat. I had some plans." He paused and then asked in a tone which had almost a suggestion of entreaty in it, "Is there anything I can do for you?"

"Nothing, my lord. My needs are well attended to always."

"Is your grandfather more kind to you—and to your mother?"

"I am not to discuss such matters with strangers."

"But, Wat, we are not strangers." His eyes were fixed on the boy intently. "You know that I am your father?"

Suddenly Walter felt a wild inclination to cry, and he had to fight hard to keep back the tears. He nodded his head. "Yes, my lord. It is a matter of great shame and is never mentioned at Gurnie."

"You are almost big enough for the pair of boots I promised you, my boy."

Walter drew himself up stiffly, and yet at the same time he had to rub a knuckle across his eyes. "I have decided I don't want them. When I am old enough, my grandfather will buy me a pair much finer. A red pair."

"So that is the way it must be." The Earl of Lessford laughed shortly and proceeded to draw on his gloves. As they talked, Walter had been looking him over, being old enough now to take a very real interest in the matter of fine clothes. The gloves were of the very latest kind, of soft leather and divided into fingers. Walter had never seen such a pair before. His father's cloak was of a rich fabric known as baldekin (because it came from Bagdad which some people called by that name), and his baldric was so beautifully chased and embroidered that the boy had found it hard to take his eyes from it. The plume in his velvet hat was blue, and it stood up as proudly as a king at his coronation.

After a moment the earl began to speak in a slow and hesitating way. "Walter, it is only by the merest chance that I see you. Who knows, I may never see you again! There is something I want you to know, and so I must speak of it now." He paused for a long time. "You are too young to understand fully what I am going to say, and for that reason I must ask a favor of you. I want you to listen carefully and remember every word. Will you make me that promise?"

"Yes, my lord."

"My son," said the earl, keeping his eyes studiously fixed at a distance, "I think it is no boast to say that I am a brave man. I took the Cross and I fought well against the Unbelievers. No one can deny that in the tilting yards I have borne a stout lance. But," he was finding it hard to continue, "in other matters it seems that I lack resolution. When you grow older you will understand what I am trying to tell you. It is often the case, I think, that a strong man is weak in matters that concern the people around him. It is true, and I say it with much inner regret, that I cannot stand out against the wishes of those who beset me day after day. I am as wax in more determined hands. I have done things I regret because I lacked the will to say no and to keep on saying it. I have—I have weakly refrained from doing what I knew to be right and just and honorable." There was so much self-reproach in his voice that Walter looked up, half expecting to find tears in his eyes. His father was still looking away, however, and it was impossible to read the expression of his face. "I have not done the things I wanted to do for you, my son. I have been weak, weak!"

After several long moments, the penitent voice went on. "All this must sound like arrant nonsense to you, Walter. But you must keep the promise you made me. Remember the words I have said. When you are older, and have seen things for yourself, perhaps you will understand better and not feel too hardly about me. That is what I hope, Walter, my son. And now, good-by."

The last time Walter had seen his father was just before he had left for Oxford. Word had reached Gurnie that the good Bishop Anselm was to say Mass at Cencaster. Thinking that Engaine was likely to be there, Walter had decided to attend the services.

From Gurnie to Cencaster is a long walk. Walter cut through the woods where the grass was springy to the feet, and so he did not mind the distance. Still he was dusty when he reached the town, and he found it necessary to spend some time washing his face in a brook and whipping the dust from his shoes and hose with a hazel twig.

It was late when he entered the church. The attendance was large, as was to be expected, and he ran an eye over the high oak stalls before seeking a seat for himself. Engaine was not there. This was a disappointment, but there was some compensation in the fact that the family from Bulaire had come. Beside the high poppy-head of the Lessford stall, he could see his father's yellow curls. The gold-mesh crestine of his Norman wife came barely to his shoulder. On her other side sat Edmond, their son and heir.

Walter had not seen Edmond for several years, and he watched the back of the boy's head with an absorption that lasted through a good part of the service. Edmond had been a sickly boy, as unlike his father as could be conceived: dark and sallow and thin, with the calculating look in his eyes that told of his Norman blood. Now he was shooting up with the promise of attaining a man's proper stature after all, but Walter noted, with some satisfaction it must be said, that he was scrawny still and of an unhealthy complexion.

As the minutes passed, Walter became uncomfortably aware that he was attracting attention. People in the seats ahead were craning back to look at him and smiling and whispering among themselves. He could think of no reason for this ill-timed amusement unless they thought the new blue tunic his mother had made for him a poor fit. This explanation he could not accept, for he had been proud of his finery and anxious that Engaine should see him in it. Had he, then, left streaks on his face after washing? Or did they think it a matter for levity that the illegitimate son of the great earl sat so close behind him?

Then the lad sitting beside him turned his head, and the reason for the attitude of the congregation became clear at once. He was a thick-set youth, wearing the breastplate and sollerets of the castle men-at-arms and with the gules crosslet on his arm. His hair was a disorderly yellow mop, his nose had an unmistakable arch to it, and his eyes were the blue of the midday sky! His paternity was stamped so indelibly on his outer shell that Walter realized at once, and for the first time, that he was not the only son Earl Rauf had begot out of wedlock. Fit reason indeed for laughter, the two bastard sons of one father sitting side by side and neither of them aware of the other! Walter sank back in his seat in such abject misery that he heard not another word as long as he remained in the church.

He did not look again at this newly discovered half brother. As soon as there was a stir of leaving in the seats, he was up on his feet and the first to walk down the aisle. He found it hard not to run, so intense was his desire to escape this fresh humiliation.

Once on the outside, however, he lingered, stationing himself behind the yew hedge where he could see without being seen. Here he stayed until the family from the castle, and all their dependents, had passed him on their way out. His father looked preoccupied, he thought, keeping his eyes on the sky above the treetops as though more concerned with the prospect of a day's sport with his hawks than with the Mass he had just heard. The Norman woman, as most people called the wife he had brought back from the Crusades and whose wealth had made days of unwonted prosperity at Bulaire Castle, walked beside him with a possessive air. She was short and a little squat, with black brows and a nose that bulked too largely in her face for any claim to beauty. Edmond, three years younger than Walter, carried himself with an air of pride that was doubly galling to the illegitimate son. The boy was dressed in rich brown samite, and his hose wrinkled at his gangling knees.

"Well," said Walter to himself, as he watched them mount their horses and canter off, "the bastard son has straight legs, at any rate, and a man's shoulders. Does my father know that his lawful whelp is a scrawny, bandy nidering?"

He struck out at once on his return trip, feeling sick at heart and cheated of his object in coming. He had not seen Engaine, and he had suffered a humiliating blow to his pride. The eighteen miles back would be a tiring walk. He had a blister on each heel already.

6

And now Rauf of Bulaire, Earl of Lessford, was dead.

Walter sat still on the side of the bed, his shoulders hunched over, his mind filled with conflicting emotions. He was thinking mostly of what his father had said the day of their second meeting. "I have not done the things I wanted to do for you, my son" and, "When you are older perhaps, you will understand better and not feel too hardly about me." He understood this much: that what people said was true, his father had been under the thumb of his Norman wife. He was trying to sort it all out in his mind, sure only of one thing: now that his father was dead, he would never again think hardly of him. He turned with a start when Giles touched his shoulder from behind.

"Some-'un to see ye, Master Walter," said the maniciple. "He comes to back door, and he says he can't come in. A chamber-deacon, I thinks, Master Walter."

Walter threw his bundle hurriedly over his shoulder. An uproar had risen suddenly in the vestibule below which warned him that some of the fellows had returned from their classes; although it sounded in full truth as if a gaggle of geese had invaded the premises. He heard someone say, "By St. Winwaloe, it is a filthy day!" It was a fad of the moment for each clerk to select one of the lesser-known saints for use in emphatic speech, but no one at the Hall had picked this pious abbot of the sixth century, so it was clear there were outsiders in the party. It would not do for Tristram to be seen.

As he turned toward the stairs, he said to Giles, "See that the messenger from Bulaire has something to put in his belly and then send him on his way."

The roke had returned in full earnest, and Tristram, standing patiently at the rear door, was already thoroughly soaked.

"I am leaving at once," he said. "Perhaps it was foolish to take the time to come here. But I wanted you to know the truth." He was breathing hard, as though from a long run. "I have had a fight with my landlord, and I am afraid he is badly hurt. This is the last of Oxford for me."

"Then you went back to the house on Sheydyard Street."

Tristram nodded apologetically. "I know it was agreed I would keep away and find other quarters. But I kept thinking about the poor badger. There would be no one to feed her, so I picked up a few scraps and took them with me, enough to last her for several days. When I got there"— he gulped before going on—"she was dead! He had taken it out on the crippled little beast. Her head was crushed in, and there was a blood-stained rule from the shop beside the body." His eyes, usually so mild, burned with a deep anger. "I went downstairs after him. He saw me coming and picked up a bucket of paste. I had him down before he could raise it to his shoulder. His wife beat me from behind with a fire-iron, and her screeching brought the neighbors in. I had to run for it then." He looked at Walter ruefully before concluding, "I hope he's not too badly hurt."

"I am leaving too," said Walter. "I'm glad you took it out of the fellow's hide, Tris. Now we can go together."

CHAPTER II

Gurnie

THE DOWNPOUR CEASED at dawn, and man's great and jovial friend, the sun, popped his head up over the horizon. There was a smile and a wink on his broad golden face, and he seemed to be saying: "Take heart, ye poor, channering earthworms, stumbling through the dark and the wet. Here I am, to drive the devil from the world again." There was an autumnal vibrancy in the air. In their sedate beauty of ruby and brown, the trees stretched ahead on each side of the winding road. Through the

up-perked ears of stone on Chanfrin Rock, they caught their first
glimpse of Gurnie, standing sturdily in the bend of Franklyn Creek.

Walter sensed at once that there was something wrong; and his pride,
which had only the greatness of Gurnie to feed upon, took alarm. He
could see droves of small black animals about the stables and was sure
they were swine. "Where are the horses?" he asked himself, uneasily.
He had a guilty fear that the expense of sending him to Oxford had
made sweeping economies necessary.

There was an equally unpleasant surprise for him when they came in
sight of the western exposure. What had once been the yew garden was
now a huge rubbish pile. He studied this fresh proof of poverty with a
sinking heart. The pile was made up of rusted shields, broken lances,
cast-off parts of horse gear, wheels of carts.

"St. Aidan!" he muttered, shaking his head. "Has my grandfather
gone mad? There used to be a garden here that was my mother's special
pride. We had a yew walk four hundred years old. There isn't a trace
of it left!"

"Perhaps your grandfather has sold it," ventured Tristram. "The abbeys are always ready to pay handsomely for yew."

To complete the picture, there were chickens everywhere. They filled
the road, expostulating as they scattered to make way. They were
perched on the pointed beams of the palisade, clucking indignantly from
this point of vantage. Even the drawbridge, lying flat and impotent with
its hoisting chains rotted clear away, was covered with their feathers.
When Walter saw that the water in the moat was coated with straw and
foul with marish growths, his humiliation was complete.

Wilderkin admitted them, looking well fed and content. In fact, he
filled his hempen shamewes with a fine roundness of belly which be-
spoke no shortage of food in the household. Walter noticed, however,
that the seneschal was beginning to show his age. He was rheumy of
eye, and time was tracing purple reminders on his nose and cheeks.
This was to be expected, for Old Will was getting close to fifty years, a
good ripe age.

"Ha, Master Walter!" he wheezed. "We looked for ye at sundown.
Ye've had the word, then?"

"Yes, Will. One of the Bulaire men was sent to Oxford to bring me
back. Simeon Bautrie sent him."

"Simeon Bautrie sent him!" The eyes of the old man opened wide at
this. "Now that makes good hearing. Simeon was the earl's man of law.
Can it mean that some land has been left ye?"

Land! Ever since the confiscation, that word had been spoken in the household with almost savage longing. Land, the one basis of prosperity, the sole means of enjoying comfort and security; how bitterly its lack had been resented!

"I know as little of that as you do, Old Will."

The low-beamed hall into which they stepped was dank and unaired. Was the inside of the house as unkempt as the exterior?

"Old Will," said Walter, laying a supplicating hand on the rough sleeve of the seneschal, "what is amiss here? The whole place is as sour as rennet. It reeks of swine and hens and rotting merd. Why is that pile of rubbish in the yew garden?"

"We are doing the best we can, let me tell ye, Master Walter," said Wilderkin, with a trace of sulkiness. "Do ye find fault with the steps taken to keep food on the board? There are only a few begster acres left; and twelve men and four women to feed, not to mention the two bordar boys and that slut of a buttery burd. Ye would not object to the hens and the swine if ye knew the jingling price we get for them in the London market. Oh yes, we sell all the way to London. As for the rubbish, it will bring wealth to Gurnie in time."

Walter heard his grandfather's voice calling from somewhere within, "Wilderkin, where are you, knave?" He asked hurriedly, "What wealth can there be in splintered lances and rusted hubs?"

"Ha, that's the surprise we have for ye," declared the seneschal, with an air of sly triumph. "Two of the men scour the countryside for the ross ye see out there. It's little they pay for it; but how different it is when the armourers come here, looking for the metal they can melt in their furnaces? Steven Littlesteven has come to us all the way from his shop in London. The right metals are hard to come by these days."

"But—but——" Walter was so stricken with horror that he found it hard to command his tongue. "Are you telling me that my grandfather has gone into dealing in old metal? He, a belted knight!"

Wilderkin laughed scornfully. "Belted knights can starve as easily as common men, Master Walter. I tell ye the profit we make is an honest one. Not that my lord Alfgar has any part in it himself, save to do the planning and keep the books." He gave vent to a sudden sigh. "It is true I have more stomach for the ross trade than for the swine. Men hold their noses when they see me now and ask, 'How sets the wind?'"

Walter's eyes were becoming accustomed to the dark inside, and he could see now that nothing had been changed. The hall, bare of all furnishings save a few ancient weapons and shields hanging on the walls, opened into the main room where the tables and trestles still stood from last night's rere-supper. Burnt-out torches sagged in the wall hooks. He could hear dogs scratching and snuffling among the floor rushes.

Wilderkin was looking him over critically. "Ye've grown," he said. "I swear ye've stretched up a full two inches. I like it little that ye resemble *him* so much. There is little trace of Gurnie blood in ye that I can see." He suddenly clutched one arm of the homecomer, "Did ye hear he was killed in Gillam's Spinney? By an arrow through the heart?"

The seneschal's words came as such a shock that Walter gazed at him for several moments in a stunned silence. He had lacked the will to ask any questions of the thrall from Bulaire. "Killed!" he said, suddenly. "It must have been an accident. My lord of Lessford had no enemies."

Wilderkin wagged his head. "No one knows for a certainty, Master Walter. No enemies, ye say? How have we regarded your good lord of Lessford here at Gurnie? His lady has no doubts. She is sure in her mind he was killed by someone poaching in Gillam's Spinney."

"That could be true, and it could yet be an accident. Do you remember the death of King Rufus?"

The face of the old retainer hinted of things still untold. He kept nodding his round head and smirking, as though savoring the effect his disclosures would have.

"Come, Old Will!" cried Walter. "Out with it, man! Tell me what you've heard."

"The widow has not been content to wait for the king's justice. Nothing would suit her but she must take the avenging of her lord's death into her own hands. All of the men who have ever been known to loose an arrow after sundown in Bulaire domain were brought in to her. Six of them, Master Walter, six stout fellows with families of their own and no fault on their consciences that anyone wotted of. They were lined up before her and charged with the murder of her lord; and with such a violence of words that even her own servants hung their heads as they listened. They were put to the torture and, when nothing was learned, she summoned them out again. It passes all belief, Master Walter! She had them hanged from one tree in full view of the castle."

"All of them! Six innocent men hanged! Were—any of them from Gurnie?"

"No. None from Gurnie. A blessing it was, for my own nephew Jack had been——" Wilderkin drew in his breath sharply. "Forget what I said, Master Walter; and lay a promise on this fellow with ye to keep a still tongue in his head."

"But has nothing been done about it?"

Wilderkin shook his head slowly. "There have been plenty of black looks and much talk. Ye may depend on it, there will be trouble for the widow when the word gets to Lunnon."

Tristram, whose face had gone white at the first telling, said in a suppressed voice, "Some day the common men of England will rise up and put an end for all time to such crimes as this!"

"The common men?" said the old servant. "The common men have little stomach for trouble hereabouts since Evesham. They were all out against King Harry then, and plenty of them swung from the gallows tree before it was over. As for the widow, they say she boasts of what she has done. Norman justice, she calls it." He clutched Walter's arm a second time. "Ye're not to go there! If ye show yer face at Bulaire Castle, the she-devil will hang ye up with the rest of them. She's always hated ye; make no mistake about that!"

2

Before leaving to answer his master's impatiently repeated summons, Wilderkin had said, "Ye'll be able to see the Lady Hild at once, Master Walter." This was unexpected good luck. His mother's health was so uncertain that Walter had not been sure of seeing her before going on to Bulaire.

For ten years or more she had not stirred from her room except on rare occasions when she made an appearance at supper or on still rarer evenings when she walked in her garden after dusk had fallen. When she graced the supper table, she sat on the dais beside her father, but no words were exchanged between them.

Walter had always been certain that she kept herself hidden away because life had lost all savor for her. Her *camera* was the largest room on the solar floor, but it was not well suited to such continuous occupancy. It was exposed on three sides, which meant that it was very warm in summer and cold in winter. No amount of persuasion could get her to change it, however. She would smile gently when Walter girded at her about it, and say that she was a creature of habit, that she could be content nowhere else. He knew the real reason for her obduracy: From the east window she could see afar off, against the black gorget of Algitha Scaur, the donjon top of Bulaire!

Wulfa, her maidservant, shared her solitude, a gaunt woman with a bitter and intent face. Walter had never been able to detect a trace of warmth in the maid. Certainly she never smiled, and as for a word passed in jest it was not in the nature of her. But she was devoted to her mistress and gave her every waking moment. She emerged from the room only when something was necessary for their use, and she would then move swiftly about her task on noiseless heels. With the other members of the domestic staff she kept up a ceaseless warfare.

It was this faithful creature who answered his tap on the door. She did not smile but gave him a curtsy so brief and restrained that he expected to hear her knees creak.

"The Lady Hild is up and will see you, master," she whispered.

He heard his mother cry: "Walter! Is it you, my son?" She was sitting in a rush-bottomed chair near the window which commanded the view of Bulaire, and she would have risen to greet him if Wulfa had not precipitated herself on her with almost frenzied cries. "No, no, my lady! You must not! You really must not try it! You have so little strength, my lady."

His mother's dark eyes smiled at Walter over the bent shoulder of her servant as though to say, "Forgive me for not getting up, but you see how it is." He stood still for several moments and watched her with a sense of surprise and even awe. She had never looked more lovely. Her hair was white, but she looked young and fresh in spite of it. Her eyes seemed enormous in her pale face, and her features were as finely etched as a saint's on a cathedral wall. Wulfa had seen to it that she was attired in a delicate cendal dress with a peplum wrapped about her neck.

There was another reason for surprise. Walter had expected to find her in the depths of despair, but instead there was a serene calmness about her. She seemed happy even.

"My son," she said, taking his wrist and urging him into a chair beside her, "you know that he is gone? At first, when Wulfa told me, I thought the end of everything had come. It seemed so cruel. He was so strong, so brave, so beautiful! But now I see things more clearly. He was not happy, Walter, and now he is at peace. I feel that he's closer to me than he has ever been, and so I know it is for the best, that it is God's will. Before you came in, Walter, I was sitting here and watching the sky, and I was remembering. I was remembering many things, and I was happy."

She went on talking in low tones. It was hard for him to follow her, for she spoke mostly of things of which he knew nothing. She had drawn her arm through his, and they sat closely together as she whispered some of her pleasantest memories. He glanced about the room and saw that Wulfa had made some changes while he was away. The bed of tapister's work (it was so high that Wulfa herself slept under it on a truckle-bed) had a turkey-red coverlet now, and there were red candles instead of white on the top shelf of the old bink in the corner. The one tapestry in the room, hanging on the wall opposite the bed, had been so neatly repaired that he could see no trace of the once familiar rents. The changes made the room seem much more cheerful.

"You look so much like him, my son," his mother whispered. "I am proud of you, so proud of you, because of that. You will become a learned man at the university, Walter. Your father had very little learning; you will excel him in that."

She began to talk then in an almost lyric tone of things that had occurred before he was born. It was all so far removed from his ken that before long he found his attention wandering. He began to think how important this room had been in his life. He had been born here (although it had not been certain at first that his grandfather would permit the event to take place in his house), it had been his real home for several years, and it was here he had first seen Engaine.

She was about eight at the time, and he three years older. The confiscation was a new thing then, and there was the blackest of blood between Gurnie and Tressling. Many stories of the self-willed little beauty had reached them at Gurnie, and she was as ill thought of as her favor-pandering father. Walter might never have seen her had it not been for an accident.

It was a cold day in the dead of winter, with snow piled up in great white drifts and a wind brawling in from the west. Engaine had been permitted to set out for a ride, or had neglected to ask for permission, which seems more likely. A single page had accompanied her, a pasty-faced youth new to the district and to the feud between the two houses. When his young mistress became thoroughly numbed with the cold, the page had rapped at the front door of Gurnie, asking that they might rest and become warm. Lady Hild welcomed the girl and took her up to her own room, where a fine blaze roared in the fireplace. She sat Engaine down in front of it and instructed Wilderkin to heat a mug of morat for her. Walter was in the room, sitting off in one corner and missing nothing about this young guest with lovely blue eyes in a small, pinched face. He was hoping, vainly, that there would be some of the morat for him.

He still recalled that she wore a tunic of a rich shade of blue over her kirtle. It had quite obviously been cut down from adult size. This was not a matter for surprise. Even in the highest families, the handing on of garments from old to young, and from rich to poor, was a common practice. Walter was quite sure that the tunic, being the exact shade of her eyes, became her more than it had its previous wearer. The tight-fitting hood on her head was of ermine, and it had a liripipe of blue velvet tied under her chin.

Even at that age Engaine had a pert and venturesome tongue. She talked to Lady Hild with an ease quite surprising in so young a girl, and many times she went into trills of laughter. She even had the audacity to nod over the mug of steaming morat and say, *"Waes hael!"* By this time she had become warm again. Color had come back into her cheeks, a most delicate shading of pink, and her eyes sparkled as she talked. He had never seen anyone so lovely in all his life, and it was no wonder that his subjugation began there and then.

The girl looked about her with a lively curiosity, not neglecting to include Walter in the inspection. What she saw did not seem to impress her, for she said, with a slight curl of her very pretty nostril: "This house is small. It's not nearly as fine as Tressling."

"No," answered Lady Hild. "It is humble compared to Tressling and Bulaire."

"Our castle is the largest in the whole world. It has six towers."

This was so far from the truth that Walter wanted to shout out a contradiction. Tressling had only two towers. He remained silent with great difficulty.

"My father has a hundred archers and fifty men-at-arms."

This was going too far. "There are only twenty archers at Tressling," Walter piped up. "And only ten men-at-arms!"

She turned around and looked him over so coolly that he was sorry he had spoken. "That boy has very bad manners," she said. Then she looked back at his mother to ask, "What is your house called?"

"Gurnie. It's an old house. It has stood, we believe, since the days of our great King Alfred."

"King Alfred? I have never heard of a King Alfred." She was thinking hard. "Now I know. I have heard my father speak of Gurnie. You have *no* archers here and *no* men-at-arms. You are Saxons."

"Yes, my child, we are Saxons."

"And we are proud to be Saxons!" cried Walter.

"Well," said Engaine, after a long pause during which she stared steadily at him, "it can't be helped, can it? I think you are really very nice. What is the name of that boy?"

"His name is Walter."

"Then he's Walter of Gurnie. It's rather a nice name. Is his hair like that naturally or do you have to curl it? *Mine* curls naturally."

"And so does Walter's."

"Do you know," she said, after another pause, "he looks much like my father's cousin, the Earl of Lessford. Do you think he will be as handsome as the earl when he grows up? But I *do* think it would be better if he combed his hair."

He saw her quite often as the years passed. Engaine would condescend to speak to him at times, and always with a tinge of liking under her disdainful manner. He was never very happy after seeing her, for she made it clear that she regarded him as of very inferior clay. In spite of that, these glimpses of her provided him with most of the memories he cared to retain of a bleak boyhood.

"Walter," said his mother, finally, "now that your father is gone, I think I must tell you the whole story. It is your right to know."

Walter looked at her anxiously, thinking how bad her memory had become. She had told him the story many times and, as she never deviated in the telling, he could have recited it word for word. He got to his feet, knowing that the usual ritual would have to be observed. Wulfa had already vanished. He went to each door in turn, opening them to make sure there were no listeners, and even visiting each window.

When she began the familiar recital, he listened with a new interest, hoping that his father's death would serve to revive additional memories in her mind.

"Your grandfather was against us, Rauf and me. Rauf was twenty-two, and I was going on sixteen. As we were both of gentle blood, and I was the heiress of Gurnie, it would not have been a one-sided match. But Rauf was of the Norman invaders and I was pure Anglo-Saxon, and so my father would not hear of it. No daughter of his would marry a foreigner, he swore. Imagine calling my Rauf a foreigner! He had been born at Bulaire, as had his father, and many generations before that. But Father hated the Normans and had never been able to forgive them the Battle of Hastings." She indulged in a long sigh. "We used to meet, of course. Oh, it was all most proper, Wulfa, who was with me even then, was always along, and Rauf would have his squire. We wouldn't even dismount, but would sit our horses side by side in some forest glade. Rauf would whisper to me. We were so sure that in the end we would marry."

She sighed still more deeply. "Then the monks came again, carrying the Cross and preaching the need for another Crusade to help good King Louis of France. They put up a wooden cross—it was thirty feet high, I remember—and set it blazing. People gathered from all around and, when one of the priests told us of the things he had seen in the Holy Land, I wanted to stand up and cry out, as all the men did, that the Sepulcher must no longer be left in heathen hands! I was glad that Rauf was the first to step forward and kiss the Cross. I could not have gone on loving him if he held back. I sang as fervently as anyone, even 'The Old Man of the Mountain.' Over two hundred of our men took the oath that day."

As usual she paused a long time at this point. So far she had told him nothing he had not heard before. He found a resentment of the Crusades rising in his mind. There had been so many of them, so much trouble and suffering. At Oxford, he was tempted to tell her, the clerks had fallen into the habit of discussing them with levity and, even, irreverence. A man who expressed his desire to see another was not looked up to as one bent on knightly endeavor. An expression was used instead, "He wants his gambeson tails free of his wife's fingers." No one had the patience any more to listen to the stories of returned Crusaders. They were all too familiar. The warriors were now called Old Cruses; sometimes the clerks would put it this way, "His head is filled with Arabian fleas." There was even an offhanded method of saying that a man was a captive in the East: "He has the Cross burned on his buttocks," that being one of the Saracen ways of treating their Christian prisoners.

His mother took up the story. "They were so brave and sweet, the young men who had sworn to win back the Holy City. They marched about with their crosses on their arms and a look of devotion on their faces. We knew that not more than one out of five would come back, for it had been that way all the other times. They would die of the heat and the thirst or they would be killed in battle; or, worse still, they would fall into the hands of the Saracens and be kept as slaves or even flayed alive. They had such a short time to live, and most of them were so young!" She let her head droop, and it was several moments before she continued. "There were eighteen children born hereabouts within nine months after they marched away; and you were one of the eighteen, my son. No attention was paid to the others, as it had always happened that way, but I was of noble blood, and that made so much talk that I thought at first I would die of the shame. But I was sure Rauf and I would be married when he returned—he would be one of the lucky ones, God and Our Lady willing—and so I withstood the tempers of your grandfather and forced myself to keep my head up."

The customary pause followed. "It was four years before Rauf returned. When he did come back, he brought a wife with him!"

This had always been the end of her story. After a few moments, however, she went on with more passion than he had ever known her to display. "He would not have married if he had known about you, my son!" A trace of color flared in her cheeks. "There was no way of letting him know. And he was so terribly in debt. He had mortgaged his lands to raise the money to go, and on the way back his ship was wrecked on one of the islands off Greece. They held him there for ransom, just as the Germans did with King Richard. His kinsmen in Normandy, *her* people, paid the ransom. So he was married and stayed a year in Normandy before coming back with his ugly Norman wife and his son. Walter, my boy, he would have shouldered his debts and remained true to his vows to me if he had known about you!"

"How can you be sure of that, Mother?"

She was very tired now, but she answered him with a rally of triumphant spirit. "He told me. Yes, Walter, he came once to see me. It was when your grandfather was riding on the Welsh Marshes. We had such a long talk; and he was very sad and contrite, and he told me then he would have come back to face all his debts gladly had he known, that he would have sold all of Bulaire if necessary. He had been away four years, and he was sure I had given him up for dead long before. The thought had been in his mind even that I had wearied of waiting and married someone else."

Walter interrupted eagerly. "You never told me before that he came to see you. I think—I think it makes a difference."

"Yes, my son. A great difference. I don't think I could have lived this long if I had not seen him at all. But he came! And he told me"—she took one of his hands and pressed it against her cheek—"he told me that I was the only one he had ever loved. I have had that to comfort me all these years!"

"There is something I have never told you, Mother," confided Walter. "I had a talk with him too, and he said that he knew he was not a strong man; that he yielded to influences easily. I see now that he was trying to explain himself to me."

There was a moment's silence, and then she said in a whisper: "I have never seen his wife, Walter. What is she like?"

The son's feelings flared out in angry words. "She is a Norman woman! Need I say more? She is determined to have her way in everything; and she is hard and grasping and cruel."

"What a sorry life he has had!"

"Mother," asked Walter tensely, "are you sure he would have married you if things had been different? And that I would then have been made legitimate?"

"Yes, my son, I am sure of it."

"Are you sure he preferred you to his legal wife? And me, *me,* to his other son?"

"Walter," she answered, earnestly, "never let yourself doubt that in his heart my Rauf felt I was his real wife and that you were the son he wanted at his right side! Never, never doubt it!"

A great sense of relief and happiness welled up inside him. He said to himself, "Now I need not go on hating his memory!"

The servingmaid came back and crossed swiftly to the side of her mistress. "You have talked too much, Lady Hild," she said in a toneless voice which succeeded nevertheless in conveying a suggestion of blame. "Now you must lie down. Come, lean on me, my lady."

His mother let herself sink back into her chair. Her eyes closed, and he could see that she was trembling.

"Oh, you have overdone it, my lady!" cried Wulfa. "I knew you would. I was sure of it." She said to Walter in an urgent voice, "You had better go, master."

She accompanied him to the door and there said in a whisper: "She is getting worse. The spells come oftener. I notice all the time how much worse she is."

The figure in the chair had straightened up. She looked at them standing there in the doorway with all the appearance of conspirators. There was neither understanding nor recognition in her eyes.

"Wulfa!" she cried, in a high and unnatural voice. "What are you saying? What are you going to do?" Her voice rose even higher. "Come back to me! Wulfa! *Who is that man?*"

3

Walter had never suspected what was wrong with his mother, and the discovery left him in such a depressed frame of mind that Tristram took him out for a walk in the hope that the exertion would lighten his mood. They tramped through a countryside as rich with regal color as an emperor's robe, and content with the fatness of a rich harvest; a land tended by faithful hands so that even the cultivated fields seemed as lovely as the woods where nature suffered no interference; a land of quiet charm where the spires of small churches were like poems written on the sky, and the only sore spots to be seen were the swine-pens and the ross heap of Gurnie.

Dusk was falling when they returned, and they heard the banging and clamping of shutters as they crossed the drawbridge. In the main hall, however, the talk was cheerful. The day's work was done, the barriers had been raised against the encroachments of evil, a smell of good food filled the air. There was much repeating of sly jokes about scholards at the *niniversity* and the likelihood that Walter himself would end up with a tonsured poll.

Walter watched the preparations for supper with an eagerness that had nothing to do with appetite. Crosswise on the dais was a table laid with a fine linen cloth, at the center of which his grandfather's chair had been placed. It was a stately chair with an overhanging canopy and pommels of shining copper. Two of lesser height had been placed on each side of it. Did this mean, he asked himself with a sudden jubilance of spirit, that the ban was to be raised at last? Was he to be allowed to sit with the family? He had suffered so intensely from his exclusion that at the moment life could offer him no greater boon.

His hopes were soon dashed, however. Wilderkin bustled by him, saying in a disapproving voice: "There are guests tonight, Master Walter. And my lord Alfgar, as usual, has insisted that we do everything well. He is a proud man, my lord. Ha, how the stores in the kitchen have been used up!"

Walter sighed unhappily. It had been foolish of him, he knew, to set his hopes so high. His grandfather would never relent to such an extent. Nevertheless he felt so disappointed that he could find no compensation in the fine appearance of the hall. His grandfather's two prized standing cups, called *John the Beloved* and *Bernard of Clairvaux* according to the custom which gave names to these valuable heirlooms, had been placed at each end of the table on the dais. His grandfather, he said to himself, would be sure to recite their pedigree again for the edification of his guests. There were silver ewers at intervals and a high candelabrum with new tapers. They were indeed doing everything well tonight.

Trestles were being set up in the lower part of the hall to form a T with the head table. Wilderkin came in with a silver salt-cellar and, with a nod for Walter, placed it several feet from the point of junction. This meant, of course, that the old compromise arrangement was to be followed. Walter had always been placed just above the salt, a contrivance of his grandfather's which did not seat him with the family but spared him the humiliation of eating with the family retainers and servants. Walter noticed that two chairs were being placed in that position, one on each side of the board. This must mean that Tristram was to be placed opposite him.

As soon as his grandfather entered, Walter knew that he held a poor esteem of his guests, in spite of the preparations which had been made. There was condescension in the gesture with which he assigned them to their seats. One was a surly and porcine sprat of a man in a dun-colored tunic. Wilderkin, whose opinions were set by his master's, whispered scornfully in Walter's ear: "The Socman of Tasker! When the pox got into our swine-pens last spring, we lost a Socman of Tasker every day." The second guest was a fattish priest who kept his cowl drawn up over his head as though he found the hall too cold for his comfort. Wilderkin whispered: "The prior of Gatherby. It takes three monks to load him on the back of a mule. Toothless old adder!"

Alfgar of Gurnie was looking well, although Walter noticed that his stomach had rounded out almost to the point of tubbiness, and that the iron gray of his closely clipped mustache had changed to white. The hair on his head had retreated until the merest fringe was left and his dome stood up high, shining with the most scrupulous scrubbing. As usual he was elegantly attired, and a heavy gold chain hung around his neck.

Walter was surprised when his mother followed into the room. She seemed, however, to have become completely normal again. Tristram looked at her in wonder and whispered: "Your lady mother is beautiful. She looks like a queen, and yet like a saint too."

Leaning across the table, she said to Walter, "I hope you will bring your companion from Oxford to talk with me after supper."

Not knowing what he should do, Tristram flushed and glanced at Walter for guidance. He was so embarrassed that he had begun to perspire profusely. When Walter rose and bowed, he followed suit with an ungainly stiffness which told how much at sea he felt. The Lady Hild bowed back to them and said, "You are very tall young men, though it seems to me, Walter, that your companion has somewhat the advantage of you."

Wulfa had dressed her in a flowing gown of green samite, with roses diapered handsomely on the bodice. To conceal its age, buttons had been sewn in rows from wrist to elbow in what was the latest feminine fashion. Her white hair, without ornamentation of any kind, was bound in braids and piled high on the top of her head. Walter thought with a surge of pride that Tristram had been right; she looked both queen and saint.

The maid had carried down all six sections of the family Bible, and she laid them now in one pile beside her mistress. Lady Hild was very proud of the Bible, for it had a glossatam and many illuminations made by patient monkly hands. She was so proud of it, in fact, that she was wont to practice a deception at times. Not being able to read, she had memorized many passages and would recite them aloud with the Book in front of her; not caring that she spoke them in English while the print, of course, was in Latin.

Agnes Malkinsmaiden was carrying in the food with the assistance of the buttery burd, a steamy-faced wench with great rolling hips. Even after the seneschal's warning, Walter was amazed at the variety of the dishes set on the board. There was a haunch of venison, a round of prime beef, braces of woodcock and bittern roasted to such a turn that the brown skins seemed ready to burst with richness, and a platter of little pig sausages garnished with black puddings. Agnes did all the cooking for the household, and she had a sagacious hand with seasonings, scorning to heap on the pepper and the cloves and fennel from the East as had become the rule and using instead all the old English herbs, basil, lavender, coriander, and marjoram. After placing the last dish on the table, she took it on herself to repeat the formula used when the family supped alone, "God and Our Lady bless this feast."

The host glanced once at Walter, and his eye softened almost imperceptibly by way of an unspoken welcome. Then he covered the bread tranchoir in front of him with a large slice of beef and called to have his horn mug filled with wine. His blue eye, so deceptively mild, began to beam. To show his scholarship (he had very little, as Walter knew), he bowed to the old prior and indulged in a quotation from Horace, "'Death grips us by the ear and says, "Drink, for I come."'"

The prior, who clearly was doddering at the very brink of the grave, accepted the invitation to drink in this form with an ill grace. The Socman of Tasker, surprised that they did not begin by toasting the King, ventured to say, "Our young ruler promises to restore our rights and give us justice such as we have not seen since the days of our great Alfred."

"Pay no heed to such idle talk, Tasker," admonished the host. "We are all of pure Saxon blood here, and so I can speak freely. Talk like that is started for one purpose only, to make us slothful and content. We are living in an age of lawyers; sharp Norman fellows with covetous minds and glib tongues. They will beguile us with words while they find means to rivet still heavier chains on us."

"I have been disposed to believe in the good intent of the young king," protested the Socman, rather feebly.

The host shook his head with a well-satisfied dissent. He cut the juice-soaked tranchoir with his dagger and threw the strips of bread into the alms-dish in the center of the table, using great care that his fingers did not become stained in doing so. The alms-dish was well stocked by this time with gristly ends of meat and the wings of the game; there would be good fare for the beggars who came to the door next day.

"That is where you make your mistake." Walter recognized this as his grandfather's favorite phrase. "We must expect no favors from this young king. He is Norman, and there you have the answer. I have said this time and again to men who, like you, should know better than to believe in the soft lies of our rulers." He shook his head from side to side. "No one pays heed to my warnings. As soon as Old King Harry died, I said . . ."

Walter could hear his voice go on and on, telling what he had said and making it clear that he had always been right. The thread of argument was lost to the grandson, who now noticed with alarm that his mother's hands were opening the last section of the Bible. Her eyes had taken on a strained look.

"I see the lake of everlasting fire!" she said suddenly in a low voice. "The day is near at hand when the Lord cometh in His wrath."

A shudder ran along the board, and even the piggish eyes of the Socman of Tasker turned toward her with a suggestion of panic. Everyone lived in dread, knowing that all the signs of the Second Coming were being fulfilled rapidly. No one failed at the end of each day to look at the western sky and wonder if there was anything in the appearance of it to suggest that the Lord would come before morning.

Alfgar paid no heed to the interruption. He was regaling himself now with slices of pale yellow cheese, and he began to talk about the standing cups.

"My good churchman," he said, turning to the priest, "I want to call *John the Beloved* to your attention. It is very old. In fact, it belonged to the saintly Lady Hild after whom my daughter is named. See, it is of the most ancient workmanship. Greek, in my opinion; and the maker undoubtedly lived in Antioch. The shape proves its antiquity, for you find here the true vase-turned body and the double handles. Fifth century, would you say?"

The prior, with the carcass of a whole pheasant in his hands, mumbled, "Undoubtedly," and went on eating.

"I prefer to think that the figure of the apostle represents him on the Island of Patmos when the gift of prophecy ran so strangely in his veins. Observe, the face is gaunt from fasting, and there is a light in the eyes——"

A loud yelping came from under the table, where the dogs were disputing ownership of a bone. Alfgar broke off his discourse to call out sharply, "Chomper! Briff! Chetwind!" Wilderkin took down the lance from the wall and probed vigorously with it under the cloth. The noise subsided.

"Now this one," continued the host, indicating *Bernard of Clairvaux,* "is not as old, but I value it because it rested once in the hands of the great saint for whom it is named."

The Lady Hild had continued to talk, but in so low a tone that no one could tell what she was saying. Now she looked up and stared straight at Walter with no sign of recognition. Her voice became clear again. "And the heavens were rent as a scroll and the mountains and the islands were moved out of their places; and the kings of the earth hid themselves in the dens and the rocks of the mountains. For the great day of His wrath had come!"

"I cannot compete with the inspired Word," smiled Alfgar. He called to Wulfa, standing back of her mistress's chair, "She is tired and must be taken to her room at once." Then he turned back to his guests. "Well, shall we have the board and pieces in and play a game of spillikins while we finish our wine? I warn you, my hand is quick at it. I suggest, for the good of your pockets, that a low stake be set."

4

Tristram slept in Walter's room on a bundle of straw. He was sound asleep before the tallow dip had been extinguished, his long legs stretched out straight. When Walter roused at dawn, his companion was in exactly the same position; apparently he had not moved a muscle during the night.

They were finishing a breakfast of venison steak when Wilderkin interrupted them with a surprise summons: Walter was to see his grandfather at once in his working room. He had always been under the strictest orders not to enter this particular apartment. It opened off a dark corner under the inner staircase, and it had one window only, diamond-shaped and iron-barred, which looked out on the moat and could be seen from the top of the palisade and from nowhere else. As a boy Walter had often climbed the palisade to look at it and wonder what it contained. Did his grandfather dabble in magic that so much secrecy was necessary?

His grandfather was not there when he arrived, and so he was able to look the place over thoroughly. It was a disappointment; a small and frugal apartment with a clayish white floor. The furnishings consisted of a table, a single chair, a brazier in which a charcoal fire glowed feebly, and some shelves on one wall filled with documents. Of mystery it had none, of comfort very little.

The owner of Gurnie entered, followed by Wilderkin. He was wearing a gray surcote trimmed with miniver, and Walter realized for the first time how much he lacked in stature. Sitting down in the one chair, he placed his well-tended hands on the edge of the table and proceeded to talk in his clipped and precise manner.

"Wilderkin," he said, glancing once at his grandson and then looking studiously away, "there are some things I must say. As I have given careful thought to these matters, it is my wish to finish without any interruptions. If Walter feels it necessary to make any comments, he must as usual address them to you." He twisted uneasily in his chair. "An oath, once made, may never be broken; to that, naturally, we all agree.

"I have a desire," he went on, "to justify the changes which have been made at Gurnie. Without a doubt it has been felt that what I have done is a complete break away from all the traditions of knighthood. That I grant. No one could be more irked than I at the level to which the once proud domain of Gurnie has been brought." He paused and smiled bleakly. "Starvation is easier to talk about than to endure, but many have said it would be better to starve than to do what I have done."

His fingers were interlocked over his stomach, and he had swung one knee above the other, emphasizing the trimness of his fur-topped boots.

"I could have said that, inasmuch as His King's Grace had seen fit to take my land away from me, it was no longer possible to make a living from the begster holding left. A knight is denied the right to be useful at anything but the honorable use of arms, the control of his people, and in the councils of his king. But there were nearly a score of people who depended on me for the food they put into their mouths. None of them had any desire to starve. They were not bound by knightly traditions; they had normal bellies which cried aloud to be filled. And there was my daughter who needed all the care I could provide for—for the perhaps short time that we can hope to have her with us still.

"I tried other means. I swallowed my pride by petitioning repeatedly for the return of some part of my land. I even offered my services to the King, believing that my experience and my judgment, which I know to be sound, would make me useful to him. It was made clear to me that none of the land would be mine again and that there was no place for me in the royal service. So I took the only course open. It should not be necessary for me to say how repugnant this was to me. The best blood in England flows in my veins, and I have always been proud and tenacious of my rights and privileges. I have tried to accept the inevitable with a good grace, and it is not too much to expect, surely, that those who depend on me will do the same."

Walter had listened with the closest attention and with a growing sense of contrition. He could see now that his grandfather had done the only thing possible under the circumstances. It should have been evident to him from the first that the consequences of dabbling in trade were more galling to the old man than they could be to him.

"I would like to say, Wilderkin," he declared, in spite of his grandfather's request not to be interrupted, "that I see my lord Alfgar's position clearly and that I consider he has taken a courageous and knightly course."

The old man nodded his head with a pleased smile. "That was well spoken. And now I may tell of some plans I have for the future. I have a logical mind and, once I have reached a decision, I am prepared to carry it out with all the vigor I possess. My equals, or rather those who claim to be my equals, look down their noses at me now. I may as well earn their complete contempt. I am having cheese vats and curd knives made for me, and I propose to enlarge the root chamber for the making of yellow vinny, which I have always considered the best of cheese. I plan to make cheese on a large scale and sell it in London where the prices will be good. There will be double profit in it; for the swine will fatten on the whey. Then there are the few acres of orchard left to me. I shall use the squillery for the making of cider, a fine strong cider from the Gurnie recipe. I shall buy apples from all around here for the purpose as well."

"But," ventured Walter, "I must ask one question, Wilderkin. Couldn't the old metal be kept farther away from the house?"

"I am in trade now, and so I must make myself the very best of tradesmen just as I was once the most sagacious of knights. True enough, the metal could be stored on the other side of Oswiu Pond, where it would not seriously offend the eye. But how then could I keep an eye on it and be sure no thieving rascals were running off with the most valuable pieces? No, no! One cannot expect to enjoy the profits without paying the full price. The ross heap must stay where it is, just as my cheese-making must be part of the household offices so it can be managed more easily—even though the odor of the rennet may prove somewhat hard to bear."

The old man turned in his chair and looked squarely at his grandson. He even went to the extent of wagging a finger at him.

"That is where he makes his mistake, Wilderkin," he concluded, with a triumphant chirp. "The bitter must be taken with the sweet. One must always be logical."

Walter was thinking, though with some reluctance: "He is quite right. What grounds have I to quarrel with his methods?"

"And now, Wilderkin," went on his grandfather, in a brisker tone, "there are other matters to be discussed. I have heard talk that it might not be wise for Walter to go to Bulaire Castle for the funeral. I see no reason for staying away. The Norman woman would not dare vent her hatred on him. Of that I am convinced."

"I have no fears on that score," said Walter.

"Even if there were risks, he would have to go." Alfgar was looking down at the table, but Walter could see that he was indulging in shrewd speculations. "There is the matter of the will. It is reasonable to expect that some provision will be made for him. The acknowledgment that must go with the acceptance of a bequest will be a bitter dose to swallow, but—he was son to the dead man, and that cannot, in his own best interests, be brushed aside. I am hoping"—he paused and sighed—"that there will be some land for him. We need land so badly! What a fine use we could put it to!"

"It is my right to have a share," declared Walter. "But if no provision has been made, Wilderkin, I shall accept the situation with good grace. I have no desire to be beholden to them at Bulaire."

"Well spoken, again. I like the spirit he shows, Wilderkin. But we must be logical about this as in all other things. It is indeed his right to have a share of these fine, fat lands. We must swallow our pride and take what we can."

The old man reached behind him and drew down one of the documents from the shelves. Opening it with a cautious motion of his hand, as though he wanted to cover it from any eyes but his own, he proceeded to study the figures it contained. He had to lean his face over closely, as his eyesight was not good.

"Gurnie is beginning to do well enough. Not," with an alarmed raise of the head, "that we have yet anything to spare. We must still live on very little and make every easterling do the work of ten. But it is quite true that our position shows some improvement."

He closed the sheets and put them away. Then he looked at Walter and smiled; a warm and affectionate smile, the very first that his grandson had ever received from him.

"He is a good boy, Wilderkin. I have always been fond of him, although it has been impossible to show it; and now I have pride in him as well. It must not be held against him that his father was a weak man, nay that he broke the most sacred of knightly vows." He leaned over and touched Walter on the arm. "I have reached a difficult decision, Wilderkin. I am going to leave him everything that I possess."

CHAPTER III

Bulaire

THE WARDER who admitted Walter into the barbican at Bulaire Castle was suspicious of a visitor who had come on foot. "Simeon Bautrie sent for ye?" he said. "What would yer name be, then?"

"I am called Walter of Gurnie."

The warder grinned and motioned across the drawbridge with his thumb. "Get on in," he said. "I should know ye by the fine hump of yer nose. Get someone to take ye at once to Simeon Bautrie."

The man of the law was found in a dark cubicle cut into the thick stone wall of the gatehouse. Very little light got through the one high, iron-barred slit which served as a window, and he was busy over some writings by the light of a small candle. His lips moved moistly as he read, and he did not look up immediately. When he did, Walter saw that he had pale squinting eyes in a face as gray and lifeless as the parchments with which he worked.

"Ye've come, then," he muttered, studying Walter with an intentness that seemed to the latter to smack of suspicion. He was much bothered with fleas, for he kept scraping at his thin, woolen-clad ribs with his elbows. "And what do ye expect, Walter of Gurnie?"

"I have come on your instructions and without any thought of expectations," answered Walter, nettled at the tone. "I have one desire, to look on the face of my dead father."

"Ye're mentioned in the will, and so it was deemed wise to summon you." Bautrie picked up the document as though prepared to resume his work, but then thought better of it and dropped the sheets on the table again. He resumed in a high, sharp voice. "There is dislike for your presence here, Walter of Gurnie; of that you may be sure. My lady must not set eyes on you. For that reason, I am telling ye that on no account are ye to show yourself at the services. There will be the public service this afternoon at the church in Bulaire village and one later on for the members of the family in the chapel here."

"Am I not one of the family?"

"That ye are not. Never think it, young sir. My best advice to you is to sing low and keep yourself well out of the range of my lady's vision. As ye may have heard, she is of a stern determination; and she likes ye not." He coughed and spat on the stone floor. "Ask for Father Nicholas."

From the cold gloom of the high-vaulted gatehouse, on the wall of which the funereal hatchment hung in solemn warning of the loss the castle had sustained, Walter walked into the sunlit activities of the outer bailey. He had never been inside the walls of a castle before, and as he looked about him he escaped momentarily from the heavy humors which had occupied his mind on the long walk over. Packed tightly in against the wall, and so facing the stone keep which separated the outer from the inner bailey, were a series of buildings devoted to the agricultural side of the establishment—the stables, the poultry-house, the tool house, the smith's shop, the root chamber, the squillery, the woodyard. They were built of wood, and rather flimsy, with the exception of the stables which were of stone and most impressive, having two transepts and a jumble of Gothic buttresses.

The space between was as crowded with life as a street in London town. Walter stood and watched, for some minutes, rather shocked at the casual air of everything and the cheerful note of the loud talk. Some men-at-arms were playing billiards at the far end of the court, slapping their mallets against the large wooden balls and sending them through the hoops or against the "king" or skittering them over the baked clay base of the yard with exuberant shouts of, "Played up!" and "A clean hit at three toises!" A juggler was practicing the difficult feat of keeping three daggers twirling in the air while walking on stilts. Funerals always attracted entertainers of this sort, and there were probably many more of them about. The castle cordwainer, wearing a cloth awl above the crosslet on his arm, had fallen into a bitter argument with the blacksmith, and the air was shrill with invective.

"Ha, Harry-bell-the-cat!" cried the cordwainer. "So ye are saying the shoes I fashioned for ye had no proper shape, ye scum o' the spittals! If ye want the truth, I'll give it to ye straight: It is not part of my trade to make shoes for feet like the hooves of a mule."

"What, ye fleeching cagmag!" roared the blacksmith, his face black with rage. "If my lord did not lie dead above us, I would bend yer backbone into the shape of a mule's shoe, ye retching sib to a Sir Reverence!"

Two men-at-arms were rolling dice on the ground. As Walter watched, a maid came by and suddenly reached down and scooped up one of the dice. With a sly wink, she dropped it under the scarf covering her breasts and then ran away, flirting her scarlet plackerds impudently. One of the men went in immediate chase, and the pair disappeared back of the keep. "The slut!" said the other man-at-arms, continuing to toss the remaining dice with a grin.

Walter leaned over him to ask, "Where will I find Father Nicholas?"

"Where will ye find Father Nick? That," said the man, blowing on the dice, "is a fair question but a hard one to answer. He is as busy today as a tomcat on a leaden roof and as hard to catch as a will-o'-the-wisp. Still, speaking o' the devil, there for a wonder is the heaven-beck himself, and coming in this direction too."

A young priest had emerged from the stables. He was carrying a list in his hands and calling back over his shoulder in a tone of voice which proved he was bitterly at odds with someone within: "You will make room somehow. I tell you, Flanders, there is another party crossing the drawbridge this minute; two draught horses, three jennets, and a churchman's mule."

When he saw Walter, he came over to him at once. His face, a handsome one with a fine straight nose and a pair of lively brown eyes, was still clouded by the argument. "Another stranger!" he said. "Well, my son, and who are you?"

"I am Walter of Gurnie. Simeon Bautrie told me to find you."

The young priest looked at him with increased interest, then smiled and laid a hand on his arm.

"*You* have a right to be here at any rate. I can see you have not been given an attentive welcome, and so I must do what I can to right the scales." Then his expression became clouded again. "Because I am in Holy Orders, do they think I can perform miracles? Am I a soothsayer that I can guess who are coming and what must be done for each one? They give me a list that is no more than half complete, and I find that the supplies are no more than half adequate! Where I am to put you for the night, my son, is an answer to which at the moment I have no ready answer. Perhaps I can find room for another pallet in one of the bastion towers."

"You will have no complaint from me, no matter what you do. All I ask is a chance to see my father."

The wrathful look under the brown cowl changed immediately to one of understanding. "Of course, my son. I will take you to the chapel now."

Walter followed him through the door of the keep. The sun had little chance to assert itself through the narrow slits in the walls, and it took him some time to make out that they stood in a room which seemed to stretch ahead indefinitely, its arched roof supported by round pillars as in a crypt. It was used as the guardhouse. There were stone benches along the walls, littered with ringed hauberks and steel morions, and there were weapons everywhere, hanging on hooks driven into the whitewashed walls or piled up in racks down the center. There were targets on the walls for the throwing of darts, and pennons slumping limply on ropes strung from pillar to pillar. Crude and obscene drawings were scrawled everywhere.

There was one occupant only, a young man stripped to his waist who was oiling a steel belt and singing off key, in a thin tenor, "Merry Maude Was a Bouncing Bawd." Walter wondered why his guide paused beside the singer, throwing a look back as though he himself had reason to be interested as well. He understood when the soldier raised his head. It was the young fellow who had sat beside him in the church at Cencaster.

"Why must you stay in here, Hugh?" demanded the priest, with some return of his mood of exasperation. "Do you want to catch the rheumatics, sitting in the damp without a shirt on your back? There won't be many more fine days like this before the winter sets in and God's season is over."

"I must be ready for the procession." The young man-at-arms lowered his eyes again and went on briskly with his polishing. "It is late, Father Nick, and I've still a great deal to do."

"I was not sure you would want to march in the procession, Hugh, and I was going to ask Swire Jennings that you be excused."

The man-at-arms looked up and smiled with childlike pride. "But I'm looking forward to it, Father Nick. I must be at my best today. I have worked for hours on my hauberk, and it shines like the glass in the chapel. You can see yerself in my helmet. Yes, I will certainly look my best today. I've a new surcote to wear and"—his eyes were beaming now with eagerness—"and it's made of red wool. *Red,* Father Nick, and what do you think of that? They've always had their jokes about me, calling me 'bastard' and asking, 'Who's yer father?' But, Gog shrivel them up, I shall show them today. They will know who my father is today, Father Nick."

When they had walked out of earshot, Father Nicholas said to Walter: "Don't permit yourself to be disturbed, my son. It would take the full staff of scriveners who made up the Doomsday Book to count all the illegitimate children in England."

"Who was his mother?"

"A maid in the kitchens. She worked in the salsarium, and how his lordship ever managed to get a good look at her is a mystery. She was a pretty enough slut, when she got the flour and salt off her face, but she had no better than half a mind. She died in child-bed." His expression sobered. "Did you look closely at my poor Hugh? The stamp of his paternity is all over him, but it doesn't penetrate beneath the skin. Hugh is a stouthearted fellow, but he has the mind of a child."

Walter hesitated before asking his next question. "Are—are there any more of them?"

"Do you mean, are there any more of your father's get about?" The priest shook his head as though surprised at being asked. "Now, my son, what do you suppose? The late earl was the sun in the heavens of Bulaire, and he had quite a way with women. You will see a few peasant faces hereabouts with fine Norman noses instead of the usual camus spread. You will find that every lord in the land has done the same thing, my son."

Walter asked no more questions as they walked down the guardroom, their footsteps echoing loudly through the arched space above. They passed through a copper-studded door into the inner bailey, and Walter was surprised to find that this court lacked the space and the bustle of the outer one. The reason was soon clear, however. The important sections of the castle hedged it in—the Great Hall, the chapel, and tall bastion towers at each end, thus turning it into a series of connected quads and lanes. The stone walls facing them rose so high that the light of day came down sparingly. The cobblestones were slippery with the refuse which had been dumped from windows above during the night. An ancient nidering, puttering along with broom and pail, was engaged in cleaning up the debris. He was singing to himself in a cracked voice, and he wore a discolored cross on one shoulder. An old Crusader, and yet reduced to menial work of this description!

Two other house carles brushed by, carrying a basket of soiled clothes between them, a baby's biggin and a fool's cap reposing together on top. One was saying to the other: "Six sin-eaters! All of them stuffing their polluted stummicks with rich foods and wine! If I could be sure as earls and such 'ud die regular, I 'ud turn sin-eater myself."

"And go straight to hell when ye die?" There was deep scorn in the other servant's voice. "I've enough sins o' my own without taking other men's on my soul; and just for a piece o' gold and a good meal!"

The door of the chapel, which faced them, had the Lessford quarterings carved in the stone on each side and a great window above with stained glass showing Moses and the Burning Bush. The priest turned a key in the lock and motioned him to go in.

"Father Nicholas," said Walter, with one foot on the steps, "I saw no tree with out-of-season fruit! I was watching all the way along the Larney."

The priest's face took on a somber air. "The bodies were cut down and buried yesterday. May God give them peace!"

"Norman justice!" cried Walter bitterly.

Father Nicholas laid a cautioning hand on his arm. He whispered: "Speak lower. It is like a well here, and the sound of voices carries up. There is no telling who may be listening." After a moment, he added in a tense tone: "I live on the bread of Bulaire. My loyalty was to the earl, and I served him well, as priestly counselor and, I think, as friend. As soon as he has been laid away, I shall shake the dust of Bulaire from my feet!"

"Bravely and truly said!"

"As for you, Walter of Gurnie, a word of advice. You must stay until tomorrow when the will is opened and read. Let nothing delay your going then! Be sure your door is bolted—and sleep lightly!"

The chapel was not large, but the roof was high and so gave an effect of spaciousness. The stillness and the gloom took hold of him at once. He stood within the entrance, unable to move further, and blinking his eyes in the light of a *gaudy* in a socket beside him. His eyes were fixed on the shrine at the far end and the bier in front of it. There were candles as thick as a ship's mast at each corner of the bier. They must have been burning now for five days, but they still reared flickering flames several feet above the grim black pall on which his father lay.

Walter began to hear sounds. There were ghostly footsteps in the side aisles and a hint of stirring in the black monuments along the walls where the sculptured figures of the dead earls of Lessford lay in their armor. Whispering reached him from high up in the clerestory, where a faint light pierced the gloom through the quatrefoil windows. A cold chill began to creep up his spine.

The whisperings became more distinct. He was sure now that he could hear voices. They were not human voices, for there was a strange quality to them, a higher note than any living throat could produce. Were prayers for the departed soul being chanted by a celestial choir?

He took several steps forward, clutching the poppy-heads on the stalls for reassurance. Then he found himself hurrying, his heels making a clatter in the blackness, and this was unseemly because so completely human. The voices still sounded about him, and he was sure the eyes of the departed noblemen on each side turned in their marble sockets and bored into his back as he passed.

He was breathless when he found himself in front of the bier, and it did not help him to regain his composure when he realized he was not the only one in the chapel. A figure, swathed in black from head to foot, was sitting beside the body of his father. A strained white face stared at him from under a funeral coif, and a hand equally white was raised in a gesture which made it clear his presence was resented.

Although he had seen her once only, he knew that it was the Norman woman. The light of the candles was sufficient for him to make out that her eyes were tense under her heavy brows and that her mouth was set in a line of suffering and grim purpose. She had never been a comely woman, and now she looked like an avenging wraith. He noticed to his great surprise that she had a large balas-ruby on a chain around her neck; and he wondered if she wore it because it had been a gift from her departed lord.

She recognized him and rose at once, placing herself between him and the bier with the intent of preventing him from getting any closer. All fear left him now that he had someone human to face. He paid her no attention but looked steadily on the calm white face of his father, etched so clearly against the black background of his shield which had been elevated at his head.

Rauf of Bulaire was attired in a silk mantle embroidered with golden threads. Beside him lay his steel helmet from Bordeax, a white cointise wrapped about it. By him also were his costly coat of Naples mail and his Touranian sword. His hands, which had been so strong, looked thin and white folded across his breast. Now that his eyes were closed and no longer dominated his face with their fierce pride, he seemed gentle and kindly, and much more handsome than he had been in life. The fine chiseling of his nose and mouth affected Walter so deeply that he felt like crying at the pity and waste of this untimely death.

He had intended to remain silent, but almost against his will his lips began to move. "Father," he whispered, "I wanted so much to see you once again and tell you——" Then he clamped his lips tight. What he wanted to say could not be spoken with the Norman woman standing between them.

She said in an angry voice: "You must go! You have no right to be here!"

He did not shift his eyes from his father's face. "I have every right to be here," he declared. "He was my father. I was kept from seeing him when he was alive, but now that he is dead I deny anyone the right to prevent me from standing beside him."

"The door was locked," she said. "Who let you in?"

He looked at her squarely for the first time. Her prominent nose, so out of proportion to her thin and intense face, was twitching with emotion. "Would you have him hanged," he demanded, "as you did those six innocent men? Do you want to show us more samples of your Norman justice?"

She raised her arms in a passion of anger. "You must leave at once," she ordered. "If you do not, I swear you will hang as they did. I will tolerate no more insolence from you, nameless rascal that you are!"

It was on the tip of his tongue to say that retribution would be exacted for the terrible thing she had done, but he realized in time that it would be useless, as well as wrong, to bandy threats in the presence of the dead.

"I have a name," he said, "an honorable name, and I am proud of it. I need none other; though I know my father would have been happy could he have righted the wrong he did. Nothing you can say can take away from me the knowledge of what was in his heart."

"Saxon cur! How can you pretend to know what was in my lord's heart? I, and I alone, knew."

He made no effort to answer her further. His voice had choked, and he knew he would burst into tears if he stayed a moment longer or said another word. He did not want her to witness his weakness, and so he turned and hurried down the aisle.

"Good-by, Father," he said to himself. "If only things could have been different! I should have been your acknowledged son, and we should have lived together, you and my mother and I. If that had been the way of it, you might not be lying here dead and my mother would be happy and clear in her mind. And this hateful Norman woman would have remained where she belonged, far across the seas from Bulaire!"

He knew now, and for the first time fully, that in spite of everything he had always loved his father.

2

Having no idea how to find his way about in this teeming town packed within the castle walls, Walter turned at random down a narrow close. A bell sounded from somewhere up in the keep. Immediately people began to pour out of doors and to walk in one direction; men-at-arms, archers, house carles, musicians, most of them wearing the iron collar of Bulaire. He fell into line with them.

At an arch which opened from the inner into the outer bailey, he met Father Nicholas again. When told what had happened, the priest shook his head wrathfully.

"Was it necessary to speak up to her?" he demanded. "I care not for myself what she may do, but—you have offended her mortally, Walter of Gurnie, and you may rest assured she will not be content until she has paid you back in her own coinage. We must now see to it that for today at least you get well out of her sight."

Saying that he thought it best to leave by a rear postern, the priest led the way to the other end of the inner bailey, where the offices were located. Entering through the glass-stores, they found themselves in a dark passage which smelled strongly of spices and fragrant herbs. Passing an open archway, Walter caught a glimpse of a great cavern, stretching almost as far as he could see, where the cooks of the castle were preparing food before blazing open fires. There seemed to be an army of them, all in white smocks, and there was much brandishing of carving knives and potclames, and much bitter argument around the fires where joints and trussed fowls were turning on spits. The voices of the head cooks were raised in continuous demands for this and that, and the scullery knaves were kept running to and from the lardarium and the buttery, dipping supplies out of the huge sowes and finding dropping-pans and paste-troughs and pipkins.

The offices, Walter realized, were far away in spirit as well as in space from the gracious world of the Great Hall, where the walls were covered with tapestries and the furnishings were rich with needlepoint and brocade, and gentle music sounded from the Musicians' Gallery. Behind its imposing front the castle was dirty and mean and makeshift, and so badly planned that everything was continuously awry. Something of this he sensed as he peered into that resounding culinary cockpit, but it was to be a long time thereafter before he would see that a system of life which created tall stone castles and malodorous hovels clustering in squalor about its walls was equally awry.

Descending a winding stone stairway, they came to a damp passage closed off with an oak door. There was no one in sight, and the door was bolted on the other side, so the priest pounded on a wooden shield, suspended, perhaps, for that purpose. This summons brought a palsied little man, covered with dust and flour, who shouted at them in the toneless volume of the deaf, "What d'ye want?"

"To leave by the postern, miller," answered Father Nicholas, impatiently.

They could see in the gloom behind him a section of the castle mill. The stones of the quern were busily grinding, and a steady flow of the crushed grain poured down through the funnel in the upper stone.

"Can a man be in two places at once?" demanded the miller. " 'Tis impossible, ye'll tell me, Father Nick, but I know better. Flour, flour, they say! Enough flour to fill the draffsacks of all these fancy guests. But can they spare one lazy, ill-begotten jobbernowl from the guardroom to tend gate? Nay, nay, they are all needed to make a brave show above, and so Hal the miller must tend gate as well."

"Take a good look at this young gentleman, Hal," directed the priest. "Some time this night he will be wanting to return, and he will give you a special knock. Three quick and then two slow. Like this." He rapped on the door to demonstrate. "Will you promise to remember that? Three quick and two slow."

"He better not be later as midnight." The miller peered at Walter. "No 'un gets in after midnight. Yes, Father Nick, I'll remember." He nodded and repeated the signal with the key ring he carried. "Three quick and two slow. I'll not forget."

Walter departed by himself, crossing the moat on a hollowed-out trunk of elm. The narrow postern in the outer wall was swinging open. He found himself in a herb garden of considerable size, surrounded by a high hedge.

Beyond this stretched an open common through which wound the road to Bulaire village. He had expected to find it crowded, but to his great surprise it was almost empty. The few people he encountered were standing about in glum knots, talking in undertones and paying small heed to the entertainers. A reciter of tales, perched on a stump and vigorously declaiming the popular annals of Good King Borgabed, had no more than a listless baker's dozen about him. The juggler he had seen in the castle was having no better luck. Even a rope dancer, always the most likely to catch the public eye, was weaving and balancing on his coil with little hope of a copper harvest.

Walter had wandered about aimlessly and in the lowest of spirits for perhaps a quarter of an hour when a small man with a bent back hobbled past him and winked.

"Follow me, an it please you, my lord," whispered the man.

He was away immediately; and Walter, wondering why the message had been delivered with such an air of mystery, followed the bobbing turkey feather in his cap. The man disappeared into the russet border of trees and, not more than twenty yards within the forest shelter, they came on Tristram, leaning against the trunk of a large oak.

Walter wondered more than ever what it was all about. "I thought you went to Cencaster," he said.

Tristram nodded slowly. "I was there and saw my father," he said in a low voice. "I came here as soon as I learned what he had to tell me. There is something I have to do, Walter, and I am setting about it at once."

Walter's surprise was heightened when he perceived that his friend from Oxford had discarded his well-worn clothes and was now attired in an almost new and decidedly handsome archer's jacket, with a scarlet baldric and a longbow over his shoulder on a leather sling. The bow was a full seven-footer, and the quiver at his side was filled with arrows.

Walter was about to comment on this new finery, but he noticed in time that the face beneath the green archer's cap wore an expression of set and saddened determination. Clearly, something was amiss.

"What is it, Tris?" he asked.

Tristram faced about. His eyes, which never before had been anything but gentle and honestly unconcerned over the hardships and restrictions of his lot, were blazing with anger and rebellion. He tried to speak, but no words came. Walter saw that the gauntleted hand resting on the baldric was trembling.

"Tell me, Tris. What sorry news have you had?"

"My brother, my only brother Peter, was one of the six!" Tristram lost control of himself, and tears of grief streamed down his cheeks. "Poor little Peter! He was three years my senior; but he was small and not overly strong, and so I always felt I must look after him. He was honest and true and with a gentle spirit in his heart. Oh, he may have brought down a few birds on the lands of Bulaire, but I swear he had no more to do with the earl's death than I had!"

Walter stepped up close and threw an arm around the quaking shoulders. "This makes sorry hearing, Tris, my friend. But rest assured that justice will be done. The Norman woman will pay for her crime. The King's men will see to that in due course."

Tristram straightened up and said in a tense voice: "Justice cannot wait on the King's ministers. Haven't you heard that she was not content with killing the men?"

"All I know is what Wilderkin told us. We have been cut off from much dealings with the rest of the country since the confiscation. They hear little at Gurnie of what is going on."

"She has seized their wives and children," cried Tristram, "and is holding them in the dungeons of the castle! Peter married young, and he had a son nearly three years old. His wife and the boy are prisoners with the rest."

"I had heard no word of that. It is hard to believe; and yet, having seen her, I am ready to think any evil of her."

"Why is she holding them? Does she expect to force from one of the women the confession she couldn't get from any of the men?" Tristram was compelling himself to speak in a more restrained tone. "It is not in anyone's power to bring the men she murdered back to life. It may be that her punishment for that terrible crime should be left to God and the King. But she is holding the families without any shadow of legal right, and something must be done to free them without any more delay."

"The sheriff——" began Walter.

"The sheriff," cried Tristram, bitterly, "is the sorriest of cowards! He is afraid of the power of Bulaire, and he has done nothing. Nor will he

do anything; of that we can be sure now. No, Walter, the time has come
to take the law into our own hands."

"What do you propose to do?"

"I am going to follow a course which will raise a barrier between us
for all time. That is why I wanted to see you first. I wanted you to
know how sorely I feel the certain consequences. You are nobly born
and I am of the common people; and yet you took me into your home
as though I had been your equal. I will never forget that, Walter. And
now—now we will be pitted against each other. You abhor what she
did as much as anyone, but, after all, the earl was your father, and it
can't be in your nature to condone a rising of the common men. You
will turn against us. I am reconciled to that, and all I ask is that you
respect the confidence I am placing in you."

"But there is nothing you can hope to gain," exclaimed Walter earnestly. "Have you any conception of the strength of the castle? What
effect will your arrows have on those walls? Come, Tris, it would be the
worst of follies. Even if a miracle happened and you got your people
out, they would hunt you down afterward. And then all these trees
would be heavy with swinging bodies. Whichever way it went, they
would hang you, Tris, my friend."

"I must take the risk." Tristram touched the bow at his shoulder with
a confident hand. "Have you any idea of the might of the longbow?
Listen to me, Walter: We have here a new weapon which no other race
wots of yet. English archers could cut any army in Europe to pieces before they got close enough to harm us with their womanish crossbows.
And the longbow belongs to the common men of England. We could
slaughter your valiant knights just as readily. The archers hereabouts
are sturdy fellows and, if I can bring them into line, they will pick off
the Norman woman's garrison with the greatest ease. Chivalry is due
for a surprise, Walter; make no mistake about that."

The rooted beliefs of a lifetime are not easily to be shaken. Walter was
sure the fletcher's son was talking impossibilities, and he strove earnestly
to persuade him from his folly. "There must be other ways," he urged.
"Send a deputation to the widow to demand that she let them go. If she
sees the whole countryside is back of you, she will be of a mind to listen
to reason."

"It has already been done. She refused to see them."

"Then lay the case before the other large landowners. They can persuade her to a more reasonable course."

"My lord of Tressling was too drunk to listen to those who called on him yesterday. The sheriff is a place-seeking fool, and he quibbles about writs. The rest are in London." Tristram shook his head soberly. "They will starve before a peaceable solution can be found in the courts. So we must take the law into our own hands. I have one request to make, Walter. Don't return to the castle!"

"I must stay for the reading of the will tomorrow."

"Listen to reason!" cried Tristram. "Go back to Gurnie at once! I—I don't want to find my best friend with an arrow through his throat."

"You said you must face the risks. I must do the same."

There was silence between them for several moments, and then Tristram said in a repressed tone: "Then it is just as I said; we are on opposite sides from this time forward. I am sorely grieved it has to be this way."

He stepped back a pace and stripped off his gauntlet. It was of heavy leather, Walter saw, with a shield of mottled horn to protect the wrist and forearm from the action of the string, and the back was elaborately embossed in red with the words *Jesus direct my aim*. They shook hands solemnly.

To relieve the tension, Walter said, "You are handsomely attired, Tris. I swear I would not have known you."

"All this belonged to my father. He is old and has sworn never to loose an arrow at the butts again, and he insisted I must take his outfit." They were carefully avoiding each other's eyes in a mutual embarrassment over the regrets they shared. "My father wore the gauntlets at Lewes and Evesham, and," with an air of pride, "Jesus directed his aim well both days. May He do the same for me." He extended his arms so Walter could gauge the full splendor of the paternal gift. The jacket was not only ornate but of extreme practicality, having metal cuffs large enough to contain all the small equipment an archer must carry—a knife, a file, a large flint, a piece of resin, even a sizable whetstone. "This bow is the finest one he has ever made. He has saved it for me for years. It has a great strength, and yet it is supple to the hand. The balance is perfect. I have three dozen arrows, some of horn beam and some of sallow wood. I pray for the power to use them well."

They shook hands again, looking each other squarely in the eye this time.

"Good-by, Tris. I wish you the best of luck."

"Good-by, Wat. God bless you."

Walter watched the tall form of his friend vanish into the thick pattern of tree trunks. "I may never see him again," he said aloud.

It had been his intention to watch the funeral procession, but he found now that he had no heart to witness any part of the last rites from which he was barred of participation. He struck off to the right and walked for an hour along the banks of the Larney. The chatter of that busy little beck as it roiled over its shallows and stones had a soothing effect on his troubled spirits. "No matter what happens," he thought, "I must return to Oxford. I must complete my studies. I owe it to my grandfather not to lose all benefit of the sums he has paid out for me." There was a fortune to be made in the trade with the East, and he must content himself with that manner of life. Knighthood, he knew only too well, was not for a Saxon who had been born ignobly into a house which rested under the royal displeasure. He must do the best he could under the circumstances.

He had no belief, after thinking the situation over, that Tristram's aggressive intentions would bring matters to the point of actual conflict. The men of the country must have still too vivid a memory of what had happened after the defeat at Evesham to join him in such a hopeless venture. Tristram would have to abandon the plan. In the meantime somehow the means would be found to bring about the release of the unfortunate prisoners. He decided he would speak to Father Nicholas and urge that pressure be brought to bear on the Norman woman from her own people to change her vengeful intent.

3

The cortege had returned from the chapel when he reached the common again and the last of the horsemen were lowering their black plumed heads under the arch of the barbican. Walter was hungry, not having eaten since early morning, and he made his way to the pits, where whole carcasses of beef and lamb had been roasted for the stomachs of the anticipated crowds.

"Eat hearty!" said one of the cooks, slashing at the ribs of a steer to get a fine slice for him. "The apple-squires wanted none o' this. Let 'em go hungry then, the dirty chaw-bacons! It'll mean fine fare for the rest of us."

The warder waved him in at the entrance without question. Walter went at once to the outer bailey, hoping to find Father Nicholas there. He was told that supper was being served in the Great Hall and that the young priest would be included in the company. The meal would be a long one, for the visitors would be served in great state. For more than an hour, Walter watched a group of men-at-arms play the Game of God, their faces avid as they squatted on their heels, rubbing the bone dice in their hands and crying, "I utter defiance!" as they tossed in their stakes. Then, with some difficulty, he found his way to the inner court.

There was an unusually tall oriel window in the Great Hall, looking into the court and directly opposite the rear of the keep. Lights gleamed through it, and he could hear the blare of horns and the twang of strings from within. Next to the oriel was a chantry which had been built, as the inscription over the door showed, by the Adam of Lessford who had fought in the First Crusade. It was to be hoped, thought Walter, that prayers were still being said for him there; for Earl Adam had been a carnal and bloody-minded man and very much in need of them. The chapel was small, though it had an imposing entrance and two tall windows. Stained glass in churches always wakened some strange fancy in his mind, and it seemed to him now that the blue in the chantry windows suggested the thresh of angel's wings against a stormy evening sky.

A surly fellow in a dusty jerkin came by and said: "Stand away. We're ready to begin."

Walter obeyed by moving further to the right where a door was sunk down into the masonry of the keep. Here, it seemed, he was more in the way than ever. The man spat savagely and shoved at him with both hands, uttering: "Out of here, ye jordan-head! I'll gut ye if ye don't, sure's my name is Jack Daldy."

Walter looked at him with both curiosity and aversion, recognizing him by his name as the head jailer of Bulaire. He had a bad reputation in the county, this Jack Daldy, although he had been given no chance to display his skill with his instruments of torture during the time of the late earl. Walter shifted still farther along until he was practically out of sight in an angle of the keep wall. From here he still commanded a view of the court beneath the oriel window. He could see an old seneschal moving candelabra close to the panes. This done, the man loosened a catch in one section of the glass and threw it wide open. When he stepped back with a low bow, the guests began to take their places in the window, vying among themselves for better positions.

All this was casual enough. The guests were staring down into the court like spectators at a church mystery or a puppet-motion. Walter was certain nevertheless that the amusement provided for them would not be pleasant to watch.

"Are we to see more samples of Norman justice?" he wondered.

The Norman woman herself was standing in the open section, gazing down intently into the court. She was dressed in a black kirtle with sleeves long enough to cover her hands and a high fur collar against which her face seemed paler than ever.

Jack Daldy opened the sunken door into the keep, and two men appeared, dragging a third between them. The third man was a little fellow with a chalky face under an uncombed mop of tow-colored hair. He was in a great state of fright, for the iron collar around his neck shook as he moved. When they reached the middle of the court, the two keepers forced their prisoner to a kneeling position.

"Bart Linkin, my lady," said Jack Daldy.

"Proceed," said the widow.

Daldy produced a quarterstave and, raising it above his head, brought it down with a thud on the back of the kneeling man. Walter could see the frame of the prisoner quiver with shock and pain, but no sound came from him. More blows were rained on him, on his neck and ribs and even on his head, each one sending a convulsive jerk through his body. The victim controlled himself until a dozen strokes had been delivered. Then a shriek issued from his lips and he collapsed on the paving stones like a shewel from which the props had been removed. Daldy looked up at the widow.

"Go on," said the Norman woman. "Twenty strokes were ordered."

The rest of the sentence was inflicted on the prone body. The victim tried to cower away from the flailing staff and screeched piteously for mercy. By the time the last stroke was delivered, the screams had fallen away to a low sobbing. Daldy picked up a bucket of water and threw the contents over the body. Bart Linkin quivered once but made no other move. The two keepers yanked him up to a standing position between them and then proceeded to drag him to the keep door.

"Take him first to the outer bailey," ordered their mistress. "I want them all to see him. They must realize the kind of punishment I exact for disloyal talk."

The heads at the window made no move to withdraw. "Is there to be more of this?" thought Walter, uncertain if his stomach could stand it.

Without pausing to remove the blood which had splattered on the paving stones of the court, the phlegmatic Daldy proceeded to set out a long trough which had been brought, quite apparently, from the swinepens. This he filled with two bucketfuls of broken food, some scraps of meat, some bread, a mess of vegetables, none of it very fresh from the looks of it. He straightened up over his shoulder: "Open up now. Let 'em come out."

The dungeon door was opened from within. For several moments nothing happened, and then a very small boy ventured out, looking about him with a sort of animal caution and drawing his body back with each hesitant step he took. His clothes were torn, and his face and hands were caked with dirt. There was a reddish streak on the front of his jerkin which might have been blood.

"Food," said Daldy, in a less belligerent tone. "Help yourself, boy."

What happened then was strange and terrifying to witness. The boy saw the trough and rushed forward, throwing himself on his knees beside it and scooping up the food in his hands. He began to eat with a frantic haste, making a horrible gobbling sound and at the same time weeping with nervous abandon.

"The poor little fellow is nearly starved," thought Walter.

Almost immediately there was a scuffling in the doorway and a flood of children precipitated themselves into the court. They were of all ages, up to perhaps twelve, girls as well as boys, and they were all as dirty and wild-looking as the first boy. They struggled about the trough as furiously as a litter of pigs and so it was impossible to count them; but Walter was sure there were at least a score. As the trough was not long enough for all of them, the result can be imagined. They screamed and fought, tearing the food from one another and bolting what they could keep with convulsive haste.

They were the children of the six hanged men, he was sure. There was an iron ring sunk into the masonry back of him, and Walter found that his fingers had clamped themselves around it. "Steady!" he said to himself. "It would do no good to interfere now. *Wait!*"

The struggle for the food continued with unabated ferocity. Several of the smaller children had been hurt and were crying bitterly on the edge of things. One, the smallest of the lot, had not been able to get near the trough at all. He was rubbing grubby knuckles in his eyes as he wept. This, Walter was certain, was Tristram's little nephew.

Walter looked up at the group in the oriel window. It seemed to him that most of them were not enjoying the spectacle. Some had already withdrawn, but the widow kept her position, her eyes fixed on the scene below with a brooding intensity.

When the food was all gone, Daldy began to drive the still ravenous children back to the dungeon door. They resisted furiously, clawing at him and shrieking for more to eat. He had to summon his two helpers to get them herded within. Not until the last child had disappeared, and the door had clanged to on them, did the widow leave her post at the window.

Walter walked over to Daldy, who was busying himself now at cleaning up the court. "Ye're still here, are ye?" the jailer grunted over his shoulder. "I didn't know it or I'd of warmed yer backsides off the place."

"I am glad to know what Norman justice means," said Walter.

The man looked up at him suspiciously. "I don't know ye from Adam's bastard son, but if ye're sensible enough to take a word of advice from old Jack Daldy, ye'll get away from here as fast as ye can."

"How long had they been without food?"

"Ever since they brought 'em in. Ye have no call to look at me that way; it's been done on strict orders. I'll rack grown men, and I'll put red-hot rivets agin their buttocks and think nothin' of it; but I've no stummick for treating childers this way. I'm a blabberin' fool to say that much to a stranger. Ye saw what happened to Bart Linkin. He had too much to say for hisself. A still tongue—that's the safe thing here."

"Where are the mothers of the children?"

Daldy suddenly became sulky. "I'll tell ye nothin' more. Get along about yer business. For all I know, *she* will find out everything we've been saying."

Walter turned and walked away.

4

He decided it would be wiser to leave by the rear postern. Hal the miller answered his summons and stared at him curiously in the flickering light cast by a cresset above the mill door.

"Ye look pale," grunted the miller.

"I have had a shock."

"If it wasn't as ye're of the nobility, I 'ud offer to share with ye a pot o' ale I've just drawn."

"I'll share it, and gladly," said Walter. "There is some doubt as to my right to claim nobility, and at this moment I am disposed to cherish the doubt. I am full of doubts, Hal the miller; doubts which beset me sorely. I am wondering if the things I have always believed right and just, which set one man above another, are of God's will and purpose."

Back in the mill, they supped their ale in silence until Walter bestirred himself to ask, "Is there a man in these parts, a common man, who could be depended on to know of any matters afoot calling for resolution and a stout heart?"

The miller answered at once. "Camus Harry, who runs the Lubber's Head in Little Tamitt. Three miles and more back. An old Cruse and a solid fellow, Camus Harry. Aye, Camus Harry's yer man."

Walter nodded and got to his feet. "How long will you be on duty here?" he asked.

"Till midnight. Knock loud if ye come back. I'm old and rheumy, and I fall to sleep easy."

Inky blackness engulfed Walter when he issued from the postern. Certain that he could get wind of Tristram's whereabouts at the Lubber's Head, he struck out in the direction that Hal the miller had indicated.

There was a light in the one window of the alehouse, by which he could make out a pentagram on the lintel to keep away evil spirits. There were half a dozen men inside seated on wooden benches and talking together in low voices. The landlord, a powerfully built fellow with a friendly eye and a flattened nose which, no doubt, accounted for his nickname, came forward at once.

"I've a bed if that's what ye seek," he said. "There are three in it now, but it holds five at a pinch."

"I'm not looking for a bed tonight," answered Walter.

A silence fell on the room. Walter could see that every pair of eyes had turned in his direction. He sensed an unfriendly wariness in their fixed regard.

"So," said Camus Harry, the smile deserting his broad face, "it's not a bed ye want. A sup of ale, then, and a nook of the rabbit ye see turning on the spit?"

"I am not hungry, landlord."

"What brings ye to the Lubber's Head at this late hour, then?"

Walter lowered his voice. "I must find Tristram Griffen, and at once. Do you know where he might be?"

There was a stir in the room at that. Several of the onlookers got up from the benches and ranged themselves by the landlord, staring at the visitor with an even more disquieting intentness. One of them drew a dagger from his belt.

"Who is this young sprink?" he demanded gruffly.

"I will handle this, Nat," cautioned the landlord. "I know the lad. He's grandson to the nip-cheese of Gurnie."

"Then he's of the nobility!" exclaimed the same man. "I don't like the looks of it, Harry."

Camus Harry motioned them back with both arms. "Easy," he said. "There's no call yet to get yer weasands rumbling. Now, Sir Clerk, answer me fairly. Why do ye seek Tristram Griffen?"

"I have something of urgency to tell him." Walter looked around at the ring of menacing faces and then added: "Perhaps you would be easier in your minds about me if I told you also. No harm can come of it. It will be all over the countryside by morning in any event."

He began to tell them what he had seen at the castle. They listened for several minutes in a glum and unconvinced silence; then suddenly they were all on their feet, surging around him and swearing bitterly, their hands pawing at their daggers. The caution with which he had first been met was tossed aside, and he heard eager voices saying that they must march against the castle without a moment's delay.

"Empty yer beds!" cried one of them to the landlord. "Rout them out! We'll need every pair of hands for the work ahead of us this night!"

"Now b'yr Lady of Walsingham," said Camus Harry, when the story had all been told. He continued to watch Walter steadily, although the latter noticed that one of his hands was trembling as it gripped his wispy beard. "And ye saw this yerself, Walter of Gurnie?"

"With my own eyes. Every word I have spoken is God's truth."

"But ye haven't told us yet why ye seek Tristram Griffen."

"We are friends, Tristram and I. I know what he has in his mind to do."

"And is it in yer mind to lend him aid?"

Walter did not answer immediately. What he must say now was a betrayal of the class from which he sprang, a denial of the rights and privileges he had never before questioned. After no more than a moment's hesitation, however, he said in a clear voice, "Any man with blood in his veins, who saw what I saw tonight, would be ready to see the castle torn down, stone by stone."

"You are a son of the dead earl, and yet ye say that?"

"I am ready to help."

Camus Harry took it on himself to pronounce the verdict. "That is good enough," he said. "Fairly spoken, young sir. I, for one, believe ye. Now go and sit down, all of ye." He paused. "We have been waiting here for Tristram to join us. He should arrive at any minute now."

There was much discussion of plans from the creaking benches for the next half hour. Walter seated himself in a corner and took no part in the talk, realizing that his position would remain somewhat uncertain until Tristram put in an appearance. Camus Harry listened with a mounting impatience.

"I'm an old Cruse," he said, finally, "and I want to tell ye all that we can't go plunging blindly into this. I've seen a plenty of sieges in my day. The walls of Bulaire won't tumble down like Jericho when ye sound yer horns. They're strong and they're high, and the Norman woman has plenty of men to guard them. Close yer bone-traps and listen to one who has worn the Cross. We must gain by stratagem what we can't by blind attack."

Walter spoke up at this. "I can be of help there."

The landlord winked for the benefit of the company. "Out with it, then, Sir Clerk. What have ye learned at the *niniversity* that old soldiers and men o' the woods don't ken?"

"Assemble the main body in the woods which mask the main entrance. In the meantime send a dozen men with me to get in at the rear postern. We'll cross to the gatehouse, surprise the warders there, and lower the portcullis. Our main body can then swarm into the castle."

"A noble plan," said the landlord, grinning broadly. "But ye've left one detail out. Which do we play, a game of stooleball or spillikins, while we're about it?"

A dusty fellow sprawling on a bulting-ark at one side gave vent to a loud guffaw and slapped his thigh ecstatically. "That puts the noble lord in his place," he said.

Camus Harry went on in a kindlier tone, having had his joke, "What makes ye think we could force the west postern?"

Walter hesitated before answering. "It may not be necessary to use force," he explained. "If we get there before midnight, the gate will be opened. A special signal has been arranged."

"Ah!" cried the landlord, suddenly alert. "That puts a new face on it. Why didn't ye tell us ye counted on help from inside? By the great Melec Ric, we may have them if this be true!"

Tristram put in an appearance at this point. He stopped dead in the doorway when his eyes lighted on Walter, then he came forward slowly. "You here?" he said. "What does it mean, Walter?"

"I want to have a share in the night's work. My eyes have been opened, Tris, and I know now that you are right. Justice can wait no longer."

The honest face of the fletcher's son began to beam. He dropped a hand on each of Walter's shoulders and shook him affectionately. "I know the sound heart of you, Walter," he exclaimed, "and yet this is better than I could have hoped for. Now we can take the risks side by side." In a moment, however, a shadow of doubt showed itself. "It's not your quarrel. Should you share a risk that is ours only? What will your grandfather say? What will this do to your chances at Bulaire? I wonder if you have weighed all these matters?"

"When you've heard what I have to tell," said Walter, "you will need no answers to any of your questions."

"The telling can wait," said the landlord. He walked to an inner door and called back to the kitchen: "Bess! Wenciliana! Come, ye lazy trollops, hoist yerselves up from off yer fat mutton-buttons and bring us food." He looked back at the company and added, "Ye need a full stummick when ye have man's work ahead of ye."

They left a full hour before midnight, Camus Harry halting the little company at the door of the inn to give them a solemn harangue. "Tris will leave us here and will see to it that the men from Cencaster and Tressling wait outside the main gate. The rest of ye will be under my orders. Wait for the signal, Tris, which will tell ye the plan has been carried out—two blasts on this horn of mine. When ye hear it, come with a rush and a shout like the stout men of Gideon. If ye don't hear it, stay where ye are until I can get some word to ye as to what must be done." He paused and then went on with sudden gravity. "And now a word of caution. Win or lose, there will be grave trouble for us afterward. They will try to hunt us down singly. Cover yer faces with mud and lay it on thick; there's no sense to being seen and recognized. Raise yer voices as little as possible, even in the middle of it. We may all take a leap from the gallows tree for what we're setting out to do. Say a prayer before the fighting starts and ask the King's Son of Heaven to look with lenient eyes on us. Take a mouthful of earth to remind ye that all men are mortal. We always did that when I wore the Cross."

He led off, carrying a lighted torch but holding it down close to the earth so those who followed could get an idea of the footing. They went slowly. When they had covered perhaps half of the distance, Walter saw ahead of them a faint pinprick of light and decided that it must be the fire in the warder's turret at Bulaire. It seemed small, and he wondered if the sentries had forgotten to replenish it. Perhaps they had gone to sleep on duty. In either case, it promised well.

Camus Harry had timed their movements so they would arrive at the western postern at about the same time as the men from the near-by villages. They crossed the common and halted outside the hedge. "Stay here," whispered their leader. "I am going to skirt around to the other side to make sure they are ready."

A long wait followed. Walter was growing more apprehensive by the moment, fearing they would be too late to catch Hal the miller on duty. Then he heard a cautious voice in the darkness near him. "We're ready. Tris has his men drawn up on the other side. Thirty men from Ashley-Buzzard have joined us, and the Engster squad are coming in from the south now."

Walter could hear their leader crawling about in the darkness and whispering final instructions. Looking about him, he saw with a sudden surge of excitement a light winking and bobbing in the distance. More men were coming! Turning in another direction, he saw more lights, torches carried in the hands of hurrying yeomen. In another ten minutes there were lights visible in all directions, tossing against the inky blackness of the sky. The sentries on the walls above must see them also. Walter expected to hear shouts from the battlements at any instant. Then he heard the landlord of Little Tamitt whisper at his shoulder: "Go along, Walter of Gurnie. Give your signal at the postern."

The outer postern was closed and locked. Walter rapped loudly three times and then twice slowly. No response came. Was Hal of the mill sleeping or had he been relieved from duty? It was an anxious moment.

He knocked again. No response. A complete silence still reigned inside. He had just about given up hope when he heard a hand fumbling at the lock inside.

"Ye're late," grumbled the miller, peering out through the open gate. "What have ye been up to? It's a cold night for wenching. And now ye'll give me the word."

"The word?" repeated Walter. "I'll give you an appropriate one. *Norman justice!*"

The miller raised his lantern, and at that moment two of Walter's companions sprang forward and pinioned his arms. A third seized the lantern, and a fourth clapped a hand over his mouth. The miller recovered from his surprise sufficiently to struggle vigorously. In the tussle which ensued, he lost his footing and fell back into the water, taking one of the men with him. It was the least desirable of all places for an involuntary dip. The castle garde-robes were located floor on floor below the mill, and the filth from them was carried to the walls in pipes and allowed to run down the outer surface of the masonry to the moat.

Camus Harry, crossing the log after Walter, whispered an order: "If he makes any noise when he comes up, chine his head wide open."

A torch was burning dimly in a wall socket. Walter took possession of it and led the way through the offices. They were dark and empty, although the presence of torches on the walls at intervals made it certain that a watchman was about somewhere. When they reached the inner bailey, they found that a few lights still showed in windows looking down on it. From one of them came a sound of male voices singing in chorus. They were rendering "Loudly Sing Cuckoo" in such perfect harmony that it was certain they were trained gleemen. Some of the guests, quite obviously, were still making merry.

Camus Harry said at his shoulder, "That's a brave chorus, but they will sing small later."

An intense exhilaration had gripped Walter. They were in the castle, and it should now be possible to carry out the full plan, his plan. The unfortunate prisoners would be rescued. "What would she think of the nameless rascal, if she knew?" he asked himself, triumphantly.

There were lights in the gatehouse but no signs of human occupancy. They looked about them, amazed at such carelessness. "It's always this way when there's a woman in charge," declared the landlord of Little Tamitt. "Things were different when your father was alive."

A sound of snoring reached them finally from a small room at one side. The leader went in to investigate and returned with a broad and triumphant grin. "Whiddled to their snouts. Get in there, Stevie, Robin, Hengist! Gag them and tie them up." His eyes blazed at Walter. "Such luck, Sir Clerk! The whole castle seems to be sleeping off the funeral wines."

He led the way out to the main gate and stared up at the massive portcullis and the raised bridge which closed off the entrance tightly. The chains hanging down on each side looked too heavy for human hands to move.

"I learned the way of these when I wore the Cross," said the landlord with brisk confidence. "They work with a double action; ye raise the portcullis and the bridge falls. Let me see now. There should be two levers extending from the gudgeon pin. Once they're released over the truss, the rest will be easy."

While he tugged at the chains with the aid of two husky comrades, Walter kept an eye on the inside passage. Two archers had stationed themselves there with arrows fitted to their bows in readiness. Would the bridge be lowered before the alarm was raised? The great castle still remained in complete silence. Walter could hear the reluctant whine and creak of the chains and the breathless orders of Camus Harry. When the latter cried out in sudden exasperation, Walter said to himself, "He can't do it, after all, and we'll be caught in here like rats!" It was too much to hope that their presence would go unnoticed much longer.

"There!" said the landlord, finally.

Walter looked back over his shoulder and saw that the bridge was beginning to swing outward. The sharp iron fangs at the base of the portcullis had already lifted several feet. The gate continued to rise, protesting with a shrill metallic screech. Camus Harry climbed under the blades and ran out on the falling bridge, his weight accelerating its descent. He had the barbican gate open within a minute after the bridge had fallen into its outer groove. Walter could see him tugging at the horn in his belt.

When the two sharp blasts sounded, Walter ran to the inner end of the passage to lend such aid as might be necessary to the archers posted there. One of the pair pointed to the lights which were now showing in the keep. "Too late," he grinned, drawing a hawthorn shaft from his quiver. "There will be bows and bills all over the place in two minutes. The castle is ours, and we have you to thank for it, Sir Clerk."

Loud shouts of "St. George! St. George!" could be heard behind them as scores of eager feet raced across the drawbridge. Walter took one look back and saw that Tristram was in the lead, tossing his longbow in the air and catching it as he ran. The next instant the door of the keep opened and some men-at-arms poured out. They were buckling on their armor, and some even were rubbing the sleep from their eyes. One of the archers raised his bow and sighted hurriedly.

"No, no!" cried Walter. "They'll give up without a fight when they find we're inside."

He was too late. The bow twanged and the arrow shot across the narrow space of the outer bailey, striking one of the men-at-arms in the neck. The victim had been gathering himself to run across the court, but the impact sent him reeling backward. For a moment he rocked on his heels and then collapsed in a heap, one leg twisted unnaturally under him, the arrow in his neck sticking straight up into the air.

"Never knew what struck him," boasted the successful marksman, fitting another arrow to his bow. "A neat shot, my bullies. Well, I've evened the score for poor Mark Githing, my kinsman, who danced on air at the widow's bidding."

There was no chance to use the second arrow. The passage behind them was full suddenly of shouting men, their faces daubed a savage black. They erupted into the bailey and in the space of seconds had taken full possession of it. The men-at-arms laid down their pikes with a willingness that suggested they had no stomach for fighting the Norman woman's battle.

Camus Harry, one hand bleeding from the furious haste with which he had worked on the chains, paused beside Walter in the arched entrance.

"We've won!" He had to shout at the top of his voice to make himself heard over the din. "In all the years I carried the Cross, I never saw a stronghold fall so easily. And it hasn't cost a life on either side."

"One," exclaimed Walter.

Abruptly all sense of elation had left him. He saw the body of the dead man-at-arms stretched out on the cobblestones, surrounded by a subdued group of his fellows. The dead man had yellow hair and a young face, and he was wearing a red surcote.

A deputation of three came down from the tower where the retiring rooms of the family were located. Two of them were knights, looking very crestfallen and not a little ridiculous with their swords buckled over the loose gowns in which they had been sleeping. The third was Simeon Bautrie. The man of the law was as white as the skin of an onion. They had sent word ahead for the leaders of the yeomen to meet them in the Great Hall, but Camus Harry would have none of that; the parley, he had replied, would be held in the open where everyone could hear. The trio accordingly had come to the outer bailey where the landlord of Little Tamitt waited for them.

"We come in behalf of the Countess of Bulaire," said one of the knights. "The countess, in turn, acts for the earl who is still a minor in years. First, we demand to know the reason for this unseemly intrusion."

Silence had fallen on the courtyard, and all eyes turned expectantly in the direction of Camus Harry.

"The reason is soon given," he answered. "We come to secure the release of the wives and children of the six men who were foully murdered on the orders of the woman ye call the Countess of Bulaire. It's not our intent to exact vengeance for the six men, though it's in our power to do so. We could hang the countess herself." A loud shout went up at this, a proof of the mood of his followers. "Yes, we could hang her if we so willed; and I for one would find great satisfaction in pulling on the rope which would swing her to her punishment beyond! But that would lead to more bloodshed, and there would be more wives without husbands and children without fathers before we saw the end of it. In that matter, we will wait for the King's law, believing he will see to it that justice is done." He made a pause. "We are yeomen of England, not thieves; and when we leave here we will take nothing with us, not so much as a bite of food for the starving prisoners ye hold in yer foul dungeons. They are held without a shadow of right, and we demand their release at once."

"I am sure," began Simeon Bautrie, "that your demand will be given consideration by the countess——"

"Listen to me, ye distraining cheat!" declared the landlord. "Our demand must be met without any consideration at all. We'll have none o' yer glib talk of writs and laws of infang. We give ye five minutes to produce them. For each minute over the five, we'll hang a member of the household from the battlements. And we'll begin with you, Sir Lawyer. By the God above us, Who hears every word we say, ye'll dance at the nubbing-post if ye're late with them!"

The neck of Simeon Bautrie was not to know the feel of the rope, for there was a full minute to spare when the last of the prisoners appeared from the dungeons. Several of the women had to be carried up, having been put to the rack to force confessions of their men's guilt. This was not known until later, or nothing could have saved Jack Daldy and his helpers from hanging. The children were too dazed and weak to know what was happening. Horses from the stables were hitched to farm carts in which the released families were placed on comfortable piles of straw.

The picture of the departure would remain in Walter's mind as long as he lived. Waving lighted torches over their heads, the triumphant yeoman marched out over the drawbridge. The men of Little Tamitt went first, Camus Harry leading them with a new strut in his heels. There were no men from Gurnie, as the word had not been carried that far, and so Walter waited with Tristram to leave with the band from Cencaster. Nobly born though he was, he felt a great pride as he watched the contingents of common men swing into line. An English answer had been given to the Norman woman with her foreign ideas of justice!

Stout of limb and broad of back, each man carried one of those mighty weapons with which, if Tristram was to be believed, the whole world could be conquered. At the moment Walter was sure of it also.

As the first files swung down toward the forest, the torches casting so great a light that wisps of straw could be seen floating on the water of the moat and even the bend of the road one hundred yards below, where a

stone bridge crossed the Larney, the leaders struck up "The Sons of
Job." This easy marching song, which had been first sung by the men
who fought under Earl Simon, was immediately taken up all along the
line. The words came rolling back:

> *"Job, in ashes, low did sing,*
> *Nor ceased cor-vee for Heaven's King.*
> *We are the sons of Job!"*

It seemed to Walter that the shades of William Longbeard and the
three bold outlaws, Adam Bel, William Cloudsley, and Clym-o'-the
Clough, marched with the men of Little Tamitt and Engster under the
arching trees. Certainly they had seen the thing done, these dead and
gone heroes of Saxon resistance to Norman aggression. Wherever they
might be, they must have indulged in much ghostly thumping of backs
and loud rejoicing!

The song was still being sung as Walter fell into step with the men of
Cencaster:

> *"The Lord, relenting, smote Job's foes,*
> *Shaped new arrows for his bows.*
> *We are the sons of Job!"*

He was the very last of the procession, and he found himself joining
in the chorus:

> *"Norman, Socman, Chapman—pray!*
> *The sons of Job are on their way!"*

5

Fearing that the Lubber's Head might be visited by forces of retribution during the night, Walter and Tristram slept in a hayrick near by.
Walter wakened first and sat up, stretching his dusty arms sleepily and
looking up into a clear October sky. Tristram roused immediately after,
shaking his head as though he thought it part of his dreams to find himself in such a position.

"There will be a sour taste in the mouth of the Norman woman this
morning," said the latter, grinning at Walter.

This reference to their success the night before pleased them so much
that they fell to wrestling and scuffling about in the hay like a pair of
overgrown schoolboys, bandying back and forth some of the catch

phrases of Oxford, "Thou utterly masterly Master of Arts!" and "Avaunt, thou very idiot!"

"And now what are we to do?" asked Tristram, when they had settled down. "I, for one, must shake the dust of the county from my feet. You also, Walter, may be in danger."

"I am going to Bulaire."

The fletcher's son tried to talk him out of this purpose, but his arguments had no effect. He had been summoned there, Walter contended, and he must be in attendance, come what may. No one, he was sure, would suspect him of a part in the events of the night.

They arranged then to meet later in the day. After washing thoroughly in a neighboring stream and brushing his dusty clothes, Walter set out. Glancing back over his shoulder, he caught a last glimpse of Tristram breakfasting on a turnip under the cover of the rick.

It was well that he had been so industrious about his ablutions, for in a short time he heard the clomp-clomp of a horse's hooves coming up behind him at a gallop. He jumped quickly to the side of the road, prepared to vanish if need be into the cover of Malley Wood.

It was Engaine. She was out early (she was always one to seek the benefit of the morning sun), and he saw that she had loosed her hawk at some prey in the air. It was a saber-hawk, apparently, for the squire who rode behind her was having difficulty in coaxing it back. He was whistling desperately and swinging the lure over his head, a mock falcon with scarlet feathers. As the recalcitrant bird wheeled and swooped in the sky, Engaine slowed down her mount and whistled also, a clear note, much higher than anything the squire had been able to produce. She had a red gorget wound loosely around her throat and was wearing a gold-mesh crestine to protect her hair from the wind. His heart thumped at the sight of her.

The hawk finally decided to return, the silver bells attached to each of its legs jingling cheerfully as it settled on her wrist. She slipped the hood on, a very gay covering of scarlet velvet, embroidered with gold thread and with a paradise plume arching up from it. The cost of this finery was more than a common man could hope to earn in a score of years!

"Saladin, Saladin!" said Engaine, reprovingly. "You are such a bad bird, such a very ill-trained fellow indeed!"

Then she saw Walter and reined in her horse, regarding him with the half-friendly, half-scornful look she always wore when they met.

"Walter of Gurnie," she said, holding her head so high that she seemed to be looking down at him the full length of her handsome nose. "Are you aware that you are out of bounds? Can it be that you have taken it on yourself to do the poaching which keeps your table at Gurnie supplied with meat?"

"Are *you* aware," he countered, hating her for her pride and arrogance but loving her at the same time for her beauty, "that all this land belonged to Gurnie at one time? You Normans were no better than poachers in France, thieving wolves of the sea with no land of your own, when my ancestors owned all of Tressling and much of Bulaire?"

"*Your* ancestors?" She tossed her head still higher. "You seem to forget that you're half Norman yourself."

"No," he answered, after a long and painful pause. "I never forget it."

She realized from his tone how much he had been hurt, and her mood changed at once. She smiled at him with the sudden radiance which was her greatest charm and which always left him breathless. "That was unkind, Wat. I am always saying unkind things and then regretting them. And now I must be still more unkind to you," she added in a penitent tone. "Walter, I am going to be married."

"Ninian warned me of it."

He had always lived in dread of this moment; knowing it was sure to come and that nothing could avert it, and yet hoping that some miracle would happen to give him his chance. The blow had fallen at last: She was going to be married; and he, the illegitimate son of the Earl of Lessford, loved her so much it did not seem possible he would ever know happiness or content again.

"Didn't you hear what I said?"

"Yes, I heard. Whom are you going to marry?"

He found it hard to get the question out, feeling that once he knew the name of his supremely favored rival the thing would become more definite. He did not want to learn any of the details, because the hearing of them would have the same effect.

She was looking at him with a trace of hesitation. "It will be a very fine match," she said. "Everyone is agreed to that. My uncle Rauf had settled it with Father before he was killed. You see, the first Earl of Lessford was given two hundred and forty-seven manors at the time of the Conquest, but not all of the land has been kept in the family. Our first holdings at Tressling were part of the original grant."

The significance of what she had said made no impression on him at first. He had given a thought to the despoiling of Saxon homes which had gone into such a large grant. No wonder the hate engendered in Saxon hearts had continued to smolder all these years!

"The marriage will nearly restore the full holdings of Bulaire," Engaine was saying. "It is a very sensible arrangement."

The truth dawned on him at last. He stared at her, trying not to believe what he had heard. "Do you mean," he asked, finally, "that you're to marry Edmond?"

"And why not? What better match could I make? We are second cousins only. I am to be the Countess of Lessford."

He did not dare look at her. "I have known it was impossible, but I've always wanted you so much that nothing else seemed of any real consequence." A fury of dissent with everything that was happening took possession of him. "You know that my father was shipwrecked on his return from the Crusades and the family of his wife paid the ransom. It was only because of this that he married her. If his ship had not been wrecked, I would be the Earl of Lessford today." He looked up then. "Because of that you are going to marry Edmond and not me."

He stepped nearer and took hold of the bridle. He had never been so close to her before, and he was finding her beauty as dazzling as the sun at midday.

"You are taking much for granted," she said. Then she smiled, and Engaine's smile was something for the memory to cherish; her eyes had widened, crinkling at the corners and glowing warmly, her lips had parted with a hint of a dimple at each corner.

"Engaine, wait for me!" he cried. "I am working hard to gain knowledge so that I may make a worthy and honorable position in life for myself. I will have land some day, much land, and a good name which you could bear without any feeling of shame. I swear that I am going to succeed! Wait, give me a little time!"

"That is the talk of a schoolboy," she said. Then her voice became more gentle and understanding, "I am sorry, Walter, but it cannot be any other way. It has been settled, and my father would not consent to any change or delay. I have always liked you, Walter. You know that. But I have always known that nothing could come of it."

"Engaine, listen to me. I will return soon, and perhaps then your father will give his consent. You are too young to wed now. Wait a year, two years; that is all I will need."

Engaine smiled again. She held out her gloved hand to him.

"Walter, come a little closer," she said.

When he obeyed, she leaned over until her face was very near his.
Their hands were tightly clasped.

"You are so tall and so handsome," she whispered. "I am fond of you,
more fond than you will ever know. If—if it had only been possible!"
She sighed, and her fingers pressed his tightly. "I wish it could be you
instead of Edmond. But—it can't be that way, Walter, and wishes are
of no avail."

Then she withdrew her hand and sat up straight again in her saddle.
Looking up at her, he realized that the distance she had put between
them was more than a matter of a few feet; it was the measureless space
between a lady of high rank and the illegitimate member of a Saxon
house, a gap he could do nothing to span.

She tapped the horse's flank with her heel. "When you come back,"
she said, "I will be the Countess of Lessford. It is not likely we will ever
see each other again. But—I hope you will not forget me, Walter."

"I will never forget you!" he cried. "I pledge you my everlasting devotion."

She was off immediately, her horse's pace settling almost at once into
a full gallop. That was the way it had always been: a few words between them, a few smiles for his benefit, some scornful and some vivacious and even kindly, and then she galloped off. This time, he feared,
it was for good.

6

Walter studied the pattern of Biblical scenes in the wall vervayer. It
was done in distemper and with considerable skill. The mottoes were
elaborately twined through the drawings, *Solyman and His Many Wives,
Simon y-hote Peter, The Last Supper.* No strolling hedge-artist had
painted them. His father had hired skilled monkish hands to do these
scenes from Holy Bible, and, no doubt, had paid well for them.

The room to which he had been escorted on his arrival at the castle
was not large but it was most handsomely furnished. The walls beneath
the pictured border were hung with cloth of gold and vermilion velvet.
The seats along the walls were heaped high with bancoves and pillows
ornamented with buttons of pearl. The floor was covered with a Spanish carpet. It was plain to see that his father's Norman wife had brought
much wealth to Bulaire.

He had the room to himself at first, and he fell into such a deep mood
of abstraction that he did not notice when the next arrivals came to

share it with him. He was surprised, therefore, when he heard the voice of Simeon Bautrie raised in a tone of exasperation.

"Why come to me, Gather? It is your concern, not mine."

The lawyer's companion was the seneschal who had opened the oriel window the evening before. "But something must be done," protested the old man. "It is forbidden that I speak to the Lady Mathilde, and now you tell me all the moneys in hand will be needed to pay the soulscat. If you won't find any for me, how am I to pay the onstead accounts? There are forty-seven house carles who have received nothing for a month, and thirty archers—nay, twenty-nine since Hugh was killed last night. The almoner tells me that his purse is empty. Father Guthide has a long list which must be sent for to London. What am I to do if no moneys are allowed me?"

"You can get along without," answered Simeon Bautrie. "The people of the castle can wait."

"There's not more than a day's supply of food left," persisted the worried seneschal.

Others began to arrive at this point. Simeon Bautrie shrugged the old man away and took his seat at a table which occupied the other end of the room. Walter remained where he was. The table, he saw, was heaped up with valuables of all kinds, jewelry, plate, standing cups, missals, the family Bible. Apparently there would be a distribution following the reading of the will.

Everyone rose when the widow came into the room, followed by Edmond. The latter looked about him with the proud air of new ownership and took a seat beside the lawyer at the table. His mother placed herself on the other side.

Walter had not been offered a chair, so he remained standing at the far end of the room. He had experienced some surprise when he saw his father's widow. She seemed to have aged overnight and was obviously tired and of dismal mood. Perhaps she realized that the ceremony about to begin marked the end of what she had prized most in life. She did not look once in his direction, but he was sure she knew he was there.

Simeon Bautrie smoothed out the document in front of him and began to read aloud. " 'I, Rauf, Earl of Lessford and lord of the domain of Bulaire and other lands to be cited hereafter, do assert that this is my last will and testament . . .' "

The arrangements for the widow's dower and the settling of the main estates were dealt with first. The farms and manors falling to Ed-

mond were listed, and it seemed to Walter that the lawyer would never
be finished with the enumeration. The longing for land of his own rose
in him as the unctuous voice of Bautrie rolled on. He would be satisfied
with even the smallest bequest; just a few virgates of land, green and
fruitful and suitable for pasturage as well as for wheat; earth that he
could feel between his fingers and work over hard and faithfully. With
such he could overcome the handicap of his birth and achieve an honest name of his own. Solidity of position and a proper dignity went with
the possession of land. It was not too much to expect, surely, that his
father had sensed his need and had done something about it.

He was so concerned with this speculation, and so distressed with Engaine's news, that he paid little heed to the reading of the clauses which
followed immediately thereafter. His father had proven generous with
his less favored relatives, leaving them handsome donations of money.
Many personal possessions were dispersed among them as well. Dimly
he heard mention of dragenalls and pottengers and trussing-beds, of
dozers and cousters and silver pelves, of panels of tapister's work and of
rugs from Asia. They were distributed with a prodigality which brought
a flush to the old-young face of Edmond. Walter could see that his half
brother had his full share of Norman frugality and acquisitiveness.

At last Walter heard his own name. " 'It is known,' " intoned the man
of law, " 'that I have a bastard son, who goes by the name of Walter of
Gurnie, for whom I have affection and for whose welfare I am deeply
concerned. To the said Walter of Gurnie I bequeath my best standing
cup, *Luke the Physician . . .* ' "

It stood on the table before Bautrie, a full two feet high, made of gold
and crystal and most beautifully and intricately wrought. It had been,
quite certainly, one of the dead man's most prized possessions. And it
had been willed to him! *For whom I have affection.* The words repeated
themselves in Walter's mind. There was a great lump in his throat, for
this was what he had wanted to hear, an assertion of his paternity and
of his father's love.

" '. . . My black boots of Spanish leather . . .' "

The boots lay on the table beside the standing cup, the pair with
the yellow leopards that the earl had worn the first time Walter saw
him. So he had remembered!

But he was not to receive land. The lawyer's voice was going on.
" 'Further, I bequeath the body of my bastard son to His King's Grace,
confident that the King will find for him a post in his royal household,

and equally confident that the said Walter of Gurnie will serve his liege lord and king faithfully and well all the years of his life . . .'"

Walter was too shocked at first to think clearly. It had never entered his mind that his father would follow the not uncommon practice of leaving him to the King's service. "Father in heaven," he thought, "have I heard right?" The pride he had felt during the reading of the earlier clauses was shattered at once. He had been handed over, body and soul, like a villein or house carle, to a king for whom he could never feel any loyalty! His hand strayed to his throat as though he felt there already an iron badge of servitude.

After a moment he said to himself that he would not serve in the household of the young king who had defeated and killed the great Earl Simon. His body was his own, and no man, certainly not a father who had never claimed him before and had never done anything for him, could dispose of him in this way. *I bequeath the body of my bastard son!* A black wave of humiliation passed over him. So this was the end of his high hopes and expectations, to be passed lightly by like the ill-begotten son of a scullery maid or a light-o'-love!

He found himself standing near the table, not conscious of having crossed the room, and quite oblivious of the unfriendly scrutiny of many pairs of eyes. The standing cup was within his reach, and he picked it up.

"My father prized this highly," he said. "And so, in giving it to me, he has done me honor. It is clear also he remembered my saying that I would like a pair of boots like these. I am happy to accept the cup and the boots."

"There are no further clauses in the will concerning you," said the lawyer. "But you will oblige by returning to your place and not interrupting until the reading is completed."

Walter refused to be diverted. "I have something more to say," he declared. "I reject my father's stipulation binding me to the service of the King. I am a free man, and my future is my own concern, and mine alone."

"The intent was to do you honor," said the lawyer, "and to provide for your future welfare."

"Honor!" cried Walter. "I see no honor in it. Can an Englishman serve a king who has made it clear that he does not intend to abide by the Great Charter?"

"This is treason!" sputtered Simeon Bautrie. A loud murmur of agreement rose from all parts of the room.

"No, it is not treason." Walter threw caution and reason to the winds. "If there is any treason, it is on the part of those who have broken the provisions of the Charter. The Charter comes before the will of any king!"

"You will hang for this!" several voices shouted in chorus.

"If I am to hang, they will have to send a long way to catch me!"

Walter turned and ran from the room with *Luke the Physician* and the pair of boots under his arm.

CHAPTER IV

London

THE STORM which descended on them the third night after they left the neighborhood of Bulaire drenched them to the skin and added much to their discomfort; but it proved to be a blessing in disguise after all. Well toward morning, when the bitter lash of the rain had stopped, they came on a small boat with a tattered sail and a single oar, resting on its side in a cove of the river. It had been washed ashore, quite clearly, after being dragged by the wind from an insecure mooring farther up the river.

"The Lord has directed it to this spot for our use," declared Tristram solemnly. "I know a little of sailing. We can get to London by water much sooner and much safer than by skulking along side roads and taking to cover every time we see a horseman approaching."

They had not a single easterling between them, and for two days they had been journeying with great discretion, certain in their minds that a hue and cry had been raised behind them. Walter's rash words at the reading of the will had marked him for summary punishment, and they had been told by Camus Harry before getting away that Tristram was spoken of as the ringleader in the attack on the castle. They were making for London in the belief that it would be easiest to drop out of sight there. It was in their minds also that, if it became necessary to leave the country, they would find a ship in the port of that great city.

The two days had not been easy ones. They had lived on apples and pears, stolen by night from orchards along the roads, and on the partly cooked flesh of a pair of ducks which Tristram had brought down with his longbow. They had slept one night in a hayrick but had found nothing better the second night than a hedge to huddle under. They were hungry and dirty and completely discouraged.

The finding of the boat was to lead to another discovery which, in turn, led them inevitably to their great adventure. The little craft yawed suddenly under Tristram's not too skillful handling, and water deluged Walter at the end of the boat. After bailing out what remained in the bottom, he was compelled to take off his boots and empty them. The idea of putting them back on again immediately did not recommend itself, but the night air was raw and penetrating and it was certain he would be chilled to the bone if he went without. In the circumstances he decided to try the boots his father had left him.

They had been hidden away with the standing cup in a sack filled with bits of old clothes. Walter produced them reluctantly, not happy at the need of putting them to so menial a use. He slid one foot in, relieved to find that the fit was perfect. The other foot, however, could not be inserted beyond the instep, and he realized that something had been stuffed into the toe. With curious fingers he drew it out: a piece of stiff parchment, folded over and tied securely with lengths of hempen thread. It was too dark to make out anything about it, but Walter was convinced that the parchment contained a message for him. What could it be?

He called out to Tristram, telling him what he had found and adding the conjecture which had come into his mind.

"It may be a letter from your father." Tristram was so busy with the crazily unpredictable sail that he spoke in instalments. "It has always been said, Walter . . . that he walked in fear of his wife. . . . Perhaps the letter is to amend the smallness of his open bequest to you."

As soon as the coming of dawn provided light enough to read, Walter drew the parchment from his pocket. On the outside it was subscribed "To my son" in an ill-formed and almost indecipherable scrawl. There was a brief message inside, in the same loose writing. The dead earl's scholarship had been of the most rudimentary kind and his hand so unpracticed with the pen that it took many minutes of earnest study on the part of both of them to determine what he had intended to say. This was the message that they finally evolved from it:

This note, dear Walter, is to be taken at once to Joseph at the Sign of the Merrytotter in London. He served me as squire in the Crusades, both bravely and well, and on our return I set him up in the —— trade [the nature of the

trade was beyond any hope of deciphering] as he had the wish to settle down.
He has done well at it. My good and honest Joseph is the only one I can
trust in this matter. He will know what is to be done.

Yr most loving father
RAUF OF BULAIRE

The mood in which Walter had been sunk ever since the reading of
the will, a combination of prideful anger and despairing certainty that
the whole world was against him, began to lift as he conned the possibilities suggested by this note from his father.

"You made a shrewd guess, Tris," he said, with a catch in his voice.
"There is a promise of better things in this."

His companion's state of mind had been equally improved. He smiled
back at Walter and said: "I have been wondering how we could expect
to live in London without a single coin between us. Joseph of the Merrytotter can be depended on, at least, to take us in and feed us."

"I have heard him well spoken of." Walter pointed up at the scudding
clouds above them and went on in a suddenly cheerful tone. "More good
tidings for us, Tris. This wind will soon clear the storm off, and it will
take us down to London in quick order. We'll get a look at the sun in
another hour." He added quickly in a jubilant burst: "I was not sure the
sun would ever shine again! And now everything seems so much
brighter already."

2

Joseph of the Merrytotter was in the grain trade. His house was tall
and shabby and built somewhat in the shape of a Christmas tree. A
block-and-tackle was suspended from the crow-stepped gable in front,
and a rickety outside stairway climbed on one side to the high roof.
The sign, which was newly painted and quite gay, showed a child teetering ecstatically.

Joseph himself was small and inclined to tubbiness about the middle.
His face looked younger than might have been expected from the gray
tumble of his thatch, and his eyes twinkled in a friendly way under sloping brows.

He met them at the front entrance. "I know ye by the boldness of yer
jib," he said to Walter. "If ye're not a son of my old master, then my
name is not Joseph Maule."

"I am called Walter of Gurnie."

"Ah, *that* one." The ex-squire studied him intently, rubbing dusty hands on the back of his tunic. "I hardly expected to see ye so soon, young sir. And how did ye leave my good lord Rauf of Bulaire?"

"My father is dead," declared Walter.

The man stared at him for a moment as though unwilling to believe what he had heard. "Dead!" he cried, finally. "My lord Rauf dead! This is bitter hearing, young sir. The last word I had of him was a month come Tuesday, and he said then he would be coming on to Lunnon and would stop by to see me. He never came to Lunnon without seeing me." He rubbed a hand across his eyes, which had filled with tears. "Ah, Master Walter, I was so deeply attached to my lord Rauf that I—I am loath to accept this sorry story ye bring."

"He died nine days ago." Walter hesitated before going on. "There is much to tell you about the manner of it, if you will take us in where we will be free to talk."

"Yes, Master Walter. Come in, come in. I am so overcome by your news that I don't know what I am saying or doing."

The grain dealer stumbled as he led the way into a room lined with bins and sweet with the healthy smell of grain. He motioned his two guests to seat themselves on stools and then leaned against one of the bins with an air of listlessness and misery. His kindly face was clouded with distress, and he kept shaking his head from side to side without finding any further words to express what he was feeling.

His attention was reclaimed immediately when Walter told of the finding of his father's body and of the sequence of events which had followed.

"That would have gone bitterly against my lord Rauf's will!" Joseph cried when the story came to the point of the hangings. "A hard and bitter woman, my lady. I had good cause to know it. She wanted no Englishmen about him. I would never have left him to come here had it not been for her. I was always glad to keep clear of her, from the very first day."

When Walter told of the raid on the castle, the kindly eyes suddenly took fire. "Well and bravely done!" he cried. "I am an Engster man, and there would be many of my kin there. On that I would stake my chance of eternal happiness!"

"All the men of Engster were with us," said Tristram.

Walter had been careful not to mention the part that he and Tristram had played. Joseph Maule looked up quickly, his glance darting from one to the other. "I was waiting to hear that," he said, "though I had no doubts ye were both in the thick of it. Brave lads! And now ye've run away to Lunnon because of it?"

Walter nodded. "It may be necessary for us to leave the country for a time."

"Ye'll be safe here in Lunnon." The ex-squire shook his head with a positive air of assurance. "I can see to that, and glad to do it. Lunnon is like the sea. Once ye drop out of sight in it, the eye of the law will never light on ye again. There will be many willing to lend ye their aid."

The wall behind him was covered with souvenirs of his crusading days; his coat of mail, furbished so recently and so zealously that it shone like glass, and the coarse linen pourpoint that had been worn with it; his gisarme, as sharply pointed as when it had been a threat to Saracen ribs, his fustibal with weight in sling, his iron solleret stirrups; and some curious bits of Eastern gear, including a curved sword and a mane-guard of purple leather. Noting that the eyes of his two visitors were fixed on this warlike display, he smiled deprecatingly.

"Brave days they were when I followed my lord Rauf to the Eastern wars," he said. "But there were two of us, and it was Wat Stander he depended on to follow him in where the fighting was thick. Oh, I had my share of the give-and-take; but I was more useful at finding food and setting up the tents in good order and looking after the horses, poor faithful beasts. My brave Wat! Lunnon born and bred he was, and as stout a hand with mace or sword as any belted knight."

"Was he killed?"

"That we never knew for sure. Perhaps he was taken prisoner, and if so I trust our merciful Father took pity on him and gave him a quick release from life. We didn't get there until the very end. The French under good King Louis had left the year before, and all we saw were border skirmishes. No good was to be done then, but the fighting was warm and bloody while it lasted. I saw Wat go down just as we were scattered by a charge of the screeching brown devils. God have mercy on his soul! He was a good comrade as well as a brave man-at-arms."

There was a moment's silence, and then Walter drew the parchment from his pocket. "We have no wish to involve you in our troubles," he said. "So I'll tell you what brought us to you, and then we'll be on our way. I was to give you this."

"Then you must read it to me, young sir. I can cast up figures in my head with the best of them. But when it comes to the writings, I can set down my mark and that's the end of it."

Walter read the message aloud. The ex-squire was deeply affected by the references to himself and brushed his forearm again across his eyes.

"I am proud he thought well of me," he said, at the finish. "If ye will come with me, Walter of Gurnie, I will carry out the instructions my lord Rauf gave to me some four years back."

He walked to the door, and Walter followed. As they turned to climb the outside stairway, two small boys came running from the yard in the rear, shouting at the top of their voices: "Gramfaw! See, we have been setting up a snare and perhaps there will be wild ducks for supper!"

"Little fellows, little fellows!" scolded their grandsire. "Ye should know by this time that wild fowl never fly through city smoke. Rats are all ye may hope to catch here. And what of yer manners now? See ye not I have a guest?"

As they climbed the unsteady steps, the grain dealer looked back over his shoulder and chuckled. "I have been blessed with grandchilder if in nothing else. A fine brood I have, twelve of the little sprats there are, no less."

"And they all live here with you?"

"Aye, all of them are here, more's the pity. It's not that I regret having them with me, it's the ill fortune that came to their parents I have in mind. My pretty little Wencie died of the shrinkage in her chest, and her husband caught it from her. And then my good Nick, who always walked with his head in the clouds, paid no heed to the shout of 'Beauseant!' behind him in the streets and a Knight Templar rode him down. Conand, my only other child, helps me here with the trade, and his Elspie has been a prolific wife. Yes, twelve I have and another on the way to make a baker's dozen of it."

A third boy, several years younger than the stout pair below, was crouching on the top landing with his head hidden behind interlaced arms. He shrank away from them and did not look up.

"Gilly!" cried his grandfather. "What do ye here, lad?"

The boy sat up at once with a look of intense relief. "I thought it was the giant after me with his bag full of snakes," he quavered. "Harry and Toby said he was coming here today and would take away all little boys he could get his hands on."

"I will dust their backsides for them," declared Joseph, patting the lad's tow-colored head. "The giant is not coming today, but if he did I would take care of him, never fear, my Gilly. I would chine his head for him as I did the wicked paynim."

"Yes, Gramfaw. I was sure you would. But I was afraid the giant might catch me first."

"Get ye down, now, with Harry and Toby. No grandson of mine should be afraid of giants."

He watched the boy's quick descent with an affectionate eye. "That one is Gilbert, my Wencie's second oldest. We call him the Gad because he is all over the place when he is feeling himself. Did ye notice I didn't say there was no giant on the lookout for little boys? I didn't want to take that away from him. The fear of giants makes life more interesting for little boys."

The room they entered was at the rear of the house. The front part was given over to bags of grain and seed, piled all the way to the ceiling. In the rear was an immensely wide bed without either head or baseboard. Seeing that Walter was surprised at the unusual proportions of the bed, Joseph explained that he had made it himself.

"The good wife died some years agone," he said. "If she had lived, she would have known how to do better for the grand-'uns. They kept coming and I was at my wit's end. I built two beds like this. The boys sleep in this one, all six—Harry, Toby, Joseph, Timothy, Gilly the Gad, and little John-Put-Upon. The other is in the room below, and the six little girls sleep there. What a clack of tongues there is when *they* go to bed!"

"I had seen nothing but boys," said Walter, "and I was beginning to wonder if you had no granddaughters."

"Aye, a half dozen of the little flutter-heads! They are taking a lesson with the needle today, and when they are through with it they will be all over the place like so many pretty butterflies."

Apologizing then for the need he was under of storing his stock all over the house, Joseph began to lift the bags of grain aside until he reached a small sack at the bottom of the pile. This he deposited on the foot of the bed. Opening the clasp knife he had worn at his belt, he placed it beside the sack.

"The safest hiding place I could think of," he said, with a satisfied grin. "Four years ago my lord Rauf gave it to me, and I stored it away in this corn. No one has laid an eye on it since. What ye'll find there was to be delivered to ye when the time came. Rip it open, Walter of Gurnie. My boys will clear up the grain after ye."

He left the room with another pleased wink, and Walter heard him call as he descended the stairs, "Come now, little fellows, less noise there."

The contents spilled out on the bed, and Walter's fingers came on a smaller bag concealed in the grains of corn. It was of velvet, tied tightly with a leather string and with the gules crosslet of Bulaire embroidered on its side. He lifted it up and heard inside a jingle of metal. Then he let it fall on the scarlet squares of the coverlet and looked at it for several moments with shining eyes.

"Four years ago!" he whispered. "Father, you were thinking of my welfare even as long ago as that!"

He knew the bag was filled with gold, but at the moment the nature of this unexpected bequest did not seem to him important at all. His mind was filled with pride and gratitude that he had not been passed over, after all, with purely token gifts and a plea to the King for his employment. Why his father had planned this way to provide for his future was not clear, but that did not seem of any importance either. "He thought enough of me to arrange it this way," he repeated over and over, his eyes brimming with this proof of his father's love. The disappointment he had felt over the terms of the will seemed petty now, and he felt shamed that he had permitted himself to think so much and so bitterly about it.

Gold coins tumbled out on the counterpane when he untied the string. Pounds, tower pounds, new and shiny with unclipped edges. Ten, twenty, an infinity of them, jingling proudly and seeming to wink at him with their golden promise of security and wealth. He tried to count them in mounds of ten, but his fingers were so unsteady that the piles kept tumbling and he would have to start all over again. It took some time to get them stacked and counted. Four hundred pounds! A truly fine fortune!

There was no doubt in Walter's mind as to what he would do with the money, but for several ecstatic minutes he let his mind revel in thoughts of various uses to which it could be put. He pictured himself riding a richly caparisoned horse, curveting proudly for Engaine's benefit, a plume in his hat and a sword of Touranian steel at his side, knightly spurs jingling as he rode. He thought of walking in boldly to his grandfather's workroom, without being summoned and without any need of Wilderkin to act as go-between in the conversation, and spilling out on the table enough coin to buy back some of Gurnie's riven acres. This last, he said to himself must be done; but, as he dared not return to Gurnie, it would have to be accomplished in a different way.

Absorbed in these pleasant speculations, he was not aware at first that an inner door had been opened a few inches and that a very small boy was watching him through the crack. Finally the youngster sniffed, and Walter turned in that direction.

"Well," he said, "and which one are you?"

"I am John," replied the boy. "I am the youngest of all. The rest call me John-Put-Upon."

"And are you put upon? Do the other boys make things hard for you because you're smaller than they are?"

"They won't let me play in all the games." Then the boy nodded his head with pride. "They are good to me when my gramfaw is around. He would dust them soundly if they didn't let me play. Sometimes he takes me up to sit beside him at the table, and then he cuts off tender bits for me. I think I am my gramfaw's favorite."

"Don't be too sure of that, John. I am not disposed to think your grandfather the kind of man to have favorites. He is a very fair and honest man. And now, John-Put-Upon, will you be good enough to run downstairs and ask your grandfather and my friend to come up?"

When Tristram and the ex-squire had entered the room, Walter pointed to the gold heaped up on the bed. "My inheritance," he said, proudly. "It has reposed here for four years in the most honest pair of hands in the world. My father knew what he was about when he entrusted it to Joseph of the Merrytotter."

Joseph looked abashed at this open praise. "My lord Rauf had trusted me in many ways," he said. Then he hesitated and cleared his throat. "Perhaps you wonder why he went about it in this way. You must know, Walter of Gurnie, that his lady never allowed him to forget that it was her gold which paid all his debts when he came back from the wars. She knew how he had drawn his will, and she would not agree that anything be left to you. He was a man of an easy nature, and he—well, he lived in a wholesome dread of her tempers. This money was saved for you in ways she knew nothing of."

"I must now write out an acknowledgment of its receipt, Joseph."

"That is not necessary, my lord Walter. The transaction was between my master and me. He is dead now. For what other eyes would I need an acknowledgment?"

"I think it wise to do it nevertheless. Have you ink and a quill pen?"

Joseph laughed. "Ink and a pen? I am a poor dealer in grain and not a clerk."

Tristram was staring at the piles of gold with incredulous eyes. "It is a fortune, Wat," he said. "I know little of the value of money, but it seems to me you could buy the whole domain of Bulaire with this."

"Hardly that. But I think there is enough to carry out a plan I have in mind. Joseph, could two men travel to Cathay on what we have here?"

The ex-squire looked startled. "To Cathay? No Christian has ever ventured that far, young sir. It is a fearsome long distance, and the road is beset with dragons and evil magicians."

"We will take our chances with the dragons and the magicians. But will we have enough to pay our way?"

Joseph nodded his head with an air of somber assurance. "Aye, ye could travel to all parts of the world on what ye have there. But ye would have to be sensible and never let it be known ye had gold in yer belts. There are robbers everywhere and sly men of the East; much more to be feared, I swear, than all the dragons and magicians."

Walter turned to Tristram. "I have a plan in my head. I want to turn this gold into a great fortune, and where would there be a better chance than in this fabulous land of Cathay? A fortune for each of us, Tris. And I want also to see the wonders of the East. The thought was put in my mind by your great man at Oxford, Roger Bacon. We must learn the secrets of Cathay and bring them back with us to England. Roger Bacon will know how to put them to good use. We will become famous as well as rich men. And I have still another purpose which perhaps you have guessed." He paused. "Well, Tris, will you go with me?"

Tristram had been watching him with troubled eyes. "It is a long journey. I wonder, Wat, if you realize fully what this plan of yours would mean?" Then his face began to light up with a slow smile. "Do you think I would let you go alone? Nay, Wat, I would go with you if we still lacked a single coin between us."

Walter clapped him joyously on the back. "My stout friend! I knew what you were going to say; I had no doubts about it at all." Then he added affectionately: "Thou very idiot! Always ready for any manner of risk and without any thought of your own gain or the safety of that huge frame of yours! Very well, then, we shall set out together. That longbow of yours, my great Tristram, will litter the road to Cathay with the bones of dead dragons!"

"I see that a word of sober caution would not sit well on your stomachs," said Joseph. "It is time for the midday meal. Some food would sit better, if ye would honor me by sitting at table with us. It will be plain fare, I warn ye, and there will be a great deal of noise. Twelve young tongues have always a great deal to say for themselves."

"I must warn you in turn that we have mighty appetites," said Walter. "We haven't had a full meal in three days. We will eat you out of house and home, and that is no light matter with so many mouths to fill. They must be a heavy burden, Joseph. I would like to leave one of these coins for each of them. What do you say? You guarded the money for me nobly."

"No, no! It makes me proud that ye think of it, my lord Walter. But I am getting along well enough in the grain trade. There will be a little for each when I pass on. That and an honest name; what more can they need?"

There was a long pause. "Yes, they will have an honest name!" exclaimed Walter. "I think, Joseph, it is the best inheritance they could ask. I know the lack of one." His feelings got the better of him, and he found himself pouring out the reason back of his plans which he had not mentioned before. "As far back as I can remember, I have been called nothing but 'bastard' and I have been treated as though I had no feelings to be hurt. My grandfather has never spoken a word to me direct. I saw my father three times only, and I was not permitted to follow his body to the grave. You saw, Tris, how things were at Oxford and what I had to put up with there.

"I am going to Cathay," he went on, with a sudden passion he could not control, "because it is the only way I know to change all that! It is a rich country, and they say you can pick up gold in the streets. Very soon I will come back with my pockets stuffed—with gold and with rubies and emeralds and adamants! I will be a famous man, and people will treat me with respect. They won't laugh at me then and call me 'bastard.' I will buy land of my own, and I will then have a name of my own as well. I may even get back in time," he added, after a pause, "to claim the girl I love."

An uncomfortable silence had fallen on the room. Tristram kept his head turned away, but it was clear he was filled with sympathy for his friend. Walter picked up his bag, which he had placed by the side of the bed, and drew out the standing cup.

"There is another matter to be seen to before I go. I must send money back to Gurnie. There is my mother's comfort to be seen to. Perhaps, Joseph, you will do what is needed to be done. It would not be safe for me to show myself either here in London or at Gurnie."

He placed *Luke the Physician* on the bed with reverent fingers. "It is the most beautiful thing I have ever seen. See how fine the silverwork is! It is very old and was made in the East, I am sure." He looked it over with the greatest care, noting that there were small rubies and emeralds in the nodus stem and that the lip of the truncated inner cup was richly chased. "How much do you think it is worth?"

"A great deal," said Joseph. "But surely ye don't think of selling it?"

Walter shook his head emphatically. "I will never sell it. My father willed it to me. But it can't be taken along, and perhaps it could be left as security for a loan from one of the Lombardy merchants. Would you take it, Joseph, and see what they would be willing to give?"

"Aye, I will make the best bargain I can for ye. Is it your wish that what I get is to be sent to Gurnie?"

"Ten shillings for each of the grandchildren must be set aside first. I insist on that, Joseph of the Merrytotter. And I want my mother to have word of what I am planning to do. I can't risk a visit home before setting out."

"It will be safer for ye to ship from some other port than Lunnon," declared Joseph. "A cousin of mine is in the French trade. He sails from Portsmouth to Brest. A word from me and he would put ye down safely on French soil."

Walter nodded in assent and then smiled at Tristram. "We are all set for our journey, it seems. Does your heart leap up inside you at the thought of it? Mine is thumping, and my feet are ready to march to the tune of 'The Old Man of the Mountain.'" He drew the leather boots from his bag and held them up. "This gift of my father's I shall take with me and wear them when I visit the court of Kublai Khan."

3

It was after dusk when Walter called on the priest who controlled the Chest at St. Frideswide's. He had left Tristram in an inn on the outskirts of town and was hoping to transact his affairs safely under cover of darkness.

"Walter of Gurnie," said Father Francis, scanning his ledgers with shortsighted thoroughness, "a balance of nineteen shillings, seven pence. A goodly sum, young man. You are not wanting the full amount?"

"Yes," said Walter. "I am leaving Oxford, Father Francis."

"It is always the way," sighed the priest. "The death of the earl, your father, has made this change in your plans. When a man comes into property of his own, he feels that learning is no longer necessary. We have to depend here on younger sons and poor clerks who desire to improve their station in life." He squinted at Walter with an abrupt assumption of sternness. "Be both humble and discreet, my son, now that you are venturing out into the world."

Walter set out with a sense of relief on his second errand in this gray town that he loved so much. The woman who directed him to the stone folly at the South Bridge, where Roger Bacon lived, crossed herself and muttered a hasty prayer under her breath. He had to confess that the place, when he located it, had a haunted look. It was partly dismantled, and he felt that eyes were fixed on him from its dark and gaping windows.

His knock echoed hollowly through the dark tower, and he had to repeat it before a voice from within called out, "Come in, come in." A winding staircase was built into the stone walls of the folly, and he started to climb them with some hesitation. He was sure that all the stories whispered about Friar Bacon were old wives' tales, but he jumped nevertheless at every sound and did not dare raise his eyes to the black void above into which the stairs dissolved.

His common sense returned as soon as he entered the room from which the voice had come. Roger Bacon was sitting at his full ease in a chair with a manuscript propped up in front of him. A frugal meal was spread on a pewter platter beside him on the floor; a wedge of manchet bread, a large onion, and a small slab of blue-veined cheese. The room was bare in the fullest monastic sense. There was the chair in which the friar sat, a pallet of straw in one corner, and a cupboard against the wall. The cupboard, solidly built of estrichboard, was packed with books and manuscripts. Walter's eyes strayed in that direction, for books were a rare sight even to an Oxford student.

"Well, my son?"

Seeing him thus closely for the first time, Walter was awed by the majesty of Roger Bacon's face. It had a quality so unusual that it amounted almost to beauty. This did not derive in any way from the features, for the nose of the friar was a jutting crag under an inordinately wide brow, and his mouth had a melancholy wryness of line. It came, Walter decided, from the eyes, which were large and dark. They were remarkable eyes, drawing you and holding you by their power. There was nothing, in fact, that was fully English, or even fully human, about the face of this strange churchman. It could have seemed in place among the wise men who made a certain memorable journey one night on camelback or at a council on Mount Olympus.

Walter looked at him with tongue-tied intentness until he smiled and repeated, "Well?"

"I attended one of your classes a fortnight ago, though my name is not on your matricula. I remember everything you told us, and most particularly what you said about the land of Cathay. I have come to let you know that I am going there."

Roger Bacon laid his manuscript aside and gave him his full attention.

"Are you aware, my son," he asked, "that no man with the temerity to do what you say you are going to try has ever returned?"

The austerity of his expression had given way to a smile of such kindliness that Walter began to feel more at home with him.

"I am sure," said Walter, "that my legs are long enough to carry me there and back."

Bacon remained in deep thought for several moments. "I dreamed of going to Cathay when I was your age," he said then. "The wish comes back at times still, even though I know now that I shall never see that great country. If I had the magic powers some people ascribe to me"—his eyes twinkled at this point—"I would use them to whisk me over the seas and the deserts and to set me down in Cathay. What a wonderful thing it would be to hear their secrets from the lips of their own wise men!"

"Perhaps," suggested Walter, "I could seek for the things you want to know."

"My son, why do you think of risking your life in this way? I judge that you are of gentle birth and that your prospects are good. You can count on a pleasant and profitable life here in England."

"On the contrary, there is every prospect that my life will come to a quick ending and in a manner that will hardly be pleasant." Walter proceeded to relate what had occurred at Bulaire, even repeating the words with which he had refused to consider himself bound to the King.

Bacon listened with close attention. "I know little about our young king," he said, at the finish. "It is said of him, *Abundat dulcibus vitiis.* But even if his faults are sweet, he will think ill of the report which reaches him of you. I agree that it will be wise to leave the kingdom for a time at least. And," he added after some reflection, "if you must travel abroad, why not try the road to Cathay? The route to the East is no more dangerous than the roads of Europe. It is a sad thing to reflect upon; but the fiercest and most rapacious of robbers are to be found in the Christian world. You can put out of your mind the stories they tell of dragons and many-headed beasts to be encountered. They do not exist."

He got to his feet and walked to the cupboard. An exploring hand found the right spot behind the books, and the click of a sliding panel was heard. From the almery thus exposed, he drew out a map.

"I am sure you expected something quite different," said the friar, spreading the map out on his knee. "Did you think I would produce

the Enneads, the books of magic from the East, the very sight of which
is death to the uninitiated? Such a very great absurdity! How could the
sight of writing, that greatest of blessings, cause death? I have never
seen the Enneads, and I doubt very much if they exist. I am sure Simon
Magus was a trickster and that Merlin was a hoary old hoax.

"I know that I am supposed to spend my time here burning gall of
cuttlefish with aloe-wood to produce earthquakes and other things
equally absurd. My son, I am a student of science, and my interest is
confined to proven facts. Clear all such rubbish from your mind if you
aim to be of service to me. It is not the charms and incantations of the
East that I want. It is the practical discoveries they have made and the
methods they have of using them." He leaned forward, his eyes beginning to burn with an intense light. "I am certain that all the things
wrong with the world—this ignorant, dirty, cruel world—can be cured
in time through the knowledge to be gained in studying the laws of
nature. And they can be cured in no other way.

"Now let me show you this map," he added, in a more normal tone.
"It covers the known world of the East from Constantinople to the land
of Prester John, which is supposed to border on Cathay. Here is marked
the best route to follow, from Antioch to Babylon and from there to the
Ilkhan, which is generally called Persia. From there it follows the hot
lands north of the Snowy Mountains. I shall give you this map, my son,
because it is the most accurate one in existence, even though it was
drawn by Mohammedan hands." The gravity of his face gave way to a
smile. "How religious beliefs can sometimes blind us to the truth! Because the men of the East are heathen, it is deemed wicked to credit
them with the skill to make better maps than we do. They are accurate
within the bounds of their knowledge. On the other hand, we Christians
go about the making of charts like tellers of fairy stories for children.
And I could be put in a dark cell for the rest of my life for saying such a
thing!"

The map was drawn on stiff parchment and, although very old, was
in good condition. The line of the silk trails were easy to follow, and the
geographical points were plainly marked. Walter folded it thankfully
and put it away under his tunic.

Roger Bacon leaned forward in his chair and stared at his companion
closely. His mood had changed. "I can read what is written in your
face," he said, in a low voice. "I am sure now you will get to Cathay and
that moreover you will succeed in coming back. Ah, my son, what a
fortunate destiny!" His eyes had taken on a faraway look. "A hand has

come and struck my stall, it has brushed across my eyes. There is a sky brighter than any blue I have ever seen, a blue shot through with fire. A man sits on a throne carried on the backs of four elephants, and thousands of other men with wise and serene faces are following after. I can see you most clearly. You are riding a small horse and you have a curved sword at your side and there is a rich stone hanging on a chain around your neck. I can see temples of a curious design, and I can hear bells sounding at a distance."

His excitement communicated itself to Walter, who listened with breathless interest as the friar went on to tell in a glowing fervor of the strange visions which filled his mind. The words he spoke conjured up a land of glowing color, teeming with strange men and filled with new sights and sounds.

After a time the voice dwindled off. Roger Bacon sighed, brushed a hand across his face, and then sat up straight in his chair again. "I am not quite clear as to what I have been saying. I am subject to these spells, and I am not sure in my mind as to what they are. Perhaps what I see is truth, a flash allowed me by the wise God who has fettered our everyday senses to an understanding of nothing but the things immediately around us. Perhaps on the other hand it is mere nonsense, a churning up of babble when the ship of reason begins to drag its anchor. I am only sure of one thing: that this trait of mine which shows itself rarely is not sib to the childish magic of incantations spoken over burning frogs' bowels and herbs gathered in the full of the moon."

He brushed his eyes a second time and then proceeded to speak in an entirely normal voice. "Now, my son, we must speak of more practical matters. Come, share my bread and onion, and while we eat I will tell you what you must look for when you reach the kingdom of Kublai Khan."

Book Two

CHAPTER V

Antioch

THE TWO TALL ENGLISHMEN had decided not to ride into Jerusalem on mules, as so many pilgrims did in memory of Christ's entry, but they stopped at a stable just outside the holy city where mounts were rented, at extortionist rates, for the purpose. Walter had learned that the keeper was a Greek, and so this was an opportunity not to be missed; he could test out his schoolroom knowledge of the classic tongue on an everyday user of it and, in addition, he might get some advice about the road to Cathay. He found to his great gratification that he could make himself understood.

The Greek shook his head when he heard they had some thought of going to the Far East by sea.

"It is much quicker and safer to follow the overland route," he said. "Take my advice, young men, and go to Anthemus of Antioch. He will see you are outfitted properly." A speculative gleam showed in his eye. "You must remember to tell him that I, Alexander on the Joppa Road, sent you to him."

"Will he charge us much?"

The renter of horses laughed so loudly that a party of pilgrims, plodding slowly past on the dusty road, turned as one man to look. "Anthemus will skin you alive," he said delightedly.

"Then why do you send us to him? We are poor men and haven't the means to fatten the purse of this Anthemus of Antioch."

The Greek pointed to the wall back of them, on which a double A was painted in large red letters. "Anthemus owns this place," he said. "I get no more out of the profits than a miserable pittance. You will find the AA on many walls in Jerusalem when you arrive, and in all cities hereabouts. I believe, verily, that he would have it on the Sepulcher itself if he dared. You will find it on the saddlebags of camels in every caravan that crosses the desert. Anthemus," holding up both hands cupped together, "has the trade with the East as close under his control as that. He's the richest man in the world."

Walter laughed in turn. "Clearly," he said, "we must keep ourselves free of the clutches of your opulent Anthemus."

The Greek shook his head several times with an air compounded of many things: admiration, envy, fear. "You must go to him whether you like it or not. In no other way can you hope to get to this far land. His caravans travel safely, for he has influence in all countries, and he pays tribute as well to the robber bands on the desert."

"My friend and I are prepared for danger," declared Walter. "We don't expect to find the journey as easy as a jaunt to Canterbury. Surely there are merchants we could go to who could be content with a reasonable profit?"

The Greek shook his dark head in vigorous dissent. "My advice to you, young pilgrims, is not to try anyone else. If you are not ready to meet the terms of Anthemus, turn around and go home after you have visited the holy places in the city." He clutched Walter's sleeve in an earnest effort at persuasion. "You would not get far if you went to any of the others. He would see to that. One night you would hear a wild shouting as a band of these devils of the desert swooped down on your camp. You would never hear anything more in this world."

"You seem determined to earn your share of the profits."

The stable keeper brushed that suggestion aside. "I would get no more than a grudging word of credit if you went to him. Listen to me. What think you would happen to any rash dealer who set himself up here as a renter of horses in opposition to us? He would be found some morning with his throat cut neatly from ear to ear. If you buy holy relics in Jerusalem, you can be sure the profit will find itself finally in the pockets of my master." His face suddenly became contorted. "He is a verminous gall under the *emeel* of the East! But everyone has to go to him."

"Well," said Walter after a long pause, "I will promise you this much: we'll go to Antioch and see him before we decide on our course."

"Put in a good word for me," admonished the renter of horses. "He has seemed not too pleased with me of late."

2

The entrance to the establishment of Anthemus was tall and imposing. Walter paused on the green marble steps and said to Tristram, "Through this portal we may step into a land of great adventure."

Tristram had found the intense heat of the East harder to endure than did his companion. His face had a scorched and leathery look about it. His once handsome archer's jacket was so soiled and caked with dust that it was no longer recognizable. The cock's feather in his cap was limp and moldy, and the lettering had worn off his gauntlets.

He replied with a doubtful shake of his head: "I want to say again that I doubt the wisdom of coming here. There must be something peculiarly wicked about a man who makes the Sepulcher a market for profits."

"But we can't hope to reach Cathay except through him. He will probably steal the very cross-garterings off our legs, but—we must take things as they come. As for the man himself, he is undoubtedly a great scoundrel, but there must be a trace of genius in him."

Tristram shook his head even more despondently. "He is a vicar of the devil, Wat. Evil will come of any dealings with him."

The gate swung open to their knock, and they were greeted within by a little man with feeble whiskers and a jeweled ring in his nose. He was wearing a red turban and a not overly clean tunic which was tied under his neck in a huge bow.

He addressed them in a tongue they did not know and then tried a second with like result. Shaking his head, he made a third attempt in Latin, "What is it you desire, young sirs?"

Tristram's knowledge of the Roman language had always been of the scantiest, and so it fell to Walter to answer. "We desire a few words with Anthemus of Antioch. We come from the West, and it is our purpose to make the journey to Cathay. Perhaps it could be arranged for us to accompany one of his caravans."

"To Cathay!" The eyes of the little man became so round that a feline suggestion about him was heightened. "That is most strange. I go to Cathay myself. You are Christians, and so we might make the journey together." Then his expression fell, and he added in a depreciatory tone: "But I am a Nestorian priest. I am Father Theodore from Ispahan. I realize you must look on me with loathing and scorn."

The two visitors regarded each other in a puzzled way. They knew that the Nestorians were an Asiatic offshoot of Holy Church, but that was as far as their knowledge went. Before they could ask any questions, Father Theodore motioned them to step inside and then ordered a sweating ebony giant to close the gates.

"You look down on us," he continued, nodding his head in an excess of humility. "It is true we have our seven mysteries and that we are not committed to celibacy. Some of us even have taken plural wives. You must understand," he added hastily, "that I am not married myself. It is not that I believe in priestly celibacy. Nay, nay, I stand firmly by our own rules. It is simply that so far no young female has—has filled my eyes, as you might say."

They were standing in a garden which had been trampled out of all semblance of its original beauty by the feet of camels. It was empty at the moment, but a distinct animal odor filled their nostrils unpleasantly. Thinking of the high arch of the palace lobby, with its handsome tiling and prismatic globe swaying at the end of a gold chain, Walter wondered at this contrast of outer grandeur with inner commercial utility.

Father Theodore paused to ask a question. "Is it true that the real purpose of the last Crusades was not to free the Sepulcher but to gain power and crush the Nestorian Church?"

"The sole purpose of the Crusades," declared Walter, with a laugh, "was to drive the Moslems from Jerusalem. Few of the men who took the Cross had ever heard of the Nestorians."

They had entered a hall so lofty that every sound came echoing back to them. Father Theodore lowered his voice instinctively. "It is said otherwise. Indeed we have heard disturbing things of the ambitious plans of your popes. But they will never succeed. We are closer to the Divine Truth than you are, and we can never be crushed." He added after a moment: "I will now seek an audience for you with Kyrios Anthemus. I serve him as interpreter, having many languages at my command. But you must understand, it is only a means to an end. I choose to do it as an easy way of reaching Cathay. It is my mission to go there and preach the true faith."

The lower floor of the palace was given over entirely to trade. They passed through rooms which literally bulged with every conceivable variety of goods: armor of all kinds, from the tough leather shields of the Mongolian horsemen to the great shining swords of bone-shearing edge which only the smiths of Damascus could weld; the lovely porcelains of the Far East, the red-glazed wares of the desert, the stamped leathers of Morocco; missals thick with gold leaf, jeweled breviaries, relics from holy places. They saw countless bolts of the richest fabrics, heavy velvets, silks into which had been spun the molten sunlight of warm skies, velours and brocades so heavy that they seemed capable of standing by themselves. The halls were filled with the odor of spices, so enticing to European tastes—ginger and cubeb and nutmeg and cinnamon, and the hot, red-grained galingal.

Walter nudged his friend and whispered exultantly: "Our first glimpse of the riches of the East! This is indeed a land of milk and honey. A love of the East is in my blood already."

He would have liked a chance to inspect these fabulous stores, but Father Theodore was urging them on, still prating in his thin, meticulous voice of church rivalries. They came finally to a large room where a number of people were waiting. It was an ornate apartment and as richly furnished as the anteroom of an emperor. The chairs and couches were of bronze and covered with soft cushions. There were three-legged tables, also of bronze, containing platters of tempting fresh fruit. Fans swung noiselessly on the ceiling, sending currents of cool air through the room.

Walter's eyes settled on one of the occupants, a huge Oriental who dwarfed the chair in which he sat. The chin beard of this hulking specimen was divided into three parts, his hair was braided and coiled over his ears, and his eyes, which he had fixed on the newcomers, seemed ready to leap out of their sockets in sheer ferocity. His costume blazed with magnificence, an amaranth tunic with golden embroidery, a belt shaped like a serpent, and high scarlet boots with golden arrows up each side.

"A very great man from the Manji country, the southern part of Cathay where the Sung emperors rule," whispered Father Theodore, noting the interest Walter was showing. "He has been engaged by Kublai Khan because of the information he can supply for the war against the Manji. His name is Lu Chung, and he is known as Bird Who Feathers His Nest."

"There is war in Cathay?"

The priest nodded. "Kublai Khan has sworn to conquer all of the country. So far he has had little success. It is rightly said that fighting the Chinese people is like plunging a fist into a feather cushion. It meets no resistance, but the cushion goes back at once to its original shape. That is why the great Khan has sent for Bayan."

"And who is Bayan?"

"You have not heard of Bayan of the Hundred Eyes?" The priest's tone suggested that such ignorance passed all belief. "He is the greatest general the world has ever seen. He is a Mongol, but as my country has been under Mongolian rule for many years, he commands the armies of the Ilkhan. His soldiers say he sees everything, a dip in the road a mile away, a speck of dust on a single arrowhead. That is why he is called Bayan of the Hundred Eyes. Kublai Khan is borrowing him from Persia. He leaves Maragha,* our new capital city, some time within the next two months."

Walter had pricked up his ears at this news. "This Bayan will ride with a large retinue, no doubt," he said. "And I judge he will travel fast."

Father Theodore spread out both arms by way of emphasis. "The greatest caravan, I declare, that has ever crossed the deserts. Anthemus goes to Maragha soon, taking gifts with him; gifts for the young general himself as well as for Kublai Khan. They are truly magnificent." The priest paused and then went on in a hushed tone. "You cannot conceive, young men, what a hard matter it is to collect gifts for the great Khan. He demands nine times nine of everything. And so, when it comes to beautiful women——"

"Women! Is that what Anthemus is sending?"

A look of avid interest crept into the beady eyes of the priest. "Naturally. It is the gift the Khan prizes most. Eighty-one of the love-liest little creatures in the whole world are being gathered together. I myself have had the great luck to see some of them. Ah, young men, such beauties from Egypt with mystery in their sloe-black eyes, such delectable fuchsia buds from Greece, such morsels of fragile gold from the Circassian country, such merry little gadflies from Georgia with enticing smiles and fine roomy hips! This gift cannot fail to win for Anthemus the concession he seeks."

"But," said Walter, "what can a merchant in Antioch hope to gain from a war in Cathay? Will it not upset his trade?"

"No, no! Anthemus is a man of vision. He realizes that the spoils will be great. When Bayan's army captures the cities of the South, the wealth of ages will fall into his hands. Anthemus desires the privilege of selling these treasures in the markets hereabouts and even in the large cities of Europe. Kublai Khan could pay the whole cost of the war out of what

---

*Maragha lies south and west of the Caspian Sea. It remained the capital for a short period only.

he would reap in this way. And as for the profits Anthemus will make! Ah, young men, they will be truly colossal."

An idea had entered Walter's head as he listened. He said to Tristram in an excited whisper: "We come at the right moment to make our fortunes. How lucky that we decided to see Anthemus first."

A loud gong sounded in the distance. Father Theodore counted the strokes and then nodded to the two Englishmen. "That is for me. I must go at once. Remain here, my sirs, and I will strive to arrange for him to see you when he has a free moment."

They took seats and waited, Walter explaining all that had been told him to his companion. The giant Lu Chung, who had not taken his eyes off them, reached out a hand and began to eat fruit from the nearest platter. Vast quantities vanished down his throat in the space of a very few minutes. Large red grapes were consumed without any regard to the seeds. Dates went in at one corner of his mouth and the pits worked their way out at the other. Pomegranates, peaches, plums, disappeared with loud crunching sounds. The belligerent expression on the face of Bird Who Feathers His Nest Lu Chung never relaxed for a moment while all this was going on.

Walter had begun to study the other occupants of the room, paying special attention to a woman who sat beside Lu Chung and seemed to be his feminine counterpart. She showed such a billowing prodigality of fat that she threatened at each move to burst the seams of her scarlet coat. Her hair was red (a curious shade, he thought, to find on an Asiatic head), and her cheeks, encrusted with ocher ruddle, sagged from cheekbones as wide as a mastiff's.

"Tris," he whispered, "that strange pair could pass for the God of War and his spouse, Pestilence."

Tristram was twisting uneasily in his seat. "I am not feeling happy about what you have told me," he said. "The Mongolian armies are the scourge of the devil. Are you planning to join them? It would be much better to fight on the other side."

Walter was silent for a moment. "Whether or not we go with this Bayan of the Hundred Eyes, he will scatter the Chinese armies like chaff before the wind. Should we let this merchant fellow have all the profits? We could take our share with completely clear consciences."

"Would our consciences be completely clear, Wat?"

"Are you thinking we should seek the Holy Grail instead?" Walter shook his head determinedly. "All the castles where the noblest knights

of Christendom live are filled with spoils. The English take them from
the French. The French take them from Spain and Italy and the Low
Countries. In every castle in Europe there are trophies of the Crusades,
and not all of them taken from Saracen towns." He looked at his companion earnestly as though beseeching his understanding. "We will
break no laws of chivalry if we take a small share of the rape of this
Eastern country. Neither of us can afford to be saintly knight-errants—
if any of that fabulous breed still exist. You must improve your station
in life, Tris, and I must find a way to acquire land." He added after a
moment: "I have no intention of setting foot again on the shores of
England until I have the means to get myself an honest name. I am not
going to be Walter the bastard of Gurnie any longer. Rather I will be a
wanderer on the face of the earth, and forced to make my living perhaps by means more questionable than following the Mongol armies."

"You really feel as deeply about it as that?"

"I think of little else. If only it can be done in time!"

"You are very much in love, then, with the heiress of Tressling?"

Walter nodded his head glumly. "Yes, heaven help me! I can't get her
out of my mind."

Father Theodore appeared in the doorway and beckoned to them.
"Anthemus will see you now. He is in a rare mood. The worst thing he
called me was an ill-begotten fleabag. Usually he calls me by all manner
of vile names and even accuses me of fleshly abominations. It is your
luck, young men, to find him in such a pleasant humor."

"Who is that large woman?" asked Walter, when they had left the
room. "She impresses me as most sinister."

The priest's red turban nodded in full agreement. "Nothing too ill
can be said of that one. She deals in *ohins,* the woman trade, and Anthemus has engaged her to take charge of his party. It will be no easy
task to keep eighty-one girls in hand, but Hoochin B'abahu is thoroughly
capable of it. It will interest you to know that the number has been
made up. Anthemus has just selected the last one. He is sending the
most beautiful of his sisters."

"A sister!" cried Walter.

Father Theodore looked at him in surprise. "And why not? He could
not pay the emperor a greater compliment than to send one of his own
blood."

"But," protested Walter, "he's sending her into slavery. I find it hard
to believe any man capable of such a monstrous thing."

"If she wins the Khan's fancy, she will live the rest of her life in the greatest magnificence. Her name is Maryam, and I hear she is a very great beauty indeed. The Khan is certain to notice her."

"Have her wishes been consulted?"

The little priest paused to enjoy a laugh. "Women must always obey the orders of the head of the household. What strange ideas you have! Does it matter so much when he has at least ten other sisters? His father had many wives, and so this one is no more than a half sister. And"—with a sly look—"it has even been whispered that there were doubts about her paternity. It seems there was a male slave in the household"—he paused again, for this was the traditional opening to most obscene anecdotes in the East—"a Western soldier who had been captured in the fighting for Jerusalem. He was tall and handsome, and many of the women made eyes at him; that much is certain. Whether the girl's mother was one of them cannot now be determined, but quite naturally Old Alexander, the father of Anthemus, took the usual steps. He had the slave killed at once."

The clash of backgrounds in this fantastic establishment, further proofs of which they had seen at every step, reached a climax when they entered the room where Anthemus was to receive them. It was in the center of the palace and, as it was directly under the *baudegeer* (a contrivance on the roof to catch the winds), a steady stream of cool air came down from an aperture immediately above the chair where the master sat. The rest of the room was stiflingly hot. The chair itself had undoubtedly served once as the throne of some petty ruler, for there was a jeweled representation of a crown on the back. One leg had been broken off and, strangely enough, had been carelessly replaced by a plain metal shaft. The floors and walls were covered with the finest of rugs, but facing the chair was a frame on which hung samples of the fabrics kept for sale.

Anthemus paid no attention to them at first. He was a young man and a very corpulent one, with a round bald head and a round white face in which heavy-lidded eyes smoldered sleepily. He was attired with the obvious intent of matching the regality of the chair. A tight-sleeved white tunic with pearl-encrusted scrollwork at the wrists covered him from his neck to the tips of his toes. Over this he wore a purple pallium, a strip of rich material two feet wide, fitting around his neck and reaching to the ground. The rear section of the pallium had been gathered up and looped over one arm. Even his purple leather shoes were embroidered with gems.

Off in a corner a trim girl with jet-black hair was roasting chestnuts on a charcoal brazier. Peeling one with a deft twist of her fingers, she dipped it in honey and powdered cassia bark and then, teetering over to her master on tiny feet, popped it into his mouth. Anthemus ground it between his large white teeth, snuffling with enjoyment as he did so.

It was not until he had finished the chestnut that he favored the visitors with a direct glance. Then he said something to the priest in an undertone which the latter translated for them with a pleased smirk.

"He asks, 'What do the Western dogs want?'"

"I know a little Greek," said Walter in that language. "Perhaps it would save time if I talked with him direct."

The sleepy eyes of the merchant slewed around. "It's unusual for a barbarian to speak the only civilized tongue," he grunted. "What are you, a half priest like this slavering little beast?"

"I studied Greek at the University of Oxford," answered Walter, speaking slowly in an effort to make understanding easier. "My companion and I intend to go to Cathay, and we were told that Kyrios Anthemus was sending a special caravan there. We thought it might be arranged for us to accompany it."

"Are you prepared to pay handsomely?"

"We are poor students and cannot pay anything. But we could be very useful to you. My companion is a great archer and would be of help in guarding the caravan."

Anthemus appraised Tristram with a hostile eye. "I could hire a dozen fighting men for the cost of the food this great hulking ox would consume." His eyes turned back to Walter. "And what can you do? Before you try to tell me, I want you to understand that every minute of my day must yield me a profit. I will have my profit out of this even if it is necessary to have you stripped of all your clothes and thrown naked into the streets. So don't mount up the toll on yourselves. Be brief."

"No European has ever been to Cathay and returned alive," said Walter. "If we can do it, we will be welcomed at every court for the tales we will have to tell. Consider the chance we would have to rouse interest in the treasures you will have for sale. My proposal is that we act as agents for you to the kings and rich men of Europe."

The girl returned with another chestnut. Anthemus consumed it thoughtfully.

"I have agents everywhere," he said. "Jews, Lombardy merchants, the very shrewdest dealers I can find. What could a shaveling like you do for me that they can't?"

Walter laughed, realizing that the plan he had thought of when the war was first mentioned was taking hold on the merchant's mind. "Is it necessary to put the answer into words? Your dealers demand their full share of the profits. You could cut what you pay us to a mere fraction of what you allow your Lombardy bankers."

Anthemus wiped his lips with a soft white hand. "You have a shrewd head on your shoulders after all, my young quail-hawk. This will bear some thought." He barked out suddenly, "What languages do you speak?"

"As you see, I speak some Greek."

"Very badly."

"I am well equipped with Latin and French. I even know a little Arabic." Walter was thinking, "How lucky I was in the course I selected!"

Anthemus went into a silent calculation. "Have you any idea how much it would cost me to fit you out properly to visit the courts of Europe? First, a retinue of servants from the East to impress them with the truth of your story. You would have to be handsomely dressed. Presents would have to be scattered about. It would cost me a fortune." He bit savagely into a third chestnut. "And I would have to do it on trust!"

Engrossed though he was in their talk, Walter had noticed that the girl was skipping about unnecessarily and that she was favoring him with sly glances from the corners of her bright black eyes. Apparently the merchant had noticed it also, for suddenly he lashed out with one hand and gave her a resounding smack on her plump posterior.

"So!" he cried. "You must display your waggles for other eyes than mine, must you? Come here! Now stand right where you are and look me in the eye. What do you think I am seeing? I am seeing that fat little body of yours staked out on hot sands and ants crawling over it. Thousands of ants and every one of them with a maddening sting. That's how I treat my girls who show interest in other men, and that is what will happen to you next time. Now go!"

The girl ran from the room, weeping hysterically. Anthemus turned back and continued his interrogation. "Where do you come from?"

"From England."

"England! Land of the great Melec Ric of ever green memory, Richard of the Lion Heart and the thick head! And Edward of the Long Shanks who was hereabouts two years back, hammering away at the Saracens like a good little soldier. You English have strong arms but weak heads. I wonder if any Englishman has the wits to serve Anthemus as he insists on being served?"

"That remains to be proven."

The merchant ran a scowling eye over each of them in turn. "Your miserable rags would bring me in little, even considering the possible value of the toy your overgrown friend carries on his shoulder. I must make my profit the other way." He shook his head as though still doubtful of the wisdom of his course. "I am sending on an advance caravan to Maragha in a few days. Make your plans to go with it. And a word of warning. A party of women will go along. Show no interest in them. To provide a feast for ants is an unpleasant way to die."

3

They had been instructed to remain in the room. As Anthemus was now busying himself with other matters, they walked over to one of the windows and sat down. Here they were screened by an abacus, a form of reckoning board much used in the East. It was so huge that ivory balls, several inches in diameter, served as the pips. Walter decided in his mind that it was used as a symbol.

"What has happened?" asked Tristram, in an anxious whisper.

"It's settled, I think. We are to go with the first party." Walter was in a jubilant mood. "Tris, we are in great luck. We will go to Cathay in half the time, and there will be no risks at all. The only fire-breathing dragon we are likely to meet is Anthemus himself."

"Without knowing a word he said, I have taken a dislike for this fellow. Can we trust him?"

Walter shook his head. "He is a cruel, calculating beast. But I have convinced him he can make use of us, and that's all that counts with a man of his stamp."

Tristram squirmed in his chair and smiled at his companion with reluctance over what he had to say. "I hope, Wat, you will not take this amiss. You haven't been yourself since we reached the East. You are so concerned with your plans that you haven't had a thought for anything else. Even when we stood at the Dome of the Rock, your mind was elsewhere. It was the same when we visited the Mount of Olives and saw where the feet of the Saviour had rested. All the way up to Antioch from Jerusalem you plunged straight ahead, and I could see you begrudged every delay, every stop at holy places. That is not a healthy state of mind, Wat. I am compelled to say this, though I fear you will misjudge my motive."

After a moment of silence, Walter nodded in somber agreement. "I

did not say so then, but I regretted the time we took in getting here.
That is a sorry confession to make. Tris, you are right about me; I am
not myself. There is an urge in me that I can't resist; a go-devil who
keeps whispering in my ear: 'Hurry, hurry! There is so little time and so
much to be done. You may be too late. Make haste!' Certes, I can think
of nothing else!"

"You must try to relax, Wat. I know how great the inducement is; but
everything is in God's hands. If you are to do the things you have set
your mind on, it will be because He has willed it."

"I know it! I have said the same thing to myself many times. But still
that voice keeps urging me on."

"You must not think I am finding fault. When I expressed my doubts
about going with the Mongols, I did not want you to believe I had any
unwillingness about it. Whatever you decide to do will be the right
thing in my eyes; or I will try very hard to believe it right. It's not for
me to question your ways or your reasons for what you do. You must
know I mean that from the very bottom of my heart."

Walter placed a hand on his friend's arm. "We are equal partners in
everything, Tris. You must always say what you think, and have no
hesitation about it. I know what a level head you have, old friend. Have
you any real doubts about the wisdom of this step? Out with them, man,
if you have!"

Tristram shook his head. "I am concerned only about what is in your
mind and your heart. Can your plans prosper if you give yourself to
them so completely? Get back your real self, Wat, and I will be only
too glad to venture out with you on this long trail; and, if needs be, to
fight with a good will under Bayan of the Hundred Eyes."

Tristram had kept his eyes on what was happening in the room while
they talked. His eyes widened suddenly in surprise. Turning in the
same direction, Walter saw that a girl had entered through an inner
door. She paused there, her eyes fixed on the corpulent man in the
throne chair.

Tristram whispered: "Look, Wat. That must be the sister the priest
told you about. She is really very beautiful."

Walter was still too full of what they had been saying to pay much
attention to the newcomer. She looked quite small in spite of the
straight line of her linen robe, which fell in a single piece from her
shoulders. There was an unusual quality about her—that much he
sensed; due perhaps to the fact that, although her hair was black and
her skin of a slightly olive tint, her eyes were a bright blue.

Anthemus was saying in an angry voice, "I didn't send for you, Maryam."

"I know. But I am here. I have just heard what you propose to do with me."

Anthemus called to Father Theodore in a loud voice, "You sickly little house rat, bring that Chinese woman here and be quick about it!"

Turning back to the girl, the merchant began to speak in angry tones. She moved slowly across the room until she was directly in front of him. If Walter had not been watching Anthemus with a keen interest in the moods of his future employer, he would have seen that she was facing her formidable brother with more courage than might have been expected. Her hair was short and was massed about her head in close dark curls. Her face was turned sideways toward them, displaying an unmistakable Grecian purity of feature, although it lacked the bold straight line of eyebrow.

She was answering her brother in low and insistent tones which sometimes rose to a note of passionate protest. Several times she appeared on the point of tears, but for the most part she held her head high and showed no signs of fear.

"She is standing up to him," whispered Tristram. "I hope she succeeds in changing his mind."

There was nothing in the scowling face of Anthemus to warrant that hope. His fingers toyed impatiently with the jeweled seam of his pallium, and the unwinking glance he bent on her was completely hostile.

When Father Theodore returned with the woman, the debate became a three-sided one. The girl showed dismay at the formidable appearance of Hoochin B'abahu, and at first she had little to say. Walter noticed that she cringed away when the heavily ringed fingers of the red-haired procuress rested on her shoulder. This was not surprising, for the small jet eyes in that broad expanse of painted face were looking her over with the cold calculation of the auction mart.

The talk was carried on in a language that Walter did not recognize. It had a guttural quality, and he was to learn later that it was the polyglot tongue of the Asiatic trails, a mixture of many languages. The girl's voice had begun to rise again on an insistent note. Once, in answer to something the Chinese woman had said, she cried out an answer unmistakable in any language. It was, "No, no!" Hoochin B'abahu said, "*Tiimu, tiimu!*" which meant, just as surely, "Yes, yes." When the girl shook her head, the woman went into a long and vehement tirade.

Anthemus became impatient. "Enough of this talk," he said, in Greek. "My mind is made up. Go back where you belong and be ready to obey when the time comes."

Maryam raised her head and announced in a clear voice: "My mind is made up also. I will not go. I will kill myself first."

"I will have obedience from you, my stubborn kokona!" cried her brother. Rising angrily, he took the girl by the shoulders and began to shake her. "You ought to know I always mean what I say. Are you going to get some sense into your head? Are you? Are you?"

The shaking increased in violence as his temper mounted. She struggled to get away but was unable to break his grip.

"Let me go, let me go!" she said, breathlessly.

His face was becoming purple with the effort, but he did not stop. "I will let you go," he puffed, "when you tell me you will cause no more trouble. And not before."

"Can we let this go on?" asked Tristram in a tense whisper. His hand had gone to the handle of the dagger in his belt.

Before there could be any attempt at interference, the girl raised enough of her skirt to reveal a bare foot in a red leather sandal. The next instant the foot was off the ground as she lunged forward with all her strength. The point of her knee must have caught Anthemus in the pit of his round and vulnerable stomach.

The wind was knocked out of him so completely that he made no sound whatever. His face had gone blank, and he settled slowly to the floor, his arms and legs limp and powerless, like a devilfish which has suffered a wound in its vital core. He fell back against a leg of the chair and remained there without any movement for several moments. By the time he was able to breathe again, the girl had vanished through the door by which she had entered.

Father Theodore ran over to the two Englishmen. "I think," he stuttered, "you had better go before he recovers himself. Wait for me outside."

Back in the anteroom, which was now deserted, they looked at each other and grinned. "Our new overlord seems to be a thoroughly terrible fellow," said Tristram. A sober expression replaced the smile on his long face. "What do you suppose he will do to her?"

"Nothing violent, I judge," answered Walter. "After all, she's a valuable asset. Unless I have misread the character of our friend Anthemus, he would never willingly destroy anything of real value."

"She showed a high spirit," said Tristram. "I—I was quite taken with her."

"Yes, she has plenty of spirit. And you think her beautiful also? I didn't look at her very closely."

"She is the most beautiful girl I have ever seen."

Walter's ideas on the score of feminine loveliness were bounded on all four sides by the golden vision of Engaine. "She seemed dark," he said. "And what a strange way of wearing her hair. Is it womanly to have it cut so short?"

"I liked it that way. Perhaps it is the proper manner here in the East."

"I noticed one thing about her," said Walter, with a grin. "She has a very small foot. And she knows how to use it!"

It was a quarter of an hour later when Father Theodore joined them. "He is in a raging temper," he reported, wiping the perspiration from his face with both ends of the bow at his neck. "It has been a most trying experience. He has decided to send her off at once. The first caravan will leave in the morning, and you are to be ready to go also." He looked at Walter with a new respect. "Anthemus seems to have taken a fancy to you, young man. At least, he is sure you will prove of use to him. Instructions have already been given to have you both fitted out for the journey. I am to wait and travel with him in the second caravan. Without me," with a smirk of pride, "he would be quite lost. In the meantime I am to give you a lesson in the language of the trails. We will have the night only to drill some of it into your heads."

When they emerged into the grounds of the place, the sun was sinking from the sky with the suddenness which was still a matter of wonder to the two Englishmen. Shadows were already growing on the vine-snared walls which marked off in pleasant irregularity the famous gardens of Antioch. The quiet of evening was settling down, and there was a welcome hint of coolness in the air. Bells could be heard chiming in the distance.

"It is an easy enough tongue to pick up," said the priest. "There has always been a jumbled means of communication for all the races who mingle on the silk trails and in the bazaars, but of late years it has been changing a great deal. The Mongols rule all of the continent, and so most of the words used are Mongolian. It has no name, but I call it *Bi-chi*. That means I-you in their outlandish tongue." He added after a moment: "There are some Chinese words, of course. You must begin to call the country we are going to China. Cathay applies mostly to the northern part, which is now under Mongolian rule. All of the southern part, the Manji country ruled by the Sung emperor, is called China, and the people Chinese."

Walter said: "You will have to give me the first lesson, as my friend has forgotten what little Latin he knew. I will teach him in turn." He added anxiously, "What is to be done with the sister now?"

The priest indulged in a careless motion of his hands. "She will be punished. Naturally. Anthemus will see to that."

"Will the punishment be severe? We feel very much concerned about her, my friend and I."

"There is nothing to be concerned about. Anthemus will see to it that she starts in good condition, although it will go sorely against his inclinations. None of the other sisters could be sent in her place. They are all fat and swarthy, and he knows the Khan would not thank him for the gift of a waddling flap-gut. No, no, the little Maryam will be lucky because of that. She will get off with nothing worse than a tender behind." He paused with a sly grin. "It's such a nice little behind, as round and soft as that of a tame bee!"

Tristram, of course, had not been able to follow any of the talk. He leaned forward now and touched Walter on the arm. "I am inclined to believe the story that her father was a Christian slave," he said. "Did you notice her closely at all, Wat? She has blue eyes. Do you know what I have been thinking? I have been thinking they are English eyes!"

4

"May God give you the kingdom of heaven. This boy will be your servant," said Father Theodore, thrusting forward a diminutive specimen with a grinning black face under an enormous and dirty turban.

The boy placed a hand on his breast and said, *"Bi,* Mahmoud ibn Asseult."

"That is his name," explained the priest. "Mahmoud is a good boy. I picked him out for you myself. He is a willing worker, and he will steal anything you need. He comes from near the Red Sea, and I think there is some Abyssinian in him."

"But will we need a servant?" asked Walter.

"Have you ever packed a camel?" There was an impatient note in the priest's voice. "Have you ever pegged one out for the night? Are you light-fingered? You can't get along in a caravan without stealing the things you lack. You may be sure of this: when Anthemus provides a servant, there is real need for one. Take him and be thankful."

The boy undoubtedly had some African strain in him, for his nose was squat and his lips thick, and the darkness of his skin was due to something more than the effect of desert sunshine. He had a twinkle in his eye, moreover, and a jaunty way of standing with his arms akimbo which was completely foreign to the stern dignity of the nomad people. His whole attitude said as plainly as words, "I like you, my masters, and I will make you a very good boy."

The priest tapped first Walter and then Tristram on their shoulders, saying in a loud tone: "Master Walter. Master Tristram."

Mahmoud repeated with some difficulty, "Masser Watter, Masser Twiss." Then he touched his breast again and said with a still broader grin, "*Bi,* Mahmoud ibn Asseult."

Father Theodore said something in a guttural tongue, and the boy turned and vanished in the crowded square. They were standing beneath the ruined walls of Antioch, which had not been rebuilt since the last assault at the hands of Egyptian armies. The place buzzed with the most intense activity in preparation for the start.

Walter motioned toward a section of the square where all the camels had white trappings and sky-blue ostrich plumes bobbing on their nose-cords. "Does that mean the women are coming with us?" he asked.

"All of them. The second caravan will have to travel much faster than this one."

"What about the sister?"

"She goes today, as I said she would."

"Is she reconciled to it, then?"

The priest drew down the corners of his mouth. "She has given in. What would you expect? Anthemus was thorough about the whipping. He had her stripped to the waist and gave her a dozen strokes himself. I hear that all the other sisters were brought in to watch because he knew that would hurt her more than the blows. She didn't make a sound."

"What is he saying?" asked Tristram.

Fearing an outburst on the part of his friend, Walter answered grimly, "I will tell you later."

"You look upset."

"We are going to have a score to settle with Anthemus of Antioch. But we shall have to bide our time."

Mahmoud returned at this point, and it was apparent he was upset over something also. He gave the impression of a pariah dog slinking along with its tail between its legs. His mouth drooped, his eyes were

filled with the deepest woe. Even his absurdly large turban seemed to
have lost all of its jauntiness. He poured out a long story to the Nestorian priest.

"It is just as I expected," reported the latter. "Anthemus has been
most frugal in his arrangements. Mahmoud here says your tent is old
and full of holes. He says everything provided for you is beneath the
touch of lepers. The camels are the worst. You have been given the three
mangiest camels to be found between here and the land of the red
dust."

"We are not in a position to complain," said Walter, uneasily. "After
all, we are to travel on his bounty."

The priest snickered. "Very spare bounty, my sirs. Here are the creatures now."

Three camels were being led toward them across the crowded square,
a grinning Arab at each nose-cord. Knowing nothing of such matters,
Walter could still tell that these were the sickliest, the most cantanker-
ous and worthless animals that ever set a complaining foot on the desert trails. The busy packers stepped back to let them pass, slapping
each other on the back and indulging in much raucous laughter at the
expense of the Christian dogs who were to ride them. Even Father
Theodore seemed to be enjoying the jest.

"I recognize each one of them," snickered the priest. "They are pro-
verbial on the trails, my sirs. The first one is Zoroaster. He is a bag of
decrepit bones, but still he is the strongest of the three, and I suggest
the wisdom of the Tall One riding him. Then there is Helen. Not," with
a titter, "that men fight over her. On the contrary. Helen has the habit
of nipping the knees of those who ride her. She does it slyly, when they
are not looking. Her teeth are like *joes;* needles, my sirs. The last one is
Doulahu, which means The Singer. You will hear him all night long."
He raised his voice in an imitation of the wail of the camel, "*O-o-onk!
O-o-onk!* It will keep you awake until you become accustomed to it."

Tristram had not understood a word, but he had grasped the situation from the scurvy appearance of the mounts provided for them. He
took the bow from his back and brought it down with a loud thwack
across the skinny shins of the nearest of the jeering onlookers. The man
yelped with pain and scrambled to get out of reach. The rest did the
same, fearing the belligerent purpose of the tall white man.

"I would do the same for this fellow Anthemus if he were here," declared Tristram, his face an angry red. "Must we submit to this, Wat?
I would rather walk every foot of the way than ride one of these flea-
bitten beasts."

"You would soon change your mind," cautioned the priest.

The girls were putting in an appearance now, dressed in white and heavily veiled. Walter thought, as he watched, of the yearly levy of Athenian maidens who had been sent so many years before to feed the Cretan Minotaur. He noticed, however, that these harem-bred beauties were not saddened at the prospect before them. They chattered among themselves and even indulged in occasional bursts of laughter.

Hoochin B'abahu was in the lead, planting her feet down aggressively as she walked and twisting her head about in all directions. That she was searching for causes of complaint was apparent when she stopped abruptly and pointed at the camels with the white trappings, saying something in her high-pitched voice to Bird Who Feathers His Nest Lu Chung. Only two words of the tirade reached Walter's ears: *"B'abahu . . ."*

"I want! I want!" mimicked Father Theodore. "She always wants something. That's how she got her name. *Old I Want!* What she really needs is a sound application of the bastinado on her ugly feet. She has worn us all out with her wants."

"Is the sister there?" asked Walter.

The priest nodded his head. "She will ride immediately after the old hellcat. She is the pick of the lot and, after all, she is his sister; so she gets the place of honor. There, the one taking her seat on the camel with plumes in its topknot."

The animals had been forced to their knees by the sweating drivers, and the girls were climbing up to the saddle-cloths. There was nothing to distinguish the one who mounted the most gaily caparisoned camel from any of the others. Walter felt some relief of mind. Apparently she had not suffered any serious effects from the whipping.

The activity in the square came suddenly to its highest peak. A Mongolian horseman raised his arm and then wheeled his mount toward the gap in the wall which had once been a gate. Hoochin B'abahu lowered her great bulk into a horse-drawn palanquin, and the procession in white fell into single file behind her. The caravan was under way.

"Up! Up!" shouted Father Theodore, who had caught the infection. "You are to ride at the end, but you must be ready."

Tristram gave his friend a rueful smile. "Well, if we must, the sooner we get it over the better. Here goes!" He swung one long leg over the hump of Zoroaster. "But I don't like serving as a butt for these heathen swine."

"Keep cool, Tris." advised Walter, taking his seat on Helen and

watching closely for any hint of an intent to bite. "We'll be out of here
in a very few minutes. When we come back we will ride blooded Arabian steeds. Set your mind on the future and it won't be so hard."

It proved a difficult ordeal, nevertheless. The onlookers waited until
they swung into line at the tail end of the procession and then burst
into louder jeers than ever. They doubled over in paroxysms of mirth,
screaming *"Nohuner! Nohuner!* [Dogs! Dogs!]" Boys scooped up rotting vegetables from the ground and pelted the hated Christians with
them. Then they used camel droppings for the same purposes, while
others pelted them with stones. Walter bent his head and motioned to
Mahmoud, who was riding behind him on Doulahu, to go ahead. The
stones were coming from all directions now, and all three had to ride
with their heads down close to the humps of their camels. *"Cruses!
Cruses!"* shrieked the mob, working up to a religious frenzy.

From the edge of the mob Father Theodore shouted: "Farewell, my
young sirs. Be of good cheer. We shall meet again."

"Anthemus of Antioch," muttered Walter, "there will indeed be a
settlement for this some day!"

CHAPTER VI

Maragha

"A MESSENGER has reached camp," announced Walter, shivering with the
cold. "From Bayan of the Hundred Eyes. It seems we are not to see
Maragha after all."

Tristram got up from his seat in the shelter of the yurt. "What has
happened now?"

"We are late, and Bayan is determined to be off without further delay. We join his main body at a junction of the road some miles from
the city gates and start immediately for the East. The messenger says
that the second caravan from Antioch is expected to reach the junction
at the same time we do—in two more days. It's also said that Bayan is
furious because he must take the women with him."

The tall archer began to pace up and down, beating his hands against
his sides to keep them warm. His lessons in *Bi-chi* had not progressed,
and he still depended on Walter for the news of the camp.

"Another camel dropped dead when it reached the lines," reported the latter. "They can't stand the cold of this high country. Some of the girls are ill. The old woman has a running of the nose and a great pain in her fat belly."

"I have never felt anything like this cold," said Tristram.

Walter's eyes were knotted up in a frown, and his nose was blue. "The Persians tell you with so much unction that the earth is divided into seven climates and that they have the fourth, the perfect one. Perfect! Two weeks ago we choked in the dust of the desert, and now we're likely to freeze to death. Still, we are getting along. Maragha is a long leg on our journey."

"The urge for speed is still on you, then?"

Walter smiled somberly. "It has not abated a jot."

Darkness was falling so rapidly that Mahmoud had scrambled in frantic haste to get their yurt up in place. It was the same makeshift affair that their patron had provided, but Mahmoud had found new wattled rods for the frame and had mended each rent with meticulous care, stitching on them by day as he rode The Singer and by night after the evening meal. He had even succeeded in finding (they had carefully refrained from any curiosity as to the source) a bolt of the sky-blue silk which all Mongolians used for the lining of their traveling homes; and so they spent their resting hours with some comfort and even a trace of proper grandeur.

In a very short time the little servant called a cheery summons to the mess kettle, and both Englishmen hurried to obey it. Mahmoud, who had wrapped a piece of camel-cloth under his red *abba* and stuffed his shoes with straw to keep warm, asked in the smattering of trail words they used between them, "Like food, good massers?"

"Fine, you rascal," answered Walter. He added in an undertone, "We have the smartest thief in the whole caravan."

Tristram dipped into the kettle again for the drumstick of a chicken and heaved a deep sigh. "Do you suppose she is all right?"

"Your lovely Maryam? I have heard no further reports of her."

Walter had seen her once only during all the long weeks since they had left Antioch, and Tristram not at all. It was late one afternoon, and with startling suddenness a yellowish gray fog had appeared above the horizon. A cry of "Sand! Sand!" had risen from one end of the caravan to the other. All rules were forgotten as they scrambled to get the tents up and to bank them with sand against the coming of the storm. Even some of the girls had joined in the frantic labor.

Tristram was helping Mahmoud to get their own quarters ready, and so Walter had hurried forward to aid the others. He could tell from the terrifying aspect of the fast-approaching cloud that no time was to be lost. He drove in pegs with the butt end of a lance until his back threatened to break, glancing up at intervals at the sky, where already the vanguard of the storm swept over them on a whistling wind. He had never seen the like of it before, and all the stories he had ever heard of mysterious and malignant forces in the East filled his mind.

The yurts of the women had all been raised and properly safeguarded before he desisted. The storm was now ready to unleash its fury on them, and he was turning to run when he became aware that one of the girls had been working by his side. On some impulse she turned and looked up at him. She was wearing a light veil, and so he could not be entirely sure, but he believed it was the sister of Anthemus.

What happened then was against all the rules. Instead of flying away to her own quarters, she said something to him in an eager voice. When he failed to catch the words, she resorted to the desert formula of introduction, touching her breast and saying her name, *"Bi,* Maryam."

When he answered, *"Bi,* Walter," she started in surprise. She said "Wal-ter?" in a voice that suggested the name meant something to her. Then she smiled and cried, "Wal-ter, Lun-dun!", repeating in a kind of ecstasy, "Wal-ter, Lun-dun!"

The wind was howling about them now, and particles of sand were blowing against them, but they faced each other with no thought of their immediate safety. Walter raised his voice to carry over the roar of the elements, shouting in Greek: "London? What do you know of London?"

"My father . . ." The rest of her answer was lost in the mad screech of the wind.

He stepped closer to her, holding up his cloak to shield her from the sand. "Do you mean your father came from London?" he asked. "And was his name Walter also?"

She nodded eagerly. "Yes, yes! Who are you? Oh, tell me you came from Lun-dun!"

"I am English."

She leaned forward and touched his arm with an appealing gesture. She was speaking so rapidly that he could not follow what she said, but he was sure he caught one word, "Help!" In spite of the biting rain of sand, she threw back her veil, and he could see that her eyes were filled with excited tears. Again he made out the one word, "Help!"

At this moment a guard stumbled up to them and yanked the girl back angrily. He shouted something at the Englishman and then proceeded to drag her after him in the direction of the women's enclosure. In a few seconds the pair were lost to sight in the stinging wave of sand sweeping across the encampment. Walter turned and ran.

It took a full quarter hour of furious buffeting in the teeth of the wind to reach his own yurt. Once inside, he said to Tristram in a breathless voice, "I have news for you, Tris, something almost unbelievable."

"What is it? I was pretty thoroughly frightened, Wat. I had almost given you up."

"You were right!" gasped Walter. "The girl is part English. I'll tell you all about it when I get this sand out of my throat."

A few minutes later he proceeded with his explanation. "I saw her, and we talked for a minute. Her father was English. His name was Walter, and he came from London. That was all I could get out of it, except that she feels desperately in need of help. Do you suppose, Tris, it was Wat Stander, my father's squire? Joseph spoke of him, you remember."

Tristram's face had lighted up eagerly. "Perhaps you have stumbled on the truth. There would be hundreds of Englishmen named Walter with the Crusaders, of course, but there's still a chance it was Wat Stander." He made a quick calculation of the years. "Your father was here in 'fifty-four. If Stander was taken captive—yes, it all fits in. But that is not the important part. She has English blood; that is what I am thinking of. Wat, we must do something for her."

Walter nodded in agreement. "Yes, we must find some way to help her. But what can we do? You've seen how closely the enclosure is guarded. If we got her out of it, where could we take her?"

"The chance to do something will come," declared Tristram, confidently. "But if it doesn't come, we must make it."

The cautious inquiries they had made after that elicited no information whatever. The guards were under the strictest orders not to discuss their charges, although the camp seethed with rumors of what was going on behind the silk walls of the enclosure. They had heard at once when a hot-tempered vixen from the Far South stabbed one of the Circassian girls in a quarrel over some trifle. They had heard that jealousy and strife had become common and that whippings were almost daily occurrences, but the name of Maryam had never been mentioned in connection with any specific story.

As they huddled over the fire, they began to talk now of Walter's meeting with her on the day of the sand storm.

Tristram shook his head despondently. "I have been racking my brain, and I have thought of a score of plans to rescue her," he said. "None of them has been worth a second thought. It is truly maddening, Wat. There she is, facing a life worse than slavery; and here we are, men of her own race, and we can do nothing about it."

"I have been doing the same. And with the same lack of result. The only satisfaction I can see is that we will soon join the main party, where the hand of Bayan will hold these Mongolians in check. They have been showing a dangerous curiosity about the women. I've been afraid they would get out of control."

"We can attend to them if they do," asserted Tris. As usual he was working on his longbow, burnishing the yew and testing the string. He now gave it an affectionate pat. "I would enjoy taking a hand if there was trouble. It would be a pleasure to loose a few bolts into their greasy hides."

Walter shook his head. "They are always dangerous, the *Tsao-ta-tse*. These stupid eunuchs would never stop them. If they do break out, the old she-dragon will have well-raped beauties to deliver at Khan Bhalig."*

Mahmoud called from the entrance of the yurt in his musical voice, "Someone comes, good massers."

It was Bird Who Feathers His Nest Lu Chung. He had been very much in evidence at every stage of the journey, acting in general as a camp seneschal and, if rumors were to be relied on, doing very well for himself on every transaction. He was gaudily attired in a silk-embroidered robe with sleeves long enough to conceal his hands and a kerchief of gold cloth wrapped around his gargoyle of a head. The double-heeled boots he wore during the day had been replaced by slippers of purple and gold.

Speaking in the common tongue, he enunciated slowly, "Lowly Lu Chung has message for ears of mighty lords from West."

Walter motioned to him to seat himself and then lighted a stone Mongolian lamp which he attached to a hook in the main support of the yurt. The lamp was filled with oil and gave forth a very hot and beautiful light. Lu Chung studied the blue lining and the blankets spread on a bed of fresh tamarisk boughs and nodded his head approvingly.

"Servant of mighty lords of West very good servant."

*The city of Pekin now stands near the site of Khan Bhalig which Kublai Khan had made his capital.

"Very good servant. But he has too much to do."

The visitor considered this information for a moment in silence. Then he said in what seemed a tone of considerable satisfaction: "That is good. Very good. Second boy needed. This humble one will see to it."

Walter asked, "What brings illustrious Lu Chung?"

The giant Chinese got up and dropped the felt flap over the entrance. He leaned over to whisper: "*Very* secret matter. Noble lords will keep silent tongues?"

Walter nodded. "You may rely on us."

"One word unwisely spoken——" Lu Chung made a gesture as though driving a blade into his own breast. Then he whispered, "This lowly one has talked to little black rose."

Knowing only that the clove, most desired of all Eastern spices, was frequently called that, Walter waited for further enlightenment. Lu Chung achieved a semblance of a smile. "I speak of lady," he said. "This lady different from others. She has great spirit, a tang like the black rose. The rest," with the greatest contempt, "are all tasteless as young squashes."

"Which of the ladies does worthy Lu Chung mean?"

"Beautiful sister of estimable Anthemus." The huge frame inclined in a stiff bow. "She is in serious trouble. She has courage, but still she cry much at night. This humble one has made promise to help. At Maragha." He asked then in a cautious whisper, "Will noble lords also help?"

Walter was taken completely by surprise. It seemed unbelievable that the reputedly venal Lu Chung would involve himself in anything so dangerous and unprofitable. He looked their visitor over carefully, thinking to himself that he had never seen guile more clearly indicated on a human face. It was several moments before he asked, "What could we do?"

"Very small part. It is possible noble lords might not know it even at time of doing. This most stupid one speaks now so noble lords be ready."

"Has the lady asked for our help?"

"Yes, young lord. She say Lu Chung come." His manner became still more secretive. "Others will help at Maragha. It is all arranged. Much pay for Lu Chung and also for noble lords."

"No pay!" said Walter, sharply. The plea of a lady in distress could not be disregarded, but he was finding it hard to accept the situation

and the danger to his own plans involved in it. In spite of that, he added:
"My friend and I will help. Tell me what we can do."

Lu Chung indulged in another of his hideous grins. "Good! Will tell
lady. Can say no more now."

Walter demanded in a tone of exasperation, "How can we help if we
are told nothing?"

"Wait. Trust unworthy Lu Chung." The giant bowed and backed
toward the entrance. Here he paused and held out an expectant hand.
"We reach town tomorrow with slave market. Lu Chung buy second
boy for noble lords." He began to twiddle his thick fingers. "Anthemus
pay. But perhaps noble lords——"

There was no mistaking his meaning, and Walter fumbled reluctantly
in the pouch under his belt. Bringing out a gold dinar, he dropped it
in the rapacious palm.

"Good!" breathed Lu Chung. "Remember. Most silent tongue."

When he had gone, Tristram asked, "What did the rascal want?"

"Come for a walk so we can talk safely."

They struck out into the night. There had been a storm in the district
recently, for the sand lay in grooves and long curling ridges, as though
the surface had been woven into a pattern by celestial needles.

"The chance we have been waiting for has come," said Walter, plodding along slowly and flailing his arms about to keep warm. He proceeded to recount all that Lu Chung had told him and wound up by
saying: "I am not certain yet that the bird who feathers his nest is not
what we have always thought him, a treacherous, lying rascal. How do
we know he won't accept a second reward by exposing the plan to Anthemus?"

"That is a chance we must accept," exclaimed Tristram. "By the Rood,
I for one am willing to take it!"

"The Slow Death isn't a pleasant way to die. They lop off a joint a
day, starting with your fingers. It generally takes a week before you
bleed to death." Walter shuddered but then managed to smile at his
companion. "Still I feel as you do. We must do anything we can."

Tristram said thoughtfully: "We are not likely to have any part in
what is done with her after she makes her escape. But I question if we
would be able to stay with the caravan."

Walter had been thinking of this certainty, calculating the cost of
striking out by themselves against the supply of gold still in the pouch
under his belt. "Tris," he said, with a rueful shake of his head, "I doubt
if we can reach China by ourselves. There will be only one course open

to us. If we get away with whole skins, we must part company. You must go back. There's plenty left for that. I got you into this and I shall insist that you return. For myself I shall strike south and see if I can get there by sea."

Tristram laughed. "Do you think I would desert you? No, Wat, whatever happens we must face the consequences together. If one can go by sea, two can go just as readily."

"To separate is the only sensible course," persisted Walter. "The East is in my blood. I must get to this fabulous country or I shall never have any peace of mind. But that is no reason for sacrificing you."

"Would we be here now if we had intended to follow a sensible course? No, let's hear no more of it. We stand together."

They walked some distance in silence. The old Oxford phrase came back to Walter's tongue. "Thou very idiot!" he said. After a further pause, he added: "Well then, it is settled. We stand together, my stubborn old hinny. I am lucky to have a friend like you."

The Sky Walker, as they had come to call the moon after so many weeks in the company of desert people, was well started on her nightly perambulation when they turned back. Mahmoud was finishing the last of his tasks, scrubbing out the mess kettle with a handful of hair from the tail of a horse. He was humming an interminable song, the only one he seemed to know. It was called, he had told them, "I Ride a Camel with a Beard Like the Prophet's."

He gave them a cheerful, "Good massers late."

Remembering Lu Chung's promise, Walter said: "Mahmoud works too hard. We must get second boy to help him."

"No second boy, master!" The little servant was both alarmed and indignant. "Mahmoud ibn Asseult only boy you need. Other boys no good." His indignation got the upper hand, and he made a motion with one finger from ear to ear. "Second boy come, cut second boy's throat."

"Well, we shall see about it. Good night, Mahmoud."

Tristram fell off to sleep as soon as he stretched himself out on their fragrant couch of tamarisk. Walter lay awake for some time, his mind full of the difficulties which lay ahead. Mahmoud was not sleeping either. Walter could hear him tossing about on his own bed behind the curtain stretched across one side of the tent.

"Masser awake?"

"Yes, Mahmoud."

"Please, Masser." There was infinite grief in the tone. "Mahmoud like work. Mahmoud like good massers. Please, no second boy!"

2

The sky was a cold gray, shot over with a coppery light from the setting sun, and the wind came racing in from the north with an edge of
steel. For once, however, the people of the camp had forgotten their discomforts. Two male camels had broken loose from the picket lines and
were engaged in a vicious conflict which brought shouts of delight from
the circle gathered around them.

Walter watched the proceedings from a point well back of the circle.
The camels, well covered now with their winter coats of long, rufous
hair, snapped at each other with their yellow-fanged muzzles and kicked
with their feet. The noise made by the eager spectators almost drowned
out the bubbling cries of the animals. It was not very exciting, he decided, and was on the point of turning away when an incident occurred
which immediately distracted all attention from the bout.

Some of the girls had been watching over the silk wall of their enclosure. One of the poles gave way, and a section of the flimsy wall fell
outward, carrying them with it. Their shrieks brought every eye around,
and the men began to jump up and down with excitement at the sight
of feminine legs and feet waving in the air. The eunuchs were on the
scene in an instant to repair the damage and rescue their charges, followed very shortly by Hoochin B'abahu herself. That angry lady had
forgotten to don her red wig and so displayed to view, for the first and
probably the last time, the dead-white dome of her head, sparsely covered by wisps of gray hair. In the space of a few minutes the whole pop-
ulation of the enclosure had gathered on the spot.

It looked at first as though the kind of trouble Walter had been fearing would result. The ill-tempered camels were left to snarl and worry
at each other as the men rushed in a body to see at close range the
mysterious beauties they had escorted across the desert. All that happened, however, was an exchange of much loud talk and a great deal of
chattering and giggling as the ruffled ladies hurried to the cover of their
tents.

To Walter's surprise, Lu Chung was standing at the entrance when
he reached his own tent at the edge of the encampment. A boy with a
face the color of mahogany stood beside him, wrapped up to the chin in
a dirty felt coat and with a woolen hat pulled well down over his brows.
The resourceful trafficker in guileful ways spoke up from a mountain-

ous sheepskin collar. "Second boy, gallant lord. Small but willing. Name Mustapha."

"Worthy Lu Chung has been prompt."

"Wind of opportunity blows quickly by doorstep," declared the Chinese. "Second boy cold. Also, perhaps, afraid. This humble one suggests he take quick shelter in tent."

"Mahmoud!" called Walter.

The ebony-colored servant had been standing off at one side, a rebellious look on his usually cheerful face. He came forward slowly, dragging one foot after the other.

"Mahmoud, this is second boy, Mustapha. Take him to tent and see he has food."

Mahmoud made no move for several moments. Then he began to walk in the direction of the yurt, motioning his new helper to follow. "This boy no good, massers," he said. "Not strong boy. See, not much back, not much legs."

"Do as you are told, Mahmoud."

Walter's tone conveyed an unmistakable warning. Mahmoud began to show more alacrity. "You, second boy, come," he muttered. Then he called back over his shoulder, "If second boy hungry, let him get food."

Mustapha raised his head and gave Walter a glance before turning to follow. His new master reacted with a start of violent surprise. In the mahogany face there glowed eyes of a suspicious lightness!

Lu Chung chuckled. "Very prompt, noble sir."

Walter recovered himself with an effort. "Did you get her out during the trouble back there?" he asked.

The giant nodded. "When wind of opportunity does not blow, find a big fan. This unworthy one paid driver to let camels out. Also saw to it that poles were not secure." He grinned with pleasure in his own cleverness. "Big fan do work. Bought a boy at slave market and brought him to camp so many could see. That boy now on way back. Plenty see him come, no one see him go. Everyone will think this one same boy. No one suspect."

"I hope not," said Walter, earnestly.

Tristram emerged from the yurt as the two small figures reached the entrance. He stepped aside to let them past.

"Our household grows, I see," he said.

Walter motioned him to come nearer. "Did you look closely at our new second boy?"

"Closely enough. I am going to find it hard to tell them apart."

When this was repeated to Lu Chung, the Chinese spread his hands out with a gesture of self-congratulation. "If Tall One did not see, no one will see."

"If you had looked a little closer, Tris, you would have noticed that the second boy has what you called English eyes."

Tristram glanced back over his shoulder and gave a loud whistle. "Already?" His eyes, when he swung around, were alive with excitement. "By the Rood, I am glad of this. Have you been told all the plans? What are we to do?"

"I don't know yet."

Lu Chung looked about him and then motioned Walter to step closer. "Tomorrow we reach roads where honorable lord Bayan waits," he said, in a husky whisper. "When young men from West go to his camp, boy must go with them. That is all." He gestured with one hand. "Boy will run away and not be seen again. Very simple."

"But where will she—where will boy go?"

"To Maragha, where ancient uncle lives. Uncle rich rug merchant. Has no liking for estimable Anthemus and so will receive runaway. As I say, very simple."

Walter was feeling very much relieved in his mind at the undoubted simplicity of the plan. "There will be no chance for us to play the hero, Tris," he said. "You will be disappointed, I am sure, but for my part I confess that I am glad. The girl will get away easily and surely. As no suspicion can attach to us, we can still count on traveling overland with Bayan."

By the time Lu Chung left, smoke was pouring from the small air space at the top of their tent, which meant that the evening meal was being prepared.

"I don't like the idea of leaving her to fend for herself," Tristram said, when the plan was explained to him. "She may not reach this uncle. What will she do then? To be sure nothing goes wrong, we should take her to Maragha."

"And give the thing away? We would be seen, and then there would be plenty with sharp enough wits to put two and two together." Walter dropped an arm over his friend's shoulder. "My old knight-errant, we must be sensible about this. Lu Chung has figured it all out carefully, you may be sure. We mustn't spoil it by doing more than we are asked to do."

Tristram sighed. "I suppose you are right."

Mahmoud, busy over the mess kettle, was in a better mood. He was keeping his assistant busy with sharp admonitions. "You, second boy, put more cow dung on fire," and "You, Tapha, plenty water quick." The assistant, keeping her head down, was doing his bidding with alacrity. She had discarded the felt coat, revealing a clean tunic and voluminous white trousers reaching to her ankles. She still wore the cap to maintain her disguise.

"Tender stew, massers," announced Mahmoud. "Young kid. Ribs, plenty fat and juicy. Put oil of sesame in water. *Very* good that way, massers."

They had finished a hearty meal and had withdrawn from the kettle to let Mahmoud and his helper begin their meal, when a hand shoved back the flap and a yellowish face with sharply slanted eyes thrust itself through the opening. The owner of the face promptly swaggered into the yurt, bringing with him an unpleasantly greasy odor. Lu Chung followed him in, nodding his head apologetically.

"Lady run away," said Lu Chung. "Much trouble in camp. All yurts must be searched."

The Mongol did not stand on ceremony. He proceeded to examine every foot of space, even thrusting his dirty hands into the boughs under the blankets. Then he looked them over with a bitter eye.

"Christian dogs!" he said. "Your faces are like the belly of a dead fish. You poison the air." Then he turned to the Chinese and said, *"Drube?"*

"Four," repeated Lu Chung, consulting a list in his hand. "That is right, Ortuh the Stammerer. Lady not here."

As the Mongol continued to scrutinize the occupants of the yurt with a suspicious eye, Lu Chung asked, "Is thought in mind of most jealous Ortuh that lady would hide in tent of infidels?"

The greasy searcher said *"Ugee!"* which meant "No!" and spat into the supper kettle before swaggering out. Lu Chung paused to say over his shoulder with a nod and a grin, "Very, very ungrateful of lady to run away."

Mahmoud resumed his meal at once, but his companion drew back from the kettle with a shudder and said, "Mustapha not hungry."

The little servant scowled over the shank into which he had sunk his sharp white teeth. "You, second boy, better eat plenty. Need plenty strength for work."

Walter said, "Come here, Mustapha." The girl joined him at once, seating herself so that she faced him directly. Space in the tent was so cramped that their knees touched. Walter began to speak in the Greek tongue, keeping his voice low in the hope that Mahmoud would not realize they were not using the camp lingo.

"Do you recognize me as the one you talked to that day in the sand storm?"

"Yes, Most Kind Grandeur." Greek people, Walter knew, were prone to use such extravagant expressions of respect. "That was why I sent Lu Chung to ask your help."

"You spoke then of London. Was your father English?"

"English?" The large blue eyes, so much out of place in her blackened face, showed no recognition of the word. "I do not know, English."

"My friend and I are English. Your father must have been also if he came from London. You said his name was Walter. Was it Walter Stander?"

She seemed at first to find something familiar in the name, but after a moment she shook her head. "I do not know, Kind Benefactor."

"Are you sure? Think! It is most important."

She shook her head again. "I only know his name was Walter. He was a Crusader and he was taken prisoner. Old Alexander, my mother's husband, bought him at a slave market."

"Where was that?"

"I think in Aleppo. Anthemus moved us to Antioch after Alexander died. Old Alexander was rich, but Anthemus has become much richer."

"I have a great deal to ask you, but we must leave it until later when our servant is asleep."

The girl reached out suddenly and touched a strand of his hair which was hanging over one shoulder. At home he had kept it cut in clerkly fashion at the level of his ears, but since coming to the East it had been allowed to grow. It was now as long as his father's had been, curling in the same golden ringlets.

"I have never seen a man with hair like yours," she whispered. "Is it not very unusual?"

"Most Englishmen have fair hair. My friend has it too."

She looked across at Tristram, who was watching them with an expression of deep interest in his serious gray eyes. The strong sun had turned the top strands of his light tow hair to the color of straw, and it hung in straight profusion below his shoulders also. She smiled at him, sensing the friendliness of his attitude.

"Yes." She turned back to Walter. "But it is not like yours. I think you look like a God of the Sun."

Mahmoud had finished his meal. He got up and said cheerfully,

"Clean kettle, second boy." The girl got up and proceeded about the task, using a clean cloth instead of the horsetails he had produced.

"She doesn't seem to know anything about her father," said Walter. "But she is half English, that much is clear. I don't suppose we will be able to find out anything more about her now."

"That is enough. I wish——" Tristram hesitated and then shook his head. "I wish we could see that she gets to England. But I suppose that is out of the question."

When a second curtain had been suspended at a side of the tent to make a niche for the new member of the household, there was little room left in the center. Tristram, as usual, went promptly to sleep with his arms folded on his chest and his powerful legs spread out, leaving something less than half of the space for the use of his companion. Mahmoud was equally quick in getting to sleep. The little black boy must have had some obstruction in his throat, for he snored loudly, a steady snuffle which never changed its inflection, *"Waa-aa-hoo, waa-aa-hoo!"*

An occasional rustle behind her curtain indicated that Maryam had remained awake. Walter waited until he could be certain there would be no eavesdropping on the part of the servant. Then he moved closer to the flimsy barrier between them and whispered, "Maryam."

She whispered back at once, "Yes, Most Kind Grandeur?"

During the talk which followed, he spoke with a careful choice of words to bridge the difference between the Greek of that day and the classic form he understood.

"Are you all right?"

"Yes, I am quite comfortable."

"We are very much concerned about you. Are you afraid? About tomorrow, I mean."

She did not answer at once. "A little. But you must not be concerned. Lu Chung has provided for everything. I am to be met. Everything I am to do has been carefully explained."

"Do you trust Lu Chung?"

"He has been well paid," she answered, after a slight pause which may have indicated some doubts in her mind. "I have given him my ring with a fine emerald. When I reach my uncle, he is to be sent much more."

"Are you content to go to your uncle?"

"There is nothing else to do. I have never seen him, but I think he will be kind. It's said he hates Anthemus. He is very old and lives in a large marble house with seven young wives. He is rich too. But," with an inflection of pride which seemed strange under the circumstances, "he is not nearly as rich as Anthemus."

"Is there nothing else you can tell me about your father?"

"I never saw him, Kind Wal-ter. He died long before I was born. He was whipped to death when they found my mother loved him." She said this in an almost matter-of-fact way as one speaks of the distant past and the tragic things which have ceased to trouble them. "My mother died when I was a very small girl. I don't remember her very well, but she taught me those two words, Wal-ter and Lun-dun." He could hear her turn restlessly. "It must have been very sad for her. I could never find out anything else. No one would talk about it. Old Alexander was very stern, almost as stern as Anthemus."

"You have your father's eyes."

"Yes," eagerly. "Everyone said that. They laughed at them, but I am proud because of the color." She added, with a sudden and vehement change of mood: "My sisters at home called me a foreign pig and other names. I spat in their own black, ugly eyes! I hated them!"

"All of them? Was no one kind to you?"

"Not one." Her voice raised slightly in a contemptuous inflection. "They were fat, sly, greedy, cruel! They thought of nothing but the husbands they would be sent to. Fine husbands they will get!" After a moment, she went on in the same bitter tone. "These girls are the same. All they think of is men. Most of them are glad they are being sent to China."

"Then you made no friends among them?"

"One. She comes from Constantinople. I am very sorry for her because the Khan is sure to like her. She has the most lovely soft eyes and hair, and she has the exact measurements." There was a moment's silence, and then she said in a repressed whisper: "We were all measured in every possible way because this terrible emperor must be suited exactly. They even watched us when we slept to see if we snored and if our breath was sweet. I felt shamed and humiliated! And that old woman! I seemed to feel her eyes on me all the time. Watching, prying, judging. And she —she was teaching us dreadful things."

Walter said, hastily, "You must sleep now."

"I don't dare sleep. I always dream of her. Sometimes I think I shall never get away from her." After a moment, she whispered in a voice husky with gratitude: "How can I thank you? You and your very tall friend are so kind to me, and so brave! It makes me proud that my real father was English too."

The snoring from the other side of the tent stopped, and they heard Mahmoud turning heavily.

"Your master for a day may be waking up. Good night, Maryam."

Walter wakened early to find that the curtain which had shielded the slumbers of Maryam had fallen during the night. He struggled up to a sitting position.

Light was coming through the hole in the top of the tent, indicating that the sun had risen. He heard a querulous chorus of "O-o-onk!" from the camel lines and the voice of a driver raised in blistering Arabic. An important, and fateful, day was beginning.

The curtain had fallen over the body of the sleeping girl, but her face was uncovered. He studied her for a few moments in the dim light, noting that her features, even under the disfiguring stain, were attractively chiseled. Her tangle of short black curls made her look very young.

"By St. Aidan, Tris was not mistaken about her," he said to himself. "This odd little creature is quite pretty."

3

The mountains of Sakhund, in which Maragha nestled, filled the view to the north.

Tristram jerked at the nose-cord of Zoroaster, guiding him closer to Helen. He was looking straight ahead. This was a mistake, for Helen promptly leaned sideways and nipped him on the knee.

"Ugly beast!" he said, striking her nose with one end of his longbow. "Why haven't you taught her manners, Wat?"

"You can't teach a camel anything. Both my knees are raw."

Tristram pointed ahead. "I can see a smudge there that seems to move. Straight ahead of us in the sky line. That will be Bayan and his party, I think."

Walter placed one hand on the hump in front of him and raised himself to gaze over Helen's bobbing head.

"I see them," he said, excitedly. "It looks like a large camp."

As they drew close to the crossroads, a man on a very small horse came riding down the line, turning his head questingly from side to side. When he saw the three weary camels bringing up the rear, he shouted a greeting. It was Father Theodore.

"We have been here a full day," he cried. "The great Bayan has been very impatient. I do not believe he would have waited any longer."

He was wearing a sheepskin coat and a cap of the same fur, but his face looked pinched and blue with the cold. In spite of his discomfort, it was clear that he was bursting with news.

"Anthemus is not to go," he announced. "He was so informed this morning, and I leave it to you, my sirs, to conceive the rage he is in. But," and his eyes popped with triumph, "I am going. The *orkhon* finds my gift of tongues most useful. It is a pity we are to part company."

Walter's heart sank. "Does that mean we are being left behind too?"

"What could you expect, young scholar? What use would you be to Bayan?" He nodded his head. "You will stay with Anthemus. It is not yet certain he will attempt to follow. At the moment he is in a mood to turn about and go straight back to Antioch, and my advice would be to keep as far away from him as you can. He spits fire like a dragon. Orders have been given for all his servants to be whipped."

"What about the women?"

"They are to go. Bayan understands too well the keen appetite of the Son of Heaven* to interfere with *that* part of the plan." He laid a hand on the nose-cord of Helen but drew it back quickly when she snapped at him. "Can what I hear be true? That the Lady Maryam has run away?"

"All we know is that the camp was searched last night. I hope it is true and that they never find her."

The Nestorian priest lowered his head to whisper, "I also hope it is true." Then he caught sight of the two figures on the third camel. "Who is that, young scholar?"

"Another servant. Lu Chung decided we needed him. He was bought for us at the last slave market we passed."

"And Anthemus will have to pay! That will cause his cup of wrath to overflow."

The camels carrying the women had been halted, and a file of watchful guards circled them; it had been decided, apparently, not to risk taking them any closer at this stage to the main camp. As he rode past, Walter noticed that Hoochin B'abahu had alighted from her palanquin and was talking, with every evidence of intense agitation, to Bird Who Feathers His Nest Lu Chung. One fat hand toyed impatiently with a string of amber beads dangling limply in the valley between her mountainous breasts. A small black slave held a parasol in front of her as a

*Kublai Khan was often called by this name.

protection from the wind, and a second one was lighting a charcoal brazier on the ground.

Father Theodore chirped with satisfaction. "That old bag of fat and sin is trying to think of excuses. She will be blamed for letting the lady get away."

A party of Mongolians came riding pell-mell across the sands and circled about them. They were screaming with excitement, standing up in their creaking red saddles and waving their short curved swords above their heads. In spite of the disappointment he was feeling, Walter watched the horsemen with interest. This was a new aspect of the East, the magic, brawling land which had laid such a spell on him. He had felt it with his first glimpse of Joppa, sweltering in breath-taking heat but full of strange sights and smells. It mounted in him as his eyes followed the riders of the steppes, reputed to be the best fighting men in the world. All of them, he noticed, carried souvenirs of the final turning back of the Crusaders, as did most people of the East. Crucifixes or missals dangled from their bridles, Christian helmets were strapped to their saddles, skin (flayed, presumably, from the hides of Western soldiers) served some of them as saddle-cloths. One slant-eyed rider carried a human skull over his shoulder which had been converted into a drinking cup, and it could be guessed that it had once perched on a Christian pair of shoulders.

Then something happened which the two Englishmen could do nothing but watch in a state of frozen horror. The Mongolian troop circled out over the sands and then came thundering back past the caravan in solid formation. One of them leaned from his saddle and tossed a coil of rope over the boy with the parasol. The little slave shrieked with terror as he was yanked from the ground and pinned to the Mongol's saddle while one expert hand tied the rope tightly around his waist. After making a loop, the rider tossed the struggling form into the air and the next in line caught the loop with a shrill whinny of delight. Up went the boy again, legs and arms moving frantically, to be caught by another of the galloping demons. The game became fast and furious, the whole troop rocking in their saddles with laughter and maneuvering to get the next turn. The cries of the boy were cut off as the violence of the motion drove the air from his lungs. Perhaps Nature decided to be merciful; at any rate his head hung limply after he had been transferred half a dozen times, and it seemed likely that he had fainted.

The sport came to an end when one grinning rider decided to use the flat of his sword instead of his hand. The blade turned with the weight and the edge cut through the rope. Falling to the ground with a thud, the body rolled over and over in the sand. A flying hoof crushed in his skull and, after a second horse had trampled over him, the form of the little slave lay as still as an empty bundle of rags. The jeering troop then rode back to camp.

Walter's hand was shaking so much that he lost his hold on the nose-cord. He looked across at Tristram, whose face was as white as a newly washed burnoose. For several moments neither of them could speak.

"Wat," said Tristram finally, in a sick whisper, "were they men? Or was it a glimpse of hell that we saw?"

Walter realized now that tears were streaming down his face. Anger struggled with fear and horror in his brain. "All the stories we have been told about these people must be true," he managed to say. "I was sure they were exaggerated; most war stories are. They can't be men, Tris; but if they are, the brand of the devil is on them."

"I am a coward!" cried Tristram, raising a shaking hand to wipe the perspiration from his brow. "I wanted to loose a shaft into them, but I couldn't move a hand. By the Rood, I shall never be able to forgive myself! I sat as still as a frightened girl and let them butcher that child before our very eyes!"

"There was—nothing we could do. Those demons"—Walter was finding it hard to speak—"ride like the wind. They were out of range—I think—in a few seconds." Suddenly he slumped over the hump of the camel, saying in a weak voice, "I am going to be sick."

The same horror had gripped the whole caravan, and it was a long time before anyone made a move. Then a stolid eunuch walked out with a camp spade and heaped sand over what was left of the boy.

When the camels fell into motion again after a long wait, Walter said to his companion, "It's hard to talk about it, but we must get our minds clear as to the situation we face."

Tristram made no response. He was riding with lowered head, and his face was still white and withdrawn.

"These Mongols are not human—not as we understand human nature. They live by a code called the Ulang-Yassa. It teaches them they are a superior race, that it's their duty to despise, deceive, cheat, and kill all other people. They have lived by this code ever since Genghis Khan began his conquest of Asia. They hate us. Are you listening, Tris?"

His companion nodded silently.

"We must recognize one thing. From this moment we are in a land they control absolutely. They rule all Asia from Persia to the ocean of Cathay. There are as many of them as the sands of the sea, and any single one of these ruthless millions would kill us as a duty and a pleasure. They will answer a word from us with a blow, and a blow with death. We must walk lightly, speak little, and keep our pride in our pockets. It is a bitter price, but we must pay it."

"Is what we hope to gain worth such a price?"

After a moment of silence, Walter set his jaw. "I am going on. I can't turn back now. The opportunity is great enough for any sacrifice, any risk. I must seem mad to you, old friend. But by St. Aidan, I am going to Cathay!"

His companion sighed. "I think I share your feeling about it now. Yes, Wat, we must go on. We must redeem ourselves."

4

For two hours they huddled behind their sprawling camels to escape the full bite of the north wind, a silent party of four. Their eyes seldom strayed from the activities of the camp, and the same fear was reflected in all of them, that another murderous outburst might be expected at any moment from these mad horsemen of the steppes. They could see the standard of the Mongolian Horde high over the main tent. Its nine horsetails and white falcon flapped in the wind; a fantastic symbol and a fitting one for a race which traveled far and traveled fast. About the standard clustered a huddle of circular felt yurts, and off to one side was a gaudy affair of silk which flaunted on one side the scarlet "A-A" of Anthemus.

Occasionally Walter turned to look at the great Castle Rewin Diz above the distant walls of Maragha and, with still more interest, at the mountain which stood to the west of the city. The top of this peak had been leveled off with mathematical precision to make room for a temple which glistened in the light of the afternoon sun. A strange thing to find in this part of the world, he reflected. Certainly it was hard to believe that the ruler of these murderous horsemen had gone to such extraordinary lengths to build a home for the study of the stars.

"If we had a wise king in England," he said to Tristram, "there would be an observatory like that for Roger Bacon. I am afraid that we will put him in a dark cell instead."

Tristram did not answer, being more interested at the moment in the profile of Maryam. Mahmoud had seen to it that she sat well removed from the rest of them. She had not presumed to take any part in their desultory talk, but Walter had been conscious of the fact that her eyes were on him steadily.

Tristram looked up at the sun. "It must be three o'clock. Do you suppose there has been a slip? It seems strange we have heard nothing more."

There was a sudden commotion in the camp, an eruption of men on horseback toward a flat plain which lay to the west, followed by a hurrying stream of people on foot. A babel of voices filled the air. The two Englishmen looked at each other with an unspoken question: what would these unpredictable Mongolians do now?

Walter felt a hand clutch desperately at his sleeve. Mahmoud had edged up close beside him, his eyes beseeching protection.

"Good masser," he whispered, "will they kill more black boys?"

"Mahmoud, there is always danger with men like these. But I don't think there is any need to be afraid of them now. It seems likely there is going to be an exhibition of their skill at arms. Perhaps they will shoot at the targets."

"Masser, Mahmoud afraid! Mahmoud not like die that way."

Walter's guess was confirmed when Father Theodore found them a few moments later. He had wrapped himself up so closely that only his eyes showed over the red band knotted at his neck. "We are not to start until morning," he announced. "To keep his restless men from getting into more trouble, Bayan has ordered games and archery. I would advise, young scholars, that you go along with me and watch. I promise you will see sights that will make you tremble for the safety of your proud Western world."

"Archery?" cried Tristram. He raised an exploratory hand. "The wind is falling off. It is cold for accurate work, but we should be able to get an idea of what they can do. I have wanted to see the crossbow in action. Well"—he grinned and patted his longbow—"we will see how they compare with our own archers. By the Rood, it would suit me well to show them the sound English magic in this noble length of yew!"

"Put it out of your mind!" cried Walter hastily. "The best thing we can do is to avoid all notice. My head suits me as it is, on my own shoulders. I don't want them using it as a billiard ball."

Tristram nodded his head sheepishly. "I suppose they would take it badly if I outshot them," he said. "Ah, Wat, if this were a stretch of English sod, with trees at each side and a mild sun at our backs! If only there were a few stout fellows here in green jerkins to assure us of fair play!"

A new cause for uneasiness caused Walter to look about him. Maryam was nowhere in sight. She had been with them when the commotion started. He was certain of that, having seen her get to her feet and wrap her felt coat more securely about her.

"Tris," he said, "our charge has vanished."

All thought of the contest they were to witness left his tall companion at once. Tristram looked at the procession of chattering people pouring past them: Arab traders with turbans of many colors, some with jewels, some with tossing plumes; shamans with cruel and crafty eyes under their cone-shaped headgear; Mongolians with felt hats, stalking along eagerly on short, bowed legs; an occasional fighting man of the desert with burnished breastplate and arrogant sword clanking at his belt; beggars aplenty, bundled up too well to show the body sores which were their stock in trade. There were women also, some veiled, but many of them with uncovered faces the better to attract the attention they had visited the camp to win. Maryam was not to be seen.

"It means she has gone," said Tristram with a sigh. "Well, it was the plan. May our Lady of Walsingham see that she gets away safely."

"She didn't wait to bid us farewell." Walter was conscious of a sense of injury, of hurt pride. "She might have done that much."

"I am sure," said Tristram, "that she felt too badly about it for that. I had been watching her, Wat; and it was clear her emotions were always close to the surface. She thought it best to slip away unnoticed. We need not doubt that she was truly thankful for the small part we played in her escape."

Walter was conscious now of a growing sense of relief. The adventure was over, and they could proceed with their own affairs. "We did all that we could for her," he said. "We must go to Maragha as soon as the archery is over and see if any other caravans are leaving for the East. But first, of course, I must have a talk with Anthemus."

"If we go to Maragha," exclaimed Tristram, eagerly, "we can assure ourselves of her safe arrival there. That, I confess, would be a great burden off my mind. Did she tell you where she was to go?"

"All she told me when I questioned her this morning was that her uncle's name was Michael Takagalou." Walter shook his head doubtfully. "We shall have to act with great caution. Anthemus will suspect where she has gone. If we were to show ourselves at the house, the fat would be in the fire. It will be wise to consult Lu Chung before we make any move."

Horse races were being conducted when they reached the flat plain.

All other thoughts deserted the two Englishmen as they watched, for
the contestants rode with a maniacal fury they had never seen equaled
before. From start to finish they went at breakneck speed, their eyes
gleaming in their yellow faces, their voices screeching out the battle
cries of the steppes. The horses, which were small but very fast, seemed
to share the frenzy of their masters.

After the races came a succession of wrestling matches. Here the contestants were professionals; mountainous fellows who stripped down
to their dark skins and did not seem to mind the cold at all. The bouts
were conducted according to a set formula. The rivals faced each other,
now advancing and now retreating, stamping their feet to a steady chant
of "Nige! Hoir! Gorba! [One! Two! Three!]" At each repetition of
"Gorba!" they would lunge forward in an effort to catch the other off
guard. Once the arms of the wrestlers had become locked in battle, a
titanic struggle resulted. Each man heaved and pushed, emitting loud
grunts and bellows of rage. The end would come only when one of them
lay unconscious on the ground.

The Mongols watched the bouts with a fierce lustiness, twisting about
in their saddles and crying, "Chisu! Chisu! [Blood! Blood!]" Their
treble voices had an almost inhuman quality.

"Do they never get enough of blood?" asked Walter.

The targets were now set up for the archery contests, and the spectators formed in two long lines. This, clearly, was to be the main event.
The horsemen were chattering and making wagers among themselves
Tristram, his face showing that he shared the excitement of the desert
onlookers, twanged the taut string of his bow. "Now we shall see," he
said. "That is a short distance they are marking off. Are their little toys
capable of nothing better? This will be women's work, Wat!"

It was true that to anyone accustomed to English archery, the distance was short. In spite of that, however, the exhibition that the men
of the steppes proceeded to give was quite remarkable. It was all done
from horseback. First they shot standing still, and the sound of the
arrows landing in the target clouts was like the rattle of hail on a
wooden roof. When this phase of the contest had been completed, and
the wagers had been settled contentiously, they began to ride down a
line at right angles to the targets, discharging their arrows while going
at top speed. The accuracy of the shooting lessened considerably, but it
was still surprising how often the shafts found their mark.

It was exciting to watch. The rider would wheel his mount with a
wild shout of "Nada Uk!" and then come pounding over the earth, a

volley of frozen clods spraying out in all directions from the flying hoofs. If the shot were straight, there would be a loud roar of approval. If it missed, the spectators jeered in delighted derision.

When the last of the shafts had been launched, Tristram leaned over and gripped his companion by the arm.

"Wat!" he said, beseechingly.

"Yes."

"I can't stand still and do nothing. Are we to let these wild beasts, these screaming child-butchers, think they are the best archers in the world? My hand is itching, Wat! I'll never forgive myself if I don't show them what the longbow can do."

He was breathing hard, and his usually mild eyes had taken on a gleam. With a hand that trembled in eagerness, he loosed the bow at his shoulder.

"We owe it to England!" he cried.

Before his companion could interfere, he sprung forward to the starting line, holding the enormous longbow out at arm's length as a signal that he desired to compete.

The spectators were beginning to disperse, but they turned back at this. A challenge from such a quarter was so unexpected that for a few moments the Mongolian archers remained in their saddles. Then several of those nearest sprang to the ground and crowded about the tall Englishman. One of them reached out suddenly and snatched the bow from his hand. Tristram made no effort to recover it, but it was clear he was controlling himself with difficulty.

It was passed back and forth, and they ran their hands over the polished surface of the yew, voicing shrill surprise at the lack of horn and metal. It was clear they considered it a very poor thing. Then one of them raised the bow and began to bend it. This proved so difficult that he threw all his strength into the effort. The confident smile faded from his greasy features, to be replaced by a reluctant wonder. He would have thrown the bow down if Tristram had not sprung forward and wrenched it from his hand. An angry push sent the Mongolian sprawling on the ground.

Watching with growing apprehension, Walter heard a sharp order issue from somewhere behind the group. He could not see who had spoken, but there was unmistakable authority in the tone. The jeering archers around Tristram fell back.

A few moments later Father Theodore weaved his way through the crowd to Walter's side. There was a look of uneasiness on his face.

"The Tall One is to shoot," he said. "It is an order. You will tell him."

"Will he be given a fair chance?"

"There will be no interference. But if he fails to better the others, they have been told his bow is to be broken over his head. They will attend to that most thoroughly, young sir! You may take it for granted they will most joyfully beat out his brains!"

Walter felt as though his heart had ceased to beat. He had never before experienced such a wave of fear as now swept over him. It was many weeks since Tristram had bent the bow in earnest, and both his arm and eye would be out of practice. In addition to that, the string almost certainly had lost its proper tautness through lack of use. The wind, which had fallen off to nothing before, suddenly fanned his cheek with a threat of returning vigor. The test would be a failure; he was sure of it; but he realized also that it was too late for Tristram to back down.

"What will be the end of this?" he asked himself.

Walter walked over to the starting mark, where he placed himself by his friend's side. Whatever the consequences of this foolhardy venture, they would face the issue together.

"You are to show them what you can do," he managed to say.

"Good!" cried Tristram. He seemed quite easy and assured.

"Keep cool, Tris. You are loosing a shaft for England. Nay, for the glory and honor of all Christendom!"

Tristram touched his glove from which the motto had been obliterated. "Jesus guide my aim," he quoted, fervently.

"Have a mind to the wind," cautioned Walter. "It seems to be freshening again."

Tristram squinted carefully down the course. "I know none of their fancy tricks," he said. "It must be a matter of distance. Well, then, I shall show them how far my bow can carry."

He smiled and motioned with his arm that the target was to be set farther back. A pair of servants followed the order by carrying it to a distance of perhaps twenty more yards. The archer smiled again and indicated that this was not enough. Three times this happened, the men responding with longer carries until finally the butt was placed at twice its original distance. Walter watched in a horrified silence, certain that his friend was sealing their doom but not daring to warn him. He was afraid his arm would lose its strength and cunning if Tristram had any inkling of the consequences of failure.

As far as Walter could determine, the target was now set at close to three hundred yards away. Stout arms had been known to send an arrow that distance, but never with any hope of reaching a fixed mark.

"Has he taken leave of his senses?" he thought in added panic.

Tristram guessed what was passing in his friend's mind. "All or nothing," he said coolly. "If I am to teach them a lesson, it must be a good one. Well, my master of Arts, we shall see."

An excited murmur was coming from the long, expectant lines. The Mongolian archers were sitting their horses in puzzled wonder.

There was tenseness in the atmosphere. Despite their surprise at the boldness of this Christian archer in setting himself such an unheard-of mark, it was clear the Mongols were only too ready to take advantage of his certain failure.

"Our Father in heaven," prayed Walter, under his breath, "look down on Thy brave servant, Tristram Griffen. Put strength in his arm and sureness in his eye. Hold back this wind that his aim may be true!"

The archer advanced one foot to the mark and began to draw back the length of yew with ease and great care. It responded smoothly to the expert and familiar hand. Walter saw that his friend's arm was steady.

A wind was blowing the felt capes of the horsemen and ruffling the plumes in the turbans of the traders. On the point of loosing his shaft, Tristram stepped back and waited. The breeze fell off as though in answer to Walter's silent prayer. Taking instant advantage of the lull, the archer stepped forward again. He raised the bow and sighted. His left arm dropped to his side.

The shaft left the bow with a loud, whistling *Swiss-sss-sh.* It raced through the air straight to whatever mark the eye of the archer had sent it, then seemed to rise in a steady and majestic parabola. It settled again, traveling with incredible speed. Walter held his breath as he watched. The target seemed so small and so far away that he could not hope the thin blackthorn shaft would find a resting place there.

But the miracle happened. There was a faint *ping* and there it was, for all eyes to see, amazed, excited angry eyes, a line of black sticking out from the white surface of the clout!

A shout went up from the crowd. Walter sprung into the air, the intense relief he felt expressing itself in a cry of joy, "St. George! St. George for England!" He ran to his friend and threw his arms about him. Tears were running down his cheeks.

"Tris!" he cried. "My old fellow, my wonderful fellow! No one has ever equaled that shot. Not Clym-o'-the-Clough himself. Your father would be proud of you this day."

Tristram smiled at him slowly. There was a look of infinite relief in his eyes.

"What a lucky shot!" he breathed. "I didn't expect to do it, Wat. I set the mark much too far. I don't know why. Something inside me kept urging me on. Perhaps I was remembering the insults which have been heaped on us. I only knew that I must show these proud heathen something they would never forget."

"You saved our lives," said Walter. He realized now that his knees were close to the point of buckling under him.

The Mongol horsemen were sitting in a sullen silence, and not one of them had given a sign of approval for the unmatchable shot. They made way when a man of somewhat taller stature guided his way through their ranks on a magnificent black horse.

The newcomer cut quite a handsome figure. He wore a long-sleeved cloak of black sable, bound in at the waist with a girdle of jade pieces. His headgear was the uptilted felt hat of his race, but he had improved it with a jaunty peacock's feather and some dangling gold ornaments. His horse was handsomely accoutered with red harness, and it moved with a jingling of much silver. As he rode forward, he studied the two Englishmen with eyes which lacked the cruel slant at the corners. They were full and large, in fact, and warmly brown, glowing with a pleasant intelligence. His nose had something of the full bold bridge of the hawk.

He motioned to Father Theodore and began to give him some instructions. The priest nodded obsequiously and then crossed over to Walter's side.

"He asks if you can make many bows like that?"

When the question had been relayed to Tristram, the latter nodded in agreement. "If we can get the right kind of wood. That may be hard here in the East. As to the making, my father taught me something of the fletcher's trade."

"He has already said," declared Father Theodore, "that the right wood can be found in the north lands where his people came from. He asks further if the young scholars could train men in the use of the bow."

Things were assuming a favorable turn. Walter took it on himself to answer. "Yes, we can train archers. But he must understand that few arms are as strong as my friend's, and still fewer eyes have his cunning. It would not be possible to train any of his men to make such a shot as he has just witnessed."

"That also he knew. Can many shots be made with this bow in quick succession?"

"At least three in the time it takes to wind a crossbow for one shot. Men with the longbow could cut a body of crossbow archers to pieces."

The Nestorian spoke again to the man on the black horse, who seemed pleased at the nature of the answers. The latter had been studying the long limbs and broad shoulders of Tristram with an approving eye. Now he turned his gaze on Walter and addressed a question to the interpreter.

"He asks can you also use the bow of great magic?"

Walter shook his head reluctantly. "No. But tell him, Father Theodore, that I have knowledge of many languages, that I write a clerkly hand, and that I could be useful in many ways."

A smile flitted across the face of the man on the black horse when this information was conveyed to him. He said a few words which caused the priest to smile in turn.

"He asks do you play chess?"

There had been a set of battered wooden chessmen at Butterbump Hall, an incomplete one which had been made usable by pieces of slate on which the names of the missing pieces were written. Walter had been slightly more adept at the game than any of his fellows there.

"Yes, I play chess."

The horseman smiled again and called out a series of orders. He gave some final instructions then to the priest and, wheeling his horse with a light touch of one hand, rode off in the direction of the camp. Two Mongolians on foot detached themselves from the sullen ranks of the onlookers and stalked over on their grotesquely arched legs.

"You will be pleased, young scholars," declared the priest, as though the excellence of the news he had to give was the result of his own efforts. "You are to go on with the caravan. When the time comes, you will be expected to train a band of archers and to see that the magic bow is ready for them. It is an order. These men will accompany you back to camp."

"There is no danger that we will try to run away!" cried Walter exultantly.

"You are to have everything new," went on the priest. "You are to have horses as well as fine young camels for your servants and goods. A warm and capacious yurt. You will travel in comfort and state."

One of their new guards said "*Hudelhu!*" in an angry voice. This was

so obviously an order to get under way that Tristram threw his bow
back of his shoulder and started off.

Walter was not slow to follow. Sure of his answer, he asked the priest,
"Who was the man on the black horse?"

"That," said Father Theodore, "was Bayan of the Hundred Eyes."

5

"Men still outside, masser," said Mahmoud cheerfully. "One in front
say he cut me up into kettle stew if I try go out. One at back say he nail
me to cross 'cause I servant of Christians. But Mahmoud not afraid now.
Great general say Mahmoud go too. Men outside not dare touch
Mahmoud."

Their new yurt was all that had been promised, a high round dome of
felt with the interior draped in rich blue silk. Compared to the old one,
it was like a palace. Mahmoud, bursting with pride, began to show the
wonders he had already discovered. "See," he said, venturing to touch
Walter's arm. "Not one hook on pole. Six hooks. See, fine silk lining.
See, rings on silk for hanging curtains at night."

"We shall live like kings, Mahmoud," said his master.

To continue his recital of the wonders of the new yurt, the little
servant went to a curtain suspended at the rear where the kettles, spice
boxes, and other utensils were concealed. He gave one look behind it
and then turned about, allowing the curtain to drop. The excessively
casual way in which he proceeded to walk to the front entrance, avoiding his master's eye in doing so as though something had roused his
apprehension, was enough to create suspicions in the least observant.
Walter gave thought to the matter, and then a startled frown took
possession of his face. He seated himself on the ground so that he faced
the curtain, his back against the center support.

"Maryam!" he called.

When there was no response, he said: "You might as well come out.
I am sure it isn't comfortable back there."

The curtain shook at one end, and her face appeared around it. She
then stepped out with the air of a schoolboy caught redhanded in some
offense. Her eyes were kept studiously on the ground.

"Did you fail to find those who were sent to take you to Maragha?"
he asked.

Maryam shook her head. "I saw my uncle," she said, in a subdued
voice. "He came himself to get me. We had a talk and then—and then

I ran away from him!" Her voice rose with the emotional strain she was under. "I was afraid of him, Kyrios Walter! He looked so much like Anthemus, only much older and even more cruel. I had not made up my mind to do this. It was an impulse. When I saw what he was like, I was suddenly in a panic, and I began to run away without realizing what I was doing. I hid from him in the crowd. And then I didn't know where else I could go. So I came here."

"But how did you know this tent was to be ours?"

"I could not find the old one. I was very frightened then, and I went to one of the servants of Anthemus; an old servant who had always liked me and had helped me sometimes. He told me to come here."

He was thinking, "What are we to do now?"—his mind filled with all manner of dire speculations rising out of her unexpected return. Realizing this, she dropped on one knee beside him.

"Kyrios Tris did not know me," she argued eagerly. "They think now that you have two black servants and that I am one of them. No one will find me out."

"No one has suspected so far. But, you must remember, it has only been one day. Such good fortune could not continue."

"Yes! Yes, it could!" She had clutched one of his hands and was looking up beseechingly into his face. "I have been thinking about it all the time I hid behind the curtain. No one would expect to find me in the caravan after this. Anthemus is not to go; and who else will there be to care about it? No one will see me, Walter. These people do not like you because you are Christians. They will have nothing to do with you. You are always supposed to ride in the rear of the caravan and to set up your tent at night on the edge of the camp. It will be easy for me to stay out of sight. Oh, I will be so careful, so very careful! I will never speak to other servants. When anyone is near, I will keep my head down."

"Those blue eyes of yours are certain to give you away."

"I will always keep them lowered. I will wear my hat down over them. Please, Walter, it is my only hope!"

Tristram came in at this point. When he saw Maryam, he stood stock-still for a moment, his jaw slack with the unexpectedness of finding her here, his eyes filled with an almost ludicrous surprise. Then he began to laugh with relief, slapping one hand exuberantly against his thigh.

"Maryam!" he cried. "You are still here! By St. Christopher, I am glad of it! I dreaded the thought of you going to Maragha alone. In fact, I dreaded the idea of having you leave us."

She did not know what he had said, but it was easy for her to read the welcome in his eyes. She got up and ran over to him. Taking one of his hands, she cried: "*You* want me, Kyrios Tris. I can see you do. Oh, please, persuade Walter I am to stay!"

Tristram smiled at Walter over the top of her head. "What is she saying, Wat?" he asked. "She seems very much disturbed, poor little child. I don't know how you feel about this, but, certes, I am so delighted to see her back that I can't find any words to tell you. I say this: She should not go to this old uncle, this Michael Takagalou. The very name reeks of cruelty and villainy. And, coming to think of it, he is no uncle of hers. None of these money-grubbing Greeks are of her blood. She is English, Wat, and we have no right to leave her in the lurch."

The same thought had been in Walter's mind, but he had brushed it aside in the light of the practical considerations against keeping her with them.

"They will find her here, Tris," he said soberly. "Forgetting what that would mean to us, should we involve her in such danger?"

"We need not stay where she might be recognized. Why not strike out by ourselves? You still have gold under your belt. And we might get to Cathay ahead of this great procession of a caravan."

Walter laughed shortly. "Did you notice the guard in front when you came in? We have no choice open to us. Bayan has seen to that."

"Then," cried Tristram, "we must go along with them and take the risk. What do we care for risks? I took one today. Nay, *we* took it; for I know how quickly you came and ranged yourself beside me. The foul fiend take the lot of them! We have stood together so far, the two of us. Now we shall be three."

Maryam was weeping by this time and clutching his arm with still more urgency. Walter rose and walked over to them.

"Very well, Tris," he said. "We shall chance it together. The three of us."

Maryam turned quickly and looked at him. He had spoken in English, but she could sense what he had said from the changed expression of his face. She continued to weep, but now it was from sheer relief. Suddenly she sank down on her knees and kissed Tristram's hand, crying, "Oh, thank you, thank you!"

A blush took possession of Tristram's face. "Come, come," he said. "I don't merit such a reward as this." Then he gave Walter a happy grin. "She seems very glad, poor little homeless waif! We shall have to be very good to her, Wat. I think we must contrive somehow to take her home to England with us."

Maryam rose as though conscious of the need of including Walter in her appreciation. He had turned and walked to the other side, where he was examining a brass Arabian lamp with listless interest. The old feeling of being apart from things, the result of his unhappy boyhood, had come back to him. He was thinking that she would always contrast his attitude with that of his friend's and that he must seem to her cautious and indifferent. "But," he thought in self-defense, "someone must consider the practical side of things."

She followed him, with hesitation in her steps, and said, "I want to thank you, Walter."

"You have my friend to thank for this, not me."

"No, no!" she cried. "You too. I thank you from the bottom of my heart."

"Well, it seems to be settled," said Tristram in a loud and cheerful voice.

Maryam began to dry her eyes. "Now I must get to my work," she said. "My most severe taskmaster will be back soon and will demand to know why the fire has not been built and the kettles cleaned." She smiled at them both impartially. "I shall try to be *very* faithful servant, *good massers.*"

She was hard at work when Mahmoud came back. He looked at her suspiciously. "Second boy going to stay?" he asked. "You say, masser, that second boy go. Then I see him back of curtain."

"Second boy stays, Mahmoud."

The servant grinned unwillingly. "Mahmoud keep him busy then. Second boy, jump." He turned to Maryam. "You, Tapha! Speck of rust on kettle. Get rag."

To divert his attention, Walter began to praise their new quarters. Mahmoud's eyes glistened with pride. He started to point out other perfections of the large yurt. It would be warm, he said, because there was no opening at the top to let in the cold air. Walter studied this arrangement with interest, noting that the upper section was of walrus skins which could be unhooked and folded back when the need of air was felt. This did not make the interior dark, for the skins had been scraped so fine that they were almost translucent.

He was still studying the structure of their new home when the guard in front lifted the front flap and announced in a scornful voice: "Fat merchant comes to see Western dogs."

It was Anthemus. He came in, muffled to the ears in a huge cloak of shaggy pony fur. His face, nevertheless, was purple with the cold. A girl followed him, carrying boxes in both hands. She was small and timid and, in spite of her thoroughly chilled condition, quite pretty.

The merchant nodded to them morosely and sat himself down beside Tristram, his fat hips demanding so much space that the latter had to move to one side. The girl took a seat near her master and proceeded to open the boxes which contained various kinds of sweetmeats.

"I am not going with you," said Anthemus in a tone of the deepest umbrage. He was so concerned over the blow which had been dealt his pride that he relapsed into a scowling silence for several moments. "There is nothing I can do to change the mind of this stubborn *noyan*. But I am taking measures, you may be sure. What I desire will be arranged at the other end, where I have agents who can go direct to the Son of Heaven. I can get along without this pestilential Bayan, and my regret now is that I gave him first the many gifts I had brought. I trust that some day the Son of Heaven will burn out every one of his hundred eyes!" He looked at Walter, his own eyes narrowing appraisingly. "As a further precaution, I shall depend on you to deliver letters for me. One is to a Chinese merchant in Khan Bhalig. You are to consider yourself under his orders and do everything he bids you. Is that clear?"

"That is quite clear."

Anthemus opened his cloak and fumbled under it with numbed fingers, finally producing a letter on cotton script secured by hemp threads. "This is the one to Kung L'aing who lives in the great suburb of Khan Bhalig. He is known as 'Tiger Who Purrs Softly,' and so it may not be necessary for me to warn you, my young cock from the West, that it will not be safe to give anything but the most complete obedience to Kung L'aing." He drew out a second letter. "If you should get to Kinsai, the capital city of the Sung emperor,* you will also deliver this. It is to another merchant of great wealth. His name is Sung Yung and he is often called 'Fire from Black Clouds.' Again you will be under his orders." He added with an air of great pride: "Do not misunderstand me when I speak of the wealth of these Eastern merchants. I could buy and sell either one of them!"

Walter took the two letters and put them away under his tunic. "You may depend on me to follow your instructions," he said. "I hope above everything else to reach Kinsai. I shall do everything possible to get there."

Anthemus dipped a hand in one of the boxes. Crunching loudly, he

*Kinsai was the ancient name of Hangchow, still one of China's largest cities.

asked, "Did you know one of the girls I was sending to the court of the Emperor ran away last night?"

"I heard it was your sister."

Anthemus gave some consideration to the inflection of this answer. "And you are glad she escaped?" he said. "I can tell from your voice. I shall remember your misplaced pleasure when the time comes to pay you moneys for what you accomplish. It will save me much, so I am glad too."

Walter did not speak. The merchant went on eating and turned his gaze in the direction of Tristram.

"I hear this stolid ox gave the Mongols a lesson in archery today." He erupted with a short, high laugh. "I was well pleased to hear it. But you must remember that they never forget a slight or an injury. See to it that his bow arm does not aggravate them further. I must be sure my letters are delivered."

"We have agreed between us to be most discreet."

"Good. Keep still tongues and never let your foul Western pride get the better of that discretion." He went on crunching noisily. "As for that ungrateful and disobedient sister of mine, you must not hug the hope that I will fail to find her. How far can she get in this country and in this kind of weather? A score of my men are searching in Maragha this very minute and in all the flea-bitten villages hereabouts. She will be back in my hands very shortly."

In the background the dye-stained arm burnishing the kettle suspended movement for a moment. Then it proceeded with its task. Walter was relieved to note that Maryam had retired as far from them as she could and was keeping her head turned away.

"Her punishment," declared Anthemus, "will be most severe, you will be unhappy to know."

Walter made no answer. Suddenly the face of the merchant, which had regained its normal color in the warmth, began to change again. A red tint seemed to center around his eyes. Then it spread, like a smolder of fire, to all parts of his broad countenance. His eyes fixed themselves on Walter with a vicious intentness.

In a low thin voice he said slowly, "You can have no conception how she will suffer for what she has done."

"I hope," said Walter, "that you will never find her."

"And is that," demanded Anthemus, "a sample of the discretion you have promised me? I shall shave still more from your moneys."

After a few moments of silence, the merchant struggled to his feet, resting so much of his obesity on the shoulder of the girl that she nearly toppled over.

"Get up!" he said to her. He looked sharply about the tent. "Very grand indeed. This *noyan* does not use any of his eyes in finding ways to save money for his master in Khan Bhalig. Two servants, I see. Your generous Bayan may pay for that, not I." He paused reflectively. "I have not made a sliver of profit from either of you as yet; and I am sure you have gold of your own. Come, we must make a deal. I will sell you a woman."

"We lack the gold to enter into a deal with one as astute as Anthemus of Antioch."

"I will sell you one so foolishly cheap that my profit will be as nothing. You are both young and lusty and will need a woman on so long a journey. I warn you that you won't care for Mongolians. They are scratching she-devils."

"We prefer to get along as we are."

Anthemus saw that he meant it and sighed. "You English are a tight-fisted race," he complained.

The Mongolians were careless of the loot they had acquired so easily, and the last occupant of the yurt had left a Chinese cord belt dangling from a peg on the central support. It was tarnished with dust but was bound with gold thread, and there was a handsome jade buckle attached to it. Anthemus saw this as he turned to go and, without pausing, he whisked it off the pole and under the capacious folds of his pony cloak. His parting remark was, "You will do well to remember that I shall receive reports of you."

"He made his profit after all," said Walter, laughing in spite of himself.

The caravan started next morning when the sun cast its first rays over a ridge in the east. It was a sight the two Englishmen would never forget: the long procession of horsemen, riding two abreast up the slope into the pale red glow against the dull purple of the sky, singing as they went. In the center of the long file came the camels and palanquins of the women, a seemingly endless stream of them, and immediately after a most curious conveyance on which Walter fixed his eyes at once. It bore some resemblance to the closed whirlicotes occasionally seen on English roads, but it was infinitely more ornate. It was a two-storied affair and was painted a glaring vermilion, with pictures of black dragons and white tigers on the corners. But what attracted Walter most was the figure of a fairy with gold-tipped wings, with an arm outstretched, perched on the top. No matter how this strange carriage might sway and twist on the rough road, the arm of the fairy always pointed in a set direction.

Father Theodore had not yet mounted. Placing a hand on Walter's stirrups—both Englishmen were riding mettlesome young horses, with new and jingling leather and blue plumes in the manes—he explained the purpose of this strange conveyance.

"It is a direction-finding chariot," he said. "It comes from China. The arm always points to the south and so makes it possible to avoid getting off the course. The roads on the great deserts ahead of us are often wiped out by sandstorms, and so the direction finder is most useful. No one knows the secret of it but an old man from China who rides inside. But that is not all. At the end of each *li*—a third of a mile—a gong sounds in the carriage." He shook his head dubiously. "Young scholar, all I can say is that the devil himself must ride in it."

"This," said Walter to himself, "is something Friar Bacon must be told."

They cantered off proudly when their turn came to fall in at the rear of the line. Tristram smiled his slow smile and drawled to his companion: "No one will laugh at us now, Wat. I feel that I can hold up my head again."

"We have your stout bow to thank for the change."

"Farewell to thee, Zoroaster! The air seems sweeter already for your absence."

They had three camels as well, one to carry their belongings and one for each of the servants. Looking backward, Walter was glad to see that Maryam was fulfilling her promise by keeping her head resolutely bent over.

"You are to have your wish, Wat. Far beyond that ridge lies Cathay!" said Tristram.

CHAPTER VII

The Snowy Mountains

THE EVENING MEAL had been finished and dogs were snarling over the bones outside when the voice of Father Theodore reached them, begging permission to enter. He came in, bowing from the waist, his face wreathed with smiles.

"An honor has come to you," he said to Walter. "The great *orkhon* desires to play you a game of chess." A look of anxiety replaced the smile. "Young scholar has washed, I trust? It would not do to carry odor of saddle into the presence."

"I always wash before sitting down to eat," said Walter stiffly.

"Very good," said the priest, after looking him over carefully. "Men from Christian lands do not bathe enough. It is said the Crusaders stank most abominably."

The nine horsetails in front of the enormous yurt of Bayan were flapping crazily in the night wind. A guard at the entrance stepped aside to let them pass, muttering, "May the retching death come to all sons of infidel mothers!"

Felt images, dangling on strings, brushed Walter's face as he walked in. The interior blazed with the light of four lamps suspended on brass chains. Bayan had just bathed, for a servant was carrying out a wooden tub at the rear and permitting soapy water to splash on the brown bear rugs which covered the ground. The commander was stretched out at comfortable ease in a three-legged chair, his scarlet-flowered robe leaving his bare feet uncovered. Walter was surprised at the smallness of his feet, but then realized that generations of life in the saddle had undoubtedly produced this effect on the Mongolian race.

A folding table had been set up in front of the general on which a map was spread. He looked over this at his visitor and said something to Father Theodore in a pleasantly modulated voice.

"Most noble lord Bayan does not deign to speak *Bi-chi,*" said the latter. "I shall remain and act as interpreter. He bids you welcome and begs you to be seated."

A servant, who had been sleeping with his back against the center pole, and snoring loudly, roused as though by instinct and placed a chair opposite that of his master. Bayan turned back the loose sleeves of his robe with an air of eagerness. With one hand he gestured in the direction of an enormous Persian cat perched in dignity on a corner of the table.

"Noble lord Bayan wonders if the presence of his special favorite Old Booghra will be disturbing to his young opponent."

"Not at all," answered Walter. "Please tell him I am fond of cats and that I think this one a most handsome specimen."

The cat accordingly remained in his place, watching the newcomer without a blink of his large orange eyes. Bayan studied his visitor also with a steadiness which was rather disconcerting.

"He asks if young scholar is versed in military strategy?"

Walter shook his head. "My knowledge is so slight that I would not dare express myself in the presence of a great master like my lord Bayan."

A nod of the wide-browed head signified satisfaction with this disclaimer. Bayan began, nevertheless, to voice some observations, based on the study he had been making of the map, the priest translating in an undertone. "We call the country of the Manji the Yellow Cushion," said Bayan, tracing a line with a forefinger. "It is formless and soft, and it yields easily. The armies of the Great Khan have sought to conquer the Manji by lopping off border provinces, by cutting in from the south, by a broad application of the *Tulughma,* which is a surprise flank attack. They have always failed." The boastful Mongolian pride flared up in his eyes. He spoke so rapidly that Father Theodore leaned forward nervously to listen, and stammered in his translations. "I have a different plan. It is no secret, for the truth of what I aim to do will be apparent from the first moves of the campaign."

Although Walter was listening attentively, he succeeded nevertheless in getting a clear picture of his surroundings. The yurt was sumptuously furnished, so completely in fact that it was a mystery how everything could be packed and carried. There was a tall mirror (Bayan's vanity showed in every gesture he made and every word he spoke), a chest of some size, a second table on which other maps were piled, a broad dais on which the general slept. The servant had gone back to his original position and was snoring as loudly as before. A trace of seductive perfume on the air and the occasional rustle of a silk curtain in the rear suggested that a woman shared the tent with its master.

"The Yellow Cushion," Bayan was declaiming, "is like a devilfish, spreading out in all directions. Cut off one of the tentacles and another one soon grows in its place. But if you strike at the head, cutting deep into the vital core, the tentacles soon cease to have life. They shrivel and fall of themselves." He leaned forward, his remarkable eyes shining. "Those who follow the armies of Bayan will see a sweep down the line of the Han River, a crossing of the mighty Yang-tse, and then a straight drive on to Kinsai itself. When Kinsai falls, the conquest of the Manji country will be a very simple matter.

"I shall be fighting against geography, not against a people. It is not even certain that the Sung emperor in Kinsai remembers the name of

Genghis Khan. He likes to watch the women of his household bathe
naked in the imperial pools, and his interests do not extend to anything
else. His ministers are cowardly and corrupt. They are all so certain
that nothing can happen to their great country. They know nothing of
war. They think if they put hideous masks on their soldiers, it will scare
off their enemies." Bayan threw back his head and laughed in whinnying
derision. "They will die of fright themselves when the Yakka Mongols
ride to Kinsai!"

His speech ended, the general clapped his hands together and gave an
order to the twice-roused servant. The map was removed from the table,
and a set of ivory chessmen took its place. Walter looked at the pieces
in bewilderment, failing to recognize some of them. There were four
tall elephants with gold howdahs, and he did not realize they were the
rooks until his august opponent placed his pair at the ends of the shah
line. The set was a magnificent one and very old, but no care had been
taken of it. Each man was encrusted with dust and flyspecks.

"The great lord Bayan always expects the first move," said Father
Theodore.

A brisk movement of the general's hand started the *farzi* pawn out as
the first step in the battle. This was completely new to Walter, and he
studied for a full minute before countering with the same move. Bayan
was lightning fast in all his subsequent plays, shifting his men from
square to square with the suggestion of a feline pounce. He had gone on
the offensive at once and the attack was so well co-ordinated that Walter was thrown back at once on defense. The latter played as well as he
knew how, considering each move with the greatest care. "If I can only
play just well enough!" he said under his breath. "I must give him a
good game so he will send for me again."

The outcome of the game was never seriously in doubt, but the
Englishman managed to provide a stubborn defense, forcing his opponent into several changes of attack before capitulation became necessary. This quite apparently was exactly what Bayan wanted of him. The
young general shifted about in his chair with every evidence of keen
enjoyment, quaffed mare's milk frequently from a silver mug, and
emitted snorts of satisfaction at each stage of the battle. Once, when the
cat reached out suddenly and whisked a piece off the board with a tap
of his furry paw, Bayan roared in delighted approval.

"My wise Old Booghra!" he cried. "He picked out the piece I intended
to move next. Was it a hint to his master? Or was it reminding me I
have not given him as much as a single pat on the head for half an
hour?"

The cat gave no hint as to which was the correct explanation. He had curled his bushy tail about his paws again, and manifested no further interest in the game.

Three games were played, all ending in victory for the general. Bayan clapped his hands together as a signal for the board to be removed. He then poured out some rapid sentences.

"He says he likes you," said Father Theodore. "He says you are a very handsome fellow and that he has never seen such a head of hair before. He is sure you are a devil among the women. As for your game, he says it is good enough. He will play with you again." The priest continued with a comment of his own. "How fortunate it is for you, my sir, that no one else in the caravan plays well enough to keep him interested."

Bayan yawned, stretched out both his legs luxuriously, and called an order.

"We leave now," said the priest, bowing so low that he seemed on the point of losing his balance.

Walter bowed also and followed Father Theodore outside. The latter indulged in one of his amatory snickers. "He has sent for another of his women. It seems he fancies a Tartary wench tonight. One he calls his *joolem siboo*, which means 'soft bird.' "

Walter returned in a satisfied frame of mind. He had won favor with the commander of Kublai Khan's armies. "It would seem," he said to himself, "that things are shaping themselves in the right direction after all."

2

The atmosphere in the new yurt continued to show a trace of strain. Walter was convinced that Maryam's preference had been given to Tristram and, because of the isolation in which he had always lived, this proved a matter for irksome thought. She would run to his tall friend as soon as the latter entered, a smile of welcome on her blackened face. They could not talk, but there was always much nodding of heads between them which indicated complete understanding and mutual liking. Maryam showed a restraint of manner as far as Walter himself was concerned. She seemed even to be a little afraid of him. Sometimes, when he turned his head unexpectedly, he would find her eyes fixed on him with an expression he could not fathom. Whenever this happened, she would look away at once.

"I seem to have no capacity for making friends," he would think, bitterly.

The situation became even more strained, in his own mind at least, when she undertook to teach Tristram the camp lingo. Her own knowledge of it seemed quite complete, having been augmented during her stay under the wing of Hoochin B'abahu. Walter was willing enough to have her assume the task, for he had tried and given it up. It had been no exaggeration when Tristram said that foreign words did not like the looks of his head and refused to enter, like a balky horse at a strange stable. After several attempts, the two friends had made up their minds it was no use going on. But with the resumption of the lessons, Walter found himself more alone than before.

He had been playing chess with Bayan the evening when the lessons began. When he returned, one of the stone lamps was still burning brightly at the end of its chain, in spite of the wind which buffeted the felt sides of the yurt and started currents of air inside; and the girl was squatting in front of the tall archer, with her feet tucked under her and her face filled with a sober determination. She was pointing out various objects and then naming them, repeating the words several times before nodding to him to repeat them.

"*Hamar,*" she said, laying a finger on her nose. When that had been mastered, she said "*Gotol,*" sticking out her foot (a very small foot, Walter observed) and indicating her shoe. "*Horoo*" came next, as she held up her finger. Tristram was struggling hard to keep pace, repeating the words several times and then numbering them on his fingers. His face had a set look.

Maryam was proving very patient. She would say, "No, Kyrios Tris, no!" or "Yes, yes, yes!" in delighted tones whenever his efforts in any way merited approval. She would smile at him as well and occasionally give a clap of her hands. Whenever this happened, a most gratified grin would spread over the long countenance of her pupil.

"How is he getting along?" asked Walter.

Maryam seemed pleased at this voluntary notice of her. "He is doing very well," she said. "He is so patient, and he is trying so hard."

"He didn't do as well when I tried to teach him."

She smiled at that. "That was to be expected. Men are not good teachers."

He sat down on the other side of the tent and watched them. "I wonder what she would look like," he thought, "if she did not have that stuff on her face?" He could not remember much about her appearance from the occasions he had seen her in her natural guise.

After a time he yawned. Maryam must have been keeping an eye on him, for she got to her feet at once. "You are tired," she said. "The lesson is over."

"No, no," he protested. "Go on with it. I am comfortable."

But her mind was made up. "It is enough for once. There will be plenty of time for more lessons." She looked at him and then glanced away quickly, stifling a sigh. "I sometimes think you are sorry that—that I will be here to give him more lessons."

The lessons continued each evening after that, with Walter in the role of onlooker and never as a participant. At first he accepted this as natural, but gradually he began to resent his exclusion. It made him think of the days at the university when his prickly disposition had barred him from so many of the activities of his fellows. "Is this always to happen to me?" he asked himself. "Here it is, all over again. They make it clear I am not needed. It must be my fault. I am a surly fellow, just as they said at Oxford."

What he disliked about it most was that he was cut off in this way from the company of Tristram. It had never seemed to him possible that a bar could be raised between himself and the only real friend he had ever had. Although he knew that it was not her fault, he began to resent Maryam because of this. "Meddling little fussock!" he said to himself once, as he watched them. "It was a mistake to let her be anything but a servant."

Maryam seemed to realize something of what was passing through his mind, for her manner to him became increasingly aloof. When the lesson was over, she would say, "Good night, Kyrios Walter," and let the curtain drop after her without as much as a glance in his direction.

That she was at least as unhappy about it as he was became apparent, however, when she got up once in the middle of a lesson and came over to him, leaving Tristram in the painful process of counting words over on his fingers.

"Walter," she said, in a whisper that was both humble and pleading, "I think you are angry with me. What have I done?"

"I am not angry with you," he answered, although he realized he was not being entirely honest. "I am in a bad humor, that is all."

"I am afraid," she said, "you would like it better if I were not here."

He denied that with more complete conviction. "After what we heard Anthemus say on his visit here," he declared, "I became sure it was the best thing after all. If you had gone to Maragha, he would have found where you were. He would have discovered some way of getting you back."

Her eyes brightened. "If I could be sure you mean that, I would feel very much happier."

"But——" He hesitated, finding it difficult to put his feelings into words. "I am sure you feel I was not very generous about it, that I was concerned too much about my own safety."

She looked at him steadily for several moments. Then she whispered: "No, no. Please, you must not think that, Walter. I have never felt anything but most grateful to you." Suddenly she smiled and reached out to take both of his hands. "The lesson is over. You must join us. I have thought of something that may amuse you. Come, I will tell your fortune."

She led him, still holding one of his hands, to the center space where Tristram sat. Sinking down beside that earnest pupil, with both feet tucked under her like a tailor, she began to draw a series of circles on the ground with her finger. Then she produced a handful of ivory dice from the pocket at her belt.

She had become quite animated. "This is something we have learned from the Persians," she said. "It is called Kherdar; that is a name they have for your guardian angel. All women of the East believe in it, and they call on Kherdar when there is anything they want to know about the future." She smiled up at Walter. "Now, what do you want to know, good masser?"

His mood had not completely thawed, and so he said, "Why not tell your own fortune?"

She seemed quite willing to do this, saying there was something she desired to learn very much. "But it is a secret wish," she added. "I won't tell you what it is."

She cupped the dice in her hands and closed her eyes, saying, "Kherdar! Kherdar!" in a rapt tone of voice. After a moment she nodded her head and whispered, "Kherdar hears!" After another pause, she said, "Kherdar listens." Finally she cried, "Kherdar, speak!" and dropped the dice on the circles she had traced in the ground.

She bent her head over, studying the messages on the upturned surfaces of the dice and the positions in which they had fallen. After a long silence, she placed a finger at the head of the outermost circle and asked, "That is the north, is it not?"

"Yes, that is the north."

She looked down again for another period of study. Clearly she was puzzled.

"Will you get your wish?" asked Walter.

"I can't be sure. It is quite contradictory." Then she shook her head. "It is clear Kherdar does not wish me to know yet."

"Is it something you desire very much?"

"Yes," she said in a whisper. "I desire it very, very much." Then she sat up determinedly. "It is too soon for me to know. Now, Walter, it is your turn. What do you wish to ask Kherdar?"

In spite of himself, Walter was beginning to feel a keen interest. "Will I get to Cathay? Will I succeed there in what I am planning to do?" he asked.

She dropped the cubes into his hand and closed his fingers over them. "You must cast them yourself. See, roll them first in your hand. Keep your eyes closed and wish. Wish very hard. Sometimes it makes the fates smile on you, and then you get what you have asked for." As he followed her directions, she whispered, "I hope, Walter, it will be as you want it."

She studied the messages on the upturned faces. "Yes, you will reach Cathay," she said finally. "That is certain, for here we see the rising sun. It is clear too that you will get back safely to your own land, for this one means, 'The well-aimed arrow goes straight to its mark.' Anything about an arrow must mean England." Then she frowned and hesitated. "I am not quite sure about the rest. I wonder, Walter, if you really know what it is you want to find there? This one—and it is the most important of all, for it has the golden rim—this one says, 'Know your own heart.' Perhaps you will find there something you have not thought much about, and then you will see it was what you desired most after all."

"I know what I want," declared Walter. "I have no doubts about it at all."

"Well," with a sigh, "I am afraid that is all Kherdar will tell you now."

Another factor was beginning to disturb the tenor of life in their curious household. Mahmoud had overcome his unwillingness to have a second servant and was beginning to take advantage of the situation. More and more he was heaping work on Maryam's shoulders. Early in the morning he would call: "Get out of bed, lazy second boy! Light the lamps. Massers can't see to dress." At night it would be: "You, Taphal Get stew in kettle. Hurry, second boy, or Mahmoud lay pothook over your back!" He was even expecting her to do much more of the heavy work of loading and unloading than she had the strength to do.

Walter became concerned about it, realizing that she must be finding it hard to meet these demands. On one occasion he examined her hands and found that both palms, although they had callus marks on them, were so soft that it was certain she had not been accustomed to work of any kind. "I shall speak to that rascal of a Mahmoud," he said. "He is getting lazy and putting too much work on you." Then he noticed that her fingernails were cracked and broken. "You haven't complained, but I know you are finding it much too hard. That black scoundrel shall be soundly whipped!"

"The work is hard," she confessed. "But, please, you must do nothing about it. I said I would be a good servant. I must keep my word." Then she smiled, rather pathetically. "Thank you, Walter, for being troubled about me."

Several days later, he came unexpectedly into the tent and found her crying over some unusually difficult task. She tried to cover up the fact of her tears at once and went on with her work.

"Maryam," he said, "I am sorry about this. I would tell Mahmoud he must do everything, but, as you know, we must keep up appearances. If you did nothing, people would see there was something wrong. You understand, of course, that neither Tristram nor I can do any menial work without losing face."

"I know." She gave up the effort to hold back her tears and began to cry openly. "I get so tired. Sometimes I hate that Mahmoud so much I want to kill him!"

"I will talk to him at once. This can't go on."

She shook her head decidedly. "No," she said, wiping her tears on the sleeve of her once clean tunic. "It would not be wise, Walter. It is kind of you to be sorry for me. But we can't let Mahmoud suspect anything." Suddenly the Eastern half of her nature gained the upper hand. "I will go on with it! I will obey this impudent little son of a sore-eyed came driver!"

He could not help laughing as he leaned over to pat her approvingly on the back. She allowed herself to lean against him for a moment and then drew back quickly. "I should not have said that!" she cried. "An English lady would not have spoken that way. And, Walter, I want so much to be like an English lady!"

Mahmoud was not to be found at the moment. When Walter returned some time later, he heard a sound of scuffling from inside the tent and voices raised in anger and pain. Throwing back the flap, he found that the disturbance came from Maryam and Mahmoud, who were rolling on the ground in a tight grapple, clawing at each other and indulging in furious recriminations.

"Stop it!" he cried, rushing in to separate them. "Mahmoud, you shall be soundly whipped for this. Maryam, let go. Get up, both of you."

Maryam rolled to one side and then sat up, weeping angrily. "Impudent slave!" she said. "I have stood as much as I can." Then she stopped, and an apologetic look spread on her face. She rose slowly and walked away.

From the other side of the tent she said to Walter: "I am sorry. You will think badly of me because I make a promise and then break it so soon. But I could not help it, Walter. He struck me."

"Tapha bit me!" accused Mahmoud. "That second boy has teeth like viper."

Walter turned toward Maryam. Whatever he had intended to say remained unspoken, for he now saw that in the struggle the wide trouser on her right leg had been ripped from waist to ankle. Under normal circumstances he could not have failed to notice that the limb thus revealed to full view was slender and quite beautifully rounded; but all he could see now was its telltale color. It was white, white, white!

He motioned to her frantically. Maryam looked down and instantly realized the danger. She drew the torn edges together and ran back of her curtain. But it was too late. Walter saw a startled gleam in the eyes of Mahmoud and knew that the explanation would soon find its way into that stunted mind. The little servant had stopped sniffling.

"Well, the cat is out of the bag," he said to himself.

He crossed over and sat down beside Mahmoud. "Do you like your masters?" he asked.

"Yes, Masser Wasser!" affirmed the boy, on the point of blubbering. "Mahmoud love good massers."

"Would you want to see them in trouble? Would you want to see them killed in some such way as that black boy?"

"No, no, masser!"

"Then can you keep a secret?"

The whites showed in a full rim around both eyes in the ebony-colored face. "Yes, masser," he whispered.

"This one you call second boy is not boy at all," said Walter, lowering his voice. "She is a lady, a very great lady. She was being sent to China, but she didn't want to go. So she ran away from them and came here to us. Now do you know who she is?"

The round eyes were rolling in their sockets. "Yes, masser. Yes, masser."

"If they found out she was here, it would mean trouble. Very great trouble, Mahmoud. All of us—even you, Mahmoud—would be held responsible, and we would all be killed. Do you understand that?"

"Yes, masser." Fear had taken such complete possession of Mahmoud that he could hardly speak.

"Now listen to me closely. We must go on as we are. Great lady must still keep her face black. People outside must still think her second boy. That means she must do some work so they won't know anything different. But, Mahmoud, she is small and not strong. She must not do very much work. Do you see that?"

"Oh *yes*, masser."

"You must keep all this to yourself. Not a word is to be said to other servants. Remember, Mahmoud, if they find out, you will be killed too."

The boy drew himself up with resolution and even dignity. "Mahmoud too busy after this to talk to other servants. Mahmoud try to do all work." Then a penitent look stole over his face. He said in a horrified whisper: "*Masser!* Mahmoud struck great lady. Mahmoud bit and scratched her! Mahmoud should be whipped."

"Yes, Mahmoud deserves to be whipped. But"—Walter walked to the pole and took down from one of the pegs a fancy leather belt he had bought in the bazaar at Antioch—"he is to have a reward first. Mahmoud is a good boy. This is his."

A smile drove the fear slowly from an incredulous face. The boy took the belt, stroked it with eagerly trembling fingers, and then pressed it ecstatically to his bosom.

"This very fine belt for Mahmoud! Oh, masser! Mahmoud happy. Mahmoud *proud!*"

"Remember this. No talk. No boasting to other boys in camp. Loose tongue get all of us in very great trouble."

The servant nodded his head several times. "Masser cut out Mahmoud's tongue if he talk." Then the horrified look came back. The full knowledge of the enormity of his offenses had entered his mind. "*Masser!* Mahmoud came up behind great lady and struck heavenly twins with pothook!"

Tristram had been instructed to give further demonstrations with the longbow whenever possible. He came in now with a tired but satisfied air and hung the bow up on one of the pegs.

"They buzzed like bees when I lodged three in the course of a minute near the center of the clout," he said. "I was lucky again. Still my eye is getting back its cunning."

"Tris," said Walter in a casual voice, "Maryam Stander will be supping with us tonight."

"Maryam Stander! Do you really think she was his daughter? But why——" The puzzled look in Tristram's eyes turned quickly to one of understanding. "Something has happened. Is the secret out, Wat?"

"As far as Mahmoud is concerned." Walter told him what had occurred, adding: "From now on we won't have to keep up any pretense among ourselves. She will take her meals with us, of course."

Tristram smiled with delight. "I am glad of that. I have always felt guilty about having her share our leavings with this rascal. But about that name, Wat. Have you learned something more of her past?"

"Nothing. I am sure we will never find out anything more. The mystery of her origin is completely buried in the past. But I sometimes find myself thinking of her as Maryam Stander. It serves as a good reason for doing everything we can for her."

3

A week passed, with the weather showing no tendency to moderate. One morning Walter wakened early and proceeded to make up the fire himself. He was sitting beside the slowly prospering flames and wondering at the straight bar of white mist which entered through two loose skins at the top and pointed down at the fire like the celestial beams he had seen in illuminated missals, when the rustle of a curtain behind him caused him to turn his head. Maryam was peering around the edge at him, her black curls still tousled from sleep.

He realized with a shock that her face was several shades lighter than when she had first joined them.

"The stain is wearing off!" he exclaimed.

The girl nodded her head. "I thought it was, but I have no mirror, and so I could not be sure. See." She held out her hands palms up for his inspection. "They are much lighter."

"I hope no one has noticed it! You must apply more of it before you show yourself outside the tent again."

"But I have no stain. It was Lu Chung who put it on in the first place." She added in a reassuring tone, "It does not matter. No one ever sees me. No one comes near us at all."

This was quite true. As she had said when he found her hiding behind the curtain, they were held in the utmost disdain by the rest of the caravan. They rode in the rear and they pitched their tent at nights well

outside the circle of the encampment. Father Theodore was their sole
contact with the life of the camp, except for Walter's occasional games
with the commander. The priest was always so full of gossip that he
never gave the servants a glance. The wily Lu Chung, not wishing to
share in their difficulties, had not come near them.

"They treat us as though we were No-noses," went on Maryam, using
the term often applied to lepers.

"Come over here. Let me have a good look at you."

She obeyed by seating herself beside him and turning up her face to
be inspected.

"By St. Aidan!" he exclaimed. "You *are* pretty."

Her face dimpled. "I have been looking forward to the time when you
would find that out, Kyrios Walter."

Tristram sat up and began to rub the sleep from his eyes. "What is
it?" he asked.

"We will soon have a lily-colored second boy on our hands," answered
Walter, getting to his feet. "I'm going to find Lu Chung and have him
apply another coat of stain before we set out today."

Fortunately Lu Chung had risen early also. Walter found him beside
the direction-finding chariot, talking through the door in the rear to
a very small and ancient Chinese. Walter looked curiously at the custodian of the mystery carriage, who was so weazened that his unsteady
head seemed in momentary danger of slipping down through the gaping
collar of his winter tunic and disappearing from sight entirely.

When they had drawn away to one side, Lu Chung said: "Honorable
scholar is in trouble?"

"Unworthy scholar has been in trouble for some time, but exalted Lu
Chung has not deigned to come near him."

The giant looked around carefully before replying. "What is in young
scholar's mind to do with her?"

"Nothing can be done with her except to take her along. Lu Chung
knows that."

A cautious whisper was the answer. "She could be placed at next *yamb*
and instructions left for her to be taken back by caravan passing for
West. It would cost much, and purse of Lu Chung is empty as pickle vat
at end of winter."

Walter shook his head. "Could Lu Chung trust those who travel to
West? He knows full well they would sell her off their hands at first
slave market."

The giant essayed another suggestion. "Accidents happen, young scholar. Tent pole could crush in head of Mustapha. Great pain in belly could bring sudden demise. Boy Mustapha dead and buried, no one learn secret."

Walter's hand was toying with his dagger. "Listen to me, Bird Who Feathers His Nest. No accident will happen to Mustapha. Try anything like that and you would pay the price with two sharp blades sunk into your own belly. Now that we are speaking freely, I want Lu Chung to know there is no trust placed in him by these guardians of Lady Maryam. What is more, this one has found favor in eyes of my lord Bayan. It would not be wise to seek reward or immunity by telling lord Bayan the secret of her whereabouts."

Lu Chung thought it over and then grinned uneasily. "When both hands dirty, why try to clean one? Honorable scholar can rest in peace. This lowly one desires nothing but to stay out of more trouble."

"There will be more trouble if Lu Chung does not help at once." Walter proceeded to tell of the new complication. The giant nodded his head and agreed that steps must be taken at once to conceal the telltale condition of the runaway's skin. He was on the point of setting out on this errand when Walter laid a detaining hand on his sleeve.

"Could Lu Chung persuade this fellow to let me see inside of chariot?" he asked.

"Few are about at this unseemly hour. Perhaps it would be agreed to. For a consideration to be shared with my ancient friend."

A coin changed hands, and the clawlike fingers of the man inside the vermilion wagon beckoned Walter to climb up. He obeyed with alacrity, finding himself in a dark hole which stank of body odor and a sickeningly acrid smell which, he was sure, was due to the use of a drug. The inside was so small that the attendant slept on a filthy pile of blankets under a table which filled more than half of the space. When his eyes became accustomed to the faint light, Walter saw that a white dish rested on the table filled with water and that on its surface a needle about six inches long was floating. He could see through the water that the bottom of the dish was decorated with two straight lines crossed at right angles. The needle pointed along one of the lines.

"*Ting-nan-ching,*" said the old man in a quavering singsong. Walter was to learn later that this was the Chinese name for a magnetized needle.

A sense of awe swept over the Englishman. This, then, was the compass Roger Bacon had spoken of in their talk in the folly at Oxford. The needle oscillated slightly but never departed from the one direction

Above the table was a wooden lever with a handle. It was painted with all manner of mystic symbols.

The custodian, he decided, kept the handle set to correspond with the pointing of the needle, and so the arm on the figure above always stretched out to the south! Could it be as simple as that? He was so certain he had stumbled on the truth that he regretted deeply his inability to question the old man.

"I must learn all about it somehow," he thought. "When I get back, I must have all the details so Friar Bacon can make compasses for use on English ships."

He was more puzzled over the function of a second lever protruding from the floor and so placed that any motion would sound a gong suspended beside it. The truth here came to him again in a sudden flash. This was the gong which sounded at the end of each *li* traveled.

"I believe," he said to himself, after some thought, "that the lever is attached to one of the wheels. They have calculated how many revolutions are used in going one *li*. At the end of this number, something moves the lever and the gong sounds."

He found at a later stage of the journey that he had been right in both matters.

As the old man seemed anxious to be rid of him, he turned reluctantly and lowered himself to the ground. The exhilaration he felt over what he had seen remained with him to the exclusion of everything else, and it was not until he reached their camping site that he thought about the plight they were in. The yurt had been taken down in the meantime and packed away. Maryam was already perched on the back of her camel, and he was relieved to see that her face had been restored to a safely dark shade.

Tristram was ready to mount his tall Khorassan horse. As he slung one long leg up over the saddle, he said: "She cried when that stuff was rubbed on her face. Easy, Sargon! Easy, boy! She said she didn't want to look ugly again."

"It was a choice between looking ugly and finding herself back in the clutches of Hoochin B'abahu."

As they cantered off along the trail, Tristram said, "I am glad you seem to like her a little better."

"I have never disliked her."

Tristram smiled proudly. "I am getting on with my lessons. I can talk to her a little. She is taking advantage of it to ask me a great many questions."

"What about?"

"About England. About life there, and the people. She seems particularly curious about English women. And, of course, she asks about you."

"What does she want to know about me?"

Tristram looked a little shamefaced. "I am afraid I have allowed her to drag out all I know about your lady Engaine. She asked me all manner of questions. I am sure you haven't noticed it, but she likes you a very great deal. She was silent, and a little sad, when I told her of your devotion to Engaine."

"Are you turning into a prattling gossip?" said Walter, half angry and half amused. "Come, Tris, you must not let your sympathy for her get the better of you. She's close to being a heathen, you know. I am sure she has never been baptized."

"I know that." Tristram sighed deeply. "But she's so brave and so loyal. I might as well go on now that I have said that much. I—I am growing to like her very much."

"Put a check on your emotions, Tristram Griffen!" laughed Walter. "How would you look, you great lummox, taking a girl of the East back home as a wife?"

Tristram said in a despondent tone: "I have never considered such a possibility. After all, Wat, if she has fixed her eye on either of us, it is on you, not on me."

4

The improvement in the relationship between Walter and the guest in their tent was due to receive a setback.

An unusual bustle pervaded the interior of their felt home that evening. Maryam had been humming as she did her share of the work and, as she disappeared behind her curtain, she called over her shoulder, "Quickly, some hot water, Mahmoud."

The servant answered with a cheerfulness which pledged a new understanding between them, "Yes, Great Lady, plenty water soon." He proceeded to fill a basin with the largest part of their water supply.

"Taffy is using a new kind of mess on her face," explained Tristram when Walter looked at him inquiringly. "Lu Chung brought it this morning. It's made of charcoal and some other substance, and it can be removed at night. She is very pleased with it."

"Taffy?"

"Well——" Tristram came close to blushing as he made the explanation. "Mahmoud has always called her Tapha, and so I fell into the habit of calling her Taffy. It seemed a rather pleasant nickname for her."

They could hear the girl using the water vigorously. In a moment she gave a cry of surprise and then appeared around the curtain, holding a mirror out in her hand.

"See!" she cried. "I have needed it so much!"

Both men went into roars of laughter, and Walter said, "You had better use it to look at yourself."

The discovery of the mirror had interrupted her in the midst of her ablutions, and there was still a smudge of black over one eye and on the tip of her nose. She took one look, stamped her foot impatiently, and vanished again behind the curtain.

A disturbing thought suddenly came into Walter's mind. He looked around at Mahmoud, who was now proceeding with a suspicious brisk- ness to prepare the evening meal.

"Mahmoud!"

"Yes, masser. Food ready soon, masser. Good food."

"Mahmoud, did you steal that mirror?"

The servant's wide mouth spread in a placating grin. "Mahmoud find glass."

"Mahmoud did not find glass. To whom did it belong?"

The boy lowered his head over the kettle and went on stirring. "Not know. Great lady need glass. Mahmoud see, Mahmoud take."

Tristram began to laugh, and a hastily suppressed giggle reached them from behind the curtain.

"This is not a laughing matter," declared Walter. "That mirror is valuable. I am sure it has a silver back. The owner will have the whole camp searched for it. We can't afford to have them coming here after stolen articles."

There was a pause, and then Maryam said, "The mirror was mine in the first place."

"I am afraid that won't help us. The new owner will raise just as much outcry as though it belonged to her. Mahmoud, you will take the glass back to where you found it."

Tristram asked what had been said. Then he shook his head. "He might be caught at it. No, Wat, the damage is done, and it will be safer to do nothing. Surely we can find a place to hide it."

An arm appeared around the edge of the curtain with the article, and Maryam's voice said: "Here, take it. Break it or throw it away. I won't use it again."

Mahmoud took it and climbed up the center pole by means of the hooks. He shoved the glass under one of the walrus skins which had been folded back to admit air.

"There, masser," he said cheerfully, after dropping to the ground. "No one find glass now."

"The real danger is in having them come to search the place," said Walter, still far from satisfied. "If they walked in now they would find our second boy with a face several shades lighter than when he came here. That would be the end for all of us."

Maryam said, "I can blacken my face in a few seconds."

"You had better put it on now so you will be ready." In answer to her exclamation of dismay, he added firmly: "I mean it. We can't take any unnecessary risks tonight."

There was no answer. Walter turned to the servant. "After this there will be no more stealing. Do you understand?"

The boy pointed to the kettle. "Mahmoud steal spices for food. Masser not want good food?"

"That is different. Stealing of that kind goes on in the camp all the time. No one pays any attention to it."

"Of course it is different!" Maryam's voice sounded as though she were on the point of tears. "Master Walter must have his food well spiced. But I can look like a scarecrow for lack of a mirror."

Walter thought to himself: "The black rose is not the right name for her. She partakes more of the nature of pepper."

They ate their meal without the presence of Maryam. When Tristram called to her that it was ready, she answered in a tearful voice that she was not hungry. Walter was assailed at once with a new fear. "That won't do," he said. "If you cry, this new stuff will run on your face. Come, you must try to be sensible." There were no further sounds from her after that.

Footsteps were heard approaching the tent. The two men looked at each other apprehensively. "Say a silent prayer, Tris," said Walter.

But it was only Father Theodore with a summons for Walter to play chess that evening. The latter sprang to his feet with a sigh of relief and reached down his surcote.

The priest had gone on ahead. Walter paused at the entrance and said, "Good-by, Taffy."

There was a moment's silence. Then she said in a more natural voice: "Good-by. You were right. We must be much more careful. Do you think me very ungrateful? I am sorry, Walter."

Of the many games he had with Bayan, the one that evening remained most in his memory because of a discussion which prefaced the start of play.

The general had previously displayed a great curiosity about the Christian world, asking a continuous stream of questions. Having made a serious effort to acquire a closer knowledge of the Mongol tongue than *Bi-chi* provided, Walter had been finding that he could catch the drift of his opponent's talk before Father Theodore began to expound it. The latter, never invited to sit down and so condemned to long periods of standing first on one foot and then on the other, would not get more than halfway through his explanation before the answer was forthcoming. Bayan often nodded his head in pleased understanding of Walter's efforts to learn.

"In the lands of the West, you are of a curious simplicity," Bayan said this evening. "You have been fighting for one hundred years to wrest Jerusalem from the Saracens. You are always beaten in time, but you always come back, singing your songs of one God, and dying miserably on the hot trails. I have never been to Jerusalem, but it is said to be a mean city—a crowded, filthy, flyblown hole between two small hills. To hold it is of no military importance. I do not understand." He shook his head in a puzzled way. "It is the same with you in everything. One God, one faith, one pope. Even one wife. Life must be very dull in the Christian world."

Walter was considering how disillusioned he had been to find what Eastern people thought of the Crusades. Raised in the belief that the Crusaders were gallant knights in shining mail, battling chivalrously in the holiest of causes, it had been hard to believe that their opponents had considered them a band of murderous invaders, disturbing their peace and sacking their cities for a cause which baffled them; nay, worse than that, an uncivilized and unclean lot who fought for loot as jealously as for Jerusalem. The hate engendered by the long series of wars had surrounded them at every step.

"No, you are wrong," he now answered, earnestly. "Because we have one faith, we have an abiding peace of mind and hearts full of hope and content. Because we love one woman only, that love becomes a priceless boon, the most clean and beautiful of all things after our trust in God and His promises."

"There is nothing beautiful about rape," declared Bayan. "And yet your Crusaders seem to have been much addicted to it."

"Our unity does not extend to everything," Walter pointed out. "We have scores of kings instead of one, as you have. We have scores of languages, all so different that an Englishman knows nothing of Spanish or Italian or German. We have different laws in all countries, not one code like the Ulang-Yassa."

Bayan pounced on this point as was his habit with any venturesome pawn or unprotected knight. "Your unity is concerned only with the things which do not count. We have one ruler, one language, one code of laws. Today we rule all Asia because of this. Tomorrow we will conquer the world. When the white falcon flies over every one of your cities, what help will you get from that one God of yours, watching somewhere up in the clouds? Will you hold to your devotion to one woman when all the desirable ones have been carried off to satisfy your conquerors?" He smiled with complete satisfaction. "You Christians are not practical. All your beliefs are like fine cobwebs which we will sweep away with one swish of our horses' tails!"

Walter asked, "It is your intention, then, to invade Europe?"

Bayan laughed easily and confidently. "After we have taken China into our hands, and broken it to our ways, we shall follow the trail of Sabutai into the West; only this time we shall not turn back. I may meet you on that island of yours, Englishman."

On the way back to his quarters, Walter began to reflect that he had not been as faithful to his own pledges as he had claimed all Christians were. During the day the attractive face of Maryam, as he had seen it that morning, had continued to come back into his mind.

"Am I proving a recreant knight, Engaine?" he asked aloud. "I must put a check on these roving fancies of mine!"

5

For weeks they had been making more distance each day, with the Mongolians champing up and down the line and railing at stragglers. *Hudelhu! Hudelhu!* was their constant cry. Move! Move! Bayan himself was burning with impatience to reach the scene of action, as Walter realized on the occasions when they spent the evening together.

"There are few horse replacements at any of the *yambs* now, Englishman," he said one night. "The desert has been stripped for war. The Son of Heaven will wonder why Bayan is so tardy." He scowled at the pieces on the board. "It is these sickly women! I am of a mind to turn them loose."

The general won the game with more ease than usual, and his mood became better. "I like you, Englishman," he said, "and I am going to make a post for you. There is much sending of envoys back and forth in all dealings with the Manji, and you could serve me well in that way." He studied Walter closely and then nodded his head. "You are tall and you have a manner. I shall have to dress you up with jewels like a Hindu god and send you to Kinsai when the need arises."

Kinsai! Walter was so excited at this prospect that he slept very little that night. He rose soon after dawn and stepped out for a look at the weather. The day before they had ridden out of the cover of Asiatic poplars, and now he could see mountains far to the south. He held his breath in wonder.

It was an awe-inspiring spectacle. These mountains, with their white tops merging into the cold blue of the sky, were not like the friendly elevations which England dignified by that name, or the scarred and hostile hills of Palestine. They gave a suggestion of terrifying height, as though they joined the earth with the mystic regions beyond the clouds. Their silence was puzzling; it would have been more in keeping, he reflected, if the mighty rumblings of unknown forces had echoed from behind their aloof peaks.

"The Snowy Mountains!" he exclaimed aloud.

"They are lovely!" said a voice behind him.

Maryam had followed him out, holding about her the blanket she had thrown over her night clothes. He turned to look at her. Her skin, he saw, had now completely regained its natural tint, and there was a suggestion of the whiteness of ivory about it. She was looking at the sublime spectacle to the south, her eyes wide with wonder. They dominated her face which tapered heartwise from wide brow to a chin with the merest hint of a cleft.

"Lovely!" he repeated, and realized with something of shock that he had been thinking of her rather than the Snowy Mountains. This, then, was an occasion of double discovery. He had set eyes on the fabulous range for the first time, and he had stumbled on the truth that never in all his life had he seen anyone more beautiful than Maryam.

She shivered with the cold and turned to go in. "There will be a surprise tonight," she said, over her shoulder.

Before the caravan got under way that morning, the Mongolians indulged in a curious ceremony. They drew up into two long lines, their horses motionless, their arms stretched out toward the Snowy Mountains. They began to chant in chorus. The cruel, shrill voices sent a chill through Walter's bones as he sat well back from the double line. At the conclusion, he wheeled Podarge, his mettlesome mare, and rode toward his place in the rear.

Overtaking Father Theodore, he reined in. "What did that mean?" he asked.

The Nestorian priest shuddered. "It's a kind of prayer," he explained. "They were saying it is their destiny to conquer the whole world and that when the time comes they will ride into the rich, warm country beyond the mountains. They will burn the cities of India and kill all the men. They will plant their seed in the women so that in time the race will become true Mongolian. I had heard tell of this custom. It makes my skin creep."

A horseman galloped by them, shouting in an angry voice: "Back into your places! By the rotting face of a dead Crusader, you are a slow and troublesome lot!"

"They treat us like pariah dogs," whined Father Theodore.

A sense of expectancy, due no doubt to the promised surprise, pervaded the home yurt when Walter put in an appearance that evening. Mahmoud was busy over the preparations for the meal, humming in an excited treble and grinning so broadly that his lips threatened to split his face in two. Tristram was grinning also and nodding his head as though to say, "Just wait!"

"What is going on here?" asked Walter, seating himself by the fire.

"This is going to be an occasion," answered Tristram. "Taffy is dressing up."

"Dressing up?" Walter took immediate alarm. "In what? Has Mahmoud been thieving again?"

"No. It seems she brought one dress with her when she ran away. She says she will now appear before us in all her glory like the Queen of Sheba."

"Then Mahmoud must stand guard outside. These courteous Mongols never ask your leave when they decide to pay you a visit. They walk right in. How would we explain the presence of the Queen of Sheba?"

They could hear the girl busying herself behind the curtain. She was in a happy and excited frame of mind, for she was singing snatches of songs as she proceeded with her toilet. Once she sighed and said aloud: "Oh, if I only had some face powder! And some salves, and my very best perfume."

Finally she called: "I am ready. Bow low before Her Royal Munificence!" A white hand swept the curtain back and she stepped forward to the center rug.

Even the revealing glimpse he had been favored with that morning had not prepared Walter for the change in her. Her eyes were shining radiantly. She bowed to them and then turned slowly so they could judge the grandeur of her dress from every side. She was wearing a tunic of white, covered with a rich blue dalmatic which fitted her form tightly but flared out at the base with a split in front as far as the knee to allow freedom of movement. Over this again was a *pallium* of golden shade, most intricately embroidered. The collar of the *pallium* fitted snugly about her slender throat, and in the middle of it was a midnight-blue sapphire.

Tristram was drinking her in, his eyes shining with pride. "I told you she was beautiful," he said in a tone of awe.

"I lacked your discernment," said Walter. "She looks like the lovely Empress Irene, come back to life."

Tristram protested at this. "Not an empress. I prefer to call her Queen Maryam."

They had spoken in English, of course, and the girl stopped her preening to demand, "What are you saying about me?"

When Walter had interpreted, she nodded and smiled. "Queen Maryam? Was she a queen of England? Then I would much rather be Queen Maryam."

Walter looked at Mahmoud, whose eyes were on the point of popping out of his head. "Outside, boy! Keep a sharp eye and let us know if anyone comes."

Maryam seated herself between them, drawing her skirts tightly about her to save them from dust and grease. "I am not hungry," she said. "But you must have your supper without more talk. I shall sit here until you are through."

Tristram dipped a hand in the kettle and began to eat. His appetite was enormous under any and all circumstances. Walter did not follow his example at once. He found it hard to take his eyes from the girl's face. He was fascinated by her lashes, which were black and of a most unusual length. She looked up once and favored him with a steady look, then dropped her eyes again to study her fingers, only the tips of which showed beneath the ends of her close-fitting sleeves.

He found that one glance disconcerting in the extreme. She was not only lovely to look at but different from any woman he had ever seen. Lu Chung had called her the Black Rose, and he was sure now that this came closest to the true explanation; she had a quality which suggested

the fine tang of that rare spice. "The Black Rose," he said to himself.
"That is the name for her."

Maryam was satisfied apparently with the effect she had produced.
She began to ask questions. Did they like her costume? Did it become
her? Did English ladies have costumes as fine? When they had finished
supper, she sprang up and disappeared behind her curtain again, busying herself with additional improvements. She was singing a measure
with a curious lilt to it, keeping her voice low as though unsure of the
fitness of the oriental turn of words:

"My name is Fatima; I am fat but unhappy.
I am the wife of Abu Omar ibn Abdallah.
He has a beard full of gnats and a palsy in one eye.
There are five other wives, but none are as round and lively as I am.
All day we sit on cushions and prod each other with needles, and think
*   about other men.*
At night we sit on cushions and wonder which of us will be summoned
*   by Abu Omar ibn Abdallah.*
And, oh, how I love my sweet young camel driver, Peter Doupadoulus!"

Tristram got to his feet slowly. "Our little rascal of a Mahmoud will
be hungry," he said. "I will take his place outside."

Maryam appeared again as soon as he had left. She was carrying a
pair of small, ivory-handled scissors. "My hair has grown too long," she
complained. "I have trimmed it in front, but I can't cut it properly in
the back."

"I haven't seen those scissors before," said Walter.

She looked disconcerted for a moment, then she smiled. "Mahmoud
see, Mahmoud take," she whispered.

"I warned that fellow——"

"Please, it was my fault. I needed them so badly, and I asked him to
get me a pair. If someone must be punished, I am the one. Are you going to beat me, Masser Watter?"

He was finding it hard to be properly severe. "Because there was no
search made for the mirror, he must not think he can steal anything
you happen to need. It would not be fair to whip him for this, but you
must promise, Taffy, not to set him to any more thievery."

"I promise," she said, lightly. "I have all that I need now, so it is an
easy promise to make." She looked at him and smiled, holding up the
scissors. "Please. Will you cut my hair in the back?"

She seated herself beside him with her back turned and her head bent down to facilitate the work. Walter put a thumb and forefinger into the ivory handles, finding them a close fit. He looked hesitantly at the jet tangle of hair.

"I am very clumsy," he objected, "and I fear I shall make a botch of this. Perhaps it would be better if Tris cut it."

"Perhaps it would be better if you cut it," said the girl determinedly.

He gingerly clipped off the end of one strand which fell on the palm of his other hand. "How much am I to cut?"

She held up one finger and touched the first joint with her other hand. "About that much. But be very sure not to cut more. My head is small, and I do not want to look like a mouse drowned in a jug."

He worked slowly, acutely aware of her nearness, of the youthful hollows in her neck and the delicate prettiness of her ears, of the barely perceptible trace of perfume which reached him whenever she moved. The perfume was a new variety to him, a very subtle kind and quite different from what Engaine had used. Once she leaned back, and her shoulder rested against him. She drew away at once, but he had caught a glimpse of the gentle curve of her breasts under the gold *pallium*. He suspended work for a few moments to regain control of himself.

Had it been intentional on her part? He put that suggestion out of his mind at once, but another thought took its place. What was it Anthemus had said? "You are both young and lusty and will need a woman on so long a journey." God in heaven, why did he think of that now! But Anthemus, perhaps, had been right. He had to fight an impulse to drop the scissors and gather her up in his arms.

He was now sorely at odds with himself. Love had always meant to him the silent and rapt adoration of his inaccessible Engaine. There had been thoughts, of course, of the other kind, which meant vulgar scufflings with tavern wenches and buttery burds. He wanted to feel sure that what he was beginning to feel for Maryam had no relation to this lower order of things. Could it be, then, that he was permitting her to share the realm of his mind and heart which belonged exclusively to Engaine?

"Why are you so silent?" she asked.

"I am concerned about the matter of the right length. Although I am sure you could never be made to look like a drowned mouse."

"I was sure you were thinking that black hair like mine is not as nice as the golden tresses of your lady Engaine."

There was silence for a moment.

"You think about her a great deal, Walter?"

He found it a definite relief to talk. "Not as much as I did," he answered. "I am shamed to say that I think so much of the future that the past gets lost in my mind."

"Then sometimes you must think of me, because I am a part of the future. You cannot get rid of me for a very long time." She paused. "But you intend to marry her when you return to England?"

"When I left, she had it in her mind to marry someone else. My half brother."

There was a long pause. "Tris did not tell me that."

"I am not sure that he knew. It—it has been a matter of great concern to me."

"Is she as lovely as I think—as I think she must be to win such devotion from you?"

"Yes, she is beautiful."

"This half brother, does he look like you?"

Walter laughed shortly. "He is on the puny side. He is very dark, and he has a long Norman nose. I feel about him as you do about the sisters of Anthemus." By way of extenuation for what he had said, he added: "When my father died, he received all the estates. His mother is a foreigner, and I have a deep hatred for her."

"Surely, then, your Engaine does not show very good taste if she thinks of marrying your brother."

"It will be a marriage of convenience, to merge their estates."

Mahmoud returned for his supper. The snipping went on, the little servant watching with round eyes while he consumed his food with a loud, gobbling sound.

"We are in very much the same position, you and I," said Walter suddenly. "I am an illegitimate son with nothing of my own. That is why I came to the East. And you——"

"And I was born with a question mark on my paternity. I am glad of it, because it means I have none of the blood of Anthemus in my veins."

Walter sat back and held the scissors out to her. "There! I think it is done. Look in your mirror and see if you are satisfied." He added after a moment, "As we are companions in misfortune, we should be good friends."

She rose slowly and returned back of her curtain. After a few moments she called: "It is good. You have been most clever with the scissors. Thank you, Walter."

"Our poor Tris is still out in the cold. It is now my turn to stand watch."

"No, it will not be necessary. I think now I must take this dress off. And it will be the last time I shall wear it. I know you think it is very dangerous. . . . Walter?"

"Yes."

She appeared at the end of the curtain and looked at him with an appeal in her eyes.

"Please. I want you to think of me just as I am, and not as I will have to look after this."

6

From that time until they reached the point where the Snowy Mountains began to fade into the horizon and the course of the Pe Lu, that great trail of the silk caravans, veered in the direction of the Manji country, everything that happened remained in Walter's mind as part of what he called the Brief Reign of Queen Maryam.

He and Maryam found themselves on an increasingly intimate footing. The evenings when he was not summoned to Bayan's yurt were a real pleasure now. He had moments of grave doubt, however, when he would see a sober and withdrawn look in Tristram's eyes, an indication that his friend had not failed to observe how far their new relationship had developed.

Walter had thrown caution to the winds by withdrawing his objection to the removal each evening of the stain from her face, although he saw to it that someone always stood watch outside. Maryam, needless to state, was delighted, and she never appeared for supper without something special in the way of embellishment. Occasionally the two men laughed at the barbaric note in the trinkets she wore.

"It is the foreign blood in her showing itself," Walter said once.

He had said it lightly, but she took instant offense. "But I am English too!" she cried. "I tell you I am English too!"

Walter was concerned about the trinkets but tried to convince himself that she had brought them with her. This explanation could no longer be believed when she appeared one evening in a bright red dalmatic. It looked so well with her dark hair that he disliked the necessity of inquiry into where it had come from; but, he knew, the issue could no longer be blinked.

"How did you get that?" he demanded.

She was so sure of his reaction that her blue eyes narrowed in a pleased smile. "Mahmoud see, Mahmoud take," she bubbled.

As Tristram had remarked on the occasion of the first theft, the damage was done. There would be too much danger in having their nimble-fingered servant return all these stolen articles. Walter seated himself by the fire and shook his head in despair.

"I know that thievery is the least considered of all wrongdoing in the East," he said. "For that reason we can't blame you too much on moral grounds. But you gave me a promise, Taffy, and you have been breaking it ever since."

She was all contrition at once. "That is true, Walter. But I knew you were angry when you made me promise. Since then you have seemed to like me, and I thought you would not feel the same. But was it wrong? They have all been my things. Everything that has been taken belonged to me. Even this dalmatic."

"If anyone stops to think that all the things being taken belonged to you," he pointed out, "they will certainly suspect that you are still with the caravan."

She nodded in rueful acceptance. "I promise solemnly I shall never let Mahmoud bring me another thing."

"In the meantime," he said, "we must safeguard ourselves. Mahmoud must collect all the things he has taken and bury them outside. I am sorry, Maryam, but it is the only safe course."

"I suppose you are right," she said, after a moment. "But I shall miss them dreadfully."

He played chess with Bayan for the rest of that evening and, when he returned, the yurt was in darkness. The steady breathing of Tristram and the snoring of Mahmoud testified that both were sound asleep. There were sounds of stirring, however, from behind the curtain. Maryam crawled stealthily to the end of it and whispered, "Walter!"

He followed her example until their heads were no more than a few feet apart. She reached out a hand and touched him to assure herself that he was near enough to hear her.

"I must tell you," she said in the lowest of whispers. "Mahmoud has thrown everything away but the scissors. I had to keep them. Do you know why?"

There was silence for a space, and then she said: "You have never talked to me about England. There is so much I want to know. You will take me back there, won't you?"

"Life in England is very different. It is not as easy as in the East, and the climate is wet and cold. Are you sure you would want to change your whole way of living?"

"All that is of no importance!" she whispered with an intensity that surprised him. "Now that I know I am English, I want to be completely English. I want to live in my father's country no matter how different it may be. And," she touched his arm again, "do you think I would want to be left behind?"

She began to ask him questions about his life at home. Once started, he told her of the strange ménage in which he had been raised at Gurnie, of his Oxford days, and finally of the events which had resulted in his departure. She was avid to know everything, but her chief interest, he sensed, was in Engaine and the relationship which had existed between them.

"Does it not seem to you possible that your Engaine has acted selfishly?" she asked.

"Because she was prepared to marry my brother? That was not a matter of choice entirely with her. Both fathers were set on the match, and that made it difficult for her to refuse."

"But did she want to refuse?"

Walter was compelled to answer, "I cannot be sure."

When she spoke again it was clear she was assuming that she would go to England. She began to ask questions of a less personal nature.

"I am so very ignorant of everything," she said regretfully. "It is not thought proper for women of the East to have learning. I have never seen a book. What would I do if I were in your country? It would be very difficult."

"English women have very little learning. I doubt if many of them have seen a book either."

"We are supposed to be Christians," she went on. "But I have never been in a church. It is dangerous to be a Christian in Antioch, and so Anthemus was very strict about it. You and Tris are so devout that it makes me feel ashamed. I wish I knew more of this Christian faith for which men are ready to fight and die. Will you tell me about it? I want so much to learn."

"Yes, Maryam. We will be happy to do that. We have been much at fault in not thinking of it."

She said with sudden vehemence: "I want to be like you in everything! It would hurt me very much if you were ashamed of me."

"And you want to marry an Englishman?"

There was a moment of tense silence. "Yes!" she whispered. "I want to marry an Englishman!"

Without knowing how it came about, he found that they were lying side by side and that his arm was around her neck. He drew her still closer until he could feel her heart beating wildly against his side.

"How weak I am!" she whispered. "I talk of learning to be like the ladies of your country, and then I—I let you hold me like this, when I know that you love your Engaine." After a moment she added, "But I think perhaps you are coming to like me a little too."

"I have been struggling against it," he answered. "I know that I have been breaking a solemn pledge."

"A pledge? Are words so important? Does not the state of your heart decide?"

He drew her around until she was completely within his arms, her whole body pressed against his. She lay there unresistingly and he was aware of the touch of one bare foot against his boot.

"Perhaps she is married," she said, in a breathless tone. "You won't know until you return, and that can't be for several years. Perhaps— you will come to think less of her as time goes on."

Suddenly her mood underwent a change. She struggled out of his arms and sat up.

"You will think ill of me," she said, her voice raised above the point of caution. "You will think me bold and forward. I said I did not want you ever to feel ashamed of me; and now I am ashamed of myself."

He had raised himself to a sitting position also. She moved further away on her couch of boughs.

"I think you had better go back, Walter," she said.

He remained silent for several moments, trying to decide what he should tell her. Finally he began: "It is true that I have loved Engaine devotedly all my life. I have pledged her my undying devotion. That is something a man of knightly birth and Christian faith regards as binding and sacred. Every time I have found myself thinking of you, I have felt guilty because I knew I was breaking my pledge. And yet I must tell you that I have gone on thinking of you in spite of that."

"But she made no pledge in return."

"None. That makes no difference, as far as my obligation is concerned. It is hard to explain. We have a code of honor which must seem strange to you but which is quite clear to those who follow it." He decided that now he must continue by telling her everything. "You see, Maryam, my father made this same vow to my mother when he went off to the Crusades; and I was the result of it. He was away for more than four

years, and when he came back he brought a foreign wife with him. My
mother had remained true to him, believing he would be equally true
to his pledge."

There was a long silence. "I think I understand it better now. But,
Walter, does it make no difference that she told you she was to wed
your brother?"

"Engaine is full of a great pride, and she is capricious and often she
is not kind. I loved her for her faults as well as the other qualities I saw
in her. I knew that sometimes she said things for no other purpose than
to hurt me. She knew how complete my devotion was, and of course
she knew how far above me she was in station. Perhaps she had not
made up her mind fully about Edmond but was willing to make me
believe she had. On that point I cannot be sure."

"And you still feel you must abide by your vow? That is very hard
for me to understand." She paused, and he could tell she was shaking
her head in a puzzled and resentful way. Suddenly she burst out, "I am
sure only that I am beginning to dislike your Engaine very much!"

When he had returned to his own narrow couch, Walter continued to
thresh the matter over in his mind. He realized that he had not told
her everything after all. Try as he would, he had always been unable
to rid himself of the conviction that Engaine had been sure of her purpose. It had been a blind hope which had made him feel she might wait
for him after all. He began to see things more clearly. His great urge
to get along with his plans had more to do now with his determination
to win an acceptable place for himself in the future than with the very
dim hope of winning Engaine. He realized that she had been very little
in his thoughts, hardly at all since the morning he and Maryam had
caught their first glimpse together of the Snowy Mountains and he had
seen how beautiful she was. He confessed also that the East, with its
far different standards, had been gaining a grip on him, that the code
by which he always lived did not hold him as firmly.

Maryam was not sleeping either. He could hear her turn on her couch,
and once he heard her sigh.

He said to himself, "Go back and take her in your arms again." There
was a pledge much more binding than any spoken word.

He listened with growing conviction and desire. Every nestling move
from behind the curtain seemed to him an invitation. He was sure she
would welcome him, that her soft arms would go quickly again about
his neck, that her slender body would respond to him.

Twice he sat up with the intention of returning to her, but both times he waited, clenching his fists on the edges of his blanket and forcing himself to see that he must hold this physical impulse in check.

After a time the sounds from the other side of the curtain stopped. Her even breathing told him that she had fallen to sleep.

CHAPTER VIII

The Pe Lu

THAT THE OCCUPANTS of the blue yurt were permitted to live thus without interruption was in no sense an indication of peace in the general life of the caravan. Too many races were represented in the enormous train for that, and the continuous bickering sometimes flamed out into open hostilities. Echoes of this daily strife reached the little party even in the vacuum in which they seemed to move. Bayan was finding it increasingly hard to hold his men in check and to keep them away from the enclosure of the women. Double the number of guards had to be stationed around the silk walls.

On his evening strolls Walter often stopped to look at the blue-draped seraglio which looked so much like his conception of the Tabernacle the children of Israel set up each night in the wilderness and which contrasted so sharply with the Hebrews' place of worship in every other respect. If he were rash enough to draw close to the walls, there would immediately be a blistering command to move along, the nearest guard throwing in some such embellishment as, "Foul sprout of the West, your breath has the abominations of a camel's after eating wild leaks!" There were always many guards in sight, pacing up and down with drawn swords.

Occasionally the ladies were permitted an evening walk. Before they appeared, however, the men of the camp would receive orders to gather far off to one side where they would have no opportunity to view the beautiful concubines at close range. The walk was invariably a short one; for the ladies, being harem-bred, were an indolent lot. They would wander briefly in two long files, their faces heavily veiled, and then come chattering back to their quarters, casting curious looks in the direction of the segregated men.

Once, when a second sand storm threatened, they made the return in panicky confusion. Walter happened to be close to the path they took in seeking shelter and, as the cutting wind had torn their veils free, he had a good look at many of them. It was a disappointing experience. Judged from European standards, they were too swarthy for real beauty. Most of them, however, had fine eyes, dark and limpid pools of oriental temperament which flashed inquiringly at him as they hurried past.

One man, a trader who had joined the caravan at Samarkand, was foolhardy enough to steal into the enclosure in the middle of a hot and uncomfortable night. Loud shrieks announced his discovery, and he was promptly taken in charge by two of the eunuchs. Next morning it was given out that the presumptuous trader would be fittingly punished before the day's journey began. It was a matter for surprise, to the occupants of the blue yurt at least, when he was placed on his camel and bidden to ride off alone into the sandy reaches of the desert. Walter saw the look of intense relief on the face of the delinquent as he pulled desperately on the nose-cord. That something more was due to happen was soon clear. The Mongols had lined up in two long files and were laughing uproariously at the efforts of the fugitive to speed the languid gait of his mount. At a signal, the crossbows came out and in an instant the air was black with arrows. Camel and rider went down, the man seeming to resemble at the distance a smoked leg of pork generously spiced with cloves.

The glowing, vibrant spring of the East came in due course, and the desert trails responded with a riot of color. Walter had fallen into the habit of rising early. One morning he found that the rising sun had unveiled a blanket of flowers as blue as the lupine, stretching as far as the eye could see. There had been not a single trace of them the night before.

"In the East things happen suddenly," he thought.

Certainly many things had been happening to him with a great suddenness. On this particular day they were to move to a most unexpected climax.

It came about through a pet Maryam had acquired. One evening a short time before, a baby screech owl had flown into the tent in search of warmth. She had caught it and, in spite of the raillery to which she was subjected, had elected to keep it. She had become fond of the queer-looking bird and had named it, for no good reason at all, Peter Doupadoulus.

Her affection for it had become a standing joke, and this had the effect of making her quite vociferous in its defense. Peter was unusually wise, she contended, the wisest of all birds. During the day he rode with Maryam on a perch that Tristram had built, and at night he slept attached to the front hump of her camel by a frayed piece of rope. Walter often heard her talking to him behind her curtain in the evenings. "Ah, Peter," she would say, "if I had something new to wear tonight! If my beautiful Walter and my nice kind Tristram could only see me in that white dalmatic I left behind me!" Once, when she did not know anyone was inside, he heard her say: "Come, old graven face of a stone image, why do you stare at me so hard? Because I am putting a touch of red on my cheeks? Don't you think I should try to look at my best?" Then there was a pause and she added in a tone of deep feeling: "You look at me as I think that very great Lady Engaine would. So proud, so scornful, so *superior!*"

This morning, as the caravan got under way, Ortuh the Stammerer rode by and noticed the owl which had perched on the girl's shoulder. He reined up and indulged himself in the usual jeering laugh. Then, on a sudden impulse, he leaned from his saddle and tried to spit the bird on the point of his spear. Tristram drove his horse between and threw an arm around the Mongol's waist. One vigorous heave sent Ortuh tumbling from his saddle. The Englishman dismounted also. When the Mongolian tried to draw the curved sword in his belt, he found himself gripped in such a powerful vise that he could not make a further move. With little effort, Tristram raised him from the ground and proceeded to shake him until the yellow-skinned head spun back and forth and the bowed legs wambled like those of a scarecrow in a heavy wind. Then he gave the body a toss which sent it rolling over and over on the ground.

Ortuh was too thoroughly winded to do anything but crawl away. A circle of horsemen had gathered at the first hint of conflict. They made no move to interfere, but rocked in their saddles with glee over the discomfiture of their comrade.

"Keep an eye on that fellow after this," warned Walter, when the Mongol had recovered himself sufficiently to climb slowly back into his saddle. "He has lost face with the rest of them, and he will never rest until he has paid off the score."

Tristram laughed easily. "The next time," he said, "I will shake his soul loose from his greasy bones."

Walter was seriously disturbed by the incident. Had he imagined it, or had Ortuh paused, before reaching for his spear, to look intently into the blackened face of the camel's rider? If Ortuh the Stammerer had any suspicions, he would now be doubly certain to investigate.

Walter rode up to Maryam with the intention of saying what was in his mind. She had been frightened, naturally, and was holding her head down. Unwillingly he thought that she looked in her stained woolen tunic and ludicrously baggy trousers like a small Negro beggar. The owl was trying to escape from its noose and was screeching loudly. It may have been due to the completeness of the contrast, but he could not help thinking of the last time he had seen Engaine, sitting her blooded horse so easily and so proudly, her hawk on her wrist, her golden hair blowing out from under its net, her blue eyes so beautiful and proud. It was a disturbing contrast.

"Perhaps this is a lesson you have needed, Walter of Gurnie," he said to himself. "Engaine is perfect in her own way. And yet you have been drawing comparisons, and not in her favor."

He gave Podarge a slight prod with his heel, having learned to ride in the Eastern way, with a loose rein. As he cantered off, his mind became filled with a surge of racial pride. This was the East, these were the ways of the East: How much finer and cleaner were the ways of England! He must put a closer check on his tendency to forget, to accept new ideas, new perspectives, new people.

A sense of release came over him, and he began to think of home. He wondered how his mother was and if his departure had affected her health adversely. How were his grandfather's money-making schemes progressing? Everything would be green at Gurnie, and the woods would be full of hepatica and bloodroot. And what of Engaine? Had she already married Edmond? And, if she had, did she ever have regrets and did she sometimes think of him?

He was in a silent mood that evening. Maryam realized that something was preying on his mind, and she in turn lost her animation. There was little conversation as the three of them sat about the fire. The fickle weather had taken a turn for the worse, and a raw wind was blowing, causing a loose walrus skin to beat against the top of the pole with the insistence of drumbeats. Finally Maryam got to her feet: "We are very dismal company tonight. Walter, I think, is not pleased with me. I am going to bed."

When she had left them, Tristram began to speak of a rumor which Mahmoud had picked up during the day. Bird Who Feathers His Nest Lu Chung was in some kind of trouble.

Walter pricked up his ears in immediate alarm. "Is his part in the escape suspected?"

"No, not that, praise Our Lady! As far as I could make out, he has been a little too disposed to live up to his name. He still does most of the buying of supplies, and Bayan has ordered an inquiry. He threatens to turn him over to his men for the Rope Walk."

They had heard much talk of the cruelty of this method of Mongolian punishment, although it had not yet been practiced on anyone in the camp. "Lu Chung would never survive it," said Walter.

"Sometimes the victim lives. Still there isn't enough resistance in that great mountain of flesh. It may be that he has feathered his nest for the last time."

The fire was dying down, and the air inside had fallen below the point of comfort. Tristram got to his feet and stretched. . . . Suddenly the owl let out a screech.

"What is wrong?" asked Walter.

Then he saw Tristram begin to circle back of him with extraordinary stillness and care.

"Sit where you are, Wat." There was both fear and repugnance in his voice. "Don't move! In God's name, don't move!"

Walter turned his eyes without any motion of his head and froze suddenly with horror. A snake had crept into the tent in search of warmth and was coiled up within a foot of him. It was a pit viper; there was no mistaking the indentations in the broad, repulsive head, pointing straight toward him, and the mottled coils under it. He had so great a dread of snakes that he instinctively recoiled at the sight of one, but now fortunately his chilled limbs remained stiffly set. Forcing himself to look away, he sat in a state of fear, expecting to feel each second the impact of the fangs on his outstretched thigh.

Tristram was reaching stealthily for the pothook. He whispered, "An ugly specimen, but I'll have it in a moment!" Walter could feel the ends of his fingers curling up in fear and suspense.

He heard a movement behind the curtain. Maryam stifled a scream and started to run out into the center.

"Keep back!" cried Walter.

But she ran behind him and with a quick flash of one hand seized the protruding tail of the snake. Fortunately the reptile was torpid with the cold and did not rouse until she had thrown it with another scream against the side of the tent. Walter was on his feet in an instant. The viper fell with a wriggling motion, and then the venomous head came up with deadly intent. By this time Tristram was ready for it, and one crushing blow with the pothook brought all danger to an end.

Maryam promptly fainted, her head falling into the ashes at the side of the fire. Walter saw now that she was naked from the waist up, and he hesitated before placing a hand under her head to raise it.

"Mahmoud, water!" he called.

But Mahmoud, who had roused at the first scream, had climbed the tent pole and was screeching at the top of his lungs. It was Tristram who brought water after tossing the mangled remains of the viper to a safe distance outside.

"Is she all right?" he asked, anxiously.

"She has fainted."

"I heard a great commotion in other parts of the camp," reported Tristram, after a moment during which he studied the pale features of the girl. "The sudden return of the cold must have brought more of them around. I'll go now and bank sand around the bottom of the tent so no more can get in."

Maryam sighed and then shuddered. "I'm so afraid of them!" she said, in a weak voice. She opened her eyes and saw Walter's face bent over hers. She asked in renewed alarm, "Where is it?"

"Dead," answered Walter. He was becoming acutely aware that he was supporting her bare shoulders with one arm and that her breasts were pressed against him "Tris finished it. Are you feeling better?"

"Yes. Yes, I am better now." Maryam sat up, suddenly aware of her condition. She sprang to her feet and disappeared between the curtain. It was several minutes before she emerged again fully clothed. Walter noticed that her cheeks were still pale.

"You saved my life," he said.

"I hardly knew what I was doing. It all happened so fast." Then she shook her head. "No, I didn't save you. It was Peter. If he had not seen the snake and warned us——" She gave a short, hysterical laugh. "I told you he was a wise one. I told you so, Walter."

"I humbly concede you were right. But, Maryam, it was not Peter who picked up the snake."

Mahmoud had been clinging all this time to the top of the pole. He came down now, blubbering, "Mahmoud not like snakes!"

Tristram returned, saying in a cheerful voice, "No more of them can get in. How is Taffy feeling?"

No answer was given for Walter suddenly raised a hand as a warning. He leaned forward, listening intently.

"I heard a step outside," he whispered. "There! Someone is coming!"

Maryam ran behind the curtain a second time and searched with frantic fingers for the mixture to apply on her face. Some of the hooks had fallen out of the metal rings and Walter began to replace them as a further precaution. He stopped in the middle of it, however, and pointed at the side of the tent nearest him, drawing in his breath sharply.

The end of a dagger showed through the blue silk lining!

Walter gave a hiss to attract the attention of the others. Their faces turned in that direction and, as they watched, the knife was shoved further in before beginning to sink. It cut slowly, and with very little sound, through the outer felt and the silk lining, until an incision of about a foot had been made. Then yellow fingers appeared in the cut, drawing the edges back far enough for a face to stare in at them. All they could see was a pair of eyes which rolled with malevolent curiosity, resting with particular attention on the partially disguised face of the girl. The fingers were then withdrawn and the slit in the side closed.

There was silence in the tent for several moments. Walter broke it by saying, "I am sure that was Ortuh the Stammerer!"

Maryam came over and placed a hand tensely on his arm. "I must go away!" she whispered. "It is the only way now. You will all be involved if they come and find me here. That must not be!"

"The truth is out," said Walter. "All we can do now is wait."

Tristram had taken down his bow and was flexing the string. "I won't be able to do much in the dark, but at least I can send a few of them back to the hell from which they came!"

He faced about quickly when footsteps were heard at the entrance, raising the arrow to the level of his shoulder. Walter ranged himself alongside, his dagger in his hand. Feeling a touch on his arm, the latter realized that Maryam had come forward to join them.

"By the Rood," exclaimed the archer, "we shall sell our lives dearly!"

But it was Lu Chung who entered the tent. He gasped when he saw the kind of reception prepared for him, and his face became even paler than it had been when he threw back the entrance flap. He was clearly in an agitated state of mind. His hands trembled and his eyes darted about uneasily in the flaccid expanse of his face.

"Was it Lu Chung who cut that hole?" asked Walter, nodding in the direction of the rent. As he did so, he gasped with fresh surprise. The dagger had been left there! Its weight had caused it to slip through further, and the whole of the blade could now be seen.

Lu Chung denied that it had been his work, but he was so concerned over his own plight that he did not at first grasp the significance of what had happened. When the truth penetrated his mind, he let himself sink down by the fire, shaking his head with redoubled foreboding.

"Now they will know all!" he lamented. "Unhappy Lu Chung will be sent to the Rope Walk!"

"If I am right in thinking it was Ortuh, why did he leave his dagger behind?" asked Walter.

The giant looked up at that, a glimmer of hope showing in his eyes. "He left it as a sign that he will return. That is clear. This lowly one does not think Ortuh will tell what he has seen at once. He will return to make a bargain. Perhaps it is in his mind to demand value for silence. He is a covetous one, that Ortuh. He may demand gold." The uneasy eyes strayed in the direction of Maryam. "It may be he will demand to see this girl when all the stain is off face. He may ask that she be sent to his tent when that can safely be done. Mongolians talk much of the pleasure in the feel of white woman's skin."

After a moment of silence, Maryam said in a low but determined voice, "I will go to the tent of Ortuh if it will save my friends, Lu Chung."

Tristram cried "No!" Walter pressed the hand beside him before saying: "We know you would make any sacrifice, Maryam, but we would prefer death to that. And there may be a safe way of escape for all of us. If Lu Chung is right about Ortuh, I am sure we can get away."

"What plan have you thought of, Wat?" asked Tristram with anxious eagerness.

"It will depend on whether he doesn't do anything more until tomorrow. If I have learned anything of the nature of these people, he may prefer to wait, to keep us in suspense."

Lu Chung nodded his head. "Ortuh will play like cruel cat which has found three small white mice. He will not return for his knife at once. He will wait, and watch, and let fear hang over you. Then he will pounce."

"We have often fallen far behind the caravan," went on Walter. "Tomorrow we will pretend that one of the camels has taken sick and be very slow in starting. When the last of the caravan has passed out of sight, we will strike due south. Everything will then depend on how much speed we can get out of our animals."

He had spoken in English and so had to repeat what he had said for the benefit of Lu Chung. The latter thought it over and then nodded his head in acquiescence. "Young scholar suggests only way," he declared. "Lu Chung will go also. This lowly one faces sure death if he stays." Clearly he was feeling better about the prospect, for he nodded his head again with a trace of vigor. "Lu Chung knows roads. He thinks it best that route to Kinsai be followed."

Tristram was frowning doubtfully. "How far, think you, can we hope to get before our absence is discovered?" he asked.

"Twenty miles perhaps," answered Walter. "Certainly not more."

"I question if it would suffice. You have seen how fast Bayan's horsemen ride. They would come after us like the wind. They would not retrace their course but would cut across country to intercept us. Is it not certain also that Ortuh, or whoever that was, will keep an eye on us?"

"It is our only chance, Tris."

"That I know. We must take it, of course. It will at least give us the opportunity to fight for our lives in the open. I swear that there will be many empty saddles before they close on us!"

Ortuh did not come back and, after much further discussion of plans, Lu Chung took his departure. Tristram, whose nerve did not seem to have been shaken by the prospect ahead of them, soon composed himself to slumber, but Walter decided that sleep would be out of the question for him. He replenished the fire and drew up close to it, feeling the need for warmth more than at any time he could remember. The plan kept turning over and over in his mind. A way to improve it had occurred to him, an idea of such boldness and originality that at first he accepted it without daring to consider the dangers it would entail. Later, doubts began to crop up in his mind and he tried resolutely to brush them aside, saying to himself: "I may die in any event. This way the others are certain to escape."

Even after he had made up his mind to try it, he was assailed by a cloud of disturbing thoughts. He might never see England again, never set eyes on his mother's face, never see the green woods around Gurnie and the winding streams he had loved so much. At the best, the chance to make his fortune, which had promised so well after what Bayan had said to him, would be hopelessly wrecked. It was a matter for surprise that he could pass this part over with little regret. Had this crisis they faced wrought so complete a change in him?

From her niche behind the curtain, Maryam whispered, "Walter!"

He went over at once. She was sitting up, and there was enough light from the fire for him to see that her eyes were full of tears. She had forgotten to remove the traces of stain from her face.

"I am very unhappy!" she whispered. "I have brought this on you. Oh, Walter, what can I do? There must be something!"

"You must not let yourself be disturbed. We will show them our heels; I am certain of that. A new plan has come to me. A very fine plan. It will make things doubly safe, I swear."

She did not say anything in response for a moment. "Is it something you must do yourself? Walter, I can read what is in your mind. You will be in still greater danger!"

He realized that it would not do to tell her the whole plan. "Yes, I must see to it myself," he said. "Come, clear that stricken look from your face. The plan is quite simple. I shall stay behind for a time and make certain that Ortuh sees me. That will keep him from having any suspicions. Then I shall drop back and follow you. I hope to overtake you long before nightfall."

"No, no, Walter! No, no, no!"

"There will be no danger in it," he urged. "I am sure Podarge can outrun any horse in the whole caravan. The only drawback I foresee is that I must not lead them to where you will be. I must take them well off the path. It might be a day or two before I can reach the place Lu Chung has marked for us."

"I will die if anything happens to you, Walter!" She was weeping now, and the stain was running down her cheeks in streaks. "I know that I will die!"

"Come, this will never do. You should see what you are doing to your face!" He lifted an edge of the curtain and began to dry her eyes with it. "If all goes well, you will never again have to put this ugly stain on your face. Think how pleasant that will be!"

She struggled to regain control of her emotions. "Are you going to be able to sleep?" she asked.

"Not for a time. I am going to sit by the fire and think things out carefully."

"Then may I sit with you? It may be—it may be the last time, Walter!"

2

Walter was out with the first hint of dawn. He looked up at the sky and saw to his satisfaction that the sun would be hidden from sight. "That much is in our favor," he said to himself. Then a somber thought chased everything else from his mind. It might be that he would never see the sun again!

The Snowy Mountains no longer stretched across the southern sky line in a jagged pattern of green and white. A sluggish stream, which occasionally burst into a loud and excited coil, came twisting down from the north and crossed the trail before gliding off in the direction of the Manji country. They had camped for the night near a village of more size and importance than the usual *yamb*. In addition to the customary cluster of yurts, there were a few buildings of wood, low and roughly clay-thatched, without windows or chimneys. Before each of these a high pole stood with horsetails blowing in the wind. To the north stretched the inevitable plain, but in the south there was a cover of stunted trees. He reflected with rising hopes that their movements would be covered.

He told Tristram no more of his plan than he had divulged to Maryam, fearing his friend would refuse to consent if he knew everything it entailed. A negative shake of the head was the immediate response.

"I know you, Wat," declared Tristram. "You've conjured up some scheme to get the rest of us safely away at your own risk. I won't agree. You might as well know that now."

"There is some danger in it. But also there is a good chance that I shall be able to show them a clean pair of heels. We were already agreed that we stood a very small chance the other way. The thing that counts is to get Maryam safely out of their clutches. That will be your duty."

Tristram laid a hand on his shoulder. "I believe only part of what you say. We will get away and you will be left to bear the whole burden of punishment."

"One of us must go and one must stay. I am the one to stay."

"I am the son of a fletcher and, though I spent a year at Oxford, I am still a simple fellow of the common people. I would be small loss. You need not shake your head; you know I speak the truth. You, Wat, are the son of an earl. You have a keen and active mind. You are bound to achieve great things in life." For the first time in their acquaintance, he was speaking with no trace of his usual slow drawl. His face was filled with a determination to impose his own way. "There is another reason, old friend. I love Maryam. That must have been clear to you for a long time. But Maryam loves you. She has made no secret of it. I have no way of being sure of your sentiment for her, but—there can be no doubt you are the one to go with her."

"If all you say were true, old friend, I would still be the one to remain. I alone can do what must be done. With all your courage and the best intent, you could not."

"Must you be the judge of that?" demanded Tristram. "What is there to be done that is beyond my powers?"

Walter looked his friend steadily in the eye. "I am going to try a little ruse that would bring a glow into the eyes of your old master, Roger Bacon. No hasty instructions for your guidance would suffice, Tris. I, and I alone, know how it may be done, and where."

The face of the tall archer was a study in conflicting emotions. He was still unwilling, still unconvinced, but at the same time puzzled as to what had been meant. "What is this great mystery?" he cried.

The camp had come fully to life. Horsemen had begun their regular morning harassment, dashing up and down the lines at breakneck speed and calling for dispatch in the name of the lord Bayan. The yurt was down already, and Mahmoud's hands moved busily at the task of packing it. Lu Chung rode up on his tall camel and said in a weak voice which contrasted ludicrously with the ferocious caste of his features, "The sun refuses to shine on our desperate venture, young scholars." Maryam's face was completely blacked again, and she was packing one of the camels, pausing every minute to look anxiously at them over her shoulder.

Walter was watching for signs of Ortuh, but so far the Stammerer had not put in an appearance.

Tristram asked in an unreconciled voice: "Are you quite sure of this, Wat? Must I do as you say?"

"I am quite sure."

A trumpet sounded at the head of the line. Camels screamed as their drivers began to beat them to their feet. Every Mongolian was in his saddle, screeching, *"Hudelhu!"*

Now that the moment had come, Walter felt his heart sink. He had little real hope that he would ever see them again. Fearing that this would show on his face, he turned away and studied the trail, which struck out from the town and on to a plain stretching with unbroken monotony north and east. That again, he thought, would be in his favor.

"If I should fail to reach you, make for Kinsai," he whispered to Tristram. He searched under his belt with cold fingers and produced the second of the two letters entrusted to him by Anthemus. "Deliver this to a merchant named Sung Yung in Kinsai. He will look after you until I arrive. You will have to depend on Lu Chung in getting there."

They stood for several moments with clasped hands. "You are the only good friend I have ever had, Tris," said Walter.

"This is all wrong! I know it, Wat; but I have always taken your word in everything." There was a pause. "If—if things go wrong, our kind Father in heaven may deem us worthy to meet in a kindlier world than this."

The most difficult of his farewells must now be said. He walked over to Maryam.

"Is it settled?" she asked, continuing with her task. "Are you to stay?"

"For a short time. Very soon I shall get away also and ride to join you as fast as Podarge can carry me."

She straightened up then and faced him. "I am not going to cry," she whispered. "It would make the stain run; and that would not do, would it? But I know—I know that I shall never see you again!" Despite her resolution, her large eyes were beginning to fill. "Oh, Walter, I love you so much!"

3

Walter rode up the line, watching, with an air he strove to make casual, for signs of Ortuh. He located the Stammerer finally and galloped up beside him.

"I have a knife that does not belong to me," he said.

Ortuh seemed reassured at seeing him. He grinned. "Knife belong to Ortuh," he grunted, adding after a moment, "Ortuh has sharp eyes. See much."

"Does Ortuh desire return of knife?"

"Soon. Ortuh call at yurt of Christian dogs. Have much to say. Filthy sons of West wait for Ortuh."

Walter spurred ahead. Luck was with him, for when he reached the direction-finding chariot, a score or more of spare horses had been collected together behind it in charge of a pair of morose servants. He sprang from his saddle and turned Podarge in with the others. Neither of the guards paid any attention when he threw open the rear door of the chariot and sprang up inside.

An acrid odor filled Walter's nostrils instantly. The old Chinese lay under the table, a blanket tucked around his emaciated form. His eyes were wide open, but fixed and without expression.

"Drugged!" thought Walter, exultantly.

The custodian had been faithful to his trust to the extent of lashing the overhead lever in position with a length of rope. Walter untied it.

He kept a firm hand on the lever after advancing it no more than an inch. He would change it slowly, he decided. There would be direction-wise eyes in the caravan to detect any radical change in the course.

There was a narrow slit in front through which a view might be obtained of the course ahead, but this, at the moment, was obscured by the leg of the driver. He could hear the Mongol muttering to himself. "I, Houlun, am as good a man as ever! I, Houlun, am as good a man as ever!" Finally the driver burst out in furious protest, "Then why must I be set to drive a stinking wooden cart behind these mangy, rump-sprung cattle!"

At long intervals Walter gave the lever a cautious turn. Each change meant that the arm above, instead of pointing due south, was slowly veering east and the following caravan was beginning to head into the north. Meanwhile Tristram was leading his party due south. Each *li* traveled now meant that nearly two *li* had been opened between them. He kept an eye on the slot in front and, whenever the disconsolate driver moved his leg, it could be seen that the plain ahead was still wind-swept of all trail indications.

"It is working out as I thought!" said Walter to himself. "If I can only escape notice long enough!"

Loud voices swelled up outside at intervals, and each time he held his breath, thinking, "They have noticed!" The shouts proved in each case to be no more than the casual bickerings of a contentious race. Nevertheless he shuddered at each sound. "Soon," he thought, "they will be screaming for my blood. How will they kill me?" It would be a cruel death, he knew, if he were caught.

The old man continued to lie without any motion. Walter began to doubt if he still breathed. "When I go," he thought, "I can leave the rope dangling and they will think it was due to that." On second thoughts, however, he decided against this. It would mean, he knew, that the old man would die in his stead.

Well away on the route to the south, Lu Chung called to Tristram: "Perhaps these not young eyes see wrong. Does it seem to tall scholar that caravan has changed course?"

Tristram squinted ahead dubiously. "I have little sense of direction in these flat wastes. Still I seem to think it is now set in a more northerly direction."

"It seemed so to lowly Lu Chung."

Tristram reined in, and Maryam's camel came shuffling up beside him. "Taffy," he said, "a miracle is coming to pass. Walter is taking them off their course. I don't know how it has been done."

She made no answer but watched with solemn eyes the fast-disappearing caravan. Suddenly a change came over her companion. He straightened in his saddle and raised a hand in the air.

"There is the answer!" he cried. "They laugh at us, these murderous people of the East. They call us dogs to our faces. They scoff at our faith. We have accepted their insults in silence. But now Walter of Gurnie is showing them the courage and the faith that fills a Christian heart!"

He turned to Maryam, his eyes glowing and yet filled with tears. "Would anyone but a believer in the One and only God have risked his life in such a way? Tonight they will not laugh!" Then, quite as suddenly, the animation died out of his voice. "But I am afraid my friend has offered up his life to teach them! And to save us!"

"I knew it," said Maryam in a whisper. "He tried to make me believe he would come back. But I am sure he never will."

Tristram made no effort to wipe away the tears which were streaming down his face. "Good-by, Wat!" he called. "Your faithful squire salutes you!"

"Hurry, young companions in peril," admonished Lu Chung. "We must take advantage of chance honorable lord has made for us."

Maryam leaned over and locked her arm tightly in Tristram's. They sat in silence until the last tiny figure had vanished from sight.

An hour passed. Two hours. The gong behind Walter sounded its signal with gratifying regularity.

He decided that the distance was not sufficiently great. Another hour passed. The gap must now be a full forty miles. Walter decided he could afford to leave.

But he had left it too long. A sharp voice outside ordered the driver to stop, and the rear door was thrown open. Suspicious Mongolian eyes peered in at him.

"Ha, Christian pig!" cried Ortuh. "What are you doing there?"

Back of the Stammerer he could see the felt hat of Bayan. The eyes of the leader were fixed on him with a frown of suspicion and surprise.

He dropped to the ground and stood still, facing Ortuh. There was no possibility of escape; for bronzed-faced riders had now encircled him, watching with eager intentness. This, then, was the end.

He looked up at the sky, which was a dark and threatening gray. A raw wind was blowing. He was glad of this. It would have been harder to die if the sun had been out.

"Ortuh has been the cause of this," he said to himself. "Since I must die, I shall take him with me."

He drew the knife from his belt and sprang at the Stammerer. What followed was a wild nightmare of violence, noise, confusion, and pain. He was aware that they were rolling together on the ground and that Ortuh was struggling desperately to pinion his arm which held the dagger. Others had joined in, for blows descended from above on his head and back. Heavy feet kicked him in the ribs. Dimly he could hear the voice of Bayan shouting commands to end the struggle, but the blows continued to rain on him.

When rough hands dragged Walter to his feet, Ortuh remained on the ground. Blood was flowing from a broad gash in his throat. "If I must die," thought Walter, grimly, "I have the consolation, at least, that I have paid off that score."

"Bring him to me," ordered Bayan.

When they faced each other, the general motioned to the men to drop back. He studied Walter in silence for several moments, his eyes searching the face of his chess opponent for the reasons back of what had happened. It seemed to Walter that, in spite of the severity of Bayan's gaze, he could detect a shade of regret.

"Englishman, what have you been doing? For the last two hours I have had an uneasy feeling that we were off our course. Have you been tampering with that thing?"

"Yes, my lord Bayan. We are many miles north of where we should be."

The general continued to watch him with a puzzled air. "Why have you done this?" he demanded. "You know that every hour counts with me, every *li*."

Walter answered in a tone of the deepest contrition. "I am sorry it has been necessary to delay the caravan. But no other course was open to me. The lives of my friends depended on me; and I did what I could for them."

"And did I not count? I thought, Englishman, you were a friend."

"Please let me tell you everything before you judge me."

Bayan nodded to him to proceed. He listened intently as Walter told his story in a low tone.

"You have played me an ill turn on many counts," he said at the finish. "A whole morning has been lost to me. There will be no chance now to make use of the magic longbow on which I have counted. That great villain Lu Chung has slipped through my fingers. The matter of the Greek girl is still more serious for an affront has been paid to the Son of Heaven and he will expect me to impose a fitting punishment. I am afraid, Englishman, you must die."

"Then let it be a merciful death."

Bayan regarded him with a rueful look, combing his fingers through his scant beard. "Only a brave man would have risked his life in this way to save his friends. I must do what I can for you, little though you deserve it. I have always liked you, Englishman. There is a way, if you are prepared to accept it. I can give you a bare chance for your life and at the same time please my men who are slavering for your blood." He frowned doubtfully. "Some have lived under the blows of the spear handles; and it is possible you have the strength for it. You will suffer as much as though I had ordered you to be impaled but—there *is* a chance this way. I shall send you to the Rope Walk."

4

Father Theodore came to Walter when the men had gathered about the supper kettles. There was a great deal of boisterous shouting in expectation of the sport which lay ahead. "I have just come from the general," said the priest, keeping his eyes averted. "He asks what food he may send you."

"I am not hungry," said Walter.

The priest lowered his voice. "If you keep a cool head, there will be a chance. It is said that many years ago a man made the walk and did not suffer a single blow. It is the rule that no one may strike with a spear as long as your feet are on the rope. Once you touch the ground, the blows will rain on you; but if you can get back again, they must stop. I saw it once, and I must tell you, unfortunate young scholar, it was not a pleasant thing to watch." He added after a moment: "There is always a judge to see that the rules are followed. Bayan is to act tonight."

Walter had been calm before, but he shuddered now and let his head fall into his hands.

"I come to you as a man of God," said Father Theodore. "As I am a humble Nestorian it is possible you would prefer to go unshriven."

"I must make my peace with God," said Walter. "Proceed, please, Father."

The rope, he saw, was quite thick and at least fifty yards long. It had been stretched out on the ground and pegged down at each end to make it taut. The Mongolians were already lined up on each side of it, frisking about and waving the butt ends of their spears in the air. They were clamoring for their victim to appear. Bayan, looking solemn and ill at ease, had taken his place at the far end.

Father Theodore walked with Walter to the starting point. "Keep a stout heart, young scholar," he admonished. "The Lord God may look down on you, and mayhap He will see fit to be merciful."

Two older men, both shamans, came up on each side and stripped off the clothes of the victim. Then one of them took a rag dripping with some black liquid and drew a mark around the base of his neck. Walter knew the purpose of this. One of the rules was that the breaking of the bones must not be accompanied by any shedding of blood. The stripe would serve as a guide.

"Let the first blows be so heavy that it will not take long!" prayed Walter, under his breath.

The eager Mongolians were screaming for the sport to begin.

"Start, Englishman!" called Bayan, from the other end.

It would have been a difficult enough feat to balance on the waxed surface of the rope under the most normal circumstances. Walter kept himself steady for perhaps a dozen paces, extending his arms on each side and setting his feet down with a desperate care. Behind him he heard loud howls of disappointment, for the men he had passed were now barred from the pleasure of beating him with their spear handles.

"Steady!" he kept saying to himself. "Perhaps I can make the full distance. Take care! No hurry! Steady!"

Then something struck him in the face and the unexpected shock set him back on his heels. It was a pig's bladder, blown up almost to the bursting point and wielded by one of the shamans who had kept pace with him. He swayed from side to side. He was sure he would have to step from the rope, but he caught his balance in the nick of time and continued to pace forward. Pandemonium now broke loose. Those in front were jeering and shaking their spears at him in invitation. Their maniacal faces seemed to stretch ahead for an endless distance. The shaman on the other side raised the bladder in his hands and struck him sharply across the eyes. He was ready this time, however, and the blow did no more than rock him momentarily. He knew that from this moment on he would not be allowed an uninterrupted second. This was in accordance with the accepted rules; it was not the intent of the torturers to give their victim a real chance to survive the hazards of the long walk.

He took another dozen paces successfully. This, quite clearly, was more than had been expected of him. The jeers grew even louder, and the bladders flattened on his head and shoulders with a squishing sting. "How much longer?" he wondered, panting with the strain. Perspiration was running down his face and threatening to blind him, but he dared not spare a hand to wipe it away. Had he gone half the distance? No, he decided desperately, not more than a third at best.

Then he felt his right foot touch the ground, not knowing how or why it had happened. Instantly there was a wild clamor of triumph, and he felt as though a huge rock had descended on his back. A searing pain raced through his whole body. He stumbled in blind agony, and his other foot touched the ground. A second blow caught him on his shoulder, delivered with all the strength of an arm hardened in warfare. The breath seemed knocked out of his body.

Miraculously he found himself back on the rope again, balancing with a dogged care. A half-arrested blow caught him on the arm, and he was sure a bone had been broken.

"Keep to the rule!" he heard Bayan cry.

The momentary recovery of their victim threw the lines into a paroxysm of fury. Shouts, taunts, obscenities filled his ears. The bladders flailed about his head. The pain was getting worse, and he could not straighten his back. He hunched along for a short spell of safe steps.

He touched the ground again, and the blow which descended instantly destroyed his balance. His whole frame was filled with such agony that it seemed that nothing more could matter. Nevertheless the instinct of self-preservation caused him to summon what strength he had left for a spring back to the rope. Another miracle; his feet were back on the waxed surface, his arms had teetered him into a renewal of balance.

Now he could do no more than inch along, his body bent over, his breath coming in strangling coughs, his tortured muscles responding to the urge of his will with increasing slowness.

Half the distance? Perhaps, but certainly not more. He knew he could never make the full Walk.

He was still more sure of this when he saw Ortuh the Stammerer waiting in the line ahead. Ortuh, his throat swathed in a bandage, was holding his spear above his head, his eyes glittering with anticipation. He was literally slavering for the chance to taste his revenge.

The sight of Ortuh had the effect of steadying Walter's lagging efforts. He shoved his feet painfully ahead, balancing drunkenly with arms through which excruciating waves of pain raced. Slowly, still more slowly, he inched past the poised figure of the Stammerer. At last he had left him behind.

Ortuh gave a screech of rage, lifting his spear still higher above his head. Unable to restrain his urge to kill, he brought the weapon down, catching the victim a glancing blow on the back of his head.

Total, welcome oblivion flooded over Walter.

An eternity was passed in unconsciousness, broken by intervals in which he struggled back to a pain-racked awareness of life in his body. These intervals were short and never complete; a few minutes, or perhaps seconds, of terrible pain and strangling moans before his shocked condition asserted its hold again. It was in one of these spells that he fancied he heard voices. One of them, which seemed to be that of the Nestorian priest, was saying: "He is still alive! Mother of Mercy, it does not seem possible!" Another voice spoke, and this time he recognized the tones of Bayan: "How fortunate that Ortuh lost his head and struck while he was still on the rope! That made it proper for me to end it before they could beat him to death." After what seemed hours of agonized stupor, he heard Bayan speak again. "He is strong, this Englishman. Perhaps he will live after all."

5

For what seemed an eternity, Walter existed in a state of semicoma. His body was a torture chamber from which he asked nothing better than to escape, even if death were the price of release. He was vaguely aware that he lay on a low couch, covered by a wolf hide. A yellow-skinned face appeared continually within his restricted area of vision, and it seemed to him that it belonged to a fiend who administered the tortures he was suffering. It was an evil face; mottled and cruel, with sharp and bony features and a high-domed skull. The thin lips were in continuous motion, although Walter's senses were too dulled with pain to catch any sound.

As he emerged from this first phase, he began slowly to grasp the details of his existence. He was lying in a square room with log walls. Little light penetrated, and the air was almost fetid in its heaviness. The owner of the evil face was a shaman, a very old one, who looked after his needs with grudging reluctance. There was also a woman who brought him food and mare's milk to drink, and who slept in a corner of the room. She was plump and not unattractive. It seemed to him that she did more clomping around his couch in her high sheepskin boots than was strictly necessary.

His broken bones began to knit, and in two weeks the worst of the pain had left. It was nearly a month, however, before he could sit up with any comfort. In the meantime he had learned that the caravan had moved and that no effort had been made to pursue the runaways. He could get no satisfaction out of the old man as to the orders which had been left concerning himself.

On one occasion, when the shaman was out, the woman came over and looked down at him. She leaned across and touched his arm.

"White," she whispered. "So white. Unakina never see before."

She seemed fascinated with the color and softness of his skin. Walter had already noticed that she was always about when the old man rubbed his back with ointments.

"What will they do with me?" he asked, using the tongue of the trails.

The woman smiled reassuringly. "Nothing. Lord Bayan left money for care of white man."

Walter was so taken by surprise that he remained silent for several moments. The woman leaned down to whisper, "Lord Bayan said to tell white man he need not fear."

On another occasion he asked her about herself. Was she married? Had she no children?

"No children. Unakina, wife Tului. He, army, fight. Perhaps come back. Perhaps not."

It was clear that Tului had been a man of some consequence. There was a lacquered chest beside the couch, and an unusual assortment of household articles. Most noticeable among these proofs of comparative wealth was a handsome high piece of furniture in one corner, obviously of Chinese make and obviously little regarded. Unakina made no use of it at all, preferring to hang everything she used on wall pegs.

As was usual with Mongolian women, she dressed like a man, with chamois breeches and serviceable boots. Her one concession to femininity was a silk shirt of a glaring red. She plaited hemp as she talked, but the work was accomplished automatically. She always kept her black eyes fixed on her guest.

Once she volunteered a piece of information that was completely personal. "If Tului die, Unakina marry again. Unakina young, perhaps have children then."

"You live here always?" he asked.

"Always here. Tului keep *yamb*." She looked at him archly. "White man like it here?"

As his condition improved, the shaman began to practice a method of cure called *champooing*. It consisted of a violent rubbing of his whole frame and pulling his joints until they cracked. At first Walter protested vigorously. It was Unakina who reassured him. "Champooing good," she said. "We learn from *Domdatu*. Make body strong again. White man must get strong." When the shaman grumbled at the exertion involved, she would continue with the treatment herself. Her hands were stronger than those of the old man and much more gentle. "Soon make white man very strong," she would say, as she labored over him.

It was Unakina's arm which went around his shoulders to guide him in his first efforts to walk. They went as far as the door. It was early morning and, although the threat of intense heat was in the air, there was still a trace of a breeze. Walter filled his lungs greedily, his eyes turning toward the east where the purple lights of sunrise lingered on the slopes of low hills. "Where are Maryam and Tris now?" he asked himself. "They must be well into the Manji country. What a surprised pair they will be when I reach Kinsai after all!"

He had walked this far with full confidence. When the time came to return, however, he found himself unequal to it. The Mongolian woman picked him up in her arms and carried him back to his couch. "White man still need Unakina," she said, bending over him.

"Thanks," he said, in a weak voice. "Unakina very strong."

"Arms strong, yes. But heart," she shook her head, "not strong. Heart, very weak."

He realized that he would have to leave as soon as his condition made it possible. He did not want to find the war finished when he reached the camp of Bayan, but there was an equally pressing reason. He knew the Ulang-Yassa fixed death as the penalty for consummation of the intent he could read in the eyes of his custodian.

Caravans passed through the village at long intervals. At first he knew of their arrival only by the sounds which reached his ears, the strident voices of many men, and the excitement which swept over the small settlement. As he grew stronger, he was able to watch the arrivals and departures from the door of the hut, and each time he longed to be on his way with them. He would have yielded sooner to the impulse if it had not been for curious seizures to which he was subject. These attacks came after a sharp warning in the form of a pain at the base of his spine. For several minutes he would be unable to make a move of any kind, and his mind would go completely blank. In the village they had coined a name for him as a result, Young Man Who Loses Himself.

He realized, however, that he would have to leave in spite of this condition. Unakina's liking for him was being manifested in everything she said and did. The shaman wore a sly smile all the time, and once he asked, "White man taking place Tului?" The chance came when a large caravan reached the village late one evening. It consisted mostly of Chinese silk merchants on their way back from the West, and a few Mongols beyond military age. He was equal to extended walks by this time, so he paid a visit to the head man and arranged to go on with them in the morning. Podarge whinnied a welcome when he went to see her. She was fat and glossy after her long rest in the *yamb*.

The next morning he was up at sunrise. Unakina had left the hut, but she returned before he had finished packing his belongings. She stood and watched him for a moment in silence.

"White man go?" she asked finally.

"Yes, Unakina. Go with caravan." He detached the buckle from his belt which contained a setting of turquoise and opals, and held it out to her. "Unakina very kind. Unakina take present. It's all white man has."

She took the buckle, her sharp black eyes fixed on him in hurt and angry pride. When convinced that his mind was made up, she turned her back on him and threw the present on the ground with a furious movement of her arm.

"Unakina no want present!" she said. "Unakina want white man stay."

He left at once. The sun was rising over the hills in the east. He felt strong and well, so well in fact that the long journey ahead had no terrors for him. As he swung a leg over Podarge's back, he whistled with a deep sense of relief.

CHAPTER IX

The Yang-tse

Bayan of the Hundred Eyes was sitting his black horse on an elevation which afforded a clear view of the great yellow river. Walter could see that his face had lighted up with a triumphant smile.

"What fools the *Domdatu* generals are!" said Bayan to the huddle of horsemen about him. "All that great fleet will soon be destroyed. Then a single army will be all that stands between me and Kinsai! We will scatter it like sand before the wind!"

Walter had missed the succession of land victories which had carried the Mongols down the line of the Han River, as Bayan had planned, and across the Yang-tse, great cities falling to them like ripe grain before a sweeping sickle. Arriving at the headquarters of the young general this morning, however, he had been just in time to see Bayan launch his attack on the Manji fleet.

The great river was so closely packed with Sung ships of war that it now resembled nothing so much as a serpent twisting across the landscape as far as the eye could see. There were war junks, twenty-five hundred of them, the mightiest vessels the East had ever produced; high-pooped and topped with enormous sails of scarlet and yellow, their hulls grotesquely ornamented in blue and green, and with the staring eyes of dragons painted on the prows. After the junks came hundreds of adroit *Hua-ma-Yangs,* white-bellied, with green and white bands, their sails a riot of color; then fast careening *Wa-Changtzus,* speedy *Wupans,* and crooked-hulled craft for the navigation of rapids; and last of all, thousands of smaller boats, sampans, open skiffs, seagoing rafts of bamboo. The river was blotted out for many miles.

It was a truly unique spectacle, a land army engaging ships of war. Walter, full of doubts, asked himself, "Can an elephant destroy a sea serpent?" But it soon became apparent that the effort was not beyond the power of the elephant. The Mongols were swarming up the sides of the first ships in line and taking possession of them with rapid and sanguinary ease. The sea serpent had begun to thresh about, its countless bright scales palpitating as though with terror.

At this critical moment, the Englishman heard a sound like the roar of the sea magnified many times over. He could see clouds of dense smoke rising from both banks of the river. The masts of the junks began to crumple, and flames broke out everywhere, as though the fires of hell were breaking through the surface of the earth to consume the long dragon.

Walter edged his horse up alongside one of the Mongol aides. "What is it?" he asked, in an awed voice.

"*Hua-P'ao,*" answered the aide, flicking foam from his sleeves. He had just arrived and had delivered a message to the general. A wide grin split his battle-eager face. "The new iron tubes which vomit fire. The

Manji make them. We take them and kill the Manji with them!" His grin became even wider. "A Chinese is directing them for us, Chang Jung."

Walter sat in silence, watching the Hua-P'ao demolish the great fleet. Here was the proof before his eyes of what Roger Bacon had surmised. Here in Cathay they had the secret of the mysterious powder which burst into flames; and they were using it, as the farseeing friar had predicted, for the making of war. It was like watching the end of the world. Perhaps, he thought with the habitual twinge of inner fear, this was the beginning of the end. The world could not go on now that this deadly secret had been found out.

After a time, however, Walter's more practical sense asserted itself. He must learn everything he could about the death-dealing Hua-P'ao. "I must draw plans," he said to himself, "so I can take them back with me."

The uneven battle ended soon. Most of the Manji ships were sunk and their crews drowned. A few of the junks managed to get turned and to sail off on the yellow river, away from the booming iron monsters and the deadly hail of arrows from Mongolian crossbows. A few hours of confusion, and the river was clear again, except for broken masts and floating wreckage and the bodies of the slain.

"Englishman!" cried Bayan, catching sight of him. "You arrived in time to see my greatest victory. The Manji back has been broken. Now I shall march on Kinsai." He smiled in easy triumph. "I did not need the magic bow you kept from me."

"My lord Bayan will never need it. What can arrows do against the fire of the Hua-P'ao?"

Bayan motioned him to ride up closer to him. "The Hua-P'ao is still nothing but a toy," he said in a low voice. "Here, against wooden hulls and at close range, it has done what I wanted. What use would it be on a field of battle with clouds of horsemen charging in? The iron tube is slow and hard to handle. Not yet, not yet! A toy, I tell you. Some day, I think, it will win battles easily, but your longbow will conquer Europe before the great Christian leaders have even heard of the Hua-P'ao. You will always be centuries behind us. Perhaps we shall use this powder to blow down the walls of Rome."

Walter was looking at the bivouac fires of the Mongolian armies that evening and thinking how much terror they must be causing in the Manji outposts, when Father Theodore joined him. The Nestorian was in rags, but he seemed to have withstood the rigors of the campaign surprisingly well.

"The men are now fed, and the women prisoners are being distributed," he said. "You will hear much screaming, but do not be concerned, young scholar. Life is dull for women in the East, and this will be a diversion for them." He added, as an afterthought, "Bayan has sent for you."

The general's yurt was much larger than the one he had used on the Asiatic trail. The nine horsetails above it seemed to flutter with augmented arrogance. A knot of men of high rank stood at the entrance, and they moved aside reluctantly to let the two Christians pass.

The interior was brightly lighted, and there were more members of the staff squatting on the floor and talking in loud and exultant voices. The felt images dangling on the flap were newly made to commemorate the victory of the day: a white falcon with outstretched wings, a figure of the Sung boy emperor dangling on a rope, the Yellow Cushion pierced by a Mongolian sword. Old Booghra sat on his master's lap. Bayan himself was in a buoyant mood.

"Englishman!" he called. "Come and sit down. I have much to say." When Walter obeyed, the general leaned toward him and whispered: "I am a proud man at this moment. I have just made a round of the advanced posts. I wore a plain cloak and no one recognized me. They were talking—ah, how my brave fellows talk after a victory!—but I heard no mention of Genghis Khan or even of Sabutai. Tonight they spoke of Bayan, and Bayan only! It made me happier than when I saw the Manji fleet go up in flames today."

"I have heard talk also. Everyone is saying that Bayan of the Hundred Eyes is the greatest leader in war that ever lived."

Bayan gave a gratified nod of his head. "My plans work out perfectly," he said. "Early in the year I shall dictate to the Sungs in the royal palace in Kinsai. Envoys have already arrived to ask terms of peace. It is clear they have no idea yet of the ease with which I can complete the conquest. They offer two hundred and fifty taels of silver and the same number of bolts of silk! They say the new emperor is a boy and cannot be blamed for what his ministers have done. The ministers at fault will be punished by death. Ha, they are still existing in a bright mist! I, Bayan, standing in the stead of the Son of Heaven, shall do all the punishing." He added in a more restrained tone: "I insist on unconditional surrender. It is the only way."

He continued in a still lower tone. "I can now make good use of you,

Englishman. The Manji are so thoroughly beaten that it is useless for them to fight on. It will add to my reputation if I have to break through to Kinsai, but I prefer it the other way. I have no heart for mass slaughter, and I would then have to deliver that great city over to the sword. My men would demand it as their right." He paused. "It is only the blindness and stubborn pride of the Emperor's ministers which keeps them from surrendering now. Chang Wu, their head envoy, has told me in great confidence that the Manji country longs for peace. He himself sees the folly of further resistance and the fate ahead of Kinsai if the war goes on. He tells me the peace party includes all the great men of the state and all the merchants.

"I want you to go with Chang Wu," went on Bayan. "You will go to Kinsai in the guise of a scholar from the West in search of knowledge of Chinese ways. When you get to Kinsai, keep your eyes and ears open and, if possible, get reports back to me. I want you to act with Chang Wu in bringing the peace movement to a head. They may listen to you when you tell them how powerful my armies are and what a terrible vengeance I must exact if they fight on to the end. I am convinced, Englishman, that very little now is needed to bring resistance to a head against the blind will of the ministers of the state."

Bayan shifted in his seat and faced the Englishman squarely. "You must think it strange that I suggest this in view of what happened back on the trail. I, and I alone, knew what you had done. I succeeded in getting the caravan back to the course without anyone suspecting we had wandered so far from it. I—I am a proud man. I value the reputation I have with my soldiers. Would they have continued to call me Bayan of the Hundred Eyes if they knew I had failed to see we were striking toward the north instead of due east? I covered up my own carelessness, and in doing so I had to keep your great offense a secret. It is over and done with now, Englishman. I have won my great victory, and I am willing to forget the past. I trust you in spite of everything. Perhaps now you will be willing to risk your life for me."

"I owe my life to you. I am glad to pledge it in your service."

"I need not tell you there will be danger in this mission. If the Manji ministers suspect the truth, they will cut off your head. They might even contrive a much more painful death for you."

"I am prepared to face that possibility."

"Good!" Bayan smiled. "I was sure of you, Englishman, and it is gratifying to have my estimate confirmed. And now I must give you fuller instructions. We must plan every step you are to take when you get to Kinsai. I am deeply concerned over the need for an early peace. That great city must be saved if at all possible. First you must travel in state so they will believe you a foreign prince of some consequence. I shall have a cloak for you of ermine and black moleskin, and a gold chain to wear around your neck. This priest will go along with you. If you return, your reward will be large."

"I am not concerned with the reward, my lord Bayan. All I ask is a chance to redeem myself in your eyes."

"I believe you, my friend. Perhaps the danger will not be as great as I have made it out. They will be more careful, since they have seen how hard and fast I can strike."

"There is a letter I am obligated to deliver to a merchant in Khan Bhalig," said Walter. "Anthemus entrusted it to me when we parted at Maragha. It deals, I believe, with matters of trade."

"The letter will be delivered by one of my messengers to the Son of Heaven."

"Then," exclaimed Walter, "I am willing to go on to Kinsai. I will go under any conditions you make. I am willing to go, if necessary, just as I am." He looked down at himself and smiled. "And, as you see, I am in rags."

2

Chang Wu was so very small that he looked like a perfectly molded miniature of a man. His beard hung in straight wisps from a minutely pointed chin, and his eyes twinkled behind brows of snowy white. He became so well disposed toward the Englishman that he made every effort to satisfy the latter's curiosity about the country through which they progressed, even when it entailed slight delays.

It was a priest who directed them to the yard with tanbark walls where paper was made. Drawing one of the daggers at his belt (they seemed always to be worn in pairs and were called male and female), the priest pointed through a break in the line of the Swine-back Mountains. It meant a jaunt from the straight route, but Chang Wu nodded and ordered the outriders to proceed in that direction.

The party rode up to the yard with so much shouting and jingling of gear and so much tooting of war horns by the heralds in the van that rows of frightened yellow faces appeared over the top of the tanbark, followed by a hasty scurry to whatever shelter the place afforded. The yard itself was a great disappointment to Walter. He had not known what to expect, but certainly he had been prepared to find the miracle of papermaking brought about with more difficulty and mystery. Entering with Chang Wu, he found that work had been resumed and that twoscore or more of workmen were squatting on the hard clay in the pursuit of the most prosaic of tasks. A row of them were beating fiber of various sorts, the inner bark of the mulberry being in most general use. They were using mortar and pestle, their sinewy arms rising and falling in tireless unison. In the center was a huge vat filled with water. When the fiber had been beaten out to a thin pulp, it was thrown into the vat. Along the far wall was a row of molds, consisting of squares of woven horsehair cloth, held in bamboo frames. The pulp, when removed from the vat, was spread out on the molds to dry.

"Is this all?" asked Walter. They conversed in *Bi-chi,* which all Chinese of official rank seemed to understand.

The envoy smiled and spoke to the man in charge. The latter spat out a stream of arica juice before walking over to one of the frames. With a deft twist he stripped off a sheet of the dried pulp and held it up for their inspection. It was white, wafer-thin, and with a firm smooth surface. Chang Wu took it, felt it critically between thumb and finger, and then handed it to Walter.

"The finest of paper," he said. "Does my young friend desire to test it?"

Walter's amazement at the simplicity of the process was giving way to consideration of how the secret could be used. It was certain that paper could be made in this way in England as readily as in China. Already improvements in method were suggesting themselves to him.

"Does it occur to Chang Wu that much of this hand labor is unnecessary?" he asked. "The fiber could be fed through wheels like grain in a mill and thus ground to a pulp. Think of the time which could be saved in that way."

"Time is of little importance in China," said the old man. "There is no end to the hours, and no shortage of busy hands to wield the pestles. Would the quality of the paper be improved by the method my young friend proposes?"

"Of course!" cried Walter. "The pulp would be rolled out more firmly. It could be fed into the water as it issued from the wheels."

The old man smiled. "You spoke then in much the tone that Bayan uses."

Walter began to examine everything with an aroused eye. He studied the quality of the mulberry fiber and the fragments of linen with which it was mixed to achieve more body, the temperature of the water in the vat, the construction of the bamboo frames.

"Certes it is all very simple and clear," he said to himself.

He still marveled at the sheer simplicity of the process, but he was beginning to see that this might have been anticipated. Miracles were never complicated; and this, he knew, was a very great miracle. As he felt of the weaving of the molds, he was thinking what it would mean if this substance called paper were introduced into England: how all men in time would learn to read, and messages writ in honest black and white would travel all over the land to the greater glory of God and the betterment of mortal minds and bodies as well. The yard ceased to be a small enclosure of hard-baked clay. The tanbark walls seemed to vanish, and shining horizons surrounded him on all sides.

He came back to Chang Wu, his eyes glowing, and said: "I think I understand how it is done. When I return to my home, I am going to make paper. If you will allow me a little more time and lend me your kind offices with this fellow, there are more questions I must ask him."

As they started back toward the main road, they passed a workman wheeling a barrow by the side of the road. He was naked to the waist and had hoisted a sail on the front. Both man and barrow were skimming over the road with remarkable celerity.

"Who is he?" asked Walter.

"A peasant. He owns a small bit of land hereabouts, no doubt."

"He owns land?" cried Walter. This was something completely new. The manipulator of the barrow was a fellow of the lowest degree. Under what strange social system could he be permitted to hold land in his own name?

Chang Wu reined in his horse and asked the man some questions. "His holding is half a mow," he reported to Walter. This was the equivalent of half an acre. "His father owned it before him, and *his* father before that. He has four sons, and it may be necessary to divide the land after he dies. It is hard work, but all his sons and their wives make a living from the land now."

"In my country," declared Walter, "all the land is held by the nobles. Much of it is under wood, and common men are barred by the law from disturbing the game. Small holdings are allotted to the common men, the villeins, but they must give much of what they raise to the lords and the clergy, and their time is never their own."

"China has been a great country since the beginning of history," said

Chang Wu. "We have learned many things through the long centuries—
one thing above all else: that the land belongs to everyone and not to the
few. Some men become rich while most remain poor; but the land must
be so used that there will be food for every belly. If we followed your
way, young traveler, the people would starve."

This was a matter for much thought—disturbing thought. What
Walter had been told did not fit with any of the beliefs in which he
had been raised. The ownership of land, he said to himself, was a
privilege of the ruling class. It had always been that way, and it must be
right because it was the law and it had the sanction of Holy Church. His
own place in life would depend on his ability to acquire land and the
name that would go with it, but this was in accordance with the accepted order; he had been born into the nobility, and it was his right.

"If all men shared the land in my country," he declared, "we would
cease to have an orderly way of life. Men of mean degree would no
longer be subject to the call of their lords. How then could armed forces
be raised for war? How could law and justice be maintained?"

"Perhaps," said the little envoy, "you would have fewer wars if the
men could not be raised to fight them. Do you have equitable laws now,
and is your justice fair for all men? Are all men well fed in this land of
yours?"

"There is much want in England," conceded Walter. "There are
seasons of plenty, and then there are times when the harvests are poor.
It has always been that way."

"When the harvests are poor, do the nobles lack food?"

"The nobles never lack food." Walter paused, seeking the words to
make his companion see that this was right and proper after all. "The
land is theirs! Why should they suffer when food is scarce?"

He realized, nevertheless, that strange thoughts were creeping into his
mind. Because it had always been that way, did it follow that it was
right? Should not all men have a share of the land, in spite of the in-
equalities of birth and rank? Should a few men live in castles and all
the rest in wattled huts or in the squalor of spital houses and the cheap-
ing places of crowded cities?

"If I could accept as right and fair this way you have of using the
land," he said finally, "then I would have to discard everything I have
believed, except my faith in the one God. It would mean that our whole
way of living is wrong, that knighthood is a false conception and chivalry no better than a sham."

Chang Wu smiled. "Take it not so much to heart. We are not so very different from you, after all. All men are not equal in China. We have our nobles and our villeins also. And we have laws that are as unjust as those in your distant land."

But the disturbing thought planted in Walter's mind persisted. He turned it over continuously as he rode his fine steed behind the arrogant heralds all the way to Kinsai.

CHAPTER X

Kinsai

IT WAS MIDDAY when they had their first glimpse of Kinsai. In the hot blaze of the sun it stretched in languid beauty across the horizon like a red-and-green velvet carpet. Chang Wu reined in and regarded the high walls and peaked towers ahead of them with an air of sudden gravity.

"The greatest city in the world, honorable scholar," he said, sighing deeply. "There it lies, peaceful and happy and filled with its centuries of knowledge. What is to be its fate? Can it now gird itself in silver armor like the Queen with the Dragon Heart and conquer those who come against it? Or must it wait like a lovely but indolent courtesan for the embrace of the crude ravisher from the north?"

To Walter the Celestial City was a symbol of hope. He was in a state of high anticipation, confident that somewhere in this vast maze of palaces and hovels he would find Maryam and Tristram. If they were already waiting for him, they could be traced through the merchant to whom Anthemus had addressed his letter.

"Illustrious Chang Wu," he said, "I have been wondering if you know ought of a trader of Kinsai whose name is Sung Yung and who is sometimes called 'Fire from Black Clouds'?"

The tiny features of the envoy puckered into an expression of the greatest contempt.

"Sung Yung!" He spat the name rather than spoke it. "Yes, lord from the West, I know much of this 'Fire from Black Clouds.' He is a wolf who devours the bodies of those of his own pack who fall in the chase. You also will hear much of Sung Yung while you are in Kinsai, for he has become the heart and soul of the war party."

"I was not prepared to find him so prominent a figure. A merchant of Antioch named Anthemus directed me to him."

"I know much of Anthemus also. Those two, they are like molting feathers plucked from the cussom of a cormorant."

"I carried a letter for Sung Yung. Many months ago, when it seemed very improbable that I would ever reach Kinsai, I entrusted it to a friend who was to follow the silk trails here. It has probably been delivered by this time, and so I have no need to see the merchant, save to find my friend."

"Inquiries can be made for your friend," declared Chang Wu. "It will be highly unwise for you to make your presence known to Sung Yung, who is too shrewd not to guess your purpose in coming with me. It has been in my mind that it will be safer for you to enter the city quietly. Your mission has more chance for success if pursued at first in the greatest secrecy."

A party of refugees blocked the road immediately ahead. While the heralds piped on their shrill horns to open a path, the two men walked their horses. Chang Wu studied the plodding people closely and clucked with dismay when he read the character marks on their soiled tunics.

"These are all of the Kung family," he said, shaking his head forebodingly. "That means they have come far. Many weary weeks lie between them and their own villages. As the Mongols advance, the country empties before them as the beaches clear before the incoming tide. Why must they all come to Kinsai, the one target of our enemies? Truly, young scholar, there is no single shred of intelligence in panic. We shall have them on our hands by the millions."

For many days now the roads they followed had been cumbered by the fleeing multitudes. They were for the most part a patient and spiritless lot, yellow gnomes trudging humbly with great bundles on their backs. The more prosperous drove farm carts piled high with household goods from the midst of which the solemn eyes of small children peered out. There was a lack of vigor about all of them which told of hunger as well as weariness. They seldom looked up, even at the passing of so imposing a cavalcade; and when they did, it was with complete apathy.

"War," said the envoy, when they had passed through the group, "ruins the many, but it enriches the pockets of a few like Sung Yung. From a dealer in silks he has become in three years the richest man in Kinsai. Perhaps it does not matter so much that the shoes he supplied the government for our soldiers fell to pieces after the first rains. We were doomed to lose all our battles, with or without shoes on our soldiers' feet. Army contractors have always been dishonest, and it may be that Sung Yung is no worse than the rest. What I bear against him in bitterness of heart is that he persuaded the imperial ministers to pay the soldiers with paper money."

"Money made of paper! How can such a thing be? There is no great value in paper."

"None," said the envoy. "We have issued paper money several times in the last few centuries, but always in the belief that there was enough silver coinage to redeem it. It has never failed to ruin trade for long, black periods. We call it Flying Money. But Sung Yung's plan had no excuse at all except the foolish belief that we could fight this very inconvenient war at small cost by issuing all the paper money needed. The soldiers have scattered it over the country." He sighed and shook his head. "Does my young friend see what this has led us into?"

"I have no knowledge of such matters," answered Walter.

"All good money has vanished from sight. Men hide their strings of silver in hayricks and in holes in the ground. Having so much paper and knowing it worthless, they refuse to pay with anything else. In self-defense sellers have been putting prices higher and still higher. Each day one carries larger bundles of Flying Money to pay for the little daily needs." He reached into a pocket and brought out a handful of paper squares of red and brown. "See, these are notes of very high value. Once I could have bought a live pig with one of these notes. When I left Kinsai, it was necessary to pay all of this for a plate of soup with a few shreds of pork floating on the top. That was months ago. How much worse has it become? By the Little Devil God, I dread what we shall find when we reach the city!"

They were passing a spot where some refugees had halted to dig a shallow grave by the side of the road. The men picked wearily and in silence at the hard-baked clay, but the women had covered their heads and were wailing in shrill anguish. It was a common sight; they had seen the same thing many times each day of their journey.

"Half of them will die before they reach Kinsai," said Chang Wu. "It is of no consequence. There will be no food for them when they get there. It would be wise to close the gates on them and save ourselves the plague they carry with them."

Dusk had fallen when they rode through the Gate of Invincible Strength into the wide, brick-paved streets of the great Manji city. Expecting to find traces inside of the panic which was sweeping the countryside, Walter looked about him with amazement. This was the marketing hour, it seemed, and a hum of chaffering rose on all sides. Men walked about with bundles of what he assumed to be paper money under their arms. Some held up rice stalks to indicate that the goods in their baskets were for sale. Idol-players had lighted their torches and the thump of the marionettes' feet competed with the dancing figures of the shadow shows. Lengthy closed carriages filled the graveled space in the center of the paving, gay lanterns bobbing on their shafts. Faces wore a casual and careless air.

"Don't they realize their danger?" asked Walter.

Chang Wu did not answer. With his thin neck bent to one side, he was watching the houses they passed with the most absorbed interest. It seemed to Walter that he was counting.

"The Household Gods have bestirred themselves in our behalf," said the envoy finally. "The signs were even when I left. Now they are five to one. We are not too late, young scholar."

At a loss to understand his meaning, Walter made no answer. The envoy pointed a triumphant finger at the door of a large dwelling. "Look close," he admonished. "What do the eyes of my worthy companion see?"

"There is a dagger planted beside the door," said Walter, after a moment's scrutiny.

'That means the owner wants the war to go on. Now observe, if you will deign to do so, the house next to it. What do you see?"

"A branch nailed to the door. I think it is willow."

"The sign of a desire for peace. I have been watching and counting. I have seen five willow boughs for one dagger. Excellent Western lord, the city wants peace!"

"But can public opinion prevail against the will of men like Sung Yung?"

"It will be our duty," said the envoy solemnly, "to see that the voice of the city reaches the ears of those who control the fate of my unhappy country. My spirits have risen mightily, my young friend. Now it may be possible to make them see that the dragon with the hundred eyes cannot be beaten." A tradesman on foot stopped Father Theodore and waved a comfit box at him, then tooted a horn to attract their attention. One of their outriders kicked him away. "We are believers in proverbs, even to the extent of basing national decisions on them. There is one very old saying which the peace party has spoken often in the ears of the Imperial Munificence, 'The Sung throne will fall when attacked by a dragon with a hundred eyes.' The mother of the Emperor has been for making peace ever since she heard that your Bayan is said to have a hundred eyes. I, Chang Wu, humble servant of our boy Emperor of Fu ture Magnificence, am not given to such beliefs, but I am more than content to make use of the old prophecy. Now, perhaps, we shall convince them."

They saw a band of soldiers crossing one of the immensely long market squares and stopped to watch. A three-tiered umbrella was carried over the head of the leader, and he had a sword with three points and steel links which rattled ferociously as he walked. The men had the heads of fire-spitting demons painted on the shields which they wore front and back, and there were links on the tips of their spears. A herald brought up the rear, pounding on a painted drum and reciting in a loud voice the great feats to be accomplished by the Ever Irresistible Company. Walter gave a thought to the grim fate such troops would meet when the Mongolian horsemen swept down on them.

Something of the same kind must have been running through the mind of Chang Wu, for he sighed and said, "A people trained to live well cannot be expected to fight well."

As they rode on, the envoy asked: "Have you seen the lists on the doors? It is the law that all who live in a house must be written there. It is a very quick method of tracing malefactors." He paused and gave an embarrassed snicker. "In the Street of Delightful Flowers there is one house which, it so happens, belongs to me. It is called the Abode of the Twelve Fuchsia Blossoms, and it is very exclusive. There are rooms at the top of the house which are never used. If my young companion would condescend to spend a short time in such unconventional surroundings, it would not be necessary to have his name on the door."

Walter smiled. "I place myself in the hands of the wise and farseeing Chang Wu."

"It would be the way of wisdom to repair there at once." The little man seemed much relieved at this easy solution of a difficult problem. "The Abode of the Twelve Fuchsia Blossoms is most quiet and orderly. There will be nothing to disturb the young scholar."

They stopped in front of tall gates, of intricately contrived copper, opening on a short street which was brilliantly lighted. A dozen or more houses made up the single enclosed block, and the space between them vibrated with activity. There were empty chairs and litters on the paving, and scores of servants who were filling in the time of waiting for their masters by frisking about and playing games of chance. A guard with drawn sword stood in front of the gates, and more guards were distributed along the entrances of the more imposing of the houses.

"Men must have their horizontal pleasures," said Chang Wu, leading the way through the gates. "Great establishments such as these are very profitable."

It seemed to Walter that all the houses had a withdrawn look in spite of the noise and confusion on the outside. Lights showed through some of the windows, and yet the effect was the same as though all were tightly shuttered. A suggestion of sly seclusion emanated from the tall fronts. The moon had come up and was peeping over the triple roofs of the houses.

Chang Wu paused in front of the Abode of the Twelve Fuchsia Blossoms. "The ladies within are selected with the utmost care," he said, in a tone of some pride. "Not alone for their beauty, my young friend; they must be able to converse with intelligence, to play on many musical instruments, to dance gracefully. The entertainment they provide is not limited to the obvious. Most of them are trained for years before they are permitted to appear before the patrons. Some even are admitted when they are children so their training can be completed before they have lost the first dewiness of youth."

They were admitted to an interior of quiet beauty, where the lights were pleasantly dim and no sound was to be heard save that of subdued conversation, lightened by an occasional burst of feminine laughter. A painted woman with a bundle of artificial flowers riding on her hips, which gave her more than a passing resemblance to a scarlet hen, minced up to them on delicate feet. There was nothing mincing or delicate about the tone she used in speaking to the envoy, however. The glances she cast in Walter's direction were distinctly hostile.

"I am being reminded that they are most careful," said Chang Wu, in an apologetic aside. "She says no foreigners are ever permitted as guests. It was in her mind that men of pale skin have an odor like an old sheep which has died in lambing, and she was not prepared to submit her ladies to such an ordeal. I have explained the purpose we have in coming here, and she has agreed."

A door at their right opened into a room where five men were seated about a table, engaged in some form of game while two of the Blossoms sat demurely on the floor beside them. One of the girls was strumming softly on a stringed instrument which resembled the zither. The other was embroidering, being careful in a thoroughly ladylike way to keep her needle pointed in the direction of the moon. Both girls were small and pretty, with delicately painted cheeks and black hair piled high on their heads.

The five men held brightly colored disks in their hands, and there was a pile of the same on the table into which they dipped in turn. All of them were too absorbed in the game to pay any attention to the visitors.

"The disks are made of paper," explained Chang Wu. "It is a recent game; in fact it was invented not more than three hundred years ago. It is called *che-tsin,* and there are thirty-two of the papers. All of the disks are named, starting with kings and knaves."

The woman began to lead the way toward the stairs. Chang Wu whispered in Walter's ear, "She is called Provider of Ripe Plums, and it will be wise to treat her carefully, for she is of an uneven temper."

On the floor above they caught a glimpse through an open door of a maid bathing her mistress. The plump round limbs rising from the tub were of a warm brown color, and the girl's huge black eyes were set in a slightly negroid face. She glanced around at them, smiled, and said something in a throaty voice.

"A sly puss, that one," cackled Chang Wu. "She would be more in place farther down the street where standards are somewhat less strict. Unfortunately she must be kept, for she finds much favor with the patrons."

They reached, after much climbing, a huge room lighted by a cresset in a bronze vase. It contained nothing but a low platform covered by a mattress and silk sheets and a peacock screen of five panels. Chang Wu gave the woman a monotone of orders and shortly thereafter two maids appeared, carrying a small tub between them filled with water.

"A bath first," said the envoy, "and then more suitable and less conspicuous clothes will be provided. Your Mongolian finery must now be discarded. After that a simple repast will be served which I humbly beg leave to share."

There had been no chance to bathe for many days, and Walter stepped behind the screen with the greatest alacrity. To his amazement one of the maids followed him and began with nimble fingers to unbuckle his belt and remove the moleskin cloak. The other girl joined her and busied herself also with the disrobing. Walter clutched the top of his under-tunic and called to his host, "It is our custom, honorable Chang Wu, to undress without assistance."

Chang Wu chuckled. "Presence of young maids need not disturb. It is the custom. Their fingers are skillful and their eyes see nothing."

Their fingers unquestionably were skillful, but the latter part of the promise was not borne out. One of the girls gasped when the scars on his back became visible and said something in a shocked whisper. The other, who was untying his shoes, looked up and touched the white

skin above his inside belt with a tickling motion, giving vent to a barely
perceptible giggle. Red with embarrassment, Walter stepped out of his
leggings and plunged into the small tiled tub with such frantic haste
that the water splashed out over the top on all sides. He expected now
that he would enjoy his bath in solitude, but such, it appeared, was not
the custom. Each of the maids picked up soap and brush and proceeded
with the scrubbing of his back and arms.

"Well," he said to himself, "I might as well reconcile myself to it. The
worst, at any rate, is over."

But when the time came to dress, he realized that the worst was not
over at all. His plan to dry himself quickly and spring immediately into
the new silk leggings hanging over the top of the screen was forestalled
by the firmness of the maids. They engulfed him in towels and proceeded to do the drying themselves. Then one of them held out the
leggings for him to step into. His embarrassment was intense until he
was fully clothed in the most lustrous and softest of silks and his feet
had been fitted into comfortably padded shoes. Then one of them took
a robe and draped it over his shoulders.

"The Robe of the Temple Bells," said Chang Wu. "To wear it is a
very high honor."

It was a handsome coat of plum-colored brocade that reached below
his knees. The maze of embroidery which covered it had been worked in
gold thread and blue satin, with temple bells as the main design and bats
on the wing for good fortune. The same design was stitched on the
edges of the white horse-hoof cuffs.

"I am unworthy of such distinguished clothes," said Walter, emerging
from behind the screen. He was more comfortable than he had ever been
in his life. The feel of the fine silk on his skin was a new and pleasant
sensation.

The food which was now brought in on a seemingly endless succession of trays was served on a table not higher than eighteen inches from
the floor. The dishes were carried by the two maids, who giggled continually (he was sure their mirth was due to his antics behind the
screen), but the serving was attended to by the manservant.

"I apologize most humbly for the plainness of the food," said the old
envoy. "There has not been time to provide a suitable meal for so welcome a guest."

There was no reason for apology, however. There was a clear soup
with fat stalks of greenish-white vegetables floating in it, a tureen of al-
mond-salt-pea soup rich with shreds of chicken, the breasts of ducks

roasted to a delicious crispness and cut into thin strips on mounds of
snow-white rice of an incredible fluffiness, shrimps floating in a dark
brown sauce of a sharpness to pucker the tongue, transparent bean curd,
cakes stuffed with sausage meat, fried chestnuts, rich dumplings of millet, pork covered with slices of preserved ginger, and finally a most noble
dish which the host called the *She Meal* and which consisted of a brown
rice filled with all manner of meat and vegetables, spiced to the very
quintessence of vivacity.

As each dish had to be tasted and commented on at some length,
the meal lasted for an hour and a half. They had been served a number
of wines in tiny gold cups. Walter recognized persimmon and date, but
he had never tasted one variety which came with their honey pastry and
sugared lily roots at the end of the meal. It was called *shao chin,* which
meant burning wine. Chang Wu explained that it was made from millet
with a heavy spirituous base. It earned its name by burning the throat of
the guest most thoroughly.

As soon as Father Theodore, who was to be accommodated elsewhere
in the house, had risen and taken his departure, Walter told his host
about Maryam and Tristram and explained the circumstances which
had led to the separation. At mention of the name of Lu Chung, the envoy showed an active interest.

"That great rascal, that fat and oily leech, that base seller of secrets!"
he exclaimed. "The activities of the Bird Who Feathers His Nest in
helping the enemy are well known. A special search will be started at
once. If he is in Kinsai, we shall soon have his obscene carcass in our
hands. Perhaps through him we can learn of the whereabouts of your
friends."

"The search will begin tonight?" asked Walter, well aware that procrastination was the bailiff of justice in the East.

Chang Wu wiped his hands carefully on a strip of fine linen and gave
a reassuring smile. "Tonight. The magistrates will all be informed, and
each district will be gone over. Discreet inquiries will also be made at
Sung Yung's—of certain persons in his employment."

The envoy rose to go. He bowed three times with great ceremony. At
the door he turned to ask if Walter desired the company of one of the
ladies below. "Young scholar need not be concerned about what the
Provider of Ripe Plums said," he added. "It must be considered that it is
their trade. Young scholar has no such desire? Perhaps later, then, when
the fatigues of our long journey have yielded to ease and bodily comfort."

From the next room, Walter could hear the Nestorian priest saying his first prayer of *d'Ramsha,* the evening. Since reaching the Manji country a change had come over Father Theodore. The tendency to pry into everything, the sly interest he had taken heretofore in all fleshly matters, had vanished. He had seemed rather appalled at the surroundings in which they found themselves and had partaken sparingly of supper, not touching the wine at all. Perhaps this sudden change could be attributed to the fact that they had reached the land where his mission was to begin.

2

There was no procrastination about starting on the mission which had brought Walter to Kinsai. Chang Wu arrived the next morning and reported that many meetings had been arranged with men of substance in the city. They were to set out at once.

"Nothing has been learned from the servants of Sung Yung," added the envoy. "It seems improbable that your two friends are here, though the search will be continued with great zeal and perseverance. In this gloom of uncertainty, there is one ray of hope. It has been learned that Lu Chung is in Kinsai. The fingers of justice will soon close on his great body of pestilential corruption. Then he will talk. Ah, how quickly and eagerly he will talk! Young scholar will then know about his friends."

Walter knew that Lu Chung was the key to the situation, and he felt certain that the presence of the Bird Who Feathers His Nest in Kinsai meant that Maryam and Tristram were in the city too. He became so convinced of this that he set out with a lighter heart.

Their first visit took them into a strange new world beneath the surface of the city. It was reached by a narrow stairway of iron steps leading down from the rear of a curio shop (which Chang Wu modestly admitted belonged to him) and which proved so long that the Englishman thought they would never reach the bottom. Finally they emerged into a corridor as wide almost as a city street. Although fans could be heard operating above them, the air was damp and fetid.

Chang Wu nodded his head pridefully. "This is like a second city," he said, his voice echoing with a hollow sound in the cavernous corridor. "Nothing in the world can be compared with it. There are theaters here and gaming houses and eating places. In some of them this unworthy one has a—a small but profitable interest. There are, of course, houses of joy too, though none of them can be compared with the Street of Delightful Flowers. Many hundred men are needed to pull these fans. They are slaves, and some of them never see the light of day. At night this city under the ground comes to life, and then, young scholar, it is indeed a strange spectacle. The corridors are as full as the streets above in daylight. But," with an admonitory shake of the head, "it would not be safe for a foreigner to venture down here without suitable escort."

They turned through a dark doorway and found themselves in a warm and well-lighted series of rooms which reflected ease and luxury. In one a group of men were seated about a circular table. The walls here, a vivid red in hue, were festooned with willow boughs.

The men about the table were elderly without a single exception and handsomely robed in quilted jackets embroidered with stars and belted with sealskin, which suggested some community of interest. Only one of them departed from this uniformity of attire, and he wore the yellow robe of a Taoist priest. His wrinkled scalp boasted no solitary wisp of hair, and his face was the tomblike black of extreme age. His exorcist wheel was on the floor beside his chair.

They were eating with open but decorous satisfaction. In the center of the table was a huge platter of rice, and arranged about it were consort dishes with a variety of rich foods. There were chickens, boned and boiled whole, francolins roasted until their skin crackled brownly, claws of lobsters swimming in a thick yellow sauce. One plate contained pears of an enormous size and of a curiously pulpy whiteness of flesh. What interested Walter more than anything else on the table was a liquid they supped with each mouthful. It was served in small cups and was of a fragrant dark brown. This was called by a name which sounded to him like *chaw*.* He noticed that the Taoist priest was confining himself, perhaps because of his extreme age, to a weak congee of rice.

The meal proceeded without interruption. Chairs were brought for the visitors, and Chang Wu then asked Walter to tell the company what he knew of the state of affairs at the war front. This he did, speaking slowly so that Father Theodore, with the assistance of the envoy himself, could relay the information to the solemnly nodding group. He told of the size of the Mongolian armies and their irresistible striking power, of the forces converging from the south in a development of the *tulughma,* of the deadly use the invaders made of the fire-belching *Hua-P'ao's*. He then went on to tell of the devastation which had already overtaken many of the captured cities and made it clear that Kinsai

---

*Tea, which was not to be introduced into Europe for many centuries.

would suffer the same fate if the futile opposition were continued. "Kinsai is the greatest city in the world," he said, earnestly. "It is doomed to fall into their hands; but must this flower of your advanced civilization be wiped out because a few old men at the head of your government are too stubborn and too desirous of holding on to their own authority?"

The ancient men about the table continued to eat as he talked, but it was clear their zest had left them. They asked many questions, which he answered with more complete details. One of them had a pile of paper money beside him, most of it in the red shade reserved for high denominations. When the name of Sung Yung was mentioned, he clawed at the paper with angry hands and proceeded to tear it into small bits.

The Taoist priest raised his palsied head and asked a question in *Bi-chi*.

"Where you from?"

"I come from a distant land called England. It is an island off the western coast of Europe."

It was apparent from the shake of the priest's head that he had never heard of either.

"Young visitor has hair of gold. Does he travel alone?"

"I am accompanied by this priest only."

The Taoist seemed disappointed. He squinted at Walter closely and then asked, "What happens to city if gates are opened to hated *Tsa-ta-tse?*"

"It has been promised by Bayan, who never speaks with a double tongue, that Kinsai will not be disturbed. Even Bayan will not attempt to enter. The lives of everyone will be spared, except a few of the ministers who have been responsible for killing Mongolian envoys. And," with a pause for emphasis, "all property rights will be fully respected. The life of Kinsai will continue to go on as at present except that the government will be taken over by the Mongolians. That will be done in any event."

This completed his share in the deliberations, although for the better part of an hour the solemn group talked with Chang Wu. The tone of the conversation was sometimes voluble and angry, but in the main he could read resignation and an acceptance of the inevitable in their voices. Chang Wu then rose and said, "Come, we have many more to see today."

All the visits they paid during the remaining hours were in quarters beneath the city. Everywhere they went Walter saw paper money lying about in large and neglected piles as though not worth the trouble of claiming it and carrying it away.

As the hours waned on toward the evening they found their listeners engaged in games of *che-tsin* or playing with dice and ivory disks on boards marked into red-and-black strips. In no case was the talk permitted to interfere with the play. Twice they talked to single individuals, and in both cases it was clear they were men of considerable consequence. They were found in secluded rooms behind doors with iron bars and heavy locks, and they spoke to Chang Wu in low and guarded tones.

After many hours of this, the diminutive envoy said to Walter in a satisfied voice: "It is well, young scholar. What we have said has made a deep impression. Soon all the important men of the city will be leagued against the bitter will to fight of the Emperor's ministers."

Walter laid an insistent hand on the old man's sleeve. "Estimable Chang Wu," he urged, "you will see that every effort is made to find my friends? I am filled with so much fear for them that it is hard to keep my mind on the work we have to do."

"Dismiss all such fears. Soon the nefarious Lu Chung will be in our hands. In a few days, perhaps even a few hours."

When Walter and the tired Father Theodore reached the Street of Delightful Flowers, dusk had wrapped the city in a mantle of stately quiet, but by way of contrast a loud din reached them from the house directly opposite the Abode of the Twelve Fuchsia Blossoms.

The priest sighed and said: "I have been asking questions about this district of opulent vice. That one is called the House of Rowdy Mirth. It is a place of the utmost iniquity."

The door across the way was wide open, and men were passing in and out freely. In response to the Englishman's suggestion that they go over and see what was causing the noise, Father Theodore shook his head. The Nestorian day, he said, began with the sunset, and there were many prayers to be repeated. Walter decided accordingly to visit it by himself. What he witnessed was neither inspiring nor profitable except that he saw the most telling evidence yet of the low esteem to which Flying Money had fallen.

A huge fellow was standing at the entrance and seemed to have charge of this least delightful of the houses. He had wild black hair, and there was an upward twist to his eyebrows which gave his blue tattooed face an appearance of complete disorder. He caught Walter by the elbow.

"Tall stranger come from foreign land?" he asked in *Bi-chi*. "He want lady? Perhaps he want lady who tosses heels and has many tricks?"

The Englishman brushed past him and found himself in a long room with air like indigo from burning incense. Girls were sitting on couches in such complete undress that he gave them a hurried collective look and then turned away. One with particularly dark skin was dancing in the middle of the floor and employing every muscle of her body with a grinning energy. The place was crowded with patrons, most of whom were drunk, and the noise was deafening.

The noise grew even greater when a slender girl walked into the room with no more in the way of clothing than a band of silk around her hips. She was carrying a tray filled with a thick substance like paste. The patrons crowded around her, dipping pieces of paper money, all of the highest red denomination, in the stuff. Then a huge and grotesquely fat black woman appeared through a door at the rear. She wore nothing at all, but on her head she balanced a red cylinder as large around as a man's arm and with a wick at the top. Around this large cylinder was a row of smaller ones. She was incredibly ugly.

The woman began to waddle about the room in what was intended as a dance and, as she passed, each patron reached out exuberantly and attached the paper in his hand with a loud slap on the nearest portion of her exposed skin. The paper stuck to her, and in no time at all she was crisscrossed from neck to toes with Flying Money. The fun became fast and furious, the patrons scrambling for more paste and tussling for chances to apply it.

The man in charge appeared again at Walter's elbow. "Perhaps stranger like nice, gentle lady," he insinuated. "None here. But can send out and get." Walter's glance happened to rest on the slender girl with the tray. The proprietor shook his head. "Not that one. That one, mine. That one not lady anyway."

The fat woman chose this moment to bring the sport to an end. She reached up and detached the string of small cylinders from her head. Holding each one in turn to a cresset at the side of the room until the wick had lighted, she proceeded to toss them about, aiming them at the feet of the patrons. They burst into flame with a loud and sharp report.

Then she lighted the large cylinder. The wick began to burn with a loud crackle, and she looked about her for the likeliest target. Suddenly she turned and threw it under a couch on which half a dozen of the girls were sitting. It burst with such an earsplitting roar that Walter thought of the *Hua-P'ao's* he had seen in action on the yellow river. The couch rocked and its occupants scattered, screaming with fright and racing in naked confusion for the stairs.

The proprietor tossed his arms about excitedly and shouted, "Always plenty fun at House of Rowdy Mirth!"

Walter had seen enough. As he crossed the street to the more sedate establishment where he was lodged, he indulged in a quick calculation. The conclusion he reached was that, if all the money plastered on the flabby body of the woman could be taken at face value, she now wore the price of a palace in Kinsai.

3

There was complete silence below, and the only sound that reached Walter's ears was Father Theodore reciting the *Shahra,* the morning prayer, in the next room.

He dressed with a feeling of suddenly revived confidence. For five days they had been pursuing their mission with every promise of a successful issue. Petitions for peace, signed with names that represented most of the wealth of the city, were pouring into the Great Interior Palace. Demonstrations were breaking out daily in the market squares. The willow boughs were nailed on nearly every door in the City of a Thousand Bridges, and it was becoming increasingly apparent that soon the court ministers would have to yield to public opinion. But for five days there had been no report of the whereabouts of Lu Chung.

His new sense of confidence was something he could not explain, but he was sure that the Bird Who Feathers His Nest would be located soon. This colored his thoughts to such an extent that he began to wonder what he was to do when Maryam was found. She had been in his mind continuously during the long months of separation; and, to a corresponding degree, Engaine had been forgotten. He realized that his affections were so much engaged with the guest who had traveled with them in the blue yurt that his lady love at home had receded into a dim memory. He realized also, however, that his new devotion must remain unvoiced. His pledge could not be broken. As he coiled his long hair up under a three-cornered brocade hat, he said to himself that he would have to keep a close check on his emotions when the reunion was an accomplished fact.

Chang Wu called for him early. It promised to be a hot day, and the envoy had clothed himself in cool black linen with plain shoes of black felt, and he was plying his fan assiduously. There was a sparkle of triumph in his eye.

"The presence in the city of my scholarly companion has come to the ears of Her Royal Splendor, the Dowager Empress," he said. "It has been commanded that he be taken to see her this afternoon so that she can hear what he has to say with her own ears. Perhaps this will be important first step to acceptance of peace terms." Then he smiled and touched Walter on the shoulder with his fan. "That is not all. Lu Chung has been found. He is now in the house of the nearest magistrate, waiting to be questioned. We shall go there at once."

They saw Lu Chung as soon as they arrived at the magistrate's house, which also served as a chamber of justice. He was being led through a lower hall, and he was stripped to the waist, with small flags attached to his ears as a sign that he was under suspicion of grave misdemeanors. This had reduced him to such perturbation of spirit that the great rolls of fat around his middle seemed to sag, and rivulets of sweat poured over them like moisture dripping from a water seller's bag.

He did not see them, but it was apparent at once that he did see the occupants of a dark chamber they passed on their way to the hearing. It was at the foot of a narrow flight of steps, but enough light penetrated into it to show that a number of convicted criminals had been sealed into hogsheads with only their heads showing through holes in the tops. As they existed in the most dire misery and with lack of any hope, their lamentations filled the air. Lu Chung shrank away as they passed, and his huge form quivered with fear.

Walter clutched Chang Wu's arm. "What will be done with those poor fellows?" he asked.

The envoy shrugged indifferently. "Nothing," he answered. "They are malefactors of the most desperate kind. Their sentences are of various lengths, but it always comes to the same thing. It is not possible to live long when trussed in so tightly, and so they all die before their terms are finished."

Lu Chung's distress mounted when they reached the chamber of justice. In a corner of the room stood a fearsome spectacle of a man wearing a square hood with a plume of raven's feathers. He also was stripped to the waist, and whenever he moved his arms the muscles rippled like young pythons climbing a sapling trunk.

"That is Hsui, the executioner and questioner by physical means," whispered Chang Wu as they took their places at the rear of the court. "He is known as 'Hand That Draws the Noose,' and it is told that he takes great pleasure in his skill. If Lu Chung proves stubborn, Hsui will question him with sharp knives heated to a white point. This tall thing will soon tell everything he knows."

Lu Chung showed an immediate inclination to avoid the attentions of Hand That Draws the Noose Hsui. He began to talk, and Father Theodore whispered in Walter's ear that he was explaining his reasons for joining the caravan of Bayan of the Hundred Eyes. "It lacks conviction in my opinion," said the priest. "It will surely not go well with him."

Chang Wu then joined the magistrate on the bench and, with that official's consent, began to question the prisoner. At the finish of the interrogation, Lu Chung was taken back to his cell and the envoy returned to his place beside Walter.

"It is good," he said, "but also it is bad. Your friend, called by the prisoner the Tall One, was carried off by bandits one morning near a town on the Wei-ho River. Lu Chung had gone to the town with the lady, and they learned of the regrettable occurrence when on the point of returning to the place where the yurt had been pitched. Since then he has heard nothing more of the Tall One."

Walter was too stunned to make any response. After a moment he got to his feet and began to pace about the room, his mind filled with the most dire forebodings. He was sure that Tristram had been killed. There was a possibility that the bandits would try to carry him off with the idea of selling him as a slave, but he knew that his friend would prefer death to that and would resist to the end. Yes, he had been killed and his body thrown into the river. Walter was convinced of it; and there was no doubt in his mind as to where the blame must rest. It had been his determination which had brought them to this cruel, strange land, and Tristram's death could be laid at his door.

His face was white and his hands shook when he returned to his seat with the others.

"Lu Chung knows more of this than he has told," he said in a tone of passionate repression. "He had made a deal with the bandits. That is clear from his absence at the time. The truth must be dragged from him." He paused as though afraid to ask the question on his tongue. "And now, what of the lady?"

"That great fat pig has been up to his old tricks," said Chang Wu. "He brought the lady to Kinsai and for a consideration turned her over to Sung Yung. It is Sung Yung's intention to send her back to her brother in Antioch. He will profit greatly by the transaction, because it is told by Lu Chung that Anthemus will pay much to have her back. She is being put on a ship today to be taken to the Great Yellow River. She will be taken then by boat up the river to the point where the silk trail starts overland."

"Then," said Walter, "we are just in time."

But Chang Wu shook his head doubtfully. "What does young scholar propose to do?" he asked. "Sung Yung has great influence in the courts. The magistrates always listen to him because it is told that he pays heavy bribes when needful. On what ground can custody of the lady be asked?"

"Her own desire. She does not want to return to the house of An. themus."

"The desire of the lady is of no consequence. The magistrates will say she has no husband and no father and so must return to live with her brother. Is honorable scholar related to the lady in any way?"

"No."

"Is it then his intention to marry her?"

Walter shook his head. "No," he said. "But she is part English, and it has been her desire to return with us to the land of her father."

Chang Wu spread out his hands in a gesture of resignation. "It is unfortunate that young scholar does not plan to marry her. That would provide some grounds on which to act. As it is, the judges will not listen. This humble one fears that nothing can be done for her."

After several moments of almost frantic speculation, Walter asked, "When does she leave for the ship?"

"In two hours. It was told by Lu Chung that she has been kept in the most close seclusion in the silk warehouse of Sung Yung. She will leave from there."

As they talked, one thought had filled Walter's mind to the exclusion of everything else. He was remembering the visit Anthemus had paid him that afternoon at Maragha. He could still recall with a sense of chill the expression on the face of the merchant and the sinister note in his voice as he had whispered, "You can have no conception how much she will suffer for what she has done." Anthemus was not one to forget. He would treat her with as much cruelty now when she was taken to him as he would have then. Walter said to himself: "She must not be sent back! I must take the only way by which she may be saved."

No pledge could stand in the way of saving Maryam from the punishment awaiting her and the sorry life she could expect thereafter. He thought of the unhappiness which had resulted from the hasty oath his grandfather had taken. Surely there was something wrong with a creed which visited everlasting grief on many people because of a few rash words spoken in a moment of anger!

"I have been responsible for the death of my friend," he said. "I cannot now add another great wrong to that. Would an intention on my part to marry the lady incline the judges to take her out of the hands of Sung Yung?"

Chang Wu hesitated. "Who can tell? Sung Yung might be prepared to influence them with the gift that weighs heavy in the hand. Only the accomplished fact would make it certain. No judge would separate wife and husband." He added after a moment: "An attempt at force would not be wise. He has great power in the city."

"Then it must be made an accomplished fact," said Walter. He turned to Father Theodore. "We will have a very few minutes at best to carry out what I have in my mind. Are you willing to use them to perform a marriage ceremony? It will be difficult, and perhaps there will be danger in it for you."

"I have come to this land on a mission which involves much danger," said the priest, with an air of injured pride. "Do you think I would hold back through any consideration of personal risk? No, no, you do me an injustice. But in the matter of a marriage service I see great difficulties. A few minutes only? Young sir, the Nestorian service is a beautiful and a sacred thing, and it takes the better part of an hour. There are many prayers to be said and anthems to be chanted. There must be a ring and a cup of wine and the *hnana* to sprinkle in the wine. I have a ring which will serve. Also, I am happy to say, enough *hnana* for the purpose; it is dust gathered at the tomb of a martyred saint. But the lack of time is an obstacle which cannot be overcome."

"Good Father Theodore," said Walter, earnestly, "this is truly a matter of life and death. I am sure the essential words of the service would suffice. The lady and I will be content to consider ourselves joined in the sight of God without the prayers and the anthems."

"I will provide the cup of wine," said Chang Wu.

"This strong Chinese wine?" cried the priest. "It should be a light and gentle beverage pressed from the grapes of our own warm hillsides. Would any other serve properly for two people of the Christian faith? Can they be truly joined by such unsanctified means?"

"We must do the best we can," declared Walter. "Come, Father Theodore. Put your scruples to one side. Look over the service now and select the passages which will do. We may have no more than a minute or two."

The priest shook his head unhappily. "It will be nothing short of sacrilege," he said. "I am very much disturbed. But—if needs be, I shall do as you say."

The silk warehouse of Sung Yung faced on one of the market squares. It was the most imposing of all the buildings there, having a high-tiered roof which towered above the rest and a golden representation of the mulberry moth over the door. The shutters in front had been rolled up, displaying an open room in which huge bolts of reeled silk were draped on a wall at least twenty feet high. The silks were rich and lustrous and in shades of such glowing beauty that they seemed to light up the whole side of the square.

A chair with drawn curtains stood in front of the warehouse. Two porters, naked save for loincloths, were standing in the shafts at front and back. Walter thought of the day when he and Tristram had watched the preparations for departure at Antioch. On that occasion they had been powerless to intervene. Would he have better luck today?

Despite the need for concentrating on the task ahead, Walter had been able to think of nothing but the fate of his friend. He was still convinced that Tristram had been killed, but the story of that day on the Wei-ho River would always be as much of a mystery as that concerning Wat Stander. There would be no way of tracing him if he had been taken captive; one might as well hope to recover a drop of wine cast into the sea as to find a man swallowed in the maw of this immense country. Even the prospect of rescuing Maryam did little to relieve the mood of self-condemnation into which he had fallen.

"There is Sung Yung," said the envoy, pointing across the square with his fan.

A man of shocking bulk had emerged from the warehouse, leaning on the shoulders of two servants. He proceeded to walk slowly toward the chair, taking each step with such care that it was clear he doubted the ability of his legs to sustain the weight of his body. He was dressed in a thin silk robe which stuck to his sweating, barrel-like torso, and on his head was a grotesque hat shaped like a wine cask.

Chang Wu said in a tone of bitter contempt, "It is told of him that he has ropes looped over his bed to aid him in rising. How much grief this Sung Yung has brought to my unhappy country!"

"It seems we have arrived at the exact moment of departure. Are you sure, Chang Wu, that those who promised to help are here?"

"Have no misgivings. The Brotherhood of the Blue Stars will lend us their aid. I shall now engage in talk this infamous thing, who profits by his country's misfortunes, while my young friend proceeds with his part of the plan."

The square was crowded, and there were many people standing about in the vicinity of the curtained chair. Walter joined them, placing himself as close to the side of it as he dared. He began to speak in Greek as though addressing the Nestorian priest, but in a voice loud enough to be heard inside the chair.

"Do not answer, Maryam, if you are there. This is Walter. Move the curtain slightly if you can hear me."

There was a moment of deep suspense. Then one of the curtains rustled softly.

"I said I would join you in Kinsai. God and good St. Aidan have made it possible for me to keep my promise at last. There is only one way to get you free, Maryam, and that is to claim you as my wife. If you wish it that way, touch the curtain again."

The curtain moved a second time.

"We must be very careful. Make no sound until you hear me say 'Yea.' Then part the curtain and step out. Be ready to do what we tell you at once, for we have little time. Have no fear, Taffy. Everything has been carefully arranged."

Walter then cast a quick glance about him and sighed with relief when he saw a number of jackets embroidered with stars and belted with sealskin edging through the crowd in his direction. He nodded to Father Theodore to begin.

The priest proceeded to read from a sheet of parchment in his hand. He kept his head lowered and repeated the words in hurried tones. It took no more than a minute, but to Walter it seemed as though the reading would never end. One of the carriers had stepped out from between the shafts with a look of suspicion on his blue tattooed face. A young man in a starred jacket promptly elbowed him to one side.

Father Theodore replaced the parchment in his robe and opened a basket he had carried over his shoulder. From this he produced a silver cup filled with wine. He made the sign of the cross over the rim and then dropped a ring and a sprinkling of fine dust into the wine.

"Drink," he said, handing the cup to Walter. "Two thirds are for you. No more and no less, if you wish for married happiness. If you drink more, you will be a tyrannical husband; less, and your wife will rule the household. Drink, and then make the response."

Walter drank part of the wine and said "Yea" in a clear voice. The curtains parted instantly, and Maryam stepped down to the ground. Walter had time only to see that she looked very small, smaller than he had remembered, and a little frightened.

Father Theodore handed her the cup, and she drank the rest of the wine. Then, on his bidding, she said "Yea" and took the ring from the bottom of the cup. When it had been fitted on her finger, the priest laid his right hand on Walter's head and then on hers.

"I pronounce you man and wife," he intoned loudly.

It had taken no more than a few seconds, and the people about them did not seem yet to have grasped the significance of it. Walter now dared to look down at his newly made wife, and he realized at once that he loved her. He knew that he had loved her, absorbingly, fervently, ever since the time of their parting and that it was only because of his feeling that duty demanded the permanence of his pledged devotion to Engaine that he had failed to acknowledge it. He was so sure that what he was doing was right that a sense of happiness swept over him.

Maryam looked up and said, "Walter!" in a tremulous voice. Her eyes shone radiantly through a mist of tears. He drew her arm through his and whispered, "Now you are safe, thanks to our ever watchful Father!"

Young men in the starred jackets which linked them to the circle of old merchants who had listened to him that first day closed in about them to form a bodyguard. Father Theodore, parchment in hand once more, led the way to the side of the square. Determined to lend a note of more regularity to the service, he began to read in a sonorous voice the prayers he had been compelled to omit before. One of the young men took a garland of white flowers from the tray of a vendor and tossed it around the neck of the bride.

Walter held his wife's hand tightly. He heard her say in a tense whisper: "We waited so long and we kept on hoping, but at last we could hope no longer. We were sure then you had been killed!" She was pale and thin, and the eyes she turned up to him seemed larger than ever. He saw also that she was shabbily dressed. Her coat had once been a deep blue, but now it was old and faded. It reached almost to the ground, revealing no more than the turned-up ends of narrow black trousers.

"There is no time to talk now," he said. "In a few minutes I must leave you. But be sure of this, Taffy: there is no more danger, and we shall never be separated again."

"I can scarce believe it yet!" she said with a sigh of the most complete happiness. "To think that you are alive, and that we are together!"

Despite his assurances, a threat of trouble now made itself evident. Armed servants of Sung Yung were pouring out of the silk warehouse, and their master was clawing his way through the crowds, angry eyes blazing in a square and belligerent face. Chang Wu was following in his wake.

Walter stepped forward and faced the silk merchant. "You are Sung Yung and you are called Fire from Black Clouds," he said. Realizing that he had spoken in English, he turned to Chang Wu. "Tell him that I am married to the sister of Anthemus whom he has been holding without any legal right. It should be clear to him that this has ceased to be a matter for the magistrates to judge. The marriage has been performed publicly with all these people watching."

"It will be a pleasure to tell what you have said to this great hogshead of rancid suet," declared Chang Wu.

"You might say to him also that I had expected to see him on a different errand. I received instructions from Anthemus which I have carried out in part. I can no longer continue the arrangement made between us, but say to him I will repay to Anthemus the money he laid out for my equipment."

Chang Wu translated at some length, and it was clear that he was elaborating the message. Walter learned later that he concluded by expressing the hope that the payment to Anthemus would be made in the worthless currency that Sung Yung himself had been instrumental in foisting on the country.

The effect of this was more than the envoy had expected. One of the zealous bodyguards drew a wad of crumpled paper currency from his pocket and threw it into Sung Yung's face. Cries of "Peace! Peace!" rose immediately from all parts of the square, and the angry populace began to close in around the silk merchant.

The trouble which started in this way developed rapidly into a full-sized riot. Sung Yung was shoved about and buffeted by angry hands, his immense quaking belly absorbing most of the blows. His shrill cries for help were lost in the rising uproar. A fish vendor struck him across the face with his basket. The silk merchant lost his balance and tumbled to the brick paving of the road. Immediately there was a furious struggle around the spot as the aroused townspeople fought among themselves for the chance to rain kicks and blows on the prostrate body.

In the meantime other rioters tore the gold mulberry moth from over the entrance and broke it into bits, which were then scrambled for frantically. A man seized the end of one of the long bolts of yellow silk and dragged it after him until it stretched clear to the other side of the square, like the fire from the sky for which Sung Yung was named. Others followed suit, and soon there were long streamers of scarlet and blue and green spreading out from the silk shop in all directions. Everyone was screaming, "Peace! Peace!" The few daggers which were still to be seen on the square were wrenched from the ground and willow boughs nailed up instead. The establishment of a *chaw* merchant, who had been one of the few to flaunt his desire for war, was invaded by the mob. Chests containing his stock were dragged out and piled in the center of the square, where fire was set to them. The sight of the brisk flames roused the rioters to attacks on all other shops whose owners were suspected of sympathy with the aims of Sung Yung.

When the struggling group around the focal point of the trouble drew away, it was seen that Sung Yung would no longer exercise any influence on the conduct of national affairs. Gravel had been piled on his head and packed down tightly until all movement of his bulky body had ceased.

Fearing that they would be made late for their audience at the Great Interior Palace, Chang Wu directed his companions down a side street to one of the narrow canals which bisected the city. Here Maryam was placed on a barge with Father Theodore and two of the bodyguard as escorts, with instructions that she was to be taken to the home of the envoy for the rest of the day. Her face, as she watched Walter from a seat in the stern, reflected so much anxiety and bewilderment that he walked down to the landing and said, "It will be for a few hours only, Taffy. I will join you as soon as possible."

The barge was already moving away, and she smiled back forlornly and waved as it disappeared around a bend of the canal.

"Come!" said Chang Wu urgently. "A golden opportunity will be lost if we are late in waiting on Her Imperial Grandeur."

4

It was midafternoon when they reached the palace and, in accordance with court custom, the gold-studded door of *Ta-ching,* the Hall of Audience, was covered with blue cloth. They passed this formidable portal, however, and were escorted on through an imposing corridor which seemed to stretch ahead of them indefinitely. Walter sensed a change in the atmosphere at once. Mystery brooded in this lofty passage, as though they were drawing near to the very center of Eastern knowl-

edge and the seat of real power. The walls were so high that words
changed into ghostly echoes in the upper reaches. The pillars were of
the most fantastic design, a succession of gargoyle faces tapering up
into the gloom overhead, where they mowed their resentment of intrusion. At the far end, in the midst of a red glare, sat the figure of an
idol, a truly gargantuan representation of the human form changed into
something which might be either god or fiend. Immense hands were
folded across the middle of the idol, and its face was turned to glare
straight down the passage.

Another blue-draped door was reached, a much smaller one, and the
court official who was leading the way threw it open with a ceremonious
flourish.

"Bow profusely!" he cried, setting the example by genuflecting his
spare frame four times in rapid succession.

They found themselves in a comparatively small but breath-taking
chamber. The walls were of marble, overlaid with gold and ivory and
jade. The ceiling was high and elaborately arched, and from it hung at
least a score of crystal lamps of curious design. At the far end was a
chair of jade, and on it sat a woman with a painted face.

She was tiny and as alert as a monkey. Her eyes, which she fixed at
once on the Englishman, had a sharp and mischievous glitter in them.
When she straightened up in the chair, the movement caused an enormous diamond to sparkle on the front of her scarlet robe, which was
embroidered with all the symbols of the Hundred Antiquities. Walter
noticed that her hands were so loaded with rings that only her fingernails were showing like curved purple beaks.

"She is dangerous, and her moods will be impossible to predict," he
thought, uneasily.

The only other occupants of the room were two men of obviously
high court rank, who hovered solicitously on each side of the woman in
the jade chair. One was a soldier, wearing a breastplate with the jeweled figure of a tiger in front. The other had a globe of opaque red coral
on his flat hat which marked him as belonging to the inner circle of imperial advisers. Both men were so old that they resembled frostbitten
fruit left to shrivel on the bare boughs of autumn.

The Dowager's eyes were still intently fixed on Walter, and she was
talking to the two ancient men in a voice which carried a suggestion of
excitement. Chang Wu whispered, "The color of your hair has disturbed
Her Unlimited Magnificence."

The envoy was then summoned to share in the discussion. Standing stiffly in front of the Chair of Audience, with his arms held down at his sides, Walter watched what was happening with a sense of mounting uneasiness. It seemed clear to him that things had taken an unexpected turn. The expression on the face of Chang Wu was a proof of this, a compound of surprise and a decided, though respectful, dissent.

Finally, the envoy stepped back beside him. "There will be no talk today," he said, in a rebellious tone. "I have strange news for you, young traveler, but this is not the place for the telling. We are to leave now."

Walter met the black eyes of the Dowager, but he did not read hostility in them. Instead she seemed a little awed, and it was clear also that her spirits had risen. She called out something in a chirping voice, and her thickly ruddled face broke into a caricature of a smile.

He bowed four times and then backed from the room, the imperial scrutiny following him every inch of the way.

The official with the red coral globe led the way through a maze of passages and then into a garden which extended for several hundred yards, with rows of small houses barely visible through the trees and shrubbery. "Officers of the court live here," explained Chang Wu, waving his fan in the direction of the houses. He sighed and pointed to one of them. "That will be yours, and it is called the Abode of Everlasting Felicity. A suitable title for one who has been newly joined in wedlock."

Walter was completely bewildered. "I don't understand the meaning of this, illustrious Chang Wu. Why am I to stay here?"

"That will be told in due time. First there are points of palace etiquette to be observed."

The Abode of Everlasting Felicity was so well concealed behind its abundant shrubbery that at first Walter could see nothing but the bright yellow tiles of the *t'ing,* a high triple roof. On closer inspection it proved to be quite lovely and very much larger than he had at first supposed, a single-storied structure of yellow walls and pillars at the top of a flight of red-tiled steps. Instead of the dragons which usually served for decoration, there were graceful flower designs in red about the high eaves. The door was wide open, the first indication of the felicity so generously promised.

Further indications awaited them inside: a smiling manservant and the pretty faces of two maids peeping around from behind him; a table heaped high with flowers and fruit; a pleasant odor of burning incense; a view of green lime trees through an open door at the far end of the hall. The manservant bowed deeply several times and then motioned them toward a sunny room opening off from the right. Chang

Wu led the way in, but the court official remained in the entrance.

Chang Wu drew his companion to the far end of the room, where they could talk without any danger of being overheard.

"The raven of ill omen sits on our shoulders," declared the envoy. He plucked at his thin beard with dejected fingers. "I have told before of the belief we have in prophecy. Her Imperial Magnificence, who has wanted peace because she feared the invincible power of the dragon with the hundred eyes, was reminded of another prophecy when she saw the yellow of your hair. It is a very old one and dates back as far as our records go, even beyond the days of the great Emperor Fohi of illustrious memory. There will be many to believe as she does. It says, 'In time of great peril there will come two birds of golden plumage out of the West, and the clouds of disaster will dissolve like the mist.'" His face reflected the dire consequences he now foresaw. "She is certain that we have nothing to fear, that the Gods in the Far Clouds have given this sign of their will to protect us and guide us to a victorious peace."

Walter was dumfounded by this strange and even ludicrous turn of events. "Is it possible," he asked, "that the fate of the country can depend on an old saying? I find it hard to believe, Chang Wu."

"There are some of us who put no trust in such things, but it is certain that our voices will not be heard now. I must even tell you that the only step being taken to quell the disturbances in the city is to distribute quotations from the writings of the philosophers, urging a return to calm reflection."

"Does the Empress forget that I have been with the armies of Bayan and that my purpose in coming here is to convince them of the uselessness of further resistance?"

Chang Wu shook his head. "That is of no consequence. You have come; and that is enough."

"But if I heard aright, there must be two birds of golden plumage, not one."

"That is the strange part," said the envoy. "You are the second to arrive. The first was brought to the palace earlier in the day."

Walter's heart gave a sudden bound. He clutched his companion excitedly. "A man with yellow hair? Tell me, Chang Wu, is he tall? Taller than I am?" He was thinking exultantly: "It must be Tris. There couldn't be another white man in China at this time. This means he was not killed. He was taken captive after all and has made his escape."

"I have not seen him," answered Chang Wu. "You will be taken to him as soon as you have received the presents Her Imperial Effulgence has selected for you."

The court official appeared in the doorway and bowed, saying something in a tone of deep respect.

"The gifts have arrived," declared the envoy. "Her Highness desires to show her great joy at the appearance of the two birds of good omen. You will find them, young scholar, well fitted to the important role you will now play."

There was a sound of excited chatter in the entrance and then a file of maidservants in white-and-purple livery appeared in the doorway. They carried ivory boxes of various sizes. The official bowed to Walter and called out an order. The servants deposited their burden on the floor and then withdrew.

When opened, the first ivory box was found to contain delicately carved objects in jade, rings, bracelets, brooches, chains, even a very small wine cup. They were in all the most valued shades, rose madder, sky-at-midnight, nightingale, chicken-bone white, dragon's-red, translucent and royal imperial green. Walter selected a beautifully wrought chain and held it up to the light.

"This will be a pleasant gift for my wife," he said. He was thinking how well it would look on her white throat in contrast to the cluster of her dark curls.

"There will be many things to adorn the pleasing person of my friend's new wife," said Chang Wu.

Everything in the box appeared ideally suited to the adornment of a bride; a green butterfly with wide wings which could be worn on the front of her hair; a white ring with the red eyes of a dragon; a belt of slender jade links, just large enough to span a slender waist; earrings of the most delicate coral shade. Certain that the other arrival at the palace would prove to be Tristram, Walter's mind had cleared itself of the depression which had weighed on him so heavily all day, and he gave himself to a survey of the gifts with unimpaired delight. "How well this will become her!" he thought, and "How her eyes will sparkle when she sees *this!*"

The second box contained a chalice of matchless workmanship. The third gift was a ring with a large and seemingly flawless emerald. The fourth box was much larger, and he opened it slowly, wondering what marvels would be revealed. He gasped when his eyes lighted on the contents.

It was filled with unset gems. The top layer consisted of emeralds, rubies, and sapphires, most of them of unusual size and all of great value. Under these was a glittering mass of all the known varieties of semiprecious stones: pink beryls, orange-hued rubicelles, brilliant sphenes, zircons of many shades, warm amethysts, large jargoons contrasting with the molten glow of fire opals and the duller tones of the rare cat's-eye. He picked them up in his hands in a state of bemused wonder, watching the interplay of color, well aware that he held a king's ransom. The fortune he had come to the East to seek was his!

Chang Wu had seemed little concerned with the gifts up to this point. When Walter had gained enough coherence to comment on the munificence of the Empress, he said, "Wait, young scholar," and nodded to the court official. The latter bowed more deeply than before and opened the largest receptacle.

"This," said Chang Wu, taking a vase from the box, "is *nan-ting*. It is not old, but is more valuable for that very reason. The porcelains we are making now are much finer than anything done in past dynasties. See, it is as thin as paper!" He touched the surface with his fingernail, and a bell-like sound was given out. "In the opinion of this humble one, there is no better piece in all China."

Walter took the vase hesitantly, fearing it might break in his hands. "Surely the Empress is exceeding all bounds," he said.

"The gods must be propitiated. In the eyes of Her Supreme Munificence, you are a god."

Walter was becoming concerned about his future movements. "But," he began, "when I return to my post with Bayan——"

Chang Wu shook his head. "It is not proposed to let you return. The birds of golden plumage must be kept here so the favorable influence of their presence will exert itself in our behalf."

"Then I will be held as a hostage?"

"The chains which bind you will be golden ones, young scholar. But it is true that there will be guards stationed about the walls of the Abode of Everlasting Felicity."

Walter looked startled for a moment. Then he smiled and shook his head. "Truly, I find myself in a paradoxical position, worthy Chang Wu," he said. "I confess that I can make neither head nor tail of it. The mission on which I came was in the best interests of your country. Now I seem fated to undo everything we had accomplished. How shall I be able to explain all this to my lord Bayan?"

"We can only hope," answered the envoy glumly, "that wiser counsels in time will prevail over the optimism created by old prophecy."

The official now clapped his hands again, and a beautiful young girl in a peach-colored robe entered the room, carrying a box of larger dimensions than any of the first. She giggled delightedly as she handed it to the Englishman.

When Walter opened the catch, a furry head popped out and a piping bark filled the room. He picked the little dog up, finding that it could be held comfortably on the palm of one hand. It was of a light biscuit shade, and its eyes, like brown agates, filled so much of its face that it was no wonder there was little room left for its flattened excuse for a nose. A pink tongue flicked out twice to kiss his hand as a token of good will.

"He is named Chi Wangti," said the envoy, "after the illustrious Emperor who built the Great Wall. His descent is of unbroken royalty and can be traced back for a thousand years. The hand of the Empress has often caressed the head of this rare one."

Walter held the small dog up close to his face, and the pink tongue touched the tip of his nose. "I am quite sure," he said to himself, "that if Maryam had one choice from all the gifts, this is the one she would want."

A cheerful air of activity prevailed in the household sections of the Great Interior Palace. When Walter and his guide reached the Courtyard of Contented Domestics, the former marveled that so much ease of mind could be found with the threat of death and rapine looming over the city. When he remarked on this, Chang Wu shrugged his skinny shoulders.

"These ox-heads live in a world that ends with the walls of the palace," he said. "It is even possible that many of them do not know there is a war. I may tell you further that there are gaming houses where princes of the blood stake great fortunes on the roll of a pair of dice; and in such places the echo of war sounds so faintly that the players look blank when the name of Kublai Khan is mentioned." He then added in an attempt at extenuation: "Our country is vast, and no man lives who can say how many millions of people we have. It is not strange, perhaps, that the flutter of the foul wings of the foreign war god is little heeded."

Most of the noise in the Courtyard of Contented Domestics came from one corner. As Chang Wu led the way in that direction, Walter saw that the center of interest was a man in a wooden cage. They came within twenty feet of it before he saw that a longbow was strapped to the top and so realized that the man in the cage was Tristram.

The prisoner was sitting in a huddled position with his head sunk on his knees. No other position was possible for him; the cage was one of the fiendishly contrived prisons in which the occupant can neither sit up straight nor stretch out at full length. It was impossible to see much of his face, but he was thin and ragged and incredibly dirty. His lank hair hung well below the level of his shoulders.

"Tris!" cried Walter, forcing his way through the spectators. It was clear now what had happened. His friend had been taken captive and had been carried across China in this portable chamber of torture. "Tris!" he cried again.

The caged man lifted a wasted face in which his eyes seemed to peer out from great depths like a cornered animal's. His features became contorted in an effort at a smile.

"Wat!" he whispered. He made an instinctive effort to raise himself, and his head struck against the upper bars of the cage. Then he sank back again, saying in a weak voice: "Is it really you? O kind Father in heaven, I thank Thee!"

Walter grasped Chang Wu's arm with frantic insistence. "He must be released at once! He is my friend. It is clear now that Lu Chung sold him to the bandits."

"Your wish is the key to his freedom. He was brought in this morning. It was not until you came, the second of the birds of golden plumage, that this one became of any importance. He will be released at once."

Chang Wu called an order to a tall Chinese standing beside the cage with a pike in his hands. The keeper took a key from his belt and inserted it in the lock. At first it stuck and refused to turn, and the man swore as he labored with it.

"Tell that fumbling fool to break the cage open!" cried Walter. He edged closer and said, "Courage, Tris. We will have you out in a moment."

The keeper finally succeeded in making the key turn. He then swung back one side of the cage and motioned the occupant to come out. Tristram tried to raise himself on his arms, but his strength was not equal to it. He fell back against the rear bars.

Walter brushed the keeper aside and knelt beside the prostrate body. "You will be all right now, Tris," he said. "You must not try to move. We will have you soon in a soft warm bed." His eyes were filled with tears, and he could not restrain himself from crying, "Tris, Tris, what have they done to you!"

Chang Wu had been issuing orders, and a servant now arrived with wine in a cup. Walter held it to his friend's lips. "This is what you need. Drink it down and it will put some strength in you."

Tristram managed a single swallow, coughing from the effect of the strong liquid. It was several moments before he could take more. After several swallows, however, he gained enough strength to open his eyes. "That's good," he whispered.

"How long have they kept you in this thing?"

"Ever since they caught me." A shudder shook the long, emaciated frame. "It seems like years. I lost all track of time after the first few weeks."

Chang Wu interposed an explanation. "The men who took him prisoner—they shall be most properly punished in due course!—have been exhibiting him. This keeper tells me he has been carried through three provinces. Fees have been charged for the privilege of seeing him."

Walter looked up at the envoy. "They have starved him. Do you suppose he has ever been out of this cage?"

"I speak without knowledge, but it seems unlikely he has ever been allowed out."

The head on Walter's shoulder shook weakly. "Not once. If I complained, they prodded me with their swords. There seemed to be faces around me all the time. They shoved sharp sticks at me through the bars."

"Maryam is here," said Walter. "I found her today. Now that we are all together again, there is nothing to fear any more."

Tristram made another effort to sit up, his eyes alive again with the relief he felt. "Maryam here! I was afraid—— Now I can have some peace of mind at last! I was sure, Wat, that she had been sold by that Chinese fellow. By the Rood, this word has put new life in me already!"

Servants had arrived with a litter. When they lifted him on it, the sick man raised his arm. "My bow," he said—"don't let them take it, Wat. It was always there where I could see it, and that was the only comfort I had. It was a reminder of our own world."

Chang Wu issued some instructions and then turned to Walter. "He will be lodged in a house next to yours. I have sent for the court physicians, and they will attend him there." He smiled in an apologetic way. "It has been commanded that you are not to leave the Palace, and so it will not be possible for you to join your wife in the humble home of your servant. As soon as my duties allow, I shall go to her and explain all that has happened, so her mind will be at rest. Tomorrow she will be brought to the Abode of Everlasting Felicity. May I voice the hope that the name given to it will prove an apt and happy one?"

CHAPTER XI

The Abode of Everlasting Felicity

WHEN TRISTRAM HAD FALLEN into a sleep of complete exhaustion, which the physicians said might last for as long as twenty-four hours, Walter decided to return to his own quarters. Two guards fell into step behind him, huge fellows with swords hanging over their shoulders and dragon helmets on their heads. "I am to be kept under close watch, it seems," he said to himself, as he stumbled along through the darkness.

The manservant met him at the rear entrance and led the way to a latticed room in the center of which was a sunken bath with water running into it from a pipe in the ceiling above. He undressed and plunged into the water, finding an intense satisfaction in the coolness of it after the heat and stress of the long day. There was a wheel on the wall beside the bath with every kind of toilet aid attached to it. The servant gave it a spin to demonstrate that any of the articles could be obtained without moving from the water.

His bath completed, Walter was helped into silk trousers and shirt and shoes luxuriantly lined with wool. The man motioned to a door in the lattice and said something in a tone which seemed to contain, in spite of the fact that it was both low and respectful, a faint trace of slyness.

Walter found himself in a long room with many windows, dimly lighted by a cresset in one corner. His nose rather than his eyes told him that the walls were festooned with flowers. There was food and a tall jug of wine on a tray on the floor but, as he was not hungry, he walked past it toward a low couch placed in the center of the room. He had taken no more than a few steps when the silence was broken by a sharp bark and the small dog Chi Wangti charged across the covers to repel any invasion. The covers moved and a sleepy voice said, "*Sai?*"

He did not need this use of the Greek word to know that it was Maryam. She sat up in bed and drew a hand across her eyes. "It is you, Walter?" she asked. "I did not intend to fall asleep, but I must have been very tired."

He sat down on the side of the couch. "Chang Wu said you would not come until tomorrow." He paused, finding himself at a loss for words. "This is a—very pleasant surprise."

She began to talk to cover an equal embarrassment. "Oh, I came in great state. I rode in a covered chair with lighted lanterns at each corner and guards all around it with drawn swords. One man rode in front and blew a horn to clear the streets. I might have been the Empress herself. That old man told me you would be surprised. I think he planned it that way. He has been very kind to me."

"Did he tell you we had found Tris?"

"Yes! Yes, he told me that. I was so happy, even though I knew our kind Tris had been through terrible experiences! What have the court physicians said about him?"

"He is very weak, but it is due to exhaustion and lack of food. He is in no danger."

Walter had at last summoned up the courage to look at her directly. To his surprise, he saw that she was fully dressed.

"Maryam!" he said, reaching for one of her hands and pressing it in his. "I am unable to find words to tell you how happy I am. Here we are, the three of us, and our difficulties seem to be behind us, for the time being at any rate. Tris will be himself again after he has proper care and rest. And," he paused, "and you are my wife!"

Although she left her hand in his, he sensed a withdrawal in her attitude. "We have much to talk about, Walter," she said. "I have been thinking and—and I am sure you married me because it was the only way to save me from being sent back to Antioch. It was generous and noble of you, and you must know how grateful I am. I will love you for it all my life. But—this must not stand in the way of your real wishes. I have made up my mind to that."

Chi Wangti had curled up on the covers beside Maryam. To relieve the tension, she leaned over to stroke his small head. "We made friends while I waited for you," she said. "I think it is a dog, but I have never seen one like it before. He must be quite young."

"No, he has attained his full stature. He belongs to the oldest breed of dogs in the world, and his lineage has the stamp of royalty. It can be traced back to a time before the Children of Israel took the land of Canaan. I intended him as a gift for you. But," he smiled, "it is clear that Chi Wangti has decided the matter for himself. He has sworn fealty to you as his lady and mistress."

"I am very fond of him already," she said, keeping her head bent over the new pet.

Walter began to speak with some hesitation, striving to find the exact words he needed. "It is true I did not intend to break my pledge as my father did. But when your danger outweighed all other considerations, I knew that the justification had been found. It would not be honest if I did not tell you that; but I want you to believe that the pledge had become a hollow one and that what I did was with the greatest gladness in the world."

"You are being still more generous," she said in a low voice. "We must be completely honest with each other, Walter. I am safe now; and if you feel as I am afraid you must, it will not be hard for you to break this tie. I will do nothing to stand in the way. It seems to me that the service the priest said may not be binding."

Walter was beginning to feel more sure of himself. He smiled. "Poor Father Theodore was very much distressed at the way it had to be done. He skipped quickly over the service. But I am sure, Taffy, that it is completely binding in spite of that."

"Not if you want to break it."

"But I have no wish to break it!" He placed his hands on her shoulders and drew her closer. She trembled at his touch and refused still to raise her head. "Maryam, I love you! It took a long separation to make me realize it, but I knew as soon as I saw you today that I had loved you from the time we parted on the trail." He drew her still closer until her head rested against his shoulder. "I love you so much that I feel thankful to Lu Chung for what he did."

"Are you sure you will have no regrets?" she asked. "Will you always feel about it, and me, as you do now?"

"The only vow with which I have any concern is the one I made today; and to that vow I shall be faithful as long as there is breath in my body. All I can think of is that I love you and that you are my wife."

Her arms found their way around his neck. "You have made me so happy by saying that! I can scarce believe it true. Do I need to say, Walter, that I love you? I feel great shame that I have never been able to conceal it." She drew a contented breath. "Now I can believe I am really your wife and that nothing is going to come between us, not even your memories. I understood about the pledge, my dearest one, and I held you in no blame for feeling as you did. I also am thankful to Lu Chung and that dreadful fat man." She laughed breathlessly. "But I think we must have a proper service as soon as we can. I cannot risk losing you now."

"I consider myself married to you in the sight of God and man. Nevertheless, it shall be as you wish. There will be a pleasure in hearing you repeat the word, 'Yea' again." He touched the sleeve of her robe. "I am greedy of every moment now that we know what is in our hearts. To part for even as long as it will take to remove this is a trial I feel unfitted to bear."

She lifted up her head, and he kissed her fervently. Then she drew herself away from him and stepped to the floor.

"But you are to blame," she charged. "I laid down to rest and you were so very long in coming that I fell asleep just as I was."

She walked toward the door in the lattice, Chi Wangti trying so hard to keep up with her that he literally bounced on all four feet.

"You must promise to hurry," Walter called after her.

"I will be back soon," she promised, closing the door. "Very soon, my Walter."

The sun was pouring through the windows of the Abode of Everlasting Felicity when Walter wakened. He sat up in the low wide couch and looked down at Maryam who was still sleeping, her face turned toward him and resting on the palm of one hand. Her tousled curls and pale delicate face made her seem very young. "What a blind dolt I was!" he thought. "How could I have failed to love her the first instant I saw her?"

Maryam wakened and sat up in turn. Her silk night robe drooped on one side, displaying all of the softly rounded shoulder nearest him and part of her arm. She corrected this by placing the arm in his and resting her head against him.

"Good morrow, my husband," she said. "I seem to remember that you made me some very pretty vows last night. I trust they linger as pleasantly and resolutely in your mind as they do in mine."

"I shall be happy to repeat them."

"I shall ask you to do so many times. But there was one thing you did not tell me. It is the custom where I was born for suitors to come with offers for their brides. What a very high price that greedy pig of an Anthemus would have demanded if you had gone to him, unworthy and plain though I may be! I wonder what you would have offered? How many sheep, how many horses, how many pieces of gold and silver? Or would you have told him I had little value in the marriage market and that he should be glad to be well rid of me?"

"It's much better I tell you the offer I would have made to you. My lifelong devotion!" he cried. "My everlasting love, my arms to shield you from all fear and danger as long as we lived!"

"That is the offer I would have wanted to hear," she whispered.

A high-pitched trill sounded from near the ceiling. Walter sat up straight and looked about him. "What was that?"

"I think," said Maryam, "it was Peter, though I cannot see where he is. I kept him with me all the time. He had saved your life, my Walter, and I could not part with him on that account. Mahmoud came with me last night, and I suppose he brought Peter with him."

"Mahmoud? I had forgotten all about that little black rascal, but I am glad to hear he is safe also."

She looked about the room, which had pale green walls and drapes of rich yellow. "What a beautiful home you have brought your bride to, Sir Knight! How fortunate these people have a prophecy about strange birds with golden plumage!"

She touched a foot to the floor and then flew to the latticed room. Walter was to realize, as the days passed, that she was filled with energy. She seemed to prefer to run rather than walk. Her fingers were nimble at any task, her movements were all gracefully brisk, her voice was often breathless in her haste to say the many things she had in mind.

From the side room she called: "Such beautifully hot water! And so many pretty things for me to use. Such perfumes, Walter! I have two maids, it seems, and am not to be permitted to bathe myself. I am going to love this place!"

A few minutes later she called to report other wonders. "You should see the clothes ready for me. Such lovely things of silk. I can hardly wait to put them on. To think that Mahmoud will never have to steal for me again! Walter, you should see my robe! It is satin and has a pattern of prunus and lotus sprays. You won't know me when I come out."

"I would know you," he called back, "if you came out with your face blackened again."

"O-oh, what a dreadful thought! I am going to spend a very long time on my toilet. There are lotions and powders I have never heard of. You will have to be very patient."

Mahmoud came in before the process of dressing had been completed behind the lattice. He was very proud of the fine raiment he was wearing, and he grinned literally from ear to ear.

"Long time since Mahmoud see Masser Watter," he said. "Very bad time. Lady Ma'yam and Mahmoud think they never see masser again." He glanced about the room with an eye of kindling satisfaction. "Fine place, masser."

"I am sure you have grown several inches since I saw you last. You are going to be a big fellow, Mahmoud."

The boy tapped his chest. "Yes, masser. Mahmoud ibn Asseult grow into very big fellow. Grow strong too." He grinned again. "Mahmoud glad masser marry Lady Ma'yam. She make him fine wife."

"You think, then, she will make a better wife than second boy?"

"Oh yes. *Very* fine wife. But masser better keep big switch over door."

Walter suddenly felt the overpowering pain which preceded one of his spells. The room spun around, and he found it hard to breathe. He had time only for a single thought, "Why does this have to happen now!" before the usual blackness closed over him.

When he recovered control of himself again, he was lying on the floor and Maryam was bending over him, crying in an extremity of pity and terror. "See his poor back!" she was saying between sobs. "What did they do to him, what did they do to him!"

He sat up with an effort. "You must not worry about it, Taffy. I am getting better all the time. This is the first spell in several weeks."

She stifled her sobbing long enough to ask, "Did this happen to you when we ran away and left you to face them?"

"I escaped very lightly. You must not waste your pity on me. Save it until you see poor Tris. He is in much more need of it."

"You did not tell me of *this*," she said reproachfully. "I know I shall feel sorry for poor Tris when I see him, but I can only think now of what those terrible beasts did to you. Walter, my dearest one, are you sure you will be better?"

"Yes, I am quite sure. Except when these attacks come, I feel no pain at all now."

"Will these dreadful scars ever go away?"

"I expect to have them always. Mahmoud was advising me to keep a big switch over the door, but it is clear now I won't need one. When you are disobedient, I will say, 'See what I did for you.'"

"I will never be disobedient!" she cried. "But I think I shall keep a switch myself. For use on that ungrateful Mahmoud!"

2

Tristram wakened as soon as Walter entered his room. His long sleep had done him good, for he was able to raise himself to a sitting position. He grinned happily.

"Ha, Wat! You are there in the flesh, so I know it wasn't just a dream."

Walter looked him over with a rueful shake of the head. "You are as thin as a crow in February! It will take a long time to get the flesh back on your bones, Tris. Those cruel devils had nearly succeeded in starving you to death."

"I have had so many dreams; and none of them pleasant ones. They were strange, mad, terrible!" Tristram looked about him with a slow and painful motion of his head. "If you were not sitting there, I would swear this was paradise. No bars! No ugly yellow faces staring in at me. No sharp sticks cutting at my ribs. Ugh, I have a low conceit of your famed Cathay, Wat!"

"Maryam is here. She will come in to see you shortly."

"I want to see her as soon as possible. But," with a wry smile, "I look like a scarecrow. I am black and blue from head to foot, and I seem to have hundreds of cuts and bruises. Two of these pudding-faced maids insisted on giving me a bath—I lacked the strength to resist, though I protested loudly—and they seemed shocked at the condition they found me in." He sank back on his couch. "Still, I am on the mend. Another sleep like this and I shall feel well enough to bend a bow with the best."

Walter laughed. "That is the first boast I have ever heard you make. The court physicians will be in to see you again, and I am sure they will knock such notions out of your head. I hope you will be strong enough to leave before Bayan's army swoops down on the city."

"Tell me what has been happening. I need hardly say I have heard nothing at all. In the towns where I was exhibited like a bear with a ring in its nose they did not seem to know there was a war."

"Bayan is moving fast. I am convinced there has never been such a captain in the world before. The last word we have is that he is setting siege to the fortress city of Ch'aing-cha. As soon as it falls, the road to Kinsai will be wide open." Walter hesitated before going on with what he must tell. "Tris, there is something you must know. I—I find it hard to say it."

Tristram had closed his eyes. He opened them now and regarded his companion anxiously.

"Maryam and I are married." The words came out with a rush. "She was to be sent back to Antioch, and it was the only way to save her. We were married yesterday. Before I saw you."

The sick man struggled up to a sitting position again. "By the Rood, I am happy to hear it. I have been sure it would happen when you came to your senses."

"I love her devotedly. I have dreaded telling you because I know you loved her too. It must seem like a betrayal, Tris; but I swear it could not be delayed, and I did not know then you had come back. There would have been no time in any event, but I wish it had been possible to tell you first."

The grave eyes of the sick man smiled up at him with complete acceptance. There was no hesitation in his voice, no hint of reservations. "You feared I would take it amiss? Come, Wat, you know me better than that! It is true I loved her too, but you must believe, best of friends, that at no time did I entertain the hope she would marry me. Her heart was yours from the very first. Even when we were both sure you were dead, I said nothing to her." He stretched out an arm and shook hands. "You will be happy together. I am sure of it."

Walter thought of the days the three of them had spent together when Tristram's devotion had been so clearly apparent. "He is the least selfish man in the whole world," he thought. "In spite of what he says, I am afraid this has been a blow."

"You are the staunchest fellow I have ever known," he said aloud. "As sound and true as an English longbow."

Tristram smiled wanly. "What I have said comes from the bottom of my heart, Wat. You must not be concerned because of the past." He added, after a moment: "You praise me for my willingness to give up something I have never possessed. Something, moreover, I never hoped to possess. I have been well resigned to it always. I think those who selected this luxurious nest for me must have had an inkling how it was. It is called the Abode of the Lonely Warrior."

Walter brought Maryam in shortly after. She gave an involuntary cry of dismay and ran to the couch, where she knelt down beside the sick man.

"My poor Tris!" she said. "How thin you are! What a terrible time you must have had!"

He took one of her hands. "Taffy!" he said. "Now that you are here,

and I know you are safe and happy, I will soon get some flesh back on
these raw bones of mine. I can see you are very happy. I wish I could
let you know how glad I am about the news Wat has told me."

He had spoken in English, and she looked at him with surprise.

"Come!" she said. "You must remember I know as little of your
strange language as I do of Chinese. Have you forgotten all I taught
you?"

Tristram looked up at Walter and shook his head. "I am back where I
started. Explain how it is, Wat. After all those lessons and so much
patience on her part, I can't remember a word of it. Everything went
out of my head while I was in that cage."

When the situation had been explained, Maryam smiled at him and
declared she would start all over again. "We must not be separated again
as we were when we couldn't talk together," she said, seating herself on
the floor beside the couch. "As soon as you are strong enough, I shall
start you again with *bi* and *chi* and you will soon have it all back. How
we will talk then! I have so much to tell you."

"He says he is pleased we are married," said Walter to her. "And
knowing how truly unselfish he is, I am certain he means it. I am very
much afraid I would have been less philosophic if our positions had
been reversed."

Mahmoud was summoned a few minutes later and, on instructions
from Walter, proceeded to set out on the floor the boxes containing the
gifts of the Empress. Tristram did not seem particularly interested,
although it was clear he was amazed at the number and magnificence of
them. Maryam was both bewildered and delighted. She looked from one
box to the other, her eyes wide with wonder.

"Is it possible!" she exclaimed. "These are all for you?"

"For us," said Walter. "They are the joint property of the three of us.
I think the bulk of my share will soon be transferred to the care and
use of someone I find myself very much in love with."

She picked up a large ruby and held it to the light. "How lovely!"
she breathed, in a tone of rapture. "This one, perhaps, you will give
me?"

"We will have it set in a gold chain to hang around your pretty neck."

Walter then turned to his friend. "Our fortunes are made!" he said
exuberantly. "When we return to England, Tris, we will ride on
prancing steeds and our pockets will jingle with the sweet music of
gold!"

"I am glad, Wat, for your sake. It seems like a great fortune."

"We are rich men. Not in my wildest dreams did I expect the equal of this. Now we shall proceed to the division. What will you do with your half?"

"My half!" Tristram threw back his head and gave a laugh which had some of the old ring in it. "I am not entitled to any of this, let alone a half. You won it, Wat. I had nothing to do with it."

"You were the first to show your golden plumage in Kinsai. It was the coincidence of our arriving the same day which led the Empress into such a lavish effort to buy our favor. Naturally you were supposed to share."

"Come, Wat, don't let your kindness of heart run away with you. I have no claim to this; and no special desire to have any of it. What would I do with it?"

"Buy land," said Walter. "You must acquire enough when you go back to set yourself up as a solid citizen. Socman Griffen! How does that ring in your ears?"

"I would never feel any pleasure in the sound," declared the other with sudden vehemence. "I want no title, Wat. My father is a free man, and so his children were never under bond to any lord; but he owns nothing. You will be the one to buy land and have a title."

"Not I. After all my talk, I have had a change of heart. I no longer have the desire for large holdings. I must win an honest name for myself in some other way."

Tristram looked at him with a puzzled air. "What has happened to change your mind?"

"I have been using my eyes and my ears since I reached this country. Land is for the many, not the few. I am sure it is far from the purpose of our Heavenly Father that a few men should own all the land in England. It is not His will that all the rest exist in servitude."

The sick man sat up straight and regarded him with shining eyes. "If that is what you truly believe, Wat," he cried, "the only bar that could ever be raised between us has been removed! I have never uttered a word to combat your purpose; it did not seem fitting that I should. But I have had troubled thoughts about the future, fearing the distinctions of class would lead us on far different paths." The puzzled expression then returned. "But why do you advise me to become a landowner?"

"What I had in mind was a goodish farm of several virgates, just large enough for you to live in comfort without fear of distrain or escuage. I was not proposing a whole rape of land, cut up into tenant farms and game preserves. I knew you too well to suggest anything of that kind.

But after all, Tris, you are of yeoman stock. You belong on the land. There would be no departure from an honest belief in what I propose."

Tristram picked up enough of the stones to cover the palm of his hand. "This will be my share then. No more, Wat. My mind is made up to that, and there is no point in trying to change it. This is more than fair." He looked at Maryam and smiled. "You have a wife to support, and I want to see our little Maryam blossom into a fine lady when you take her home. And now that we have the matter settled, what do you plan to do with yours?"

It was Walter's turn to show a pair of shining eyes. "I have great plans!" he exclaimed. "I am going to introduce into England some of the wonderful things I have seen here in China. These people could learn much from us; but, make no mistake, we have much more to learn from them. Some of the things I have found will change the whole life of England, particularly the making of this magic thing called paper. I have not yet learned how it is done, but I am told they have a way of setting down writings on paper from blocks! Can you conceive what it would mean if the Bible could be set down in that way? In time every family in England would have a copy. And then there is the magic compass—I have a story to tell you about *that*—and the *Hua-P'ao* for the use of Roger Bacon's fire-making powder. England will become the first land in Christendom if I can teach our people how to make these things.

"And now I am through with speechmaking," he said. He took a number of the unset stones and handed them to Maryam. "These are to be sewn in the hem of a jacket. I never intend to let you out of my sight again if I can help it; but we are in a strange land and must be prepared for anything that may befall us. With these you could never be in want, even if we should be separated at any time."

Maryam looked at the gems in her hand with a worried frown. "I think it is time you began to teach me to speak English," she said.

"One thing at a time, Taffy. I haven't fully mastered your modern Greek. Let us finish that first."

"I know just two English words," she said solemnly.

He nodded. "Walter, London. The first word, spoken in the tone you use when you are thinking well of me, is a gratifying foundation in itself. I hope the whole language will sound as sweetly on your lips as my name does."

"If we were separated, what would I do?" There was a trace of panic in her voice. "How would I ever find you again?"

"We must have our first English lesson soon. But grant me a little delay. We must have a little time to ourselves without any thought of such serious and laborious matters."

In the wall which separated the two houses was an openwork gate with brass carving. The carving took the form of a dragon with fierce eyes and scales bristling in defiance. Maryam stopped and clutched Walter's arm.

"See!" she said. "It is looking straight at me! It doesn't want to let me in."

Walter laughed. "I would give battle to a live dragon in behalf of my lady. Have you no faith in my power to defend her from one of brass?"

"I think," she persisted, "that this dragon has decided I am not worthy to be the wife of a brave knight and to live with him in the house it guards. I am very sure it is an obsequious dragon and that it would wag its tail in welcome like a faithful dog if I were your noble lady Engaine."

"What foolish fancies you get in that small head of yours!"

"No, it is not a fancy. I am afraid there will be dragons like this one wherever we go in England. Dragons who can talk and who will sneer at the unworthy wife the great lord Walter brought back with him from the East."

"Everyone will say you are the loveliest lady in all England!" he assured her.

He swung the gate open. Maryam shrank away from it as they passed through, eyeing the mythical beast with an air that still lacked conviction. "I won't care about anything else if *you* will always feel that way," she said. "If I could only be sure! I lay awake last night after you had gone to sleep, thinking about it. I was dreading what might happen. Will you see me with the same eyes in England that you do here?"

From the inside the scaly brass figure presented an entirely different aspect. It seemed suddenly to have become benevolent, and its protruding eyes were fixed on them with the regard of a faithful guardian.

Maryam began to laugh with relief. "I feel better already!" she cried. "Everything seems so right and secure when I feel these lovely walls around us. Just you and I, Walter, with the whole world locked out! Must we ever leave?" She turned and threw her arms around him with a fierce possessiveness. "Why can't we stay here always? We could be so happy here."

"That is impossible, Taffy," he declared. "I fear all this pleasant world will soon be swept away by an ugly storm. But even if we could be sure that things would go on just as they are, it would not do for us to stay. We belong in England. I have so much work to do at home."

She nodded her head and sighed. "Of course," she said. "I know that we must return. I was not really serious about it. I shall be happy to go with you anywhere in the world, my Walter."

She looked about her, nevertheless, with a longing eye. A light breeze was stirring in the lime trees and the green foliage which closed about them on all sides. They could see no more than the friendly roof of the Abode of Everlasting Felicity. The whole world seemed indeed shut out.

She sighed again. "But it is lovely here. It is *so* lovely!"

3

The last sonorous "amen" echoed through the Abode of Everlasting Felicity. Father Theodore replaced the parchment slip in the pouch under his girdle. Maryam leaned into the support of Walter's arms, and their smiles met happily.

"You did not drink your full share of the wine," she protested. "That is supposed to mean something, I think."

"It means I shall be an overindulgent husband. But I would be that, wine or no wine." He looked down at his boots which had upcurling toes and the figures of yellow leopards in the frets. "I am wearing for the first time a gift left to me in my father's will."

Maryam reached down for Chi Wangti, who had been frisking about the hem of her skirt with a querulous conviction of neglect. She held him against her cheek. "My little Chi," she said, "your mistress is now a most thoroughly wedded woman." She turned to the priest. "Thank you, Father Theodore. The service sounded beautiful and most solemn. I wish it had been possible to follow the words."

"All ritual of the Nestorian Church is beautiful," declared the priest, looking covertly at Walter as though he half expected a contradiction. "I am to begin at once on my work here in the East, the winning of converts to a belief in what you have just said."

Walter drew him aside. "It is well known that Kublai Khan has an open mind in matters of religion," he said. "On the other hand the Sung government regards all missionary work with an eye of suspicion. I have a selfish interest in what I am going to suggest, but it is true that you will be in a freer position if you continue to hold the good opinion of

Bayan." He studied the priest closely. "It has become necessary to send a messenger to the Mongolian camp, and I am sure it would be wise for you to go. You can return when the city is in Bayan's hands and begin your work without interference."

Father Theodore nodded his head shrewdly. "There is good sense in what you say. What is the nature of the mission?"

"We want Bayan to know the proportions to which the peace movement has grown in Kinsai. I have prepared a report for him which should reach his hands as soon as possible. I desire him to know also the nature of the obstacle which has arisen, so he will not think he has been betrayed when he learns I am living luxuriously in the Great Interior Palace. Chang Wu will provide you an escort and guides. The journey will be a safe one and a quick one."

"I will go," decided the priest, after consideration. Then he added with some hesitation: "I have one regret only at the need to leave so soon. At last I have seen a woman who fills my eye. I have always fancied them of a size, and this one is of most noble proportions." His face began to glow, and he cracked the joints of his fingers enthusiastically as he talked. "I have seen her twice only. Ah, what a straight line to her back! What solidity, and yet what grace when she walks! The wise absorption of her eyes! She is a cook here in the palace," he added, "and both times when I saw her she was rolling dough in a pastry trough."

"Are you sure, good Father Theodore, it was your eye she filled?"

"She is a widow," went on the priest, his exuberance mounting as he recounted her superior qualifications. "It is better that way. It is only in selecting wives that men put value in lack of experience. With that I do not agree. I prefer a partnership of maturity to the vexatious mewlings of virginity."

In the days which followed it became evident that the yellow house in the thick green garden had been aptly named. The felicity of the newly married pair was so complete that it promised to be everlasting. Nothing happened to mar the happy hours, not a shadow of a quarrel, not a ripple of dissent between them.

The days followed a set pattern, and yet there was never a dull moment. Maryam would be up and bathed and dressed before Walter turned an unwilling head on the satin pillow they shared, and her cheerful, "Good morrow, honorable husband," would evoke protesting groans from him. He would not be permitted a respite, however; Maryam

would have plans made which required his immediate assistance, and
he would soon find himself in the lattice-shielded bath, reaching from
the comforting steam for towels on the wheel.

The mornings were spent for the most part in the garden, which was
quite extensive and contained among other attractions a good-sized
pond full of fish with reddish scales and fins flashing brilliantly in the
still water. They were intensely interested in the nature of the palace
buildings which towered above their own walls, but it was a curiosity
they had no means of satisfying. They were not allowed to leave their
own grounds. Three guards stood on the outside of the walls, and when
they approached the boundaries they were always conscious of at least
one pair of slanted eyes watching them from under a grotesque helmet.
Maryam dubbed the trio Aeacus, Minos, and Rhadamanthus after the
dread judges of the underworld, and sought to placate them with offer-
ings of food and fruit. It was hard to tell if this was having any effect,
although at times she had some small progress to report. "Minos smiled
at me today," she reported once. "One more good meal under that
enormous belt of his, and I think he may allow us as much as a walk in
the Vista of Eternal Spring." One thing was certain; the clank of swinging swords and the shuffle of padded feet never ceased on the outside
of the walls.

Maryam had fallen into the habit of aping Chinese manners and
speech. She had an amusing gift of mimicry. Often on their walks she
would fall a few respectful paces behind Walter, teetering along with
short steps, her hands folded under her cuffs. She would ask in a singsong tone, "Does estimable husband still esteem small and humble
wife?"

The afternoons were invariably quite warm, and Walter devoted them
to the writing of notes on what he had observed of this fabulous
country, setting down all the details he had learned of its most practical
innovations. Maryam would sit beside him, stitching at some embroidery
or playing with Chi, who had become so attached to her that he would
whine piteously if she deserted him for a moment. She would watch
with a jealous eye the busy quill scratching over the sheets of paper,
but she never interrupted him. Such distractions as occurred were always of his own making. At intervals he would lay down the quill and
study the dark head bent over the embroidering frame. "Do you know
how much these Chinese costumes become you?" he would ask. Or,
"How can I work when you are here to remind me of pleasanter ways
of spending the time?" She would smile then and say, "Obedient wife

knows when hint has been given." Snatching the dog up and dropping him into a capacious pocket, she would be off with a brisk clatter of heels. He would hear her harrying the servants out of their slothful ways or busying herself at some task in the house. Sometimes he would hear her laugh from far out in the garden, and then it would seem no more than a moment before she would come racing across the floor toward him, crying: "My very tall and very beautiful lord and husband, I haven't seen you for a full ten minutes. I am a sadly neglected wife!" He would then toss the quill to one side and say in a reproachful voice, "It is hard to work when you are away, my heart; but impossible when you are here!"

Her energy seemed boundless, and her moods were as varied as the shades in the rainbow they once glimpsed over the high walls of their garden. She would become ecstatic over something he said to her, and her eyes would light up until her whole face seemed to dance; and in a few moments he might find her in abject misery because one of her birds had no appetite for his seeds. One moment she would be crooning over a stringed instrument, and the next instant she would charge out to the servants' quarters to upbraid them for making the master's bath too warm that morning.

Observing these mercurial twists of temperament, he was sure she took as much after her mother as her English father. She had a great sense of fairness, however, and an appreciation of the humorous side of everything, and these traits he ascribed to her Anglo-Saxon heritage.

She had filled the house with birds. He never found out where they all came from: parakeets with blazing polls and green wings, shy little couples sitting side by side in solemn devotion, yellow-breasted singers who threatened to tear out their throats in harmonious delight. There were so many of them that Peter the owl had precipitated a tearful scene by giving up in disgust and disappearing forever.

Peter's place in her affections was taken thereafter by a large parrot. She called him Hector because it was clear, from his habit of indulging in round Grecian oaths, that he had once had a master from her own country. He would mutter, *"Diavolus! Diavolus!"* as he crunched his seeds. Mahmoud came in occasionally for unfavorable attention because of a tendency to neglect the bathing of Hector. "That Mahmoud!" she would say. "He is a lazy little beast. I will have his bones ground as food for the ravens!"

She dramatized everything. The world would rock on its base for her if she found too few dumplings in the wanton soup. She would burst into tears if Walter were unwise enough to let her catch a glimpse of his scarred back. But for the most part she existed in moods of the highest content, full of affectionate traits, as demonstratively pleased over any attentions he paid her as Chi Wangti who battened on her kindness. She would preen herself happily when her husband interrupted his work to squeeze her hand. She sang a great deal, in a throaty and not too sure voice. Often, when she tired of the inactivity imposed on her by his absorption, she would wander away to practice dance steps, humming a Chinese song, "Black bean, black bean, ripen slow," or catches of her own composition from native words, "When the fung bird sings in tree, then-my-lover-comes-back-to-me."

They enjoyed the evenings most of all, for the exhausting heat of the day had subsided then and Walter would be through with his work. As soon as the sun had vanished behind the massive bulk of the Hsuan-te Tower, Maryam would run to dress herself in her very best, the Robe of Sixteen Summers. It was a gorgeous thing of white satin with blue and gold decorations, a gift from the Empress, and she looked so well in it that Walter was never content with anything else. "Ah, if you like me in this," she would sigh, "you should have seen me in some of the robes I had at home in Antioch!"

"I find it hard to wait for the time," he would answer, "when I shall see you in an English kirtle, with a blue gorget to match the color of your eyes."

Her Imperial Munificence was losing no chance to please the visitors of good omen. Baskets heaped with fruit arrived every day, and great masses of flowers, enough to fill the main rooms of the house. Once there was a bowl of blue glaze from the Brothers' Kilns of Lung-Ch'uan, an offering of such magnificence that Chang Wu clucked with amazement when he saw it. Once the daily gift took the form of a ring for Maryam, a band of plain gold set with a splendidly large sapphire.

Once it consisted of a hundred colored duck's eggs. Chang Wu dropped in unexpectedly, and his eyes sparkled slyly when he explained that this was a custom known as "urging the birth."

"It is perhaps a little early," he conceded, "but it is clear that domestic accord has settled in the home of my young brother. Marriage is the greatest of all lotteries, and I am happy my brother has drawn a prize for himself. Let us hope this wife will fulfill the expectations of Her Imperial Munificence by giving him many sons."

"It is a consummation much to be hoped for, kind elder brother," said Walter

"Let us hope also that the accord will continue even when other wives have been taken into this house."

It proved a memorable visit, for the envoy had brought gifts of his own; a magnetic needle especially designed for maritime use, with a dial on which no fewer than twenty-four points were marked on a reckoning from the south, and an ivory tube filled with glass. Walter spent some time studying the needle and thinking what great uses it could be put to when he returned to England with it.

Then he picked up the ivory tube. It was over a foot in length and an inch and a half in diameter, tapering slightly at one end.

"It is called 'Eye That Sees Far.' Look into it, my friend. Point it at some object and observe the effect."

The Sung vase was standing near at hand. Holding the small end of the tube to his eye, Walter looked in that direction. At first he could make out very little. Then the picture seen in the glass became clearer, and he drew in his breath with surprise. The pattern on the face of the porcelain was so minutely sketched that to the eye it had seemed no more than a few very delicate lines; but now the lines were large and clear, standing out boldly on the white face. He could see small imperfections on what had seemed a flawless surface, and even some tiny cracks.

"Look at my hand." Chang Wu held out his right hand with fingers extended. "Study it with care and tell me what you observe."

Walter turned the tube in that direction. "I see a hand almost twice the natural size!" he cried. "I see a countless number of small lines gathered into curling patterns. Will honorable Chang Wu move his fingers? It is true! The fingers move also in the glass."

Chang Wu smiled. "I know nothing of such matters, but it has been told me that the strange things one sees are the result of placing together pieces of glass of different shapes."

Walter lowered the glass and gazed at it with increasing wonder. "It cannot be magic," he said. "There are no cabalistic signs on it."

"It is said to be a matter of the greatest simplicity, a freak of nature which was stumbled on by the merest chance. If my young brother desires Eye That Sees Far, it is his."

When the visitor had gone, Maryam ranged herself by Walter's side and smiled as a signal that the final ritual of the evening might begin. He loosened the jade clasp at her throat and the Robe of Sixteen Summers slid slowly from her shoulders and then dropped to the floor in a shimmering heap, revealing a pure white tunic of silk which left her shoulders and arms bare. As they were of a whiteness to match the tunic, there was always some slight delay before the next step was undertaken, but this evening he seemed even slower than usual.

"The strings are delicate, and you are going to break them," she said, as he fumbled at the intricate lacing of the under-tunic. "Are you really so clumsy or is it just an excuse?"

He was even less adept in unraveling the entwined cords, which confined the white silk trousers at the waist, with the result that they finally became snarled. He pulled and tugged at them without result until she was compelled to take the task in hand herself.

"Is it possible," she demanded, "that an impatience makes the matter of untying two simple cords such a matter of difficulty? I think after this I must place myself in the hands of the maids. Then I can come to you with my disrobing an accomplished fact."

As this threat was voiced at some stage each evening, Walter paid no attention to it, but he gave particular care to the removal of her garters. Maryam had made them herself in the fashion of the West, and as she was not sure she could achieve another pair, they had to be drawn over her knees with the utmost care. What remained after that, however, was comparatively simple, for her Chinese stockings slipped off with the astonishing ease of silk.

"As far as I have heard," he said, holding up one of the stockings and fingering it cautiously, "it has never occurred to ladies of the West to have them made of silk. How envious they would be if they could see this! The wife of our king, who comes from Spain, has brought many new things to England. Perhaps Queen Maryam will introduce silk stockings."

Any comment on the ways of the ladies of the world to which she expected soon to be translated had always been of the greatest interest to her. The remark passed unnoticed, however. She had fallen into deep thought.

"There is one question about your country I have never asked," she said finally. "Do the men ever have more than one wife?"

Walter laughed. "So that is what has made you so thoughtful all evening! Have you been disturbed over what Chang Wu said? Know then, my heart, that men of the West have one wife only. What is more, marriage is the most sacred of covenants, and nothing can loosen the bond when once the words of the service have been said."

She sighed with relief. "I thought it was that way, but it is good to know. As to the old man's other suggestion, I hope there will be sons in our house. It is my lord Walter's wish too?"

"Yes," he answered. "But not too soon. There is something I must see to first; the matter of a name for them."

If she realized what he meant, she made no comment. Her mind seemed occupied still with the first point.

"Have you realized yet that I am of a jealous disposition?" she asked. "I must tell you, my Walter, that I would have made great difficulties if the time had ever come when you thought of bringing in other wives. I could not share you with another woman. You belong to me." She paused. Then she managed a smile. "I am afraid I would make things most uncomfortable for any woman who tried to steal a share of our happiness!"

4

Chang Wu paid a visit to the Abode of Everlasting Felicity one afternoon, wearing an expression of intense anxiety.

"Ch'aing-cha has fallen," he announced. "Bayan built great mounds around the walls so his mangonels and the *Hua-P'ao's* could have full play. The walls crumbled, and then our gallant garrison was powerless to defend the city any longer." He shook his head sadly. "Bayan rode to the largest breach and held out his sword, and his men gave a great shout and went in. They killed every man, woman, and child in the place. Have you ever observed with your own eyes what happens when a city is delivered over to the sword? No sight in the world can equal it for horror."

"This means," said Walter, slowly, "that the road to Kinsai is wide open."

"The Mongol armies are already on the march. They are spreading out like locusts over the low country, and our army has broken before them. There is nothing to hold them back." The envoy paused for a moment of bitter reflection. "The Empress and imperial ministers still refuse to see the light! They are like children flying kites to hold back the tornado."

"What is to be done? This is your last chance to make a peace and save the city from the fate of Ch'aing-cha."

Chang Wu nodded somberly. "The time has come," he declared, "for the birds of golden plumage to disappear. If that vain hope is denied them, they may come to their senses. But if they persist in their folly, honorable scholar, the forces working for peace will act. The men of the city will see to it that the power to control the destiny of the country is taken away from the Great Interior Palace!"

After a long pause, Walter asked, "What can be done about getting us away?"

Chang Wu answered ominously, "Plans are being made, younger brother, of which I will tell in due time."

When he had gone, Walter went in search for Maryam, dreading the necessity of telling her of the new danger which hovered over them. At first he could not find her. He looked all through the house and then made a tour of the garden, finally catching a glimpse of her perched on a corner of their ten-foot wall. She was looking over into the Vista of Eternal Spring, which lay on the other side, with the most absorbed interest, but she turned as soon as she heard his step.

"How did you get up there?" he demanded.

She smiled down at him. "I jumped across from that limb you are standing under."

He measured the distance from tree to wall with a worried frown. "You must never do anything as risky as that again, Taffy. And now how do you propose to get down?"

"You will help me down, of course."

"But suppose I decide to leave you up there for a time as a punishment?"

She began to drum her heels against the wall and continued to smile. "I never realized before how very tall you are," she said. "This light makes your hair seem more golden than ever. You are really a very handsome man, my Walter. I am regretting the distance which separates us."

"The only way to correct that is to come down."

"Come closer," she instructed. "Hold out your arms."

"Be careful!" he exclaimed.

Before he grasped her purpose, she had sprung from the wall, landing neatly in his arms. Not having had warning, he was unable to brace himself in time, and they fell together to the ground. Fortunately there was a heavy growth of ferns to break the force of their fall. They rolled over twice, locked in each other's arms, before coming to a rest. Then they both began to laugh.

"What a gibbety little hoyden you are!" he exclaimed.

"And what a very solemn old sobersides you are! You have never learned to play. I see that I shall have to teach you."

Walter forgot the troubled situation which had filled his mind. They lay in a soft bed of the fragrant fern, her head on his shoulder and one of her arms still clasping his neck. The tall fronds on each side rose up so high that they could see nothing but the waving green tracery and a very thin slice of the sky above. Never before, not even in the seclusion of their couch, had they seemed so completely cut off from the rest of the world. Not a sound was to be heard but the chirp of a bird far away in the trees. Their eyes met in mutual realization. When he gathered her closer to him, she seemed to go limp in his arms.

"Walter!" she whispered, breathlessly.

"Was there ever a better place for making love?"

"No." Her head buried itself on his shoulder. "Not even the sun can see us."

When they were strolling back to the house, some time later, he told her of the fall of the fortress city which had barred the way to Kinsai.

"This Bayan you are always praising," said Maryam, with a shudder, "must be as cruel as all the other Mongol leaders."

Walter shook his head in dissent. "I am sure he was acting under pressure. He has been criticized for his leniency many times. Before I left, orders had been received from Kublai Khan that examples must be made of Chinese cities which resisted. Perhaps he selected Ch'aing-cha so Kinsai can be spared. In a very short time now he will take this city also.

"The court has been ordered to wear white," he added, after a moment. "They are hanging white curtains everywhere in the palace."

"What does that mean?"

"White is the Sung color of death. It means they are beginning to realize their danger. But still the ministers will not give in. Maryam, we must be prepared for anything now."

"The guards are still around the walls," she whispered fearfully. "I could see one of them as I sat on the wall. Perhaps it was my imagination, but he seemed less friendly."

"We will have no friends now. Perhaps not even Chang Wu."

A little later, in an effort to divert her thoughts, he asked what she had been watching so intently while she sat on the wall.

"I saw the Emperor. He was riding in a queer little two-wheeled carriage with a red umbrella over his head. There were cords attached to the carriage, and two rows of girls were drawing it. There must have been fifty of them. And they had almost no clothing on at all."

"Kung Tsung is losing no time in falling into the ways of his ancestors, it seems."

"He looked like a very silly and bad-tempered boy," said Maryam. "He had a long whip, and he kept curling it around their bare ankles. It must have hurt, for some of them were crying. He was laughing all the time. I'm sure he will be a very cruel ruler when he grows up."

"I don't think he will be allowed to grow up. But even if he does, there will be no part of China left for him to rule. Bayan will overrun this whole country in another year."

They did not enjoy their supper of "Sweet and Pungent Pork" that evening. After an unsuccessful effort to appear unconcerned, Maryam laid aside her chopsticks. "I have no appetite," she said, placing a small platter of the meat on the floor. "My little Chi will benefit. He is very greedy when it comes to sweet dishes."

While the tiny dog snuffled hungrily over the meat, they walked to a window where they could see the last rays of the sun tracing a pattern on the graying sky.

"Walter," she asked in a whisper, "will you be blamed because things are going wrong?"

"It's impossible to say what strange ideas they will get into their heads. One thing we may depend on: we will no longer stand in high favor with either party."

Maryam looked up resolutely. "I am not afraid," she declared. "After all that has happened to us, we need have no concern now."

Chang Wu returned during the evening. Maryam had been playing a plaintive air on a musical instrument which had been one of the daily gifts from the Empress, and she rose at once to leave. The envoy's face was so wrinkled with dismal thought that he bore a striking resemblance to Chi Wangti, but he relaxed into a smile when he greeted her.

"Your wishes have been heeded, most magnanimous lady," he said, with a low bow. "The life of Lu Chung is to be spared."

"I am so glad!"

"He is getting off better than he deserves," said Walter.

Maryam protested at this. "You are forgetting that he did me a great service."

"At a price."

"A great service still. You are forgetting also, my Walter, that you added your request to mine that he be dealt with leniently."

"Only because you cried, my dearest one." Walter turned to the envoy. "What will be done with him?"

"Lu Chung is not to escape punishment. He will be imprisoned and, naturally, he will be heavily fined. There will be no feathers left in the nest of Lu Chung."

The two men sat down to talk, and Maryam went to the other end of the room, where she curled up on a cushion. The instrument fell to the floor beside her. The dog Chi bounced from the side of the couch, where he had been sleeping, and ran over to her.

"Tonight we will come for you," said the envoy in a whisper. "A day of meditation, starting at sundown, has been decreed for the court, and so there will be few about. It will not be difficult to overpower the guards. It is my hope that they will listen to reason and be ready to stand aside. If that cannot be arranged, we must accomplish the escape without raising an alarm in the palace."

Walter had been watching him steadily, aware of a change in his attitude. It seemed to him that the old man was reluctant to meet his eye.

"And if the palace is aroused before we can get away? What then?"

Chang Wu twisted about uneasily. "In the peace party," he said after a moment, "there is a mood of determination. Everything is at stake: their lives, all their possessions. They will stop at nothing now."

"Which means that, if our escape cannot be accomplished, other steps will be taken."

The envoy nodded his head reluctantly. "Under no circumstances can you be left alive in the palace," he said. "It is to be regretted that this must be told my younger brother. But such is the decision which has been reached."

"Have you no fear in telling me this that I will go to the ministers of the Emperor and throw myself on their protection?" asked Walter.

There was a moment of silence. "It would be of no use, younger brother. The favorite of today is the scapegoat of tomorrow. If the Mongols pound on our gates, the ministers will seek an excuse for their failure, and then it will go hard with the birds of golden plumage. But," added Chang Wu, "I feel it in my heart that the brave young lord from the West will not desert the cause which brought him here. Even if it involves this much of risk."

After another long pause, Walter said: "I knew what you had to tell me as soon as you came in. Rest assured, worthy Chang Wu, I will not seek protection in the court. I have been giving much thought to the possibility of an escape, and I see no reason why it cannot be accomplished."

"'The servants must have no suspicion," cautioned the old man. "It might be well if we partook of a few dishes of wine while we talk."

Maryam had been watching with nervously observant eyes. When they began to drink *shao chin,* the hot millet wine, she concluded that the errand which had brought Chang Wu was not as serious as she had at first feared. She became anxious for him to leave so she might learn what Walter had to tell her. But Chang Wu showed no intention of leaving. He sat cross-legged on the floor and imbibed dish after dish of the wine, talking steadily in a low tone.

Finally she became sleepy. She stifled a yawn with difficulty and rose to walk about the room. She examined the water-wheel clock on the wall. It was an intricate one, and she had always been a little afraid of it, never having seen a clock of any kind before; a feeling which Walter had shared to such an extent that he had not dared investigate the delicate springs which made it go.

Chang Wu seemed impervious to indirect suggestion. She gave up the effort and returned to her cushion, where she fell into a doze. She did not hear when he took his departure.

She roused when Walter called her. Going over to him, she curled up on his lap and rested her head sleepily on his shoulder. "I thought honorable old nuisance would never go," she murmured.

Walter did not begin, as she expected he would, on their usual evening ritual. Instead he looked down at her gravely and said, "We must leave tonight, Taffy."

She sat up at once, all thought of sleep gone.

"What has happened? Are you—are you in any danger, Walter?"

He nodded his head after a moment. "Yes, there may be some danger in what is ahead of us. But I am glad it has come to this point. We could not stay here any longer while all our plans were ruined. But you must not be concerned. We have planned everything as carefully as possible; and I feel assured that our escape will be successfully carried out. We can do nothing until the servants are all asleep. Then we must pack what we are to take with us. It must be as little as possible, only such things as we will need. I must go now and speak to Tris. Don't let any fears get into that little head of yours while I am away; and, of course, do nothing to arouse the suspicions of the servants."

Maryam stood up. "Of course, Walter, I shall be most careful. And I will try not to be afraid."

The brave front she had maintained as long as he was there left her as soon as he had gone. With a white and set face she moved stealthily about the house, having many things to do before he returned. First she made the rounds of her bird cages, saying in earnest whispers: "Farewell, my Leander. Farewell, Ganymede. Good-by, my precious little Echo and Narcissus; *your* felicity will be everlasting, I am sure." She paused beside the cage of Hector. "Ah, how I will miss you, my old voice of Jove from Olympus!"

The dog had pattered anxiously at her heels. She took him up now and whispered: "You, at least, I shall take, my little Chi. But you must be a brave fellow and make no noise."

Then, as usual, she sought the guidance of Kherdar. She took the cubes in her cupped hands, shook them gently, and repeated the formula before letting them trickle through her fingers to the floor. For several moments she studied the messages on the upturned surfaces, and then frowned.

"I threw them in too much haste. I must be more careful this time." She shook them again, saying: "Kherdar, the truth! Let them so fall that I can read the future."

There was another pause as she read the results. She picked up the dice a third time and rattled them with more vigor before letting them fall.

"They come up the same each time!" she whispered unhappily. "If Walter were here, he would laugh and say there is no truth in it." She studied the symbols on the dice for the third time. "Separation—long journeys—perhaps even death. I am afraid! I am terribly afraid!"

5

Maryam swung a bundle of clothing over her shoulder. The house was in darkness, and she reached out for Walter's arm, whispering, "The long journey begins, my love." He was carrying two large bags. In one he had packed the presents from the Empress and in the other everything he had collected in his study of the country, the compass, the Eye That Sees Far, specimens of paper, some Chinese writings, his voluminous notes. Mahmoud was somewhere near them, also loaded with bags.

"I feel very sad," whispered Maryam. "We have been so happy here! Do you think we will ever find the equal of this again?"

"Gurnie will seem like a cow byre compared with the palaces of China," he said. "But there will be compensations. Wait until you see the green of the land your father came from, and the wonder of the English woods! It is always so fresh and cool and lovely there! The Eng-

lish blood in your veins will race when you are unhooded and get your
first glimpse of it all."

They made their way in the dark with the greatest caution. As the
copper gate swung to after them, Maryam said: "I am sure the ugly
old dragon is gloating at my expense. He knows I am leaving and will
never come back." Then she turned back and whispered, "Farewell,
Abode of Everlasting Felicity!"

Walter asked cautiously, "Did you sew the gems I gave you into the
lining of your coat?"

"Yes. I have done everything you told me."

Tristram was waiting for them. It was clear from the tone of his low
greeting that he was glad to be leaving. "And now, away for England!"
he said. "Those words ring happily in my ears."

Walter halted uneasily when they reached the rear gate, which opened
out on a marketing street. So far not a sound had been heard. Did this
mean that the plan he and Chang Wu had concocted between them had
been carried out successfully? His heart bounded with relief when he
heard the envoy whisper in the dark: "The guard has been enticed away,
younger brother. Come, the gate is open."

Closed chairs were in readiness a short distance down the street, and a
dozen discreetly silent carriers waited. They set off at once.

The street was not as deserted as they had hoped. Peering through the
curtains, Walter saw prone figures along the walls and in the shelter of
projecting doorways. There were a score of people sleeping in the entrance to a small *chorten,* huddled together as though to share their
misery. These were refugees, he knew; the city must be full of them,
with the invading armies drawing so close.

When they reached the neighborhood of the river, the streets were
filled with noisy, milling crowds, and there was a threat of conflict in the
air. They came to a halt. Chang Wu put his head through the curtains of
the chair Walter shared with his wife. "There have been riots," he said.
"There are rice stores along the river, and the people have been fighting
to break them open. A slight delay will be unavoidable."

They were taken to the curio shop which the old man owned, and he
left them there while he went to investigate conditions at the wharves.
It was a small shop, lighted dimly by a cresset near the back. Maryam
looked about her and shivered. Hideous masks gibbered down at them
from the walls. An enormously fat idol stared belligerently from a dark
corner. A jade snake, looking very much alive in the flickering light,
coiled along the top of a screen. The air was heavy with incense.

"Kherdar told the truth," she thought unhappily. "There will be great trouble for us tonight."

Walter was thinking of the danger in the carrying out of their plan created by this delay. The Great Bore, the high tidal wave which swept up the narrow course of the Ch'ien-tang River, was due very soon. It was essential that they reach their ship on the opposite bank before it arrived. Would there be time?

It was a full hour before Chang Wu returned. "My humblest apologies for the long wait," he said. "There have been difficulties, but at last they are resolved. Will you condescend to follow me?"

They started out on foot, their full escort still in watchful attendance. Walter looked at the tall fellow who paced along beside him and thought, "If it is found we cannot reach the boat, they will cut our throats without a qualm." He reached out for Maryam's arm and drew her closer. Their danger was not confined, however, to the avowed purpose of the peace party. Rioters surged about the edges of the slowly progressing group, shouting threats. A sound of fighting reached them from the direction of the waterfront. There would be great difficulty, without a doubt, in getting away.

When they reached the entrance to the moorings, a sentry challenged them with the end of his pike on which a lantern was suspended. Chang Wu whispered to him, and the pike was swung back obligingly, the lantern tossing giddily with the motion. They passed inside, and Walter sighed with relief when he saw a pair of triangular sails against the sky ahead.

"The good St. Aidan, to whom I have been praying all night, has answered," he said, fervently.

He stopped, half believing that he could hear in the distance a humming like the muted beat of drums behind a hill. Had the Bore started?

Chang Wu had heard it also. "You must start at once," he said. "The Bore runs sometimes as high as twenty feet, and no skiff could face it; but there is still time to reach your ship on the other side."

Walter felt his arms gripped on each side and rough voices commanding him to step ahead. He saw that Tristram also was being briskly propelled in the direction of the waiting skiffs. The face of Chang Wu appeared out of the darkness for a moment to say: "Farewell, younger brother. You and the Tall One must leave in the first boat. We dare not delay for the passing of the Bore. The others will follow later."

He tried to free himself, but his guards held him so firmly that the effort proved useless. He looked back over his shoulder desperately but could not see his wife. He felt himself being dragged down the steps of the mooring toward the waiting skiff. Then he was unceremoniously shoved aboard to find that Tristram was already there. Two guards jumped in after them, cutting the rope with their swords. They moved away from the shore.

It was not hard to fathom the purpose of this. If they got safely to the other side, all well and good; but if, on the other hand, they failed to do so, the Great Bore would accomplish what the peace party knew to be necessary: the disappearance for all time of the two birds of golden plumage. It was not essential for Maryam to leave at once, and so she could be sent across in the second skiff as soon as the tidal wave had passed. Walter found himself wondering if the delay had been deliberate, if the peace leaders had arranged it for this very purpose. They would be better suited if he and Tristram were swallowed up in the water, never to come back.

The Great Bore was a rare spectacle in the daytime, with crowds lining the banks to watch its majestic sweep up the river and expert divers with colored plumes in their caps diving into the high white head of water. At night it was a different matter. They could hear a roaring in the distance as though all the *Hua-P'ao's* in China had gone into action at once. It was too dark to see anything, but the boatmen had broken out their oars and were pulling at them desperately. Tristram leaned over to shout in his ear, "I don't think the river is very wide here, but it will be touch and go."

They made it with no more than a scant second to spare. The hull of the ship on which they were to sail up Kinsai Bay loomed up suddenly above them, a chain ladder dangling within their reach. Scrambling up, they could feel the ship give a convulsive lurch as the wash of the great wave reached it. Looking back over his shoulder, Walter saw that the whole face of the river had turned white. The next instant the water engulfed him, and it took all his strength to maintain his hold on the swaying links. He hung on desperately for what seemed to be an eternity of time, fearing that he would be swept away. His lungs were filled with water. Then the chain slackened and he knew that the first impact of the wave had been spent.

They were drenched when they reached the deck. Tristram shivered and said in a voice of intense relief: "Well, here we are. Now we can wait until the tide subsides and it will be safe for the other skiff to come across."

The deck was lighted with torches and so crowded that they had to remain close to the rail. The cries of the other passengers, frightened out of their wits by the fierce impact of the Bore, made it impossible at first to talk. When the din subsided somewhat, Walter said to his companion, "I suppose every ship leaving the city now is filled like this with people fleeing for their lives."

The pitching grew less as the water gradually lowered. The two Englishmen, conscious of the fact that their guards were still beside them, leaned over the rail and tried to see into the dark wall which cut them off from the city on the other side of the river.

"Our skiff could not live in that water," said Tristram. "Do you suppose the boatmen were able to get aboard?"

"It would suit the men who sent us out here if they were drowned," answered Walter. "The fewer witnesses left to what has happened tonight, the better they will be pleased."

Tristram nodded glumly. "The same thought has been in my mind. Well, if they were counting on drowning us too, they have been well deceived. It was not in the stars, Wat, for us to die like rats in this filthy river." A moment later he asked, in a tone of sudden anxiety, "Do you think there will be any delay in sending the other skiff across?"

"I have been able to think of nothing else," said Walter. "Chang Wu is still friendly to us, and I am sure he will do everything he can. But," his voice trailing off to a whisper, "there may be trouble back there. The mob was in an ugly mood. The city is full of men with empty bellies, and they may have tried to storm the rice warehouses."

After a long pause, Tristram asked, "Will they hold the ship, think you?"

"Of course!" cried Walter, although he felt none of the assurance he tried to put into his voice. "Every detail was arranged with the greatest care. The captain has orders to wait."

"Where are we headed for?"

"The mouth of the Yang-tse. From there we can reach Bayan's army by land."

"And return to Kinsai with him?" Tristram's tone was full of doubt. "They hope never to see us again, Wat. Even with the Mongols in control of the city, there would be questions asked if we came back. These men do not want it known they arranged our escape. The fear is in my mind, Wat, that this vessel will head for the southern route and not the mouth of the Yang-tse."

After a moment's consideration, Walter found himself in agreement.

"I am prepared to believe almost anything," he said. "If they have done as you suspect, we will be home the sooner; and so perhaps we should not quarrel with their desire to save their own skins. But I am getting more concerned about Maryam by the minute. Do you hear anything yet of traffic on the river?"

"I don't believe any boats have ventured out."

An hour passed. It was still so dark that they could see no more than a few yards in front of them. "The river is falling," said Walter. "It should be safe to make a crossing now."

As he spoke there was a sudden commotion on the deck above, a sound of shouted orders and running feet. The ship heaved and shook. They could hear voices up on the shrouds and the flapping of canvas which meant that sails were being set.

"We are under way!" cried Walter. "They are not going to wait!"

He fought himself clear of the restraining arms of his guard and plunged madly into the crowds about him. He must reach the captain and see that the sailing was delayed. Full well he knew that a separation now might mean he would never see Maryam again. In a few weeks at most, the Mongolians would be at the gates of Kinsai; and even if he and Tristram succeeded in getting off the boat and making their way back to the city, how slim the chance would be of finding her under such conditions!

Tristram followed after him. The two guards were on the point of going also, but they stopped, grinned at each other, and seated themselves comfortably on deck. The ship was pitching with an unsteadiness which meant they were now well astream; their charges could not get away.

The first signs of dawn were showing in the sky when the two Englishmen gave up the effort. They had been all over the slatternly vessel, fighting their way through people packed in as closely as salted jackbarrel. They had twice invaded the crazily high poop deck, where the captain might be expected to have taken his station, and had been roughly expelled without catching a glimpse of him. They had even climbed part way up the masts on which the patched orange sails flapped in the stiffening breeze. No one had paid any attention to them. No one had understood a word of their clamorous demands. The ship had continued to plow ahead into the rough waters which followed the lead of the Bore, drawing further away every moment from the mooring where the second skiff would arrive. Walter had considered jumping overboard and attempting to swim back, but had given the idea up, knowing that he lacked the capacity to survive long in such troubled waters.

They sat down on the deck in a desperate silence. All about them were refugees with their worldly goods: bundles and bags, prayer wheels and mats, food basins, blankets, mattresses, even gamecocks trussed up in canvas. There were fretting women and noisy children clamoring for the rice which was being cooked amidship in an iron tub. A life-sized idol of brass was suspended from one of the masts, swaying with the motion, a suggestion of active malice in its glaring eyes and wide sickle smile.

Tristram looked out across the water. "We are hugging the coast of the bay," he said. "The southern coast, mind you. It is just as I suspected. The ship is heading into the southern route."

Silence settled over them again. "Maryam is alive," said Walter tonelessly. "We have that much consolation. But we are as far removed from her now as though she were dead. It's certain they have no intention of letting us off this ship; and even if we escaped, where could we go and what could we do? Could we reach Kinsai, knowing nothing of the language?" His voice rose on a note of deepest despair. "I have no hope at all that we can ever find her now! It's as though she were at the other end of a great strange world."

The sun had risen in the sky ahead before anything further was said. Then Walter noticed that his companion had one of the bags beside him, and he roused to a sudden show of interest.

"You salvaged something at least from the wreckage," he said. "I seem to have lost the bag I was carrying. God grant this is the one with my Chinese material. At least we must have the chance to accomplish some good by our mad venture."

Tristram opened the sack. It contained the presents of the Empress.

Walter stared down into it for a moment and then rose and walked to the rail. His unseeing eyes were fixed on the muddy coast line. After a time he gave a short, harsh laugh.

"What an ironic trick fate has played us!" he said bitterly. "I came to China to make my fortune. I had no real thought at first beyond the gold I hoped to take back with me. But after these things fell unearned into my lap, I found I cared for them least of all. And this is all we have saved! All the gold and precious stones in the world can't bring Maryam back!" He turned back fiercely. "For all I care, Tris, you can take that worthless stuff and throw it into the sea!"

Book Three

CHAPTER XII

England

ALTHOUGH the shores of the estuary were the green of late May and the English countryside seemed at its very best, it was a dismal pair of travelers who went ashore in London. They had not been able to shake off their low spirits on the seemingly endless journey home. It had been Walter's intention to rewrite his notes from memory, but both mind and hand had rebelled whenever he thought of making a start. As for Tristram, the condition of his longbow was the surest indication of his state of mind. He had worn it negligently over his shoulder and had tossed it into the corners of ships' cabins and the rooms of inns; the string was frayed and limp, the bow itself lacked polish.

They turned into a tavern and called for ale and for cuts off the haunch of beef turning on a spit. The landlord gave them a rib apiece, and they fell to work with a silent enjoyment which had a touch almost of fury about it. It was not until he had swallowed the last morsel of red meat garnished with crisp fat, and had emptied his second tankard of ale, that Tristram smiled at his companion and said, "By the Rood, it is good to be home, Wat."

Walter nodded rather more soberly. "I still have my doubts. Oh, I grant you we did what we set out to do in one sense. We have been to Cathay and we have returned safely. Our pockets are full and we have tales of wonder to tell. But what kind of reception will we get, think you? Will they hold our offenses against us? Will the hangman's noose be our reward?"

"I'm not concerned about the safety of my neck. Last night I had a talk with Captain Camoys, and he spoke in glowing terms of the young king. This Edward the First is making new laws to protect the rights of common men."

"We have nothing to show for our five years except our full pockets and our well-tanned skins," said Walter glumly. "If I tell about seeing the Empress at Kinsai, they will say, '*Hic vigilans omniat*—he dreams awake.'" He consumed the remnant of his noble slice of beef. "I was becoming addicted to Manji food, but now I am prepared to admit that duck cooked in the lees of wine and pork seasoned with ginger cannot be spoken of in the same breath with the roast beef of England."

Tristram lolled back on the bench and gave a sigh of repletion. "What do we do first?" he asked.

"We must see Joseph of the Merrytotter." Walter had been carefully mapping out their course in his mind. "There's the matter of redeeming *Luke the Physician* and turning all our oriental gauds into solid Tower pounds. That must be seen to first of all. I think also our good Joseph will have a shrewd notion as to how the legal wind sets. Then it will be wise to get well away from London."

They paid their reckoning and set out in a westerly direction. Walter kept a close eye on the huddled houses and the noisy throngs on the streets. Finally he sighed and shook his head.

"Wat Stander was London born and bred," he said. "Perhaps he lived hereabouts. If he had not gone on the Crusades with my father but had stayed at home and raised a family—think of it, Tris, we might see Maryam come tripping out of one of these houses! It is inconceivable she would not have been born; though she might have lacked, with an English mother, some of the sweet contrasts of mood I came to love in her so much. I think it inconceivable also that there would be no recognition between the three of us if she came out now, with an English coif on her hair and that eager look in her eyes, even though none of us had ever seen each other before!"

Tristram laid a hand affectionately on his sleeve. "I know no sight that would be more welcome," he said. "But things were better as they were, even though—you lost her that night on the river. If she had been born a squire's daughter in London, you would never have learned of her existence. If you had seen her in that guise, you would have thought her a pretty wench of low degree. I swear you would never have given her a second thought. No, Wat, we had to go all the way to Cathay to bring you to your present way of thinking. And," he added, after a moment, "for you to know Maryam for what she was."

"Perhaps you are right. If I had stayed in England, I wouldn't have been able to get Engaine out of my mind."

The life of great London flowed about them with its noise and lusty

vulgarity and its hint of lurking malice under the surface. They stopped
and watched a company of town-pinders ride a baker off to the pillory
with his short-weight loaves tied around his neck. In the Vintry Ward
they saw people groveling in the mud to sup up the wine which had
been spilled when a cask, craned out of a lighter, fell and broke open.
Trulls accosted them, and a beggar, whose whines they had brushed
aside, shrilled a volley of typical London abuse after them, "Ye fleeching
apple-squires, ye dribblings o' vice . . ."

In the neighborhood of Temple Bar they heard a flourish of trumpets
and were caught in a rush of townspeople in that direction. Tristram,
who had brought his bone along and had gnawed at its marrow as he
walked, tossed it hurriedly into the gutter and said, "Wat, that means
the King is riding into London!"

They ran as fast as their legs would carry them, hoping for a look at
this much praised Edward the First. The streets were so densely packed
that they could not get very close, however, and had to be content at
first with a view of the bobbing plumes of horses and the helmeted
heads of their riders. They missed all of the ceremony which preceded
the lowering of the bars to admit the royal party into the City.

They edged close enough after that to get a single glimpse of the tall
monarch. He rode under his azure flag of St. Edmond with its three
crowns or, the only open indication of his rank. They were amazed at
the extreme plainness of his accouterments. There were common steel
poleyns on his shoulders, and a cloak of worn scarlet velvet was tied
carelessly around his neck. The humblest squire at the end of the procession was as well attired as this unconventional king.

Walter studied the face smiling gravely under the raised vizor. It was
an earnest and thoughtful face, and yet it in no way lacked the kingli-
ness which was the distinguishing mark of the Plantagenets. He had the
quick sparkle of eye, the handsome cast of features, accentuated rather
than marred by a slight droop of the left brow, the truly royal carriage
of the head. Edward was very tall, and he sat so straight in his saddle
that he seemed better suited to lead a charge of mounted horsemen than
to nod his way through this stilted ceremonial.

There were tears in Tristram's eyes when the procession had passed.
"Wat," he declared, "I would know him for a king if I had seen him first
in a falding camise and bare legs among all the common men of London! Everything Captain Camoys said was true. He may be the king we
have waited for so long."

Walter was silent for several moments. "He has a Norman face," he said finally.

"But the English stamp is on it! Make no mistake about that."

"You think then I was wrong in refusing to enter his service? That I blabbered myself that morning at Bulaire into the need of running away?"

Tristram shook his head. "It was God's will that everything happened as it did. But now I have seen him I am sure he has strength to take away the power the barons have seized. Will he have the inner strength to give it back to the people instead of keeping it himself?"

A fat merchant, with the embroidered tun of the Vintry guild on his sleeve, had heard what they were saying. He now gave them a somewhat sour smile. "I won't say he's a good king," he declared, "until I see in my hand the two pund I had to pay to help him off to the Crusades. Give me back my two pund and I'll agree with you that he's Alfred and Ed'ard the Confessor and stout old Rick rolled together into one suit of armor."

The crowds were beginning to thin out, but some remained as though a new attraction held them. To Walter's surprise, he became conscious that he and his comrade were supplying the interest that kept them together. The idlers had gathered close about them and were watching every move they made.

The fat vintner seemed to share this curiosity. "Well, rove a bow beyond my reach!" he exclaimed. "I think ye must be the pair all London has been looking for. Young men, did ye spend several idle days in Calais before taking boat across the Sleeve?"

Walter nodded in assent, having no idea what this was leading to.

"Then ye're the two Englishmen that's back from Cathay!" The merchant's face, which had normally a bluish cast as though underlaid with a smear of woad, had turned reddish with excitement. "A ship came in two days agone with reports of ye. Is it true ye saw the Great Khan riding on four elephants? Is it true ye fought a dragon with eyes in all its scales?"

Walter knew what to blame for this untimely recognition. He still wore the hat he had on his head when they left Kinsai, a round-cornered one of an apricot-yellow shade with a peacock's feather. It smacked unmistakably of the East and, as further evidence, their faces carried the brown of sea winds and the fierce beat of the Eastern sun.

"We were in Cathay, my friend and I," he said. "But we are on an errand of great urgency and cannot linger here."

Joseph of the Merrytotter was at work in his yard when they arrived. They heard the steady tap of a hammer behind the outside stairs and saw his rime-frosted head bent beside the framework of an addition to the house. Catching sight of them, he gave a shout and tossed the hammer over his shoulder.

"I knew ye were back," he said, coming forward with a beaming face, "when the word went all over London about the two Englishmen as had been to Cathay. Ah, my lord Walter, and you, my brave Tristram, how glad I am to see ye! There should be a fire-bavin lighted in honor of this day!"

"And not a march to the gallows?" asked Walter.

Joseph shook his head emphatically. "After what ye have done?" he cried. "Give it no second thought, my lord Walter. We have a king now as believes in justice for everyone. He calls himself an English king, and he's giving us English laws. Ye're more likely to feel the tap of his sword on yer back, dubbing ye knight, than the fingers of the rope-beck on yer neck."

It was proof of Walter's absorption in his own bitter concerns that he began immediately to speak of Wat Stander. "We may have word for you of your old comrade," he said. "An Englishman named Walter was taken captive and killed soon thereafter. It was in Aleppo that it happened. Tris and I are disposed to think it was your fellow squire."

Joseph rose to this hint like a goshawk to a partridge. "Ye have word of Wat Stander!" he cried. "Come in, come in! I can't wait to hear it. How much anxious thought I have given him, that brave Wat!"

When the story had been told, Joseph nodded his head confidently. "I believe it is the truth at last. He was a great, strutting fellow like a skewbald in a mail jacket, and the women always ran after him. He was the father of your lovely wife, my lord Walter, I would wager my head on it." He wagged his own head solemnly. "The hand of God took ye to Antioch, that we may be sure. To think a son of my lord Rauf should take to wife the daughter of my old comrade!"

"Is there any way of being sure?"

Joseph shook his head. "None as I know. Wat's parents died before he was old enough to play bob-apple. He had no kin. As for his looks, he was a tall zany with eyes as blue as a woman's. He was as shifting in his moods as April weather."

"Everything you tell me makes me more certain," said Walter. He turned then to the other anxieties which weighed on his mind. "Have you any news from our part of the country?"

Joseph's face sobered at once, and he looked at Walter with a solicitous air. "Aye," he said. "There is news, and none of it makes good hearing. Your half brother, the young earl, is as full of Norman rancor as his evil mother." He paused and then asked, "Ye know already, I take it, that yer good mother has been dead these four years?"

In the silence that fell on the room, the ex-squire looked from one to the other, his face a picture of the deepest dismay. "My lord Walter!" he cried. "It sits ill on me to be the bearer of such tidings!"

Walter walked to the window and stared out into the busy street. It was a full minute before he spoke. "I thought I had become reconciled to the—the certainty of it," he said then. "It was clear when I saw her last that she could not last long, but in spite of that I—I was hoping I would return in time to see her again." There was another long pause. "Perhaps it has been for the best. She had little to live for, and her mind could not contend with the troubles of living. I am sure she was glad to go."

He turned back from the window and dropped into a chair. "You spoke of my half brother. I have little stomach now for the tale of his wrongdoings; but we must hear about everything before we return, and so we might as well have it now. What has he done?"

Joseph plunged into his story as though glad to relieve the tension. "It is not known whether he acts under the thumb of his thrice-cursed mother or whether his deviltries are of his own choice and contrivance. However that may be, men have begun to call him the She-devil's Cub and Edmond the Cussom. He set himself at once to have revenge for the raid on the castle. Two of the men known to be with ye that night were taken on writs of outfang and hanged at Bulaire."

Tristram leaned forward to demand in a tense voice, "Do you recall their names, Joseph Maule?"

"I knew them both. Tom Aske and Rob Tallson. Stout and honest fellows they were, and incapable of the crimes laid at their door."

Tristram was filled with such a consuming anger that he found it impossible to speak above a whisper. "Cencaster men, both of them. They were good friends of my father. I think it certain they were picked because of the part I had in it. I was beyond reach; so they were hanged as proxies for me."

"That was only the start of it. Camus Harry slipped through their fingers, but the earl burned the tavern at Little Tamitt, applying the torch with his own hand. Camus Harry has been a fugitive ever since. It's said as he runs with the trailbastons of the country."

"No, no!" cried Tristram, his voice rising vehemently. "That I will never believe. Camus Harry is an honest man. Even though he was forced to take to the woods, he would never bear a hand with a crew of robbers."

"There have been great changes," said the ex-squire. "The heavy hand of the earl has driven many honest men to join them. I hear a round score have thrown away the iron collar and gone to live the life of free men. It's open war between the castle and the trailbastons. The free bands almost got their hands on the earl's young son not more than a fortn't agone."

Walter's mind had been so filled with his personal grief that he had not been listening with any degree of attention. Now he turned sharply and asked, "His son?"

Joseph nodded. "Aye. A boy of two. It's said he's a handsome lad and resembles his grandsire muchly. Which is a good thing, for his father has a black-a-vised look and a piot nose to match his greediness."

"Who is the earl's wife?"

"She was the Lady Engaine of Tressling. A great beauty, as ye must recall." Joseph paused. "Of course, *you* would remember that, from all I have heard. The story is that they don't agree. She can outride him, and she has a rare hand with the hawks. She has no great love for him, it's said. God wot, I hope it is true."

Realizing now that he was proving a lax host, Joseph left the room in search of food. Walter looked at his companion and gave his head a rueful shake.

"Poor Engaine!" he said. "I am afraid she finds her life a difficult one."

"I wouldn't waste too much sympathy on her, Wat. A lady of such high spirit can always carry things her own way. And she has the life she wanted. She is the Countess of Lessford."

"It won't be a pleasant homecoming for us, Tris. It's certain you will find things most unhappy, and I dread the thought of going back to Gurnie now that my mother won't be there to greet me."

"There will be work for me to do," said Tristram slowly. "I left my friends to bear the brunt of it. Now I must see that the scales are balanced."

"Keep an open mind," warned Walter, "until we see with our own eyes how things are."

Joseph returned with a large pewter platter heaped high with stewed mutton and wheaten dumplings speckled with suet. "My Conand's Elspie is a rare good cook," he said, with pride. "She has the secret of a proper dumpling. You will taste them all the way down, and they'll land in yer stummicks with a healthy thump."

There were tankards as well of a light, nut-flavored ale. In spite of the ill tenor of the news they had received, they fell to work with the appetite of youth. The mutton was toothsome and the dumplings all that had been claimed for them. Nothing much was said as they plied their knives, the minds of all three being occupied with the problems facing them.

A boy passed through the hall, glancing in with a curiosity that had to do with the food quite as much as the appearance of the visitors.

"That will be either Harry or Toby, I think," said Walter.

Their host laughed heartily. "Time has been flying, my lord Walter," he said. "My boys seem to grow an inch every day of their lives. Harry and Toby are great louts of fellows now and bound to trades. Even Gilly the Gad is creeping up on me and is well up to my shoulder. That one was John."

"You mean little John-Put-Upon?"

Joseph shook his head. "We never call him that any more. John is not one to be put upon any longer. I think I'll have to make a chafewax of him, for he's a keen one to figure and reckon. Aye, he'll be a clerk, that one. Sometimes we call him John-Ask-All."

"I saw you were making an addition to the house. Does that mean you have a larger family now?"

"My Conand's Elspie is a faithful wife. Aye, there are three more of them now. It irked me to see them go, but it's a boon that Harry and Toby live with their masters. The room I am adding would never suffice if they were all here. One of my fine boys, Gilly perhaps, will have to sleep with me there, so I am trying to make it snug and warm." He raised his voice and called, "Anne! Anne!"

A very small girl, of a plumpness to provide the dumplings with competition, appeared in the doorway. She was not four years old, but very alert and fully conscious of her clean white tunic and the blue liripipe with which her bonnet was tied.

"Anne, tell the fine gentlemen who *you* are."

"I am my gramfaw's own girl," answered the child, with a lisp of pride.

"Aye, that ye are." He took her up on his knee and smiled at the promptness with which she dipped her fingers into the dish for pieces of dumpling floating on the top. "She is her gramfaw's own girl. She is going to be her grandmother all over. I am so fond of this one that I dread the day as will see her grown up and leaving me. But," with a sigh, "they all do. My big fellows are so bound up in their own affairs they seldom come to see their old gramfaw any more."

The home of Haggai had a poverty-stricken entrance with worn wooden steps, but they found themselves in a different world when they left the dark outer hall. The luxury of the room into which they were shown caused them to look at each other in surprise. A silver lamp swung from the ceiling, and there were rich hangings on the walls and a deep carpet on the floor.

Haggai greeted them with the haughtiness of the English Jews of that day. Not being subject to the laws of the country but only to the personal will of the King, they walked apart and treated those who came to deal with them in an unbending scorn. Haggai had laid aside the yellow gaberdine with its two woolen tablets, which Hebrews wore on the streets as the badge of their race, and appeared before them in a shimmering robe of white samite. His beard, newly washed and perfumed, curled in fluffy profusion almost down to his waist.

"What is your pleasure, young Christians?" he asked, in lisping Norman French.

"It will be necessary to speak in English," said Walter. "My companion lacks French."

Haggai nodded as though this confirmed him in his rather poor opinion of them.

"We are newly back from Cathay," went on Walter, "and we bring many articles of great value which we desire to convert into gold. There is also the matter of a standing cup which was left with you some years ago and which we propose to redeem."

Haggai nodded indifferently. "I was on the point of disposing of the standing cup, not expecting to hear from you after so many years. There is heavy interest standing against it."

"Have you the cup here? I am anxious to see it again."

The merchant left the room and returned in a few minutes with *Luke the Physician,* which he placed before them on a table. It had been kept in excellent condition and gleamed richly in the light of the swinging lamp. Walter stepped closer to examine it.

"I had forgotten how beautiful it is," he said in a reverent tone. "I shall be happy to have it again."

Haggai gave a glance at Joseph, who had remained respectfully in the background. "This merchant brought it to me five years ago. Have you the moneys now to repay the loan and the interest which, as I have said, has grown to a considerable sum?"

"The amount of the interest," said Joseph, sharply, "was clearly understood between us."

"I trust the memory of this merchant is not faulty. I shall not relent from the full moneys due me."

Walter opened the leather bag he had been carrying over his shoulder and began to place on the table beside the resplendent standing cup the gifts of the Empress. Haggai's eyes opened with surprise, and he glanced at the display in silent calculation. After a moment he held up the Sung vase in front of his face for closer inspection.

"It is good," he admitted grudgingly. "But it is not old, and it is the antiquity of porcelains which sets their value. Still it is good."

"That is not for sale," declared Walter. "It is my purpose to present it to the King when he grants me an audience."

"His King's Grace might think better of this," said the Hebrew, picking up the emerald ring with a hand which trembled in spite of himself. "The value is much more apparent to the eye.

"It is clear," went on Haggai, after many minutes of careful study of the glittering array, "that you were in the city of Kinsai. And yet my reports were that no looting had been allowed."

"What you see here were all gifts from the Dowager Empress. We were in Kinsai, but it was before the arrival of the armies of Bayan."

Haggai studied him with his head on one side. "The conviction grows into a certainty in my mind that you are the two Englishmen of whom I have heard much. I did not suspect it when you first came in, as it had been thought you did not escape from Kinsai alive."

"Another conviction is growing in *my* mind," said Walter, looking at Haggai with quickened interest. "I think you must be acting in England for Anthemus of Antioch."

Haggai nodded indifferently. "That is true. It is a thankless task, as Anthemus demands everything by way of profit for himself. I am expecting soon to receive a consignment from him." He waved a hand in the direction of the table. "Of what use, then, are these to me?"

"Nothing you receive from Anthemus," declared Walter, "will equal what you have here in front of your eyes. I should not need to tell you that nor to remind you, worthy Haggai, that the profit on what we offer you will be all your own. You will be under no necessity of sharing with the rapacious Anthemus."

Haggai conceded merit in this by giving the articles a second close scrutiny. At the conclusion he suggested a figure which brought no more than a laugh from the three visitors. A second offer followed, to be rebuffed in the same manner. Finally he reached a figure which seemed to Walter within the outer rim of the boundary of reason. He hesitated.

"It is not enough," spoke up Joseph of the Merrytotter.

Haggai turned on him with almost breathless indignation. "Does this ignorant dealer in grains pretend to know aught of the value of precious stones?" he demanded of the ceiling.

"I know thievery when I see it tried."

The chaffering continued then until a much larger offer had been made. Walter hesitated a second time.

"It is not enough," repeated Joseph.

"Must I suffer the barbs of this grasping and infamous meddler?" cried the Jew, raising his arms in an outraged gesture. "I shall have a grievous loss at the sum I have named. Not one maravedi more do I dare offer you."

"Put them back in your bag, my lord Walter," advised the ex-squire. "There are merchants from Lombardy who will like a chance to bid."

"Am I to be ruined by this low dealer in horse food?" Haggai ran agitated fingers through his silky beard. "I will be rash enough to mention one further figure. But I swear by my belief in the only living God that this is my last word." He swallowed and, with an almost piteous effort, whispered his last suggestion.

"Take it, my lord Walter," said Joseph.

"I accept," said Walter. "I shall require a quarter of the sum in gold now and the rest on demand." He turned to Tristram. "Do you want to dispose of your share also?"

Tristram shook his head. "Not yet, Wat. I'll have no need for money until my plans are more definite."

"But you will come to me?" asked Haggai anxiously.

"I can make no promises."

When Haggai had handed over a bag of gold and had signed a paper covering the terms of the transaction, Walter counted back to him a column of small coins.

"This," he said, "is to be sent to Anthemus. It is to pay for the hire of the three least valuable camels on the whole desert, the price of one black slave, the cost of a secondhand yurt riddled with holes and filled with fleas. You will let him know, worthy Haggai, that I have settled my account with him."

2

The journey home had been disillusioning in many ways. Often the ships they were on had remained tied up in port for many days because of cloudy weather, and Walter had paced the decks, berating himself for his carelessness in losing the magnetic needle which would have freed commerce from such delays. It had galled him to see the mariners strain their eyes at distant objects and to know that it had been in his power to introduce to the backward Western world the marvel of the Eye That Sees Far.

A fatuous sense of confidence had been apparent as soon as they set sail from Alexandria and so left the East behind them. The attitude of the men of Europe said as plain as words: Perfection has been attained and is to be found in us and in the life we live. We are right in everything in the sight of God and man.

When he walked through the Arsenal at Venice and on the teeming docks of Genoa and Marseilles, he found it hard to listen to the idle tenor of the talk, to accept the deep-rooted superstitions which seemed to dictate every action. He reflected continually on the great changes which could have been brought about if he had returned with proofs of the new things he had seen.

One hot day they were riding on a sunny road in Provence, and they passed a knight in full armor. A long train cantered behind him— squires, pages, men-at-arms, archers, a spiritual comforter, an almoner, a jester, a juggler, several gossips, a full dozen servants. The knight rode proudly, with his lady's favor flaunted on the tip of his lance as a sign of his willingness to do battle with any cavalier of equal rank who might desire to oppose him according to the established practices of chivalry, and a patch on one eye in accordance, no doubt, with some vow he had made.

They drew to one side of the road to let the proud cavalcade pass. Walter caught the glitter of an arrogant eye behind the bars of the steel vizor and knew that the gallant traveler counted him of low degree and so unfit for as much as a passing hail.

"Tris," he said, when the last of them had passed, "we have just seen a perfect example of the futility of our civilized ways. That trussed-up popinjay was of the very essence of chivalry. He is riding on some absurd errand which has to do with—what is the silly phrase?—worshipfully winning worship. He will risk life and limb to gain favor in the eyes of some noble lady and joyfully maim and kill others in the doing. He would have ridden us down on any pretext and never given us a second thought, except perhaps to regret some splash of blood on his steel sollerets."

"If he had fallen from his horse, he would never have been able to get up unaided," said Tristram, with a laugh.

"What a spectacle of absurd pride! That shewel, that great unthinking zany, propped up on a long-suffering steed, sallying out to fight in the protection of his armor! I shudder to think what will happen if the Mongols decide to invade Europe next. Bayan of the Hundred Eyes would drive his horsemen through the ranks of these armorer's puppets like arrows through the sheets of paper we shall proceed to make as soon as we reach England."

"Before the Mongols come," declared Tristram, "these brave knights may find what it means to face the longbows of England. In that case they will not survive to meet the armies of the East."

Walter waved an arm toward the fields on each side of the road, where patient peasants toiled with bent backs. "It takes the labor of hundreds of these," he said glumly, "to feed that pack of lazy knaves who rode by so proudly. Yes, Tris, the truth grows on me all the time. This is a topsy-turvy world, a cruel and foolish world."

The disillusionment became complete when they reached Oxford on on their way from London. Their eagerness to finish the journey resulted in an all-night ride, and the sun was rising when they cantered into the university town. A stillness lay on the gray streets, although smoke was rising here and there from chimney tops. Suddenly, as though the place had been wakened by a magic touch, the air was filled with voices, and clerks came pouring out into the open, books and manuscripts under their arms, their faces still moist with sleep.

Tristram grinned when they reached Butterbump Hall and said he would wait outside.

"You are not a chamber-deacon now," protested Walter. "You are a great traveler, and these young masters of arts will gaze on you with eyes of wonder."

"I am still the son of a fletcher. No, Wat, I have no desire to stir their class resentments. There's an inn just down the street. I'll see what they have to offer in the way of breakfast. Join me when you are through here."

So Walter went in alone, marveling at how little the Hall resembled the fine house of his remembrance. There had been some horseplay in the entry the evening before. A chair had been broken, and the seat of the *necessaria* had been brought in from the shed behind the offices and hung now on the oak screens. No one was about. He walked up the stairs and into the solar room. A bucket, of the kind known as a skeel, had been carried up as usual for the ablutions of the clerks, and it now stood in the center of the floor, a damp flake of soap beside it. Two students only were still in the room, snoring off the effects of a carouse. Neither had gone to the trouble of undressing, and their faces looked blotchy and repulsive in the dim light. The windows were clamped tight, and the air in the room was foul.

After descending the stairs, he called "Halloo!" and waited. The face of Master Hornpepper popped out through a door in the rear. The principilator had grown stouter with the passing of time, but Walter recognized his clothes as the same he had worn five years before. The seams, as might have been expected, were threatening to burst wide open with each move. It was several moments before the shabby master accorded the intruder the accolade of recognition.

"I remember you. You are Walter of Gurnie." A sour bob of the head accompanied this speech. "What an unseemly uproar we suffered when you left! Men-at-arms clattering up to our door and asking questions about you. It was a great disgrace." He studied Walter's bronzed face with reluctant interest. "Have you been at sea?"

"I have sailed all the seven seas!" declared Walter pridefully. "Draw in your breath and prepare for the surprise of your life, Master Hornpepper. I have been to Cathay."

The principilator frowned with injured dignity. "I am a man of intelligence, I think. Do you consider me capable of believing such an extravagantly bald falsehood as that?"

"I lack the time to convince you I am speaking the truth, good Master Hornpepper. My purpose in returning to Oxford is to see Friar Bacon, and it was only the urge of pleasant memories which brought me here. I am sorry I came. The Hall of my dreams was far different from—from *this!*"

Master Hornpepper blew his nose scornfully with his thumb. "You came on a fruitless errand then, young sir. The sins of Roger Bacon have found him out at last. He has not been in Oxford for several years, and it is said he has been put in a dark cell from which he will never be released. We were delighted when we heard it, I can tell you! That vicar of the devil will have plenty of time now to ponder on his iniquities."

Walter laid an agitated hand on the patched sleeve of the principilator.
"This is an idle story you tell me, Master Hornpepper. It cannot be true!
That great mind shackled! Surely, surely, the ignorance of those who
rule this benighted corner of the world has not led them into such a
crime!"

"You have learned nothing!" cried the master of the Hall. "You have
come back babbling the same rank heresies. Curb your tongue, young
sir, or there will be another hue and cry after you." He brushed his moist
brow with a greasy forearm. "In any event, it was not here in England
that the hand of tardy justice dealt with that ungodly apostate. He went
back to Paris to teach, and from the reports we received he became even
more unregenerate. He denounced the great Thomas Aquinas as 'a
teacher of puerile vanity' and the saintly Richard of Cornwall as 'an
absolute fool.' He prated of astronomy and the need for his infamous
experiments, meaning that scholars should dabble in the blackness of
magic calculations. It is well they decided to put him away."

Walter felt sick at heart. "It would have been of no avail, after all, if
I had brought back my proofs," he thought. "Who but Roger Bacon
could have made use of them?"

He brushed violently by the principilator and walked out into the
street, where the morning sun was warming the slate roofs of the town.
He looked about him and shook his head. "This is the seat of all learning in England," he said aloud. "I will warrant that no one here realizes
what a great crime has been committed. They are all like that stupid
donkey, and they think of what has happened with smug approval."

Tristram was breakfasting on soup and a bone of ham. He looked up
when Walter joined him and asked, "Have you seen a ghost?"

Walter began to eat, feeling disdain for himself that he could have an
appetite under the circumstances. He told his companion what he had
learned. "Roger Bacon was right when he called this a dirty and ignorant world," he said. "Content and stupidity rule. The only man who
knows how to set it right has been imprisoned in a dark cell!"

"The heart of mankind is sound," declared Tristram. "We heard
peasants singing in the fields as we passed yesterday. There is honesty
in them, and a great courage. Perhaps the change will begin at the bottom, Wat. It will take longer that way; but it will come surely."

3

Walter arrived at Gurnie alone, his companion having stopped at Cencaster. The first glimpse he had of his home told of many changes in his absence.

There were several new buildings of good size grouped about the house, and a great stir of activity pervaded the place. Smoke poured from all the chimneys, and there was a clatter of grinding mill wheels. On the edge of Oswiu Pond he saw many horses behind a new wattled fence.

"My grandfather's plans seem to have prospered," he said to himself.

Equally marked proofs of well-doing were apparent when he approached the entrance. The ross heap had vanished, not a single vagrant hen was to be seen, and the outer palisade had been scraped clean and newly pointed up. A pennant with the oak leaves of Gurnie hung drumly above the drawbridge in the absence of any breeze, but its presence there was like a token of victory.

Again it was Wilderkin who greeted him. The seneschal had shrunk into a desiccated husk, and his voice had the scranniness of old age in it.

"Master Walter!" he shrilled, his key ring shaking in his hands. "Ye've come back to us at last! We gave ye up for dead long ago. St. Walburga, this will be a happy day for my lord Alfgar."

"And I am happy to be back, Old Will," said Walter, slapping him on the back with so much exuberance that the old man buckled and wheezed like a punctured bellows.

"Have a care, Master Walter! I am an old man, and my bones are brittle."

"You will outlive all of us. And how is my grandfather?"

"Ailing, Master Walter; but most careful of his health indeed. He has had ulcers, and so he must drink oil of wheat in great quantities. We must send to London for pomegranates and boil the rinds in wine for him. It is supposed to do something, but what it is I can't remember. He tries everything, master, and talks of little else. Now he is complaining of pains in his arms and says his hearing is bad. What can he expect? He is a very old man."

The interior of the house showed even plainer signs of the rejuvenation of Gurnie. Through an opening in the screens, Walter saw a tapestry covering much of one wall in the Great Hall, an eye-filling panorama of the chase in strong russets and blue. Beneath it there was a brassbound chest of the kind known as a standard, with the Gurnie oak on the lid. There were new dosseret chairs and a high cupboard with the twin shelves that denoted the knighthood of its owner. In spite of his penuriousness, his grandfather had always liked to make a brave show.

Most surprising of all was the fact that the door of the master's workroom was wide open. This once mysterious apartment had become the center of much activity, with servants bustling in and out. Inside the room a man was seated behind a table piled high with documents, his spindling legs stretched out under it. The long nose of this stranger was buried in his work, but Walter was conscious as he passed of the scrutiny of a keen pair of eyes.

"Who is that?"

"A booker." Wilderkin shrugged his low opinion of the occupant of the room. "My lord Alfgar cannot attend to everything now, and he brought this chafewax fellow from Shrewsbury to look after the accounts. He is as sly as a whole skulk of foxes put together, and he sticks his swinking nose into everything."

"Things have changed at Gurnie, Old Will. It is more like a countinghouse."

The seneschal's expression changed to one of high satisfaction. "Aye, Master Walter. We are prospering. The seven lean years are over. Like a countinghouse, say ye? That is better than starving in proud idleness. He is a man of rare vision, my lord Alfgar! Now he is buying horses and selling them in London. But that is nothing as compared to what we are doing with the washbrew."

Walter was puzzled. "What profit can there be in washbrew?"

The old man nodded his head in an ecstasy of appreciation. "The washbrew is made from oats, and it is a rare dish, as wholesome as oatmeal but much tastier. He calls it flummery, and we sell it to merchants in all the big towns. The scaldinghouse had to be torn down to build a shop for the making of it."

"I noticed many new buildings as I rode up."

"We have our own mill now. My lord Alfgar talks of branching in other ways. 'Branching' is his favorite word."

"Where is he now? I hope he can see me at once."

Wilderkin looked uncertain. "He took to his bed yesterday, but I misdoubt he is very ill. He has thought of more things to be done than when he is up and about. He has kept us all on the jump, I can tell you! 'Do this,' 'See to that,' 'What are those lazy, lowborn knaves doing at the mill?' and 'Do ye think I can be cheated because my eye isn't on the pack of ye?' It is a busy time when my lord Alfgar takes to his bed."

"Tell him of my return, Wilderkin."

The seneschal came back almost immediately and announced that Walter was to repair to his grandfather's bedroom at once. However, he proceeded to give a report of the conversation. "He sat right up when I told him, and it'll please ye to know I saw tears in his eyes. Never before has it happened save when I had to tell him your mother had died during the night. 'You lie, you rascal,' he said to me. 'I swear to ye he is here, my lord,' I said. He looked at me hard and said, 'I was sore afraid my fine boy was dead, Wilderkin.' 'Yes, my lord,' I said, 'but he is very much alive and as brown as a heathen.' He said, 'By good St. Wulstan, I am glad to hear it. Bring my grandson to me at once.'"

The bedroom was small and bare. There was little space, in fact, for anything but the wide bed in which the master of Gurnie was sitting when Walter entered. There was a definite look of age about him, a suggestion of shrinkage about the neck and shoulders. The eyes fixed on the homecomer, however, were as alert as ever, and smiling in welcome.

"Wilderkin, he has become a man!" he cried. "How he has filled out! I verily believe he has a full inch the better of me in height now." There was a difference of five inches between them, in point of fact. "It is a pity his mother is not here to see him. She would have been proud. As proud as his grandfather is, Wilderkin."

A lump had come into Walter's throat. "Tell my lord Alfgar for me, Wilderkin, that I am happy to be home with him again. My happiness would be complete if only—if only——" It proved impossible for him to make any reference to his mother's death. He blinked back the tears and waited.

"Wilderkin, where are your wits?" cried the master. "Ask him where he has been, you knave! I cannot wait to know."

"Tell my grandfather," said Walter, "that I have been to Cathay."

A silence settled on the room. "Wilderkin," said the old man, finally, "my grandson would not lie to me. Of that I am certain. And yet—and yet—no man has ever been to that distant land and returned to tell of it. My mind rebels at what I have heard."

Walter sat down and began to recount the story of his adventurous five years. He confined himself to the record of his travels and the part he had played in the war, reserving the more romantic episodes for later telling. The old man listened with an open amazement which turned gradually to acceptance as the corroborative detail drove doubts from his mind. Occasionally he asked a question, and all through the recital the hand with which he conveyed pieces of pomegranate rind to his mouth shook with excitement. Such was his agitation at one point that he neglected to give the customary neat whisk to his white mustache after eating. The sound of a tail thumping on the floor under the bed was proof of the presence there of Chetwind, and that the ancient hound sensed the exhilaration of his master's mood.

When the matter of the presents from the Empress was mentioned, the old man sat straight up in bed for the first time.

"It passes belief!" he exclaimed. "Wilderkin, have I heard aright? There were emeralds and rubies and pearls in the lot? Of a large size, perchance?"

"Tell my grandfather, Wilderkin, that there were many precious stones and all of a large size. I still have several of them. There is an emerald ring I shall give His King's Grace if I am granted an audience to tell my story. There is a ruby I desire to give my grandfather in the hope he will have it set in the gold chain he wears around his neck. Most of the gifts I have already disposed of to Haggai, the Jewish merchant in London——"

A stricken look leaped to the old man's eyes at this piece of information, and Walter hastened to explain the circumstances.

"I had the advice of Joseph of the Merrytotter in the transaction. He dealt shrewdly with the merchant and saw to it that the price paid was a proper one."

A great sigh of relief issued from the ancient lungs, and the master of Gurnie permitted himself to fall back against his pillows. "Ah, that is better! Joseph knows how to chaffer and bargain. For a moment I was afraid—I was sore afraid!—that my grandson had gone alone. That would indeed have been where he made his greatest mistake!" There was a tense pause. The old man's hands were trembling more noticeably than before. "It—it must have been a very large sum of money that changed hands, Wilderkin."

"A very large sum." Walter reached under his belt and drew out a slip of paper, folded over and sealed. This he handed to the seneschal. "Give this to your master, Old Will. He will find the amount specified therein."

The master of Gurnie slit the paper open and looked at the figures. For several moments he studied them with the deepest care.

"It is a goodly sum," he declared finally. "I could have done better. But I have no serious quarrel with Joseph over the terms. Haggai is a hard man, a bitter hand at a bargain. I could have overreached him, but on the whole I concede that the good Joseph has not allowed my grandson to be robbed." He struggled up again to a sitting position, and it seemed to Walter that years had dropped away from his shoulders. He tapped his thumb with his middle finger several times. "I approve. It is a good stroke. Yes, a good stroke."

"I would like to tell my grandfather now of certain plans I have made. Is he strong enough for further talk, Wilderkin?"

"Strong enough for further talk of this kind? Yes, Wilderkin, you may reassure him on that point. My body is growing old, but not my mind. I expect, when my time comes, that I shall be found dead with my ledgers around me."

"I have already mentioned the secret of making paper," said Walter. "It is my purpose to set up a yard here at Gurnie. There will be a great demand for the paper, from the abbeys and merchants and the officers of the Crown. I believe all we can make will be taken off our hands quickly and at a good round price. It is my hope that my grandfather will see the possibilities in it and be prepared to guide the enterprise."

The old man gave some thought to this quite revolutionary proposal. Then he nodded his head.

"Granted, Wilderkin," he said.

"More land will be needed for the purpose. I hope my grandfather will use what is needed of the money to purchase additional acres from our neighbors."

The answer came much more quickly. "Granted, Wilderkin."

"Many helpers will be needed. We could hire free men and build additional houses on the property for their use. The cost would be considerable, but there will be plenty for that. I have thought also of trying to crush the mulberry pulp between millstones to avoid the slower process of hand labor."

After lengthy thought, the old man nodded a third time. "Granted again, Wilderkin."

The master of the house studied the note in his hand with particular care, feeling the texture of it between his fingers and testing its strength. "A veritable miracle," he whispered. He then went into a long monologue on ways and means, finding occasion twice to catch up his grandson on some point and to exclaim, "Ha, that is where he makes his mistake!"

It was a full hour before Walter rose to leave. The seneschal showed a tendency to linger and said in a tone of some trepidation, "May it

please my lord Alfgar, I have a good report to give of my nephew, young
Peter Wykes, to whom another son has been born."

"What!" cried the old man. "And is that what you call a good report?
Am I right in believing he already had three sons and even two daughters? How can he hope to feed such a litter? Wilderkin, I fear your
nephew lingers overlong at home. Can he be diligent in his work if he
is so persevering as a husband?"

"My lord!" protested the seneschal. "Peter is one of your very best
men. The day before his son was born—even though the anxiety natural
at such a time weighed on his mind—he sold ten sacks of the washbrew
to merchants in Oxford. Ten sacks, my lord! No one has ever sold that
many on a single day before. I have been hoping you would condescend
to give him a—a small reward."

The master of Gurnie studied his servant with a cold and unfriendly
eye. "A reward?" he repeated. "Because on one single day he performed
his duties reasonably well? Have you taken leave of your senses! Tell
me, Wilderkin, how many sacks did he sell the day after his son was
born?"

There was a pause.

"How many, Wilderkin? Come, out with it."

"None, my lord."

The master cackled with triumph. "I will give him a reward for the
good day, but my sense of fairness makes it essential to fine him for the
day when he celebrated his son's arrival by filling his draffsack with ale
and so did nothing for me at all. The one cancels the other, Wilderkin; and the matter is resolved in all fairness and to the satisfaction of
everyone concerned."

Walter turned to the right and went down a stair of three steps which
his feet found unerringly in the dark of the hall. The door of his mother's room was closed. He tapped on it with his knuckles and then shoved
it open.

Wulfa was sitting under one of the windows with a billowing mass
of blue silk over her knees. She was stitching at this with such care that
she did not look up at once. When she saw him, she gasped and dropped
her needle.

"Master Walter!" she cried.

He stepped into the room, aware that there was something different
about it, but too filled with emotion to be capable of determining just
what it was. It took him several moments to realize that the change was

due to the maid having placed many of his mother's belongings around the room. The chain she had worn at her neck was hanging on one wall, flanked by her silver-mesh crestine and the chased plate of the mane-guard she had used in riding. Gloves hung from different points on the walls, and peplums and gorgets were suspended on the posts of the bed. The five-part Bible, which his mother had loved so much, occupied all of the table with the exception of a vase filled with early yellow roses, her favorite flower.

He took a chair and looked around, a feeling of regret growing in him that he had come. To see this familiar room without his mother in it was the most poignant reminder of his loss. The pathetic efforts of the maid to retain what she could of the well-loved presence made her absence even harder to bear.

"I am sure you were good to her, Wulfa," he said. "And so I want to thank you."

"I did what I could, master."

The maid had continued to stand beside her chair, holding the blue dress in her hand. He asked her to sit down, and she obeyed with obvious reluctance, placing herself stiffly on the edge of the seat.

"That is one of my mother's gowns, is it not?" he asked, after several moments of silence. "What are you doing with it?"

"I found a rent, and I was repairing it, Master Walter."

"For what purpose? Is it to be given away?"

Wulfa's face flamed an agitated red.

"No, no, master! None of her things are to be given away, none. But I cannot bear to think of them needing attention because—because she no longer uses them. I look them over as carefully as ever. Have I permission to go on with my work?"

"Yes. Of course."

He looked at her with interest for probably the first time in all the years he had known her. Her face looked much older and sharper, and her hair, under a plain linen coif, already showed traces of gray. It was a severe and uncompromising face, with nothing on the surface to indicate the depths of feeling of which she was capable.

"Did my mother leave any message for me?"

The maid shook her head. "My lady Hild died in her sleep," she whispered. "She did not know the end was so close, and so—she left no messages of any kind. But she spoke of you all the time, Master Walter."

"I am afraid my absence may have hastened her death," he said, with a deep sigh.

"No, master. She could not have lived longer." Wulfa's face showed no signs of softening, but a red glow had taken possession of the sharp tip of her nose. "The night before she died, she had a dream. She told me about it the next day, when it happened that her mind was quite clear. It remained clear all that day, and I should have known it was a sign."

It was only after urging on his part that she was able to go on. "She dreamed she was riding up a very steep road. There were no trees, and the sun was shining straight ahead. She was riding straight into it. She said: 'I was very happy because all three of us were there, and that had never happened before in any of my dreams. We rode in single file. My lord Rauf was in the lead, I came next, and behind me was my son. It was wonderful to ride into that great bright light in the company of my two tall men.'" The maid looked down at the work in her hands and gave the merest suggestion of a sniff. "I was not surprised, master, that she died so peacefully the next night."

Walter stood up and gazed out of the window for several minutes. As it happened he had chosen the one where his mother had always sat, and so he could see the black towers of Bulaire against the afternoon sky.

Without turning around, he said: "I shall see to it, Wulfa, that you always remain in our service. The care of this room will be your chief concern. Always take as good care of her things as you do now."

As he left the room he heard his grandfather calling, "Wilderkin! Wilderkin!" There was so much urgency in the summons that he rushed to the other door, fearing that something had happened to the old man. Then, through force of habit, he hesitated; it had always been a rule that he must not intrude on his grandfather without a direct summons.

The door was partly open, and Walter could see that the master of Gurnie had risen from his bed and was drawing on his long woolen undergarments with every evidence of haste. The old man heard his step and looked up.

"Walter, come in!" he cried.

Then he stopped and suspended the work of dressing. One spare white shank was still naked, and the gray garment trailed along the floor as he took an involuntary step forward.

"I have spoken to him!" he cried again, in a stricken voice. "God and St. Wulstan, forgive me. I have broken my oath!"

Walter remained where he was, not daring to speak. He saw now that a man was standing respectfully in a corner of the room. The black boots and naked legs of the stranger marked him as a dependent, and on a second glance Walter recognized the insignia of Bulaire on his sleeve.

The master of Gurnie did not proceed with his toilet for several tense seconds, and when he spoke again it was to the carle from Bulaire.

"Take yourself below, knave. Keep a still tongue in your head and let no one know the errand which brought you here. Say nothing of what you have just heard, or I shall see to it you never speak again."

The man left in such haste that he brushed against Walter in the doorway. The latter's mind was filled with uneasy conjectures, and he gave no thought to his grandfather's slip of the tongue. Nothing less than a tragedy could account for the presence in Gurnie of a dependent of Bulaire. Did it concern Engaine?

His grandfather continued to dress himself with unsteady hands. "I must see the good bishop at once and lay my case before him," he muttered. "What has come over me? Am I losing my mind? I have broken my oath!" Then he raised his head and shouted frantically, "Wilderkin! Wilderkin!"

When the seneschal arrived, his master began to berate him passionately. "It is your fault, you lazy rascal! Where have you been? Did you not hear me call? You have betrayed me into an act of the most utter baseness, and I am of a mind to hang your useless old carcass up from the palisades for the crows to peck at. What were you doing, knave?"

"My hearing is no longer good, my lord Alfgar," quavered the servant.

The anger of his master seemed to subside, and he shook his head. "That is true, and I add to the enormity of my offense by blaming you for what I have done. Can I expect forgiveness because I am old also and no longer able to keep a close check on my tongue? Ah, Wilderkin, the hearing of the One, to whom I made my pledge, is good. He cannot fail to have heard me." The fingers with which he was tying up his points shook with the dismay which filled him. His anger mounted again. "Come, rascal, help me with these devices of the devil! Have you lost your sight also, you doddering old fool?"

"My lord, what has happened?" asked the seneschal, too frightened to move.

"Ask no questions, but do what I tell you."

When the difficult task of adjusting the undergarments had been finished, the old man sank into a chair. He looked at Walter and smiled wanly.

"Well, the fault has been committed. What am I to do now?" He pondered the matter at some length, shaking his head continuously. "I must do penance. The good bishop will see to that."

Walter plucked up courage to say, "Perhaps, Wilderkin, my grandfather will deign to tell me the word which has been brought from Bulaire."

"Yes, yes, you must know at once, Walter," said the old man.

Another tense silence followed. Then his grandfather threw up his arms in despair. "I have done it again! Twice have I broken my solemn vow! God wot, I am so careless of my knightly word that I am unfit to offer assistance to a lady in distress!"

"A lady in distress!" Walter could think of nothing else. "Tell me, Grandfather, is Engaine in need of our help?"

"My fault is beyond redemption now." The master of Gurnie looked at Walter directly. "The fellow rode on ahead of the Countess of Lessford with word of her coming. She is leaving Bulaire. She brings her young son with her and asks us to grant her sanctuary here!"

CHAPTER XIII

Konkan (Bombay)

THE LIME-DAUBED RIBS of the firwood ship, which had brought the strangers from the Far East, were sticking up from shoal water like stumps in a burned forest; the ship would never go to sea again, and already the crew had managed somehow to disappear. The three strangers had found lodging in the house of Chilprat and were becoming a problem to him.

They were a curious trio. One was a woman who wore a veil over the lower part of her face, thus allowing nothing to be seen of her but a most unusual pair of eyes, blue eyes, a deep and unmistakable blue. Now blue was the color of the sky and of the skirts worn by women at religious festivals, but never the color of eyes. It might have been assumed that this small woman had actually dyed her eyes, as women in the seven islands dyed their toes and fingernails and even their hair, had it not been that the year-old infant with her had eyes of exactly the same shade. Clearly, then, they came from some strange land where natural laws were reversed. The third stranger presented no reason for speculation; he was a servant with a black face and an abiding broad smile.

The concern of Chilprat was rooted at first in a habit of the woman. Whenever there were ships in, she would pace up and down the waterside, crying in a voice of appeal and distress, "London! London!" There was no way of telling why she behaved in this unaccountable way, for there was no single word in the language she and her servant spoke which meant anything to the people of the islands.

Chilprat often discussed the matter with Marukya, the Palshikar Brahman. "Does she seek one of the name of London?" he would conjecture. "Is it a blessing she calls on the ships or, perchance, a curse? These are points which stay in my mind and cannot be resolved."

"Is it possible," suggested the priest, "that there is a place somewhere on the earth called London and she seeks a ship sailing there?"

This was a new thought. Chilprat revolved it in his mind as slowly as he turned the tembul leaf under his tongue. "It may be," he agreed. "She has many saggi of gold and could pay for a passage. It would be well if she went, Marukya. My house is crowded, and I cannot keep them here much longer."

The house of Chilprat was surrounded by a bamboo fence, and over the entrance was a tiger skull as a sign of his wealth and high standing in the community. Maryam had a corner of one room, closed off by a tall screen, and a window from which she could see the temple in the rocky hill on the Island of the Elephant. Here she slept on a far from comfortable mat. The only other article of household use that she possessed was the cane basket in which the child had spent much of his time during the wearisome relay from port to port. Now that he was a full year old he was becoming very active and had begun to walk a little on a pair of sturdy legs, mostly in pursuit of Chi Wangti. That tiny aristocrat liked the boy and often curled up in the basket with him, but in the main showed a cautious regard for the untrained strength in the groping fingers. The curled beige tail of the dog was the chief object of interest, and the child would totter after it, saying with a happy grin the one word his tongue had mastered, "Chi! Chi!" Although always thwarted in his quest, he continued to pursue it with unabated zeal.

Except for the disappointing spells when she patrolled the waterside, seeking a ship which would take them to London, Maryam devoted herself entirely to the boy. She bathed him twice a day, prepared his many meals with the greatest care, and stitched at clothes for him made

out of the gay pieces of cloth she found in native shops. This last was an
endless task. It seemed that she no sooner finished one than his wrists
would be too long for its sleeves and she would be unable to fit his
plump little backsides into the trousers. In spite of the continual heat
and the upsetting nature of the life they lived, he grew with bewildering
speed.

"He is such a fine fellow, my Walter," she would say to Mahmoud.
"He is so much like his father. See, his hair is so golden and it is beginning to curl already. He will be a very handsome man."

Mahmoud, who slept outside and whose chief duty was to obtain the
rice and vegetables on which they lived, was fully as devoted to the new
member of the family. He called him Masser Boy and would take him
out for long jaunts twice a day, once in the morning before the heat became excessive and then late in the afternoon, when the sun was close
to the blue rim of the sea. The boy looked forward to these excursions
into the world and would perch happily on Mahmoud's shoulder,
digging one hand into the folds of the turban for added security and
kicking his heels against the servant's chest. He always knew when the
time had come to start, and he would sit perfectly still, watching the
end of the screen around which Mahmoud was due to appear. If for any
reason the servant was late, he would pucker up his face and look at his
mother as though to say: "What has happened to the black one? This
is indeed very annoying."

Mahmoud talked to him incessantly when they were out together, and
he would report their conversations to his mistress on their return.

"Mahmoud tell Masser Boy about el'phants. Masser Boy understand.
Oh yes, he know what Mahmoud say."

"How can you be sure? What did he say, Mahmoud?"

"He not say *much*. But Mahmoud know. Small boys like el'phants."

Mostly, however, the talks were about ships. They would saunter
down to the beach, and if a vessel happened to be at the moorings the
servant would chatter excitedly about the tall patched sails of many
colors, and the steering chains, and the dark holes below decks from
which the strange smells came. When they got back to the house of
Chilprat, he would inform Maryam that her son was going to be a sailor
when he grew up. "All settled, Lady Ma'yam," he would say. "Masser
Boy like ships. Eyes get round like buttons when he sees. Masser Boy
and Mahmoud go long journeys together when he gets to be big fellow
like his father."

Maryam would protest angrily at this idea. They were having such interminable journeys now that she hoped and prayed her son would never have to go on another as long as he lived.

The hope which had kept her spirits up during the eternal sailing, and through the anxious periods in port when she would seek another ship by haunting the wharves and saying, "London?" whenever she passed a sailor, was beginning to fade. Had the captains who accepted her gold known in what direction lay the distant city of the English? Or was she penetrating farther and farther into a strange hot world far from the right course? There was no way of telling. A high and blank wall of silence had closed them in and, for all she knew, they were farther away from London than when they started.

"Mahmoud," she would say, with a despairing shake of the head, "will we ever find a ship to take us away from these dreadful islands? And if we do, will it take us to where Master Walter is waiting? And, oh, Mahmoud, *is* he still waiting for us? Don't you think he is sure we are lost forever? Perhaps he thinks we are dead."

Mahmoud would nod confidently. "Masser Watter waiting for us. He very fond Lady Ma'yam. And when he see Masser Boy—ha, how glad he be then!"

"I am beginning to fear we will never see him again."

But Mahmoud had no doubts on that score. "Sure we see Masser Watter again." He would tap his chest. "Mahmoud know here we get there very soon."

2

Maryam had not failed to observe that Walter and Tristram had been compelled to leave in the first of the skiffs on the night when the Great Bore was racing up the river. After that there was an inevitability about everything that happened to her. She followed Chang Wu silently to a dark room at the rear of one of the rice warehouses. Mahmoud was frightened when it became apparent that the hungry mobs were trying to break in, but she did not share his fears. She was sure that Walter's departure had been timed to make sure that the Bore would complete the disappearance of the birds of golden plumage. She had no hope that he was still alive; and so she asked for nothing better than to suffer a like fate.

She lay on a hard couch and stared with unseeing eyes at the dark objects about her. Rats scampered around on the floor, but she paid no attention. No one came near. The sounds of conflict drew closer and then receded, finally dying out entirely. She was to live after all, but she felt no relief when this became a certainty.

Hours passed, and a faint light began to penetrate through a narrow slit in the wall high up above her. Day was breaking.

Chang Wu came to see her finally, carrying a small lantern which caused curious streaks of light to dance on the bamboo walls. She sat up at once, striving to read the expression of his face in the uncertain light.

"Your worthy husband and his friend are safe," he announced. "One of the boatmen was drowned, but the other has returned. He says they reached the ship in time."

The fears she had kept within herself through the long hours of the night found relief now in a sudden flood of tears. "Oh, Chang Wu!" she cried. "I am so happy! I was sure they had been lost in that dreadful flood. All night long I have thought of nothing else. Are you certain they are safe? Quite, quite certain?"

The old envoy smiled reassuringly. "There is no doubt about it. I have questioned the man, and he says he saw them on the deck with his own eyes." There was a pause. "The ship could not wait. It sailed at the appointed time. Because of the trouble here, we could not send another skiff across, and now we are in a great difficulty."

Maryam's joy was so profound that the difficulties of her own position made no immediate impression on her mind. She smiled at the old man and said, "I am so happy!"

Chang Wu said nothing further for several moments. There was an expression in his eyes that suggested both regret and penitence.

"Great difficulties have arisen," he repeated. "It has been ordered that no more ships are to sail. They are to be held for use of officials of the court, in case it becomes necessary to leave quickly. All I can promise the wife of my estimable friend is to strive to find a place for her on the first that leaves."

Maryam now realized the full significance of the situation. She gazed at the old man with horror-stricken eyes.

"How soon will that be?" she asked in a whisper. "If there is a long delay, I might never—I might never find him. Good Chang Wu, I am sure you have thought of everything. Tell me I need have no fears."

The envoy shook his head slowly. "It is a matter for extreme regret, but I must say I do not know. The young lord from the West, for whom I had a great affection, is not to be allowed to land at any near-by ports. The situation demanded that he be removed to a safe distance from

Kinsai. Let us hope the next ship for the South will overtake the one on which he sailed."

As soon as it was light enough, she was taken to his home for a second time, and there she stayed for three weeks in such a state of anxiety that at times she doubted whether she could withstand the agonies of suspense. She had no way of knowing if any ships had left for the South in that time. The envoy saw her at rare intervals and reported he was doing everything possible for her. When he finally announced that she was to sail the next day, Maryam's hopes of overtaking her husband had vanished completely. She knew, however, that she must make every effort to find him, even if it meant following all the way to London. By that time it had become clear that the present of the colored duck's eggs had been prophetic.

She sailed from Kinsai a week before the gates of that great city were peacefully opened to admit the first of Bayan's men.

3

One day Chilprat summoned his friend Marukya for a very special conference. It was clear that the strangers were the cause of it, for, as the two men talked over their platter of curried rice and sea food, he kept a wary eye on the screen behind which Maryam and her son carried on their restricted existence. To lend importance to the occasion, Chilprat wore a string of small pearls around his neck in addition to the red loincloth which usually constituted his attire.

"Something must be done," he said, scooping up shrimps with his right hand. With his left, which was reserved for the less dignified functions of life, he gestured in the direction of the screen. "The blue-eyed one is causing trouble among the men of the island."

The priest laughed scornfully. "That little shive of cold white flesh? Why do the men of the island think of her?"

"You have forsworn the lusts of the flesh, and so you cannot understand. She is small and full of grace, and men cannot get those eyes of hers out of their minds. I grant you that her full-of-the-moon is not more than half as wide as that of a mature woman of our own race; but even I, Chilprat, whose blood begins to cool with age, feel a desire to give it a friendly pat whenever she passes. There will be trouble if she stays here any longer. Our women are beginning to talk bitterly among themselves, and my own Altima gives me no peace at all."

Perhaps Maryam had sensed the purpose of the conference. At any rate she chose this moment to emerge from behind the screen. She walked over to the two dignified elders and seated herself cross-legged near them, a thing no woman of the seven islands would ever dare do. She reached out a hand and laid in the palm of her host one of the gems she had carried in the hem of her skirt. It was small, but its ruby red color caused both men to draw in their breaths.

"London," said Maryam, fixing an earnest look on Chilprat. In a beseeching voice she repeated the name of that long-sought city several times.

Covetous eyes studied the gem for a full and tense minute. Chilprat then moistened it with a wet finger and held it up to the light. He tapped it with his long fingernails, rubbed it on the wool of his loincloth, and finally said in a whisper to the priest: "It is a good one. It is of the exact shade, the red of the pigeon's blood. Does she offer it to me to get her passage to this London?"

His use of the name made her hope that he was beginning to understand what she wanted. She nodded her head several times, repeating the word with each nod.

The two men bent their heads together over the stone for another period of close absorption. "It is a fortune, Marukya," whispered Chilprat.

"Yes," answered the priest. "What plan has my sagacious friend found for keeping possession of it?"

Suddenly Chilprat threw his head in the air and laughed loudly. "Horteema!" he cried. "He is the answer to this, good Marukya."

"Horteema?" Clearly the priest had failed to understand.

"Do you not see? What a perfect plan is this one I have conceived! We will send her with Horteema. After all, he is in no position to make great demands, and so we shall be able to satisfy him and still retain a good share of the stone's value for ourselves."

Comprehension dawned at last in the close-set eyes of the priest. He also threw back his head and laughed. "By the bull of holiness, you have found the answer. But," he went on after a moment of further thought, "Horteema was to take a load of horses to Aden before his misfortunes overtook him. Does this strange place she seeks lie in the direction of Aden?"

By the standards of the seven islands Chilprat was an honest man, but he proceeded now to make it clear there were limits to his probity. He raised both hands in the air. "Perhaps not. But she cannot stay here any longer, this woman of disturbing white skin. If Horteema does not take her in the right path, the next captain will. Come, we have much to do."

Horteema was a sea captain with a flat round face which had been sliced across at some time by a sword blade. At this particular moment he was the victim of cruel circumstances. Owing money to an islander which he could not repay, he had been careless enough to let his creditor steal up and draw a circle around him while he stood on an exposed part of the shore. Barred by a sacred Konkan law from stepping outside the circle until the debt had been repaid, the sea captain had already spent several days in open-air captivity. His bed of cane, with its net overbody, had been brought to him and was standing within the circle. Flies buzzed around the dishes of food set out for him, and a lizard slithered around the outer edge of things as though desirous of sharing. Horteema himself wore an unwashed and unhappy air.

His two visitors went into a long and excited debate with him. As Chilprat had predicted, Horteema was in no position to haggle successfully, and in the end he nodded his head glumly. It now remained to compound the debt which held him in thrall, and the creditor was summoned. He was a merchant of sorts, for he carried a stone bottle and pen; and he was, clearly, a harder nut to crack. The debate grew in violence.

Standing off at one side, Maryam saw the creditor produce a small square of cloth and spread it on the ground. The four men then squatted on the sand, each placing his right hand under the cloth.

What were they doing? This curious ceremony puzzled her very much until she became convinced that this was the native way of reaching a difficult agreement. She could see their fingers move under the cloth. After each stealthy gesture there would be a long spell of immobility, all four faces intent and strained. Then another finger would move slowly and unwillingly.

This went on for the better part of a half hour, and then, suddenly, the creditor raised his hand and tossed the cloth in the air. An agreement had been reached. The four participants stood up.

There was such a note of absurdity about it that Maryam, in spite of her anxiety, began to laugh. The men paid no attention to her. Horteema sprang outside the circle and proceeded to obliterate the markings with his bare heel. The creditor completed the transaction by tracing with a finger in the sand the Marathi phrase for *Paid in Full*. The onlooker sensed something of the meaning of all this and laughed again, certain now that her long period of waiting was drawing to its close.

Chilprat laughed also. He then nodded to her and said: "We have all sworn by the *Shri-gundi,* the Lucky Stone. It is settled. My small guest of the pale skin will soon take ship for this mysterious destination."

Maryam did not understand a word, but there was the promise of good things in his tone. "I believe we are going to London at last!" she breathed to herself.

Two anxious days followed while the ship was being loaded. They were more comfortable days in one respect, for Chilprat became friendly in his attitude, and even his wife relented to the extent of sending in platters of food. A dozen times each day Maryam clasped her son in her arms and crooned over him, "At last, my little Walter, we are going to take you to your father." She kept him dressed in his best, so that he would be ready when the time came to depart. In his white coat and baggy trousers he would have passed for a very small gentleman of Antioch if it had not been that she had fashioned his cap, quite unknowingly, after the order of an English biggin.

She was so concerned over the possibility of a slip that she did not permit Mahmoud to take the boy out of her sight. Understanding nothing of this, the round eyes of the child grew weary with watching the end of the screen. He refused to move until sheer fatigue made it impossible for him to keep his eyes open any longer. Maryam had stepped out for a moment, and when she returned he was sleeping with his head on the edge of the mat. Chi, sensing the unhappiness of his friend, had settled down beside him.

At last, however, the horses had all been taken aboard and tethered below, and the moment of departure arrived. The strangers were escorted to the ship, Mahmoud stalking in the lead with the boy perched on his shoulder. They found that a tiny wooden kennel on the deck had been sloshed over hastily with whitewash and furnished with a canvas bed and a chipped water basin. This was to be their home.

Maryam could see Horteema, naked save for a yellow loincloth, standing on the poop deck and sweating profusely as he directed a blistering volley of orders at his crew. Mahmoud sniffed and said, "Dirty ship, Lady Ma'yam."

Her spirits were not to be dampened, however, by any hint of discomfort. Certain in her own mind that this would be the last leg in their long journeying, she looked up at the sky, where the sun blazed fiercely, with a happy look at last on her pale, thin face.

CHAPTER XIV

Little Tamitt

WALTER DECIDED not to be on hand when Engaine arrived at Gurnie. It seemed to him likely that she would have chosen a different sanctuary had she known of his return. His presence certainly would serve to complicate the quarrel with her husband; for Edmond, he knew, had always hated him and would be doubly angered if his wife were to live under the same roof with him. It would be better to let his grandfather explain. If she chose then to leave, as he expected she would, she could do so without the embarrassment of a meeting between them.

He stationed himself, therefore, in a clump of evergreen trees at the edge of Oswiu Pond and watched her come jingling up the road with several men-at-arms in attendance and four servants on mules bringing up the rear. Her departure from Bulaire had been no hasty matter, quite clearly. It had been carefully planned, or she could not have ridden away with so much company.

He could not see her closely, but he got the impression that she had not changed. Her carriage in the saddle was as haughty as ever, and a strand of golden hair tossed in the breeze. He heard her whistle to a windhover and saw the hawk settle down to its perch on her wrist. She called an order to one of the servants in a clear, high voice. Whatever her reason for leaving Bulaire, she had not come away with a broken spirit.

He waited two hours, keeping a close watch on the house and fully expecting to see the party take to horse again and ride on to a more suitable place of refuge. Nothing of the kind happened. The horses and mules were led out to the pond and turned loose in the wattled yard. A groom with the crosslet on his arm stopped whistling when he saw Walter and pulled his front locks in humble greeting. A storm was threatening by this time, and a black helm of cloud showed above Algitha Scaur. Walter decided he might as well go in.

Servants were working on the drawbridge when he passed through the outer palisades, replacing the rusted chain with stout new ropes. His grandfather, it seemed, foresaw a need to defend the old house. The men talked and whistled as they worked, happy in the prospect.

He encountered Wulfa as soon as he entered. Her face was full of bitterness, and her hands clutched her skirt on each side with an intensity that told of some deep inner disturbance. She did not venture to address him, however.

"What has happened?" he asked.

"Master! She is in your mother's room."

"There is no other camera suitable for her entertainment," he said, after a moment's consideration. "It's the largest room we have, and the lightest."

"But, master, she—she is making changes!" Wulfa spoke as though she had witnessed acts of sacrilege. "The child is with her, and two maids are there too. It has become like the common room of a tavern."

"There is nothing to be done about it, Wulfa. The countess is our guest, and we must do everything we can for her comfort."

"It seems," said the maid, moistening her lips as she spoke, "that the room is not good enough. The blankets have been removed from the bed, and it has been made up with tawny silk she brought with her. A Tartar hanging has been put up on one wall. To make things more cheerful, she said. Master! I cannot abide it!"

"As long as the countess is in our house, her desires are our law. You must reconcile yourself to that."

The door of his mother's room was open when he passed, and a cheerful clatter of voices reached him. He heard Engaine say: "Agnes, my toilet articles are not unpacked. And where, stupid girl, is my pomander? Hurry! I must make a good appearance tonight."

Walter decided that he must make a good appearance also. The rough wooden cupboard in one corner of his room was filled with new clothing, and many handsome articles overflowed on hooks driven into the unfinished oak walls. All this finery he had purchased during his stops in Venice and Paris. With plenty of gold in his pockets, he had given rein to temporary lifts of mood; but never up to the present had he felt like wearing any of his fine acquisitions.

The costume he elected to wear was decidedly extreme, but he hummed excitedly as he put it on, confident that he would cut a fine figure. A tunic of blue satin, padded at the shoulders and tufted with seed pearls, covered him to a point not more than eight inches below the belt. It fitted him so snugly that he handled the row of gold buttons down the front with great care. The padded sleeves were long and elaborately embroidered, the dagged cuffs showing no more than the tips of his fingers. Beneath this tunic he wore stockings of white damas which fitted his long legs from hip to heel with the tightness of an onion skin. This was a daring innovation, for Englishmen covered their legs with loose hose and concealed them under long outer garments falling almost to the ground. But he had no qualms; this new fashion would soon reach England, and he rather fancied the role of pioneer.

Blue shoes with curled-up toes completed his attire, and he felt quite content as he paced up and down his room. As a matter of habit he thought, "If Maryam could only see me!" The words had no sooner formed in his mind than all sense of pride left him. He went to the window and gazed out unhappily at the gathering storm. "My sweet wife, where are you tonight?" he asked aloud.

He remained at the window for several minutes, and when he turned back it was with the intention of stripping off his finery and donning something less festive. Then he sighed and said to himself: "No, I may as well go down as I am. It is fitting that I look my best before Engaine. She seems to have a poor opinion of Gurnie, and that must be corrected."

The Great Hall had been lighted with double the usual number of tallow dips. He was the first down, and he looked at the arrangements with an eye to the impression they would make on their guest. *Luke the Physician* stood in the center of the table, towering above *John the Baptist* and *Bernard of Clairvaux* which flanked it. There were three chairs at the head, placed close together, and the tall saltcellar faced them instead of resting as always before on the trestles. Walter's heart gave a satisfied bound. He was to sit with his grandfather and Engaine! For the first time, his position as a member of the family was to be openly acknowledged.

He was aware that the servants and plowfolk at the other end of the long room were indulging in loud whistles of amazement over his appearance. One said in an audible tone, "Pluck the molting rooks if he an't come back a strutting peacock!" Another chimed in, "Young master, ye must be proud o' those long legs o' thine." He did not mind, for he knew that underneath they were as proud as peacocks themselves that he had returned from his travels in such handsome guise. He grinned back at them and said, "You lousy shewels, you should have seen me in my robes in Cathay!"

His grandfather entered the room at this point, with the help of a stout thorn-apple cane, and complete silence fell. The old man blinked at him for a moment and then, unexpectedly, he smiled.

"Solomon in all his glory!" he said. "Never have I seen the equal of your hose, my boy. By St. Wulstan, I must have a pair of them myself! My legs are still full enough to bear such arrogant exposure."

Walter bowed. "It is the custom in Venice, my lord," he said. "They will soon be wearing them at the court of His King's Grace."

His grandfather drew him aside. "I have spoken to Father Clement," he whispered. "He says a heavy penance must be exacted for the broken oath, but that, once broken, it lacks all further validity. The matter of the penance will be left for Bishop Anselm to decide, and I fear it will be both trying and costly. But in the meantime I am free to address you as much as I like. I am very happy in that prospect, my boy."

Engaine now entered. Walter's memory of her had dimmed, and it was with real pleasure that he saw how very beautiful she was. Her hair was confined on each side in a close net under a thin circlet of gold. She wore a deep blue kirtle which swept the floor as she walked, and over this a trim-fitting bodice of yellow velvet, open in front and edged with a broad band of ermine. A cloak of dull maroon was clipped around her neck with a gold chain, falling behind her shoulders and leaving her canary-buttoned sleeves in full view.

If he had expected to find her in a subdued mood or weighed down with the troubles which had brought about her flight from Bulaire, he would have been in error. She came forward, her blue skirts rustling, with both hands held out to him and a warm smile of welcome.

"Walter!" she cried. "This is a very great surprise, and a most pleasant one. I had no expectation of finding you at Gurnie; nor indeed did I know you had returned."

Her eyes, which he was finding as dazzling as ever, were taking him in with wide-open pleasure. He became confused and could do no more than stammer that he was happy to be home and to see her again.

"You are very likely to see much of me," she said. "I have left Bulaire forever. Never, never shall I return to that most unhappy place. As I have no other plans as yet, I may take advantage of your grandfather's generous hospitality for some time."

"It will make me most happy, gracious lady," said the master of Gurnie, at Walter's shoulder, "if you remain here as long as it may suit your inclination and your plans. It has been a dull house for many years. Your beauteous presence will be a boon to us indeed."

She bowed and smiled her thanks as she accepted his arm. He led her to the chair on his right and motioned to Walter to seat himself on the other side. The latter did so, acutely aware that the servants below him were winking broadly and that Agnes Malkinsmaiden, brushing past him with a silver platter on which reposed a joint of venison, said in a hoarse whisper, "Glad I am to see ye raised to yer proper place at last, Master Walter."

The old man was in the highest of spirits, and he began to talk at once, cutting Agnes off when she tried to pronounce her customary sentence of grace. As he carved the venison on his tranchoir into long strips, he steered the conversation into his favorite channels. Engaine devoted herself at first with a good appetite to her slice of venison and the half of a roast bird, drinking two glasses of wine. Then she laid her knife aside and leaned forward, ostensibly to listen more attentively to the rambling anecdotes of her host, but in reality so she could enjoy a better view of Walter, sitting silently on the other side. She took advantage of the slightest pause to ask questions across the old man. Was Cathay as fabulous a land as everyone supposed? Had he brought many curious things back with him? Had he not gained a better opinion of the fine king? To all of these he replied in the affirmative.

None of her ventures was permitted to lead into any sustained talk between them. With a hasty, "That reminds me, gracious lady," the head of the household would be off on another story. Finally she abandoned the effort and said, with a well-feigned air of weariness, that it had been a trying day. Had she her kind host's permission to retire to her room?

"We will be quite desolate without you," said the old man, rising ceremoniously. "I have one consolation, however. My grandson and I," turning his head to smile and nod at Walter, "have an enforced silence of more than twenty years to make up for. Ah, how our tongues will wag! We shall sit late tonight."

Walter escorted her across the dais. At the door she paused and touched his arm briefly and lightly. "What a very handsome creature you have become," she whispered. Then her voice took on a more serious tone. "I am in great trouble, as you must have divined. I want to tell you about it. Could you contrive to meet me alone in the gardens early tomorrow morning so I might have the benefit of your advice? It is indeed sorely needed, Walter."

"I rise at the hour of prime, Lady Engaine," he answered. "I shall be at your service and happy to do whatever I can in your behalf."

"Not as early as that!" she laughed. "My complexion would not be proof against such uncivilized rising. Still I am not one to lie abed, and I shall join you soon thereafter. I am most anxious as well to hear of your great adventures."

2

Walter had been up and about for two hours before Engaine appeared
swinging a pomander in one hand as she walked. It was made of an
orange skin filled with perfumes and tied at the top with a most
frivolous bow of black velvet.

"Good morrow," she said in a somewhat constrained tone. "I did not
sleep well because my mind was filled with all my worries. That is why
I am so late."

Walter scanned the score of faces on the old stone sundial. "You are
much earlier than I expected. Shall we walk down to the pond? There
is no cover that way, and the grass will be less damp. Your shoes look
as fragile as fuchsia buds and not fitted for walking in the wet."

Engaine raised one foot a few inches off the ground to display the toe
of a red shoe. "They are my greatest weakness," she said. "If I were
Queen of England, I would have hundreds of pairs and never wear the
same ones twice."

They began to walk slowly in the direction of the pond, and Engaine
adjusted her hood to protect her face from the sun.

"I have the room where I was taken the first time I came to Gurnie,"
she said. "You were there that day, Walter, if you care to remember
that far back. What a sulky little boy you were! And a contradicting
boy; albeit a very good-looking one."

"You were boasting, and I had to contradict you."

"I can still recall how you looked. Your hair was tangled up in curls
and was hanging down into your eyes."

"As a matter of truth," he declared, "I was always rather tidy. I am
certain my hair was well combed."

"Perchance it was. I am not sure. But I *am* sure you were quite argu-
mentative and even rude to me."

"You were showing yourself disdainful of us. You have always carried
an air of disdain with me, Engaine."

"And now," with a sigh, "I have come to Gurnie in my extremity.
There is no disdain left in me, Walter. I have not been happy since I
married Edmond." Her voice raised. "I am sure you hate him, but I am
equally sure you can have no idea what a grasping, cruel, despicable
man he is!"

"Little as I have seen of him, I will accept anything you have to say about him. And about his mother. What report have you of the Norman woman?"

Engaine tossed her head angrily. "I think I could have managed Edmond had it not been for her. He was very proud of me at first; but she, his mother, resented me from the beginning. She wanted to continue as the mistress of Bulaire. It was two against one, Walter, and I could do nothing against such odds. Their heads were always together, scheming and contriving. They seemed to think of little else but to save, to hoard, to add another bag of gold to the great store they have laid away somewhere. Have you noticed how alike their noses are? Long and covetous and quite vulgar. They would bend their heads over the table until the tips of those ugly noses almost touched, and they would whisper. They were always whispering, so I could not hear." She began to laugh in angry exasperation. "Would you believe me if I told you I have never had a single coin in my hand or my purse since the day I was married?"

He gave her an incredulous look. "But, Engaine, your father is dead, and so you must have come into your inheritance."

"Edmond claimed all of Tressling as my dowry. He took over the control at once, and he went himself to collect the rents and the share of the crops. It was because he went there yesterday that I was able to leave. He was to return last night. What a storm there must have been!"

"What you tell me passes belief."

"They are an unbelievable pair. His mother is a little crazed. She has refused to have your father's bier moved from the chapel. The candles had burned down to the sockets, but she won't allow them to be touched. She even wanted to keep his body with her." Engaine took his arm and bent her head close to whisper. "I could see madness in her eyes whenever she looked at me. I am sure she wanted to kill me, and she might have done it had I remained at the castle any longer."

"Edmond will ride against us in force when he discovers where you are," declared Walter. "My grandfather and I talked it over last night and decided it would be wise to keep all our men on the place as long as you are with us."

"You need have little fear on that score. He is so parsimonious that he has been cutting down the number of his retainers. There are no more than a dozen archers at the castle and the same number of men-at-arms. Those who came with me are my own people from Tressling. But even the Bulaire men have little love for their lord. He is in no position at this time to attempt force."

They paced along for several moments in silence. "What a sorry mar-

ried life you have had!" he said, finally. In his mind he was contrasting
what had happened to her with the great happiness he had known in
the Abode of Everlasting Felicity.

"But I have not told you the worst," she said. "He is so cruel. He
grinds his people down and punishes them terribly if they go against
his will. Jack Daldy has been busy in his dungeons! The King's law is
set at naught in Bulaire Castle."

"I heard something of this when I was in London."

"He has been repaying the peasants for what they did after his father's
death. One hundredfold, Walter." There was a pause. "And that still is
not all. We—we have lived apart since my son was born. He brings
women to the castle and flaunts them before my face. Some of them are
unwilling victims. Edmond seems to believe in *droit de seigneur!*" She
indulged in another bitter laugh at her own expense. "It is hard to believe that this could happen to Engaine of Tressling, the proud young
heiress, so very sure of herself and her power to captivate and hold all
men! Perhaps I should have been content with Ninian. Or even"—she
glanced at him quickly and then turned her head away—"listened to
another suitor."

"What are you planning to do?" he asked after a moment.

"I don't know. All I could think of was the need to get away. I do
know this: I shall never return to Bulaire. What do you advise?"

"You should go to London at once and lay your case before the King.
I have heard glowing reports of his fairness. He would give you a hearing, and I think it certain he would see to it that you receive back some
share at least of your own holdings."

"Go to London! It would not be possible to go alone; and how, think
you, could I live there with my people? Walter, it is as I told you. I
haven't as much as a single groat in my pocket."

"That," he said, "need not concern you. I did not return empty-
handed from the East. I can supply you with what you will need to live
in London while the case is under consideration."

She looked up at him in wonder. "You would do that for me? And I
always treated you so badly, dear Walter! How can two brothers be so
different?"

"We are half brothers only. I insist," he added, "that the limited scale
of our relationship must always be stated."

He had been keeping a wary eye on the landscape ahead, and he now
came to a full stop.

"Here he comes," he said. "He has lost no time. Your knightly lord and master rides with a dozen men at least to claim you. We must get back to the house at once."

Engaine watched the approaching horsemen in silence for a moment. "I have nothing but contempt for him," she said then. "No, I prefer to wait for him here. I cannot allow him to think I fear him in the least."

Walter did not make any effort to change her mind. However, he turned and gave a loud hail through cupped hands. An answering signal came back to them from behind the wall of the palisades.

"At least," he said, "we must have some men with us."

Eight stout men of Gurnie were ranged behind them when the Earl of Lessford rode up. Edmond reined in and motioned to his own men to stay back. The intervening years had wrought quite a change in him. His face was mature, with a heavy, brooding look, and his figure had thickened perceptibly.

He scowled at his wife in silence for several moments.

"So," he said then. "This is where I find you, sweet partner. In the very best of company! Are you prepared to mount your horse and return with me to Bulaire at once?"

"I shall never return to Bulaire."

"That," said the young nobleman, "is not a point for you to decide. It rests in my hands. And I am commanding you to summon your people and to be ready to ride within ten minutes."

Engaine laughed scornfully. "Have you become deficient in your hearing, my lord? I have left you forever. No power on earth can make me change my mind. I may add that I despise you so utterly I would die rather than live again under the same roof with you."

The earl made no immediate response. He transferred his regard to Walter. "I was not aware," he said, in an even tone, "that the bastard of Gurnie had returned from his travels. Can it be that his presence accounts for this sudden resolution on your part, my fair one?"

"I arrived at Gurnie yesterday," declared Walter. "Not even my grandfather knew in advance of my coming."

"Still it is a strange coincidence. A most curious thing indeed. The regard in which you have held my wife," went on the earl, with his first trace of anger, "has always been a matter of my knowledge. You have been urging her, no doubt, to this attitude of disobedience."

"I am under no obligation to make you any explanations. But I think it only fair to my lady Engaine to say that her decisions have been entirely of her own making."

"You have my son," said the earl, turning back to Engaine. "That is something I cannot tolerate for another hour. What you do yourself is of much less consequence."

"He is my son!"

"The law does not say so."

"The law?" cried Engaine. "This is the first time you have given it a thought, my sweet Edmond!"

There was a long pause. The master of Bulaire sat hunched over in his saddle, his eyes darting back and forth from one to the other. "Then it seems I must use force," he said finally.

"Think well before you make any move," said Walter quickly. "My men, as you must have seen, have arrows fitted to their bows. The archers of Gurnie are good marksmen."

"I could ride you down, bastard of Gurnie!" cried Edmond. "It would be a task much to my liking."

"You might be beautifully spitted first, half brother," laughed Walter. "An arrow through the throat is a most final matter, even when it is a noble throat."

The earl drew his reins in with a sudden fury. "Engaine, I am giving you one last chance! Make yourself ready and bring my son home with you."

"Can it be you add cowardice to your other faults?" Engaine laughed easily. "You spoke of force no more than a moment ago. Have you lost all desire for a display of it?"

"Do you think," cried her husband, "that I would honor this baseborn knave by matching my strength with his?"

"I am on foot and so are all my men," declared Walter. "You have that advantage, good half brother. Baseborn, you say? We sprang from the same loins, though in all respects save one I vow that our father did better by me. You are the Earl of Lessford, Edmond, but I must remind you that you trespass on the lands of Gurnie. Unless I see your back at once, you will have a shower of the deadliest of fruit falling about your ears."

"You will live to regret this, both of you," said Edmond. He scowled at them for a moment and then wheeled his horse around.

"Farewell, sweet husband!" called Engaine when the dust of their departure rose.

She was in high spirits as they walked back, swinging her pomander and even humming a light air.

"I feel very much better now that the die is cast," she said. "What a poor-spirited creature he is! How could I have made such a mistake as to marry him? It was your fault, Walter. You should have dragged me from my horse that morning and carried me to the nearest priest."

"It was in my mind to do it. But you had always treated me with such scant respect, and laughed so at my pretensions, that I could not believe you had the smallest liking for me."

"You knew I liked you! And now," she said, turning the full regard of her brilliant eyes on him, "I hear you have been so forgetful of me as to get yourself married. Was it necessary to dignify your relationship with this heathen girl by going through a form of wedding service with her?"

"So you have heard about it! I told no one until last night when I talked with my grandfather."

"Of course I heard. I have a great curiosity in all matters that concern you, Walter. You must know that the words said over you by that Eastern priest were neither sacred nor binding. You are not really married to your heathen girl."

"She is not a heathen. She had a Grecian mother and an English father. As to the service, it was performed by a Christian priest of the Nestorian order. It was fully binding."

"It is becoming clear you thought yourself in love with her at the time."

"Yes, I was in love with her. I still am. She remains my wife, even though the whole world separates us and I know I shall never see her again."

"Come, Walter, is so much vehemence necessary? Are you telling me this as—as a warning?" She turned and looked at him with a smile which had a trace of her old mockery in it and, at the same time, a hint of anger. "You will get over it, though I must say I resent your lack of constancy. No, that is not fair. I had made up my mind to marry this poor excuse of a man who has just ridden away in such high dudgeon. I told you so, and you are not to be blamed for seeking whatever consolation you might find." Her smile grew deeper. "But, Walter, I think you are being ridiculous when you profess an everlasting devotion for this little heathen whom you can never hope to see again. Are you going to content yourself for the rest of your life with an empty vow?"

"My mind dwells so much on the past that I have given little thought to the future."

Engaine laughed and gave the pomander another swing. "We must all conspire to win your thoughts away from the gloomy past, my most resolute Walter," she said.

3

For three days thereafter Walter worked on his plans and saw Engaine at supper only; when, as usual, his grandfather monopolized the conversation. She would lean forward and flash him an occasional smile, and he would escort her to the door, but in no other way was it possible to inject a note of intimacy into their contacts.

They proved to be trying days. Something in the atmosphere at Gurnie puzzled him. The men assisting him in the preliminary work at his proposed paper yard were aloof and even morose. Their faces wore a detached look, and they seldom spoke to him. He was sure there was no personal animus in this, for an occasional word would be dropped which indicated they still had affection for him. The first hint he had of the reason came on the third morning.

Swire Gilpin, one of the oldest of the men, suddenly dropped the axe with which he was driving in a post. He straightened up and shook his fist in the direction of Bulaire.

"Master Wat," he asked, "did ye know as Cecily Tomsmaiden threw herself from top o' keep last night?"

It was then no later than eight o'clock. Walter asked in turn, "How could news of what happened at Bulaire last night reach us here so early?"

"Bad news travels fast, master. And these days it travels often!"

"Who was the girl, Swire?"

"Daughter to the forger o' Cencaster. As honest a man as ever beat out a horseshoe. And as honest and pretty a girl as ever breathed, master."

"Had she been taken against her will?"

"Aye," answered Gilpin, picking up his axe and returning to his work. "The same has happened afore, master."

It was clear to Walter now that the tyranny at Bulaire weighed so heavily on the countryside that even the dependents of more favored domains had been driven to a hostile attitude.

Late in the afternoon he heard Gilpin whisper to one of his fellows, "Here he comes, Bart." The other glanced quickly over his shoulder and whispered back, "Aye, our tall one'll have tidings for us."

Walter turned himself and saw Tristram striding down the road from

Chanfrin Rock. A second conviction took hold of him, that Tristram had already established himself as the focal point of local discontent. It seemed clear, in fact, that he was recognized as a leader among the common men.

Walter dropped his work and hurried forward to meet his friend. The longbow was back in its accustomed place on Tristram's shoulder, and when they came close Walter saw that it was newly strung and shining to an excess.

"Hallo, Wat!" called Tristram. Then he stopped and looked about him with a puzzled air. "Is my memory at fault? You seem to have grown into a village here."

"My grandfather has won his spurs for a second time and in a manner particularly his own," answered Walter. "He has set up many profitable ventures here. I could be happy over what has been happening if I had not found our people unhappy and restless. Things are not at all to my liking."

"You have noticed it already?" The smile of greeting faded from Tristram's face. "We sowed seeds of hatred that night, and the poor fellows hereabouts have been reaping a bitter harvest ever since. The hand of the new earl lies heavily on the county."

He was attired in a new archer's suit of green, and wore gloves on his hands of the same kind his father had given him on his return from Oxford. Walter saw that the motto they bore was worded differently, *Jesus Amend All Wrongs*.

"First fruits of the spoils of China?" asked Walter, touching his friend's sleeve.

Tristram nodded indifferently. He produced a bag from his belt and held it out. "I wish you would be custodian of my wealth. I shall have no need of it for a time. If anything should happen to me, you would be better able to realize well on it for my father." He paused and favored Walter with a wry smile. "You have a guest, I hear. This attitude you mislike can be traced in part to that."

"But she has left Bulaire and refuses to return."

"It is hard to understand the minds of these downtrodden people, Wat. They all think, and with good reason, that the gentry are united against them. They dislike and fear your lady Engaine, and yet they see her sitting at your table. They don't want her here, and that is the plain truth. They have been so unhappy over the persecution of their friends and their relatives that their minds are warped with suspicion."

"It will soon be clear to them that there is nothing but the deepest enmity between Bulaire and Gurnie."

"Wat," said Tristram, after a long pause, "the things these people have suffered have brought the day of reckoning closer. Something must be done."

"The new laws will take care of that."

"Many of the barons pay no heed to the new laws. They intend to keep all their old power, and they still treat their people as though the laws did not exist. Your half brother is one of them." The look Tristram turned on his companion was startling in its suggestion of a determination from which he could not be swayed. "We must back the King by fighting his lawbreaking barons."

"Tris, you must have patience. The King will soon set the nobles in their places."

"But in the meantime the people groan under illegal exactions. They are treated worse than the beasts in the fields. Must we sit still and see young girls taken from their homes and ravished? The laws," cried Tristram in a sudden fury, "are on our side at last! We are poor subjects if we stand humbly by and see them broken!"

Conscious of the curious eyes and ready ears of the workers, Walter took his friend by the arm and led him in the direction of the house. "What do you plan to do?" he asked, when they were at a safe distance.

"Tonight I am meeting Camus Harry, and we'll talk it over. It is as we heard in London: he has thrown in with the trailbastons. We must not judge him harshly, Wat. A man has to live, and he can't exist alone in the forests for as long as our good Harry has been under the ban. He is sound at heart, and I find he has kept in touch all along with the men at home. I want first to have his advice."

"Let me go with you tonight."

"You are not in a position to help us," said Tristram, with a negative shake of the head, "and, mayhap, your presence would be a hindrance. You must think of the consequences. By taking in the countess you and your grandfather have involved yourselves already to the limit of safety. No, no, you wish us well, I know; but I can't let you go any further than that."

"I played a part before. I can't with honor stand aside."

"It is different now," said Tristram quickly. "It goes right to the roots of class differences this time. They won't have you, Wat—you might as well know it. But Camus Harry would be glad to see you again. As your purpose in coming would be to sound a note of warning

—well, he would be ready to listen to you. I promise you it will have no effect. Come, then, if nothing else will content you."

"Where do we meet Camus Harry? And when?"

"At the ruins of his tavern at Little Tamitt. He visits the place, I am told, quite regularly. The sight of its charred walls serves to strengthen his resolution—for the wild life he has to live and for the purpose he never forgets."

"Come to the house with me now. You will have the pleasure—a doubtful one to you perhaps—of supping with the lovely Countess of Lessford. We will have a chance then to discuss what you want me to do with your bag of valuables."

But Tristram was firm in his refusal of the invitation. He had many things to do still. They would go separately to Little Tamitt and meet there at eleven o'clock.

"I must prepare you for one thing," he said, in parting. "You must not be discomfited if you find a fourth man there. If he comes, Wat, you will find him a strange wreck of humanity and with a sorry story to tell —if he had any way of telling it!"

Engaine left the Great Hall earlier than usual that evening, and the master of Gurnie took advantage of this by ordering out the board for a game of spillikins. He won every game, for his play was as sharp and incisive as the stroke of a fang, and Walter's mind was elsewhere; and so the old man departed for bed in a highly pleased frame of mind. It was nearly ten o'clock when Walter found himself at liberty to leave. He ordered one of the men to have a horse waiting for him at the first turn of the road, and then started for his room to find a cloak.

A shaft of light poured into the upper hall from the partly opened door of his mother's room and the first sound of his hurrying footsteps brought Engaine out into the passage.

"I fail to understand this sudden haste," she said. "For an hour and a half I have waited for a word with you. If you could linger so long, why do you come racing now as though the devil is at your heels?"

"I am going out. Had I known you wanted to see me, Engaine, I would have found a way to shorten the game with my grandfather."

"Walter," she said, eyeing him reproachfully, "it may be that your work is so urgent you must give all your time to it, but it is my opinion you are using it as an excuse. You are avoiding me purposely."

"I have much to do. But even were I free, it would hardly be fitting for me to see much of you."

Engaine indulged in an amused laugh. She had changed the red robe in which she had appeared at supper for a long and loosely flowing one of blue silk with a square-cut low neck. Her hair was not confined and fell in golden-spun profusion to her waist. The effect, he acknowledged uncomfortably, was breath-taking.

"Are you thinking of my reputation? By running away from my lawful lord and husband, I have exposed it already to the tongues of all the scandalmongers in the kingdom. They will tear my fair name to shreds. If I am seen much in the company of the handsome grandson of my host, it may add a fillip to the talk; but I have no concern, Walter, for what they may say or think." She paused and shook her head at him in reproof. "You are not being honest with me. You are trying so hard to be fair to that dusky wife of yours. Is her skin quite dark, Walter? I have not dared to ask you about her before; but now I am angry with you, and so I don't care."

"Her skin is white," he answered shortly.

"How curious! Well, I think I understand what fills that very proper mind of yours, and I am sure you avoid me because you have decided that absence is the best aid to constancy." Then her mood sobered. "Seriously, Walter, I must have a talk with you. I have decided you gave me good advice. I must go to London and lay my case before the King."

"It is a wise decision, Engaine. In your own interests, it is best you go as soon as possible."

"Tomorrow morning, then, you will allow me a few moments? I shall defer to your convenience by rising with the sun." She was studying him with an active curiosity. "I am disturbed by this midnight errand of yours. There will be danger in it, I think."

"No danger at all, unless the devil should whisk me off my horse. I can't tell you anything about it, Engaine."

"You are being most mysterious." She was watching him with genuine anxiety. "Promise me you will exercise every care. I realize that I—that I am depending on you very much."

4

Earl Edmond and his men had been most thorough in the demolition of the tavern at Little Tamitt. The roof was gone, and there were gaping holes in the walls; it was, in fact, no more than a pile of rubble which looked ghostly enough in the light of the full moon to send shivers down the spine.

Walter reined in his horse some distance away and viewed this proof of Norman vindictiveness with the uneasiness which always sat on the shoulders of nightly travelers. He saw that some waggish member of the earl's party had suspended a heaume, the sign of hospitality, over what had once been the door. There was a brisk breeze, and so the iron heaume, which had once covered the head of a warrior in action, clanked against the pole supporting it with a sound like a muted bell.

He tethered his horse and approached the ruined building cautiously. A murmur of voices caused him to divert his steps to a malthouse in the rear which still boasted a roof. Here he found Tristram and Camus Harry, and a third man who crouched in a corner and manifested his presence only by his heavy breathing.

Camus Harry welcomed him with a thwack on the back with a hardened palm. "The wily planner of sieges!" he exclaimed. "Well, Walter of Gurnie, look on yer handiwork. If ye had not shown us the way to enter the castle that night, the tavern of Little Tamitt might still be standing and I might be a respected innkeeper instead of an outlaw skulking in the woods." He looked up at the tall figure beside him in the dark. "Ye've put on size, young gentry. I would not care to mell with ye in a test o' strength."

"He has come to preach caution," said Tristram.

The tone of Camus Harry's voice changed perceptibly. There was an ominous edge to it. "We'll lend an ear to what he has to say, but he'll find our minds are set. I warn ye, Walter of Gurnie, that I live only for the day when I'll see the body of the Earl of Lessford swinging up among the medlars." He turned to the man in the dark corner. "Come out, Will Ferryman. Perhaps he will change his mind when he sees what they've done to ye."

Tristram lighted a torch and held it up in front of the stranger's face. It was a frightening thing in the dim light thus afforded, as white as an uncured cheese, with rheumy red lashes and pale eyes which stared fixedly without any trace of expression. It did not look like a human face at all, but resembled rather the clay daubs which mummers carried on poles in holiday parades.

"He can't speak," explained Tristram, gazing at the man with the deepest compassion. "The first thing they did was to cut out his tongue."

"Will Ferryman," said the ex-landlord, "open yer tunic, man, and let him see the rest of it." Turning to Walter, he said: "The noble earl charged this honest fellow with killing one of his hawks, and he set the punishment by an old Norman law."

The man had bared his chest. Walter drew in his breath sharply when he saw that the whole surface had been scraped down almost to the bones and was covered with the black and red of unhealed sores.

"Two pounds of flesh," intoned Camus Harry. "Cut from his chest and weighed on the dungeon scales at Bulaire! It was fed to the hawks, and it's said as they made a greedy breakfast of it."

There was a long silence, and then Tristram spoke up. "Will Ferryman was with us that night, and there you have the whole story. It is just one case, Wat. We could show you many more, and all as fiendishly contrived as this. Do you understand now why our minds are set?"

Walter decided to make one effort. "But can't you wait a few weeks longer while the evidence is gathered to lay before the King?"

"There is another innocent girl held in the castle!" cried Tristram passionately. "Can we stand by and wait until she throws herself from the top of the keep?"

Camus Harry seized Walter by both wrists. "Listen to me, Walter of Gurnie. Before ye arrived, we had made our plans. It's not in our minds to attack the castle again, but I'll not tell what it is we mean to do. I'll say this: Ye could talk to the day o' doom without changing our minds."

Tristram took his friend by the arm and led him to one side. "Others will be here any minute now. You had best not be seen with us. Take my word for that and get yourself out of sight before they arrive."

Walter walked back to Camus Harry. "Tris tells me I must leave now. I'll spare you any further talk, except to say how deeply I feel about what has been happening."

"Aye, spare yer breath." The ex-landlord held out a hand. "Will ye shake with an outlaw? Ye're the only man o' noble birth I 'ud offer it to. I've allus had a warm regard for ye, and more than ever since Tris had told me tales of yer travels together." He nodded his head grimly. "He has pledged himself to a riskier course than the road to Cathay."

The two friends walked to where the horse was tethered. Nothing was said until Walter had mounted.

"This is a different homecoming than the one I dreamed of, Tris! I pictured you as a contented landowner and neighbor, raising a family of fine sons to use the longbow as well, perhaps, as their sire." He added in a tense whisper, "What will be the end of this?"

"God in heaven alone knows the answer," answered Tristram solemnly.

"Is there nothing I can do for you?"

"Nothing, Wat."

They could hear footsteps coming up the road and a voice raised cautiously in a song.

"That will be Lob Cant from Engster," said Tristram. "Stay back in the shadow, Wat. He's one of us, but he's a crowder, and he sings and plays his fiddle in all the taverns. He's a free talker, and I don't trust him overmuch."

The fiddler was singing:

> "I am the buzzard,
>   Waiting on death below.
> I am the hovering vulture,
> I am the carrion crow.
>
> "I am the maggot,
>   Last of all to be fed,
> For I crawl and sup within
>   The rotting bones of the dead."

"Lob is a carrion crow himself," whispered Tristram. "He snatches at any bit of gossip to liven up his entertainment wherever he goes. I'll see to it he gets no hint you were here. It's not a pleasant song he sings; but a fitting one for the work we have ahead!"

5

"Edward going home," lisped the boy, who was perched in front of one of Engaine's servingmen. When they turned off the side road and set themselves in the direction of Bulaire, he laughed and clapped his hands. "Edward *very* glad. Not like dark house."

"He takes after his mother," said Walter, who was riding beside Engaine. "I remember the unfavorable opinion she formed of Gurnie on her first visit."

Engaine turned her head to look back. "I have become very fond of it," she said. "You took me in, and you have been most kind to me. I shall always remember it." She glanced at her lively young son, who was now scolding the servingman because he would not set his horse to a gallop. "His father is fond of the boy. That is the one consolation I have in giving in to you. He will be treated well when he reaches home."

After two days of discussion, some of it quite heated, Walter had wor his point. He had contended from the first that it was a mistake to keep the son and heir of Lessford, because by refusing to return him she would create a prejudice in the minds of the King's advisers. The law was all on the side of the father in the matter of the child and would compel her to return him; and so it was wise to lay her case before them without the handicap of his illegal possession. Engaine had given in with the greatest reluctance. It had been decided to have little Edward escorted to the castle when she herself, with the balance of her party, took the road to London. Walter was to turn back as soon as he had witnessed the safe arrival of the earl's son at Bulaire.

Engaine sighed. "You were right about it. I realize that now. But I can't help being angry at you every time I think of that terrible old woman gloating over my son's return. She will have what she wanted: her grandson back and her hated daughter-in-law out of the castle." She sighed again. "He does not favor his father in looks. Is he going to take after him in other ways?"

After a spell of thought, she dismissed the matter from her mind and propounded a question about Maryam: "Is she quite small, this savage who stole your allegiance from me?"

"She is not as tall as you. I think there might be a difference of two inches in your heights."

"Ah," triumphantly. "Then she is squat and thickset, no doubt."

"On the contrary, she is quite slender."

"How can you be sure she hasn't changed?" demanded Engaine. "You haven't seen her for over two years, and the women of the East, I have heard, fade quickly. By this time she has become heavy and dark and with a trace of a mustache on her upper lip."

Walter threw back his head and laughed. "I forgive you the malice in that because—well, you are much alike in one respect. You are full of questions about her, and Maryam was equally curious about you."

"You told her about me, then?"

"From the very first. I made it clear I had pledged devotion to you."

"And you had!" cried Engaine. "How can you justify yourself for breaking that pledge?"

"You had married Edmond. Was that not justification in itself? As things turned out, however, it was the only way to save her from being sent back to a life of worse than slavery. It is too long a story to tell."

"I am not interested in the story at all. But I am glad it was a marriage of convenience—of necessity—after all." She proceeded then to make it clear that she was intensely interested in everything concerning the wedding. "If you care to tell me the story, I will try to listen. But first, what did you say about me?"

"I said you were very lovely, and very proud, and that you had all the accomplishments of an English lady of high birth."

"I am sure," said Engaine, "that she hated me."

"Yes, I think she did."

"What," quickly, "did she say or do to make you think that?"

"I can remember one thing only. But—I can't tell you about it."

"I must know, Walter. I insist."

"Well," after some hesitation, "you will be very angry. I had been critical of her because she had danced in a robe that was rather short. She was hurt, thinking I meant you would not have done such a thing. She answered that—— Come, Engaine, I refuse to go on with this. You won't be at all pleased and, of course, she spoke only because her feelings had been hurt. She did not mean it."

"What she said," declared Engaine, furiously, "was that I would not have *dared!* That I would have reason to be ashamed."

What Maryam had said was, "I am sure her legs are like shapeless strips of gristle." Walter now regretted that he had allowed the subject to come up at all, and he declared hastily, "I refuse to say another word."

"How unfair of her!" cried Engaine. "And—and *untrue!* I feel quite justified now in telling you I dislike this—this heathen woman very much."

When they passed the burned tavern at Little Tamitt, Walter involuntarily reined in his horse. In the light of day it did not look unlike any other dismantled building. All of his fears about the future came trooping back into his mind. What was the decision reached that night? When would the blow fall?

Engaine turned her head to ask, "What do you find so interesting here?"

"This is all that is left of the tavern of—of a friend of mine, the landlord of Little Tamitt."

It seemed to be an effort for her to recall the circumstances, but she nodded her head finally. "He was one of the ruffians who raided the castle on the night of Earl Rauf's funeral. Edmond burned the place, but the man slipped through his fingers. I remember how angry his mother was."

"All those who took part, those ruffians, have paid a bitter price. All but one."

She turned quickly. "Who do you mean?"

He did not answer at once. "Engaine, what have you thought of all this? Have you known of the men and women he has tortured and hanged?"

"They had no right to rise against their liege lord," she protested. "They deserved to be punished. Surely, Walter, you believe that too." Then, after a moment, she shook her head. "But he has gone too far. I have been sorry for some of them. I think it was his cruelty which made me begin to dislike him."

"I am glad to hear you say that. You see, I meant myself when I told you there was one who had escaped all retribution. My friend Tristram Griffen and I were responsible for what happened that night."

"I wondered." She was watching him steadily. "What a great dolt you are! One can never tell what absurd thing you will venture on next. You have such strange ideas in your head." The severity of her regard changed to an unwilling smile. "I am very much afraid I don't disapprove as much as I should."

The ride was pleasanter after that. Walter, full of pride in the prowess of his friend, began to tell of the cold afternoon at Maragha when Tristram astonished the Mongolians by planting an English arrow in the most improbable mark ever set. Engaine listened with the liveliest interest.

"He seems to be a stout fellow, this Tristram Griffen," she said. Then, inevitably, she asked, "Where was the dusky maiden of mixed blood all this time?"

"As it happened, she was hiding in my tent. You see——"

"I am quite sure," she interrupted, "the creature made it a point never to be far from your tent."

Finally, standing up black above the cover of the forest in the Valley of the Larney, they caught their first glimpse of Bulaire Castle. "I think," cried Engaine, "I must disregard your sage advice after all and ride away with my son as fast as our horses can carry us!"

He laid a hand on her bridle. "Come, if you yield to that impulse, you may ruin all chance for a fair settlement. The law will see to it that the boy is returned to his father sooner or later; and the parting will become harder all the time."

They continued to dispute the point with such absorption that they rode clear of the green blanket of trees without realizing that they had ventured closer than had been planned. Walter reined in as soon as he saw what had happened.

"The time has come to part. You must strike east from here. I will stay until I see the boy and his attendants ride in over the drawbridge, and then I shall lose no time in getting back to Gurnie."

He heard her give a sudden gasp. Her face had gone white. She raised an arm as though to point something out and then dropped it inertly.

"What is it?" he asked.

"Walter! There, that oak tree! O God, what is it I see?"

He glanced in the direction she had indicated, and it seemed to him that his heart stopped beating. The tree was a familiar one. It had been pointed out to him as they marched past by torchlight after the attack on the castle. The shape of it had stayed in his mind ever since, but now there was something different about it. No, it was not different after all; he had always pictured it as a tree bearing unsightly fruit.

A body dangled from one of the branches, with an arrow sticking out from the breast. It swung slowly in the breeze, winding and unwinding, and they could hear the rope creak. He needed no more than one glance to know that it was the body of Edmond, Earl of Lessford!

When he was able to regain some control of his senses, he whispered, "That is the tree from which the Norman woman hanged the six yeomen."

He saw now that a second body lay under the tree, doubtless the squire who had accompanied the earl on his fatal ride that morning. His mind cleared then, and he shouted to the servant who carried the heir of Bulaire: "Turn your horse! Ride to the south. The boy must not see!"

He motioned to Engaine to follow, but he made no move to leave when he heard the frantic beat of hoofs down the road. His eyes had detected signs that convinced him the killing had taken place a very short time before; a cap on the ground near the edge of the cover, a single glimpse of a green-clad figure behind the trunk of a tree. He knew that watchful eyes were fixed on him from the forest screen.

He turned his horse and rode fast after the rest of the party, keeping his head turned back over his shoulder for signs of hostile intent.

"Heads down!" he shouted in an urgent voice. "They are still back there in the woods. Ride fast!"

He heard a single shout from the depths of the forest, but that was all. No one ventured out, and no arrow was loosed after them. When he overtook Engaine, a safe margin of distance had been attained.

"I have been expecting something like this," he said, as they galloped side by side. "Hate, like a two-edged sword, cuts both ways."

It was several minutes before she began to speak in an unsteady voice. "Somehow I feel that I am responsible, that what I have done has caused his death."

"No, no! That arrow would have found its mark just as surely if you had been still in the castle. You need have no other thoughts on that score."

"I hated him while he lived," she whispered. "I cannot play the hypocrite now and say that I feel any different because he is dead. But what a dreadful thing!"

"Things just as dreadful have been happening hereabouts for the past five years."

She pulled passionately on the reins, and her nervous mount tossed its mane-guard and neighed. "We must get as far away as we can! Far, far away!" After another moment, she asked, "Walter, what am I to do?"

"There are many things you must do, and none of them will be easy. Things are in your hands now, Engaine."

"There is no need now to send my son back."

Walter indulged in a short and unmirthful laugh. "The scare seems to have robbed you of your usually keen wits. The boy must be taken back at once, and you must go with him. Don't you realize that he is now the Earl of Lessford?"

She gave him one startled look, and then a full comprehension of the situation dawned on her. She reined in abruptly.

"Of course! My little son is the Earl of Lessford."

They sat their horses in silence, staring into each other's eyes. Her face began to lose its first strained look.

"Walter!" she cried. "Everything is changed! I can go back safely now. The power is in my hands. I—I am now at last the real mistress of Bulaire!"

CHAPTER XV

Venice

MESSER MARCO DANDOLO, brother of the doge and the richest merchant of Venice, was in an exultant mood. He was setting a world record in ship-building and winning a wager with Giovanni de Florentia.

That morning, when the Marangona bell had signaled the start of the working day, a trained crew of artisans had poured into the Arsenal and had begun on the hull of a huge bireme which Messer Dandolo would use in the Western trade. Everything had been in readiness for them: the oak planks for the ribs and the keel, which had been immersed in sea water outside the Lido for ten years to season them properly; the fir for the masts, the walnut for the rudders, the elm for the capstan; the nuts and the rivets, already cast in the Arsenal, where everything needed for ships was fashioned and stamped with the Winged Lion, the badge of the great Republic; the huge bolts of colored sail cloth, and the cordage, and the leather-wrapped oars to be fitted into the locks at the benches of the rowers. It was now sunset, and in three more hours the rialtino bell would ring for the end of the day's labors; and then the bireme must be finished if the wager was to be won.

Messer Dandolo had attired himself handsomely for the occasion in a ruby-colored cassock which covered him to his feet, and over that a mantle of white with a gold brooch on his right shoulder. He looked exactly what he was, a wealthy and urbane citizen of the highest rank with a finely developed appreciation of the artistic; but if anyone had watched when his cassock was disturbed by the breezes sweeping the Arsenal lagoon, it would have been seen that beneath it his undergarments were old and shapeless and even unclean. In fact, this anointed and perfumed gentleman was the very personification of Venice itself, that glittering and showy city which sparkled on the surface and was so wicked and malodorous underneath.

He had been standing all day on the edge of the lagoon. The amount of the wager was large and, to give more edge to the contest, he felt for his rival the bitter hate that again was typically Venetian. He kept saying to himself that he would give anything he possessed to win, except perhaps his white palace on the Piazza of St. Geminiano or the beautiful slave girl he had recently purchased for a very large price, after critical appraisal of her naked charms at the slave market of Kaffa. He was so set on winning that at intervals he increased the bait held out to the sweating artisans, more and more *soldi* for each of them if the bireme reached the end of the lagoon before the rialtino sounded.

It would have been a fascinating spectacle for outside eyes to watch, except that no outsiders were ever allowed inside the Arsenal. The lagoon stretched between two islands with broad work streets on each side. Supply warehouses faced the streets. The work of construction had begun at the far end. When the ribs of the hull were in place and had been nailed and calked, barges had towed the base of the wooden giant to the next station, where the fabricated wood for the superstructure was piled. When the time came to tow it still further ahead, the *opera-morta,* a species of outrigger deck, was in its place, bulging out from the lower hull and supported by stout and elaborately ornamented brackets. Another move forward and the *corsia* had been hammered into place as well as the castlelike structures at each end in which the cabins were located. Finally it had been moved to the last station and the work of erecting the four masts was in progress.

Would it be finished in time? Messer Dandolo stroked his scented beard and said to himself that it would. How chagrined Giovanni de Florentia would be when he handed over the stake that evening! His satisfaction went even deeper, however; the Venetians were the greatest shipbuilders in the world, but never before had a fully equipped and seagoing vessel been turned out in one day.

During the last hour his mood of satisfaction had been somewhat ruffled by an interruption from outside. An old gondola had been circling the crenelated walls of the Arsenal, and a tired female voice had cried at monotonous intervals, "London! London!" It was nothing new, in reality. For over a week this same veiled female had been parading the docks and the Square of St. Mark's and even the Rialto, with her interminable cry of "London!" It had become the standing joke of the city. The woman, clearly, sought passage to London, and the gayer blades had made a point of driving her away from such ships as were ready to sail for Western waters. She was small and weary-looking; and so these same gallant gentlemen, though always avid for fresh victims, had not bothered themselves to appraise her desirability. Sitting at their games of chess and tavolette and la tria, they had watched her limp along and had contented themselves with speculating idly as to who she was and from where she came.

She had no right to invade the sacrosanct precincts of the Arsenal, however, and finally Messer Dandolo went to the workman in charge of the construction, who was called, misleadingly, the high admiral.

"Vanni," he said, "this piping little pest annoys me. Send her away or I will see to it she swings in a wooden cage on the Campanile of St. Mark's."

When the high admiral returned, he said: "She has gone, Messer Dandolo. Am I permitted to say I felt sorry for her? She has with her a small boy who is not well. Would it not be a Christian deed to set her on a ship for London?"

The wealthy merchant scoffed at this. "Curb your easily stirred sympathies, Vanni. Here she is, in Venice, the hub of the known world. Why does she long for London, where there are fogs and snow and a people of the utmost barbarism? Clearly the silly creature is demented. She mews like a sick sea gull."

"But," said the high admiral hesitantly, "it does not seem right. The woman also is not well. She is thin and very tired."

2

Maryam had come to Venice on a ship from Alexandria which carried spices and rich fabrics and slaves. Her first vision of the stately city on its maze of canals had convinced her that the end of the long pilgrimage had been reached. Here for the first time were people with white skins who dressed in most respects like her two Englishmen. London at last!

But the illusion faded quickly. Her eager "London? London?" met with uncomprehending scowls from the people she addressed. There was nothing kindly about them. They jeered at her, shoved her aside, threatened her. She felt here a more hostile attitude than in any of the teeming Eastern ports, even in sun-baked Aden or in callous Alexandria, the center of the slave trade. "Surely," she said to herself many times, "this cannot be a Christian city. And yet it comes so close to all the things my Walter told me."

She obtained possession, by the silent proffer of a small piece of gold, of a single dark room in a house of such great beauty that she was surprised at the willingness of the owner to take her in. The beauty, she discovered at once, was all on the surface. The room was damp and bare, with a ramshackle bed and a brass pan in which all household refuse had to be stored before committing it to the waters of the canal washing against the marble outer wall of the house; and nothing else. However, there had been an abundance of fresh flowers in the pan when she took possession, and that had pleased her, even though the room reeked of garlic.

There was something furtive about the neighborhood. Maryam sensed it at once. She had no way of knowing that the house was on the edge of the castellette, but there was no mistaking the purpose of the dark-eyed women who slept all day and came out in the cool of the evening to flaunt themselves in tarnished robes of gold web with bands of ermine and vair from hem to hem and the gaudiest of buttons made of enamel or crystal. She considered finding another resting place, but gave the idea up in sheer weariness.

She was more concerned about the health of her eighteen-months-old son. The long overland trip from Aden had sapped his strength and drained all color from his face. He took no interest in food and was restive with the pain of his final tooth cutting. The only interest he seemed to take in life was manifested in his devotion to the dog Chi. He even refused to be parted from it when Mahmoud swung him up on his shoulder to follow Maryam on her daily quests.

Her relief can be imagined when he roused her one morning with an urgency she had never seen before in his large blue eyes. He reached eagerly for her hand.

"Mudda," he said. "Come."

He led her to their one window which looked out on a small court. Perhaps it was a feast day and the common people were at liberty to enjoy themselves; at any rate, for the first time, the court was filled with children. They were noisily engaged in a game of *zoni,* and they were laughing and shouting noisily as they strove to bowl over the wooden pins. The boy was so excited that she could feel his hand trembling in hers.

"Modda!" he whispered. "Boys!"

She picked him up in her arms so he could see better. "At last my Walter is going to have friends of his own," she said to herself. "Perhaps that is what he has needed. He has never been able to play."

This, of course, was true. He had never possessed a toy of any kind—nothing, for that matter, he could call his own but his much loved Chi. His short and unhappy life had been lived on the hot decks of dirty ships and in the stifling discomfort below decks, or for short intervals in hovels ashore. He had seen brown children about the wharves but had never been in close contact with them.

A real difficulty now presented itself. The boy's clothes were old and ragged, and her pride rebelled at letting these Christian children see him in them. Somehow she must contrive to dress him more suitably.

She sat down to figure out a way and, after much thought, came to a reluctant conclusion. Opening a weather-beaten bag in which all their belongings were packed, she drew out the sole remaining reminder of her gracious life in the Abode of Everlasting Felicity. It was the Robe of Sixteen Summers, and she gazed at it with tear-filled eyes.

"I wanted so much to keep it," she whispered. "I wanted him to see me in it again. If he is—is beginning to forget, it might remind him of how happy and loving we were."

But the sacrifice had to be made. "It is all I have, and the money cannot be spared to buy new things," she murmured unhappily. "I must forget my pride—and my hopes. I must make my son something in which he will look well."

For two days she cut and fitted and stitched in her spare time, reducing the once gorgeous Robe of Sixteen Summers to fragments, but producing finally a garment in which the boy looked like the sober little son of a Chinese nobleman. The coat, reaching almost to his heels, fitted him very well, as did also the black satin trousers with their wide turned-up cuffs. She even fashioned him a round flat cap which looked very jaunty on his yellow curls.

She clapped her hands gleefully when she studied the final effect and no longer felt regret at the loss of her cherished finery. "My worthy and beautiful son!" she cried, falling back into the Chinese way of speaking. "These small boys will think you very grand, my Walter. They will envy you your handsome coat."

There is in even the youngest of boys a liking for fine raiment. His eyes laughed up at her, and he patted the rich satin of the coat in a way that rewarded her completely for the sacrifice she had made.

The next morning the court was filled again. She took him by the hand and led the way to the door which opened into it. Another game of zoni was in progress, but all the children stopped when the strangers appeared. They ranged in age from mere infants, sitting or rolling at the side of the court, to boys and girls of eight and ten. Several were of Walter's own size, and these were as active and noisy as the older ones.

Maryam detached her hand and gave him a gentle shove.

"Go, my son," she said. "Join in the play of these new friends. But be most careful not to get your fine new coat dirty. Your father must see you in it, and it must be at its best then."

He looked up at her, and she could tell that he was frightened as well as expectant. Then he smiled. After a moment of hesitation he took several slow steps forward.

A swarthy boy of perhaps five was the first to take active notice of the newcomer. He came over to Walter and looked at him critically. Others joined him then, grinning at each other and passing remarks in shrill appraisal. The first boy threw back his head and gave vent to a loud and derisive laugh. The others joined in immediately.

Maryam was watching in rising uneasiness, for it was clear they considered her son a very curious specimen of boyhood indeed. Suddenly one of the girls plucked the cap from his head and put it on her own, striking an attitude which said plainly, "What a silly thing this is!" Two others took him by the arms and tried to drag off his coat. They were shouting now in loud glee at this new victim offered for their amusement.

Walter turned a pair of stricken eyes on his mother, but he did not permit himself to cry. He struggled to save his coat from his tormentors and, even when he was knocked down and the garment was ripped from his arms, allowed himself no more than one urgent, "Modda!"

Maryam rushed in to rescue him, demanding in strident tones that they leave her son alone. She lifted him up in her arms, patting him comfortingly with one hand and saying to him: "Never you mind, my brave boy! They are savages, and not fit to play with!"

The children danced around them, screaming their contempt for the outlandish newcomers. Maryam kicked at them angrily and shoved them away with her free hand. One of the boys had drawn the satin coat over his own and was parading up and down. She had to chase him all around the court before she recovered it. To her dismay she found that it had been ripped up the back and was soiled with mud. "Beasts!" she cried furiously. "See what you have done! I could kill you all!"

A sound of laughter from the windows looking down on the court made her aware now that adult eyes had been watching the sport and enjoying it as much as the noisy urchins. She carried her son to the door, and here she paused for a moment to look up at the grinning women. All the rebuffs she had suffered since coming to this hard, beautiful city caused a deep anger to well up in her.

"I do not like these Christians," she said to herself bitterly.

Maryam took the boy back to their own dark room and sat him down on the floor beside the dog. "Play with Chi, my little Walter," she said, fighting to hold back her tears. "He is the best friend for you, after all."

The boy looked up at her. He was puzzled as well as unhappy, and she knew he was wondering what it had all meant, why this first glimpse of children like himself had brought him nothing but disappointment and pain. Then the discomfort of his teeth took possession of him, and for the first time he abandoned himself completely to dismal crying.

"My son, my poor little son!" she mourned. "What kind of a cruel world have I brought you to?"

After that he contented himself with the companionship of the dog. He paid no heed to the loud voices and laughter which occasionally sounded from the court, and he never went near the window.

3

The supper to celebrate the building of a seagoing bireme in one day was a brilliant affair. All the richest and most influential citizens were there, including the doge himself with his round cap of office. The food provided was sumptuous, the chief dish being a roasted boar's head surrounded by spitted nightingales. There were many kinds of fish covered with highly spiced sauces, a kid baked whole, pickled duck's eggs, confections of every kind. The wines were many and rare.

Messer Dandolo sat at the head of the board in the highest of spirits, emptying his jeweled wineglass with such regularity that his eyes began to sparkle and a rosy glow showed at the tip of his nose. At the other end was the loser, Giovanni de Florentia, a saturnine young man with a very long face and a heavy scowl. The feasting and drinking irked the chagrined Giovanni, for the cost of the meal was part of the wager.

When the last dish had been removed from the table, Messer Dandolo signalled to the musicians to stop playing. The entertainment would now begin, he announced. There was an Egyptian magician to show them some new and baffling tricks, a singer of ballads from Provence, and a dancing girl from the East who would display her amazing sinuosity for their delectation. But first he proposed to solve for them the mystery of the crying woman.

"She has been fetched and will now appear," he said. "An interpreter accompanies her, a man of many tongues. He will be able to unravel her story for us."

When Maryam entered the room, a buzz of surprised comment rose from the company. She had removed her veil, and they found her as unexpectedly pretty as a Michaelmas daisy. She had become very thin, but this had the effect of making her eyes seem quite enormous and to give a haunting quality to her face. The well-fortified and somewhat besotted merchants sat up in their chairs with new interest and watched her with greedy eyes.

Maryam, for her part, was dazzled. She gave a quick glance about her, at the dim room where the candles had been allowed to burn low and the tall windows through which the light of the early evening moon now poured, at the richness of the table appointments and the gorgeous robes of the company. A second glance did much to destroy the effect. She saw then that these well-dressed gentlemen were well along in the middle stages of intoxication, that their eyes were heavy with the wine fumes and their fingers too unsteady to handle their jeweled flagons without spilling some of the contents on the tablecloth and the heavy carpets on the floor.

The interpreter, a yellow-faced Levantine, began to question her in various languages, trying her finally in the Greek tongue. Maryam answered him then with an eagerness born of the long months of travel through walls of silence.

"She says," announced the interpreter, for the benefit of the company, "that she is of Greek birth, though her father was an Englishman in the Crusades. She is now striving to reach London to join her husband, who is also an Englishman."

The gentlemen looked disappointed. The explanation was simple enough and left them with no shred of mystery to ponder.

"She says moreover," went on the Levantine, "that she has come all the way from Cathay and has been traveling for two years."

If a merchant named Polo had been of the company it might have been that this announcement started a train of thought running in his mind; but there is nothing of record to show that this was the case. The statement had plenty of effect as it was. The gentlemen showed revived interest at once.

"This lady with the perplexing blue eyes," declared one man, "must be a very great liar. Permit me, Messer Dandolo, to make a suggestion. As a punishment for her mendacity we should see to it that she is put at once on a ship sailing in the opposite direction from London."

The idea seemed to find considerable favor. But not, as it developed, in the sulky loser at the far end of the table. He had not taken his eyes from Maryam's face since she had entered the room.

"It must be acknowledged that she is a very pretty liar," he said. "I give my compliments to my opponent who has succeeded after all in making this supper a pleasurable experience for me. I confess to a liking for her, and I hasten to assert a first claim. She must bear me company for a time. Then she may be shipped to Tunis or the Black Sea or even to famed Lough Derg at the discretion of the company."

Messer Dandolo was watching Giovanni de Florentia so intently that it was clear a purpose was forming in his mind which did not conform to the intentions of his amorous rival.

"I am afraid," he said, "that the plans of my good friend, who is quicker to see the charm in an alien pair of eyes than the great merit of our Venetian shipbuilders, cannot be fulfilled."

The loser looked up sharply. "Does my lucky opponent fancy her for himself?" he demanded.

Messer Dandolo shook his head. "I am not thinking in terms of personal satisfaction," he said, "but of the good reputation of the merchant fleet of Venice. The ship laid down today and finished in record time is the finest vessel yet to issue from our wonder-working Arsenal. I am sure you will all agree we should strive to send her out on her maiden voyage to Marseilles under the most favorable auspices. I say to all of you, my very good friends, that the hand of fate is in this. What better luck could we insure for our great bireme than to send this lady along as our first passenger?" He glanced around the board and found to his satisfaction an answering gleam in every face but one. "It is more important that this traveler, who has come to us by something more than chance, should bring good fortune to our venture than that Messer de Florentia be granted the satisfaction of a suddenly conceived desire."

CHAPTER XVI

Scaunder Clough

A HEAVY SNOW HAD FALLEN, and there was ice an inch thick on the moat at Gurnie. Rheumatic pains took possession of old bones, and Wilderkin hobbled about on a cane while his master took to his bed.

Inside what had once been the malthouse, however, the air was dry and warm. The sheets of pulp on the frames needed warmth, and so a large reredos had been placed in the center, and the logs in it blazed briskly. Walter's plans to harness millstones had not passed the experimental stage, and all the work still was done by hand. Half a dozen pairs of brawny arms plied pestles vigorously. The place hummed with talk.

On his first visit of the day, Walter halted beside old Swire Gilpin, who had charge of the frames.

"It is six months, nay seven, since I have seen my friend, Tristram Griffen," he whispered. "No word of him has reached me. Tell me, Gilpin, has anyone heard where he is and how he fares?"

Gilpin made a pretense of deep absorption in his work. "I know nothing of him, master."

"Come, Gilpin. He must have sent some word to his father at least. I hear you see the old man often."

Gilpin stripped a sheet from the nearest frame and held it up to the light. "As smooth as glass, master," he said. "The monks at Abbey'll have no more complaints."

Walter turned away impatiently. He walked over to the large vat in which the sheets were immersed after being pounded out to wafer thinness. Here a tall fellow was bending over to test the temperature of the water.

"Jack," he demanded, "what do you hear of Tristram Griffen?"

The man's face became sulky and withdrawn. He did not answer at once, but continued to dabble an arm as thin as a skrayle pin in the water. When he spoke it was in grumbling tones.

"Naught have I heard, master."

It was always the same. A veil would seem to drop when any mention was made of the events following the death of Earl Edmond of Lessford. Tristram and two other men had disappeared immediately thereafter, and it had been assumed they were with Camus Harry and the trailbastons. There had been nothing to confirm this, however. Try as he might, Walter had failed to secure any word of his friend's whereabouts.

He returned to the house in a depressed frame of mind. This deliberate secrecy was natural enough, but it seemed more than strange that Tristram himself had made no effort to communicate with him. Was he still alive?

He went to his grandfather's room for their regular morning discussion. The master of Gurnie was suffering, quite clearly, from rheumatic aches. His face twisted at intervals, and he kept the bedcoverings wrapped up closely around his neck.

"Last week's tally showed a falling off," he said sharply. "Thirty sheets fewer. It is not to be borne! What has come over the lazy knaves? Are you coddling them, Walter?"

Walter explained that the cold weather had been holding the work back. "After all," he added, "we can't expect them to do well when they are packed in like salted jack-barrel. Come spring, Grandfather, we will show you a real increase." He nodded his head with pride. "The quality of the paper improves all the time."

The old man continued to prod him with questions. Could the same quality be attained without using a mixture of linen scraps? Would the monks pay the same price for sheets a little smaller? Why should they not shave a fraction off each side of the sheets? What luck was Joseph Maule having in his efforts to sell paper to the merchants of London? Could it be that he, Walter, had made a mistake in persuading the good Joseph to give up the grain trade and act for them as a seller of paper?

The answers he received evoked nothing but grunts from the master of Gurnie. Walter did not allow this to disturb him. He never expected to see the day when his grandfather would give him an unqualified sign of approval.

The old man turned, then, to another, and more personal, grievance. "Walter," he sighed, "Father Clement gives me no peace. Does he think I can pay the penance exacted of me in such weather as this? It is beyond reason to expect a man of my age to walk barefoot to his church, and with snow on the ground. I am contending with him, moreover, in the matter of the candles. Six of them, a foot thick, to be kept burning for a full month. It would make me a beggar! I must get a mitigation from him. It is beyond reason!"

Walter spent the latter part of the afternoon tramping in the snow, his mood sinking to greater depression every step of the way. He thought of Maryam and Tristram, both lost to him now in a shrouding of mystery. "Surely," he repeated over and over again, "there is something I can do to find out about them. Can I do nothing but wait?" He wondered if his wife had become reconciled by this time to the inevitability of lifelong separation, and if so, had she found a new way of living? Was she in want?

He arrived back in time for supper and found the Great Hall fairly bursting with a spirit of good cheer. The servants chattered as they took their places at the board, and Agnes was bearing in a platter with an enormous roast of beef, garnished with a wreath of laurel. What had happened? Walter looked at his grandfather, unexpectedly ensconced in his chair on the dais. It was surprising enough that he had summoned up the strength to come down; but, in addition, he was festively attired in his best velvet cloak with wide bands of miniver and a collar of the same.

"Walter!" cried the old man. "It has come at last!"

Walter observed now that a document, loaded with impressive seals, lay on the table before his grandfather. Even the standing cups had been shoved aside to make room for it. He knew without being told what this meant.

"The lands have been restored?"

"My lands have been restored to me!" The master of Gurnie touched the seals with a hand that trembled visibly. "The messenger arrived from London three hours agone. Here it is, my boy, signed and sealed and settled beyond all legal dispute for all time! God and St. Wulstan be praised!"

Walter sat down, rather stunned by the unexpectedness of it. He shared his grandfather's delight, of course, but he could not help thinking, "I would rather hear word of Maryam than have all the lands of Bulaire signed and sealed over to us by royal decree."

"He is a good king," declared the old man. He was eating nothing, but his horn of wine had already been emptied. "I acknowledge I was wrong in my first estimate of him. A wise and just and courageous king."

Walter nodded in assent. "The first English king we have had since Hastings."

The look the old man turned on him now had more than triumph in it. A trace of sly shrewdness could be read in his eyes.

"The letter which accompanies the official writ makes it clear," he said, sipping from his replenished horn, "that the restoration is made with the full knowledge of the Lady Engaine. As the land forms part of her Tressling inheritance, she is the loser by this. I gather, nevertheless, that she urged the restoration be made."

"That was most generous of her!" exclaimed Walter.

"Generous?" The master of Gurnie smiled. "Yes, it was generous. I think, however, it was something more. It was wise on her part and— well, farseeing."

"I do not follow your reasoning, Grandfather."

"Come, you must see it too. She likes you, Walter, and she is a widow. I never miss anything, my boy. I saw how often she leaned forward to look across at you. It was in her eye, even before the death of the earl released her providentially from an irksome tie. Clearly she favors you as her second husband, and she knows that this," indicating the royal writ, "will make you incline still more favorably to her. But there is more to it than that, I swear. As heir to the restored domain of Gurnie, you are now in a position to court her openly, which you could hardly have done otherwise. It becomes a much more even match, and one at which no one can cavil. Yes, our lovely Engaine has been both wise and far-seeing."

"If what you surmise is true," said Walter slowly, "she has overlooked one point. I am not in a position to court her. I am a married man."

His grandfather protested this with an impatient frown. "An annulment must be secured at once. It may involve a pretty sum, but, with our lands restored and such bright prospects in addition, we must not count the cost. The time has come, my boy, to apply to the Church for your release."

Walter remained silent for a moment. "I love my wife," he said finally. "It will sound to you no doubt like utter folly, but I—I must wait longer. A miracle may happen to bring her back to me."

"A miracle! Do you think," exclaimed the old man passionately, "that the Lord will vouchsafe a miracle to restore a heathen wife to a Christian man? I shall be very wroth with you, very wroth indeed, if I hear any more of such nonsense. You must take the necessary steps without further delay. I insist."

"There are some points in connection with the land on which I must insist," said Walter, after a pause. "The men who work on it must not wear iron collars. They must be free men, Grandfather. They must be given adequate holdings and a chance to profit decently by their labor. I have never said this to you before, but I believe that the land is not meant for the sole benefit of the few. It is for the use of all."

"Have you been giving ear to the teachings of mad hedge-priests?" demanded his grandfather, a look of astonishment on his face. "Such talk smacks of treason and heresy. I think you must have lost your senses."

Both men were so absorbed in the points at issue between them that neither had touched a morsel of food. Agnes Malkinsmaiden appeared at the edge of the dais and said in an indignant voice, "The good food is getting cold, masters." They paid no attention to her.

"I am convinced," Walter went on, "that we will benefit in the long run. Give them a chance to live decently and they will do so much better that in time the land will increase in value. You will have a better return if you don't grind them down and demand so large a share of the crops that they will have no possible incentive. Think how well they are working for us in the paper yard."

This line of argument was well conceived, for the old man was certain to listen when the question was one of returns. After a few moments of silence, however, he shook his head as resolutely as before. "I still say that what you propose is not only wrong but dangerous." Then he leaned back in his chair and sighed deeply. "I am an old man and a sick one. I lack the strength to contest the point further with you now. Later I shall take the time to convince you of your folly."

Swire Gilpin lingered after the lower table had been removed and the rest of the serving people had gone. With many cautious looks over his shoulder, he edged his way slowly to the foot of the dais.

"Master Walter," he whispered.

Walter descended the steps and asked, "What is it, Gilpin?"

"Master, if ye followed the Larney west'ard and turned off on the old stone road as leads north, where 'ud ye come out at?"

"At the edge of the village of Little Engster."

"Aye." Gilpin nodded his head and took another look around to make sure no one was listening. "And if ye struck west again and turned at Three Forks into Bramway Spinney and walked for matter o' five mile nort', where 'ud ye be then?"

"At the south end of Scaunder Clough."

Gilpin nodded several times. "Aye," he said, "there ye 'ud be, master, in Scaunder Clough. Few 'uns goes there, master. It's wild land, and the footing's bad, and it's said as how evil speerits is to be met there. I went there once as a boy and I was frightened, I give ye my word. Aye, 'tis not a place to be sought, master, 'less ye had a purpose in going."

Walter waited for him to go on.

"But if ye had a purpose and went halfway up the Clough, ye 'ud come to rock as juts out into water. The Witch's Head it's called, master, and I never wants to set eyes on it. But if ye went that far and whistled one tune as much as three times——"

"Do you mean 'The Sons of Job'?"

An excited shake of the head this time. "Aye, that's the one. If ye did that now, what d'ye suppose as might happen?"

Walter laughed and thumped him thankfully on the back. "I understand, Gilpin. You will have reason to be glad you've done this for me."

2

He had never been to Scaunder Clough, and he felt a chill in his blood when he arrived there late the next afternoon. The black water was running like a millrace and raising a turbulent coil as it swirled and tossed over the ugly heads of jutting rocks. So fierce was it in its haste to be down and through this weird slash in the hills that the ice had formed for no more than a few inches on the sides, and yet the weather was bitter and the snow was banked so thick on the path that he sank deep into it with each labored step. The banks rose steeply on each side, and he remembered, as he observed the unnatural shapes in which they were fashioned, that men said it was the devil who had designed Scaunder Clough and that he was poll-mad when he did it.

It was an unearthly-looking place, there could be no manner of doubt about that; and it needed only the leering face of the Witch's Head, with its two deep crevices for eyes and its outgrooving layers of rock like a Medusa mane, to convince him that evil hung over this valley. It was a perfect sanctuary, but only for one in whom a determination of spirit outmatched the imagination.

He turned his back resolutely on the Witch's Head and strove to whistle "The Sons of Job," with small conceit of his courage when he found his tongue balking at the task. It was only on the third attempt that he was able to make his thin whistling rise above the roar of the stream. Nothing happened in response, and he repeated the effort. Then, as a final resort, he cupped hands to his mouth and shouted, "Halloo! Halloo!"

In a few moments he heard a sound behind him which might have been caused by a foot scraping on rock. Without looking around, he began to whistle again. He was barely through the first bars when the air was taken up and whistled back to him on a high and jubilant note. He turned then and saw Tristram climbing down a snow-packed path which led directly to the Witch's Head.

"You've come at last! How much I have wanted to see you!"

Tristram shook Walter's hand with the delight of one to whom the best of all possible things has happened. Walter was too stunned at first to return any form of greeting. His lost friend had not returned in the guise of a picturesque bandit of the woods clad in Lincoln green like another Robin Hood, with bow on shoulder and a gay song of the woods on his lips. He carried his bow over his shoulder, but the resemblance to the accepted picture stopped there. What Walter saw was a gaunt figure in dirty clothes so full of rents that he looked like a scarecrow; a saddened apparition who was cold and, perhaps, hungry and certainly most miserably run to seed.

The eagerness of his next words was an index to the real gravity of his situation: "What have you brought me, Wat?"

Walter replied, with a sinking of the heart at his own lack of foresight: "Nothing. Forgive me, Tris, but it never occurred to me that you —that you would be in need of things."

Tristram indulged in a laugh which sounded very much like the croaking of some ancient bird. "You thought of me as living in a bower concealed in a vine-tangled glade, feasting jovially on the choicest cuts of venison and in the evenings watching the wodehouses dance? That's a myth, Wat. Life in the woods is not like that. It's a dirty and grim business, if the truth must be told. When I saw it was you, I was delighted. I had wanted so much to see you, my old master of arts. And at the same time I thought, 'Wat will have some salt in his pocket.'"

"And I came empty-handed, thoughtless fool that I am!" cried Walter. "I am most thoroughly shamed. I was sure you had gone with Camus Harry and that the trailbastons had comfortable quarters somewhere in the woods hereabouts."

"They do better than I do, I think. I have never seen their camp. Camus Harry wanted me to join, but I could not bring myself to it. There is a stubbornness in me which makes me want to remain an honest man. The others went with him."

"You mean you are here alone? Tris, I had no idea how things were with you! I've never stopped trying to get some word, but all the men who might have helped have been leagued together in a conspiracy of silence. I went to see your father, but even he professed to know nothing."

"I had impressed on them the need for silence," said Tristram, "but I had no idea they would carry it so far."

"It's one class against another. They suspect even me. It was not until last night that one of them broke the silence."

Tristram nodded soberly. "Yes, I am alone. I found a cave back in the face of the rock, and there I live by myself. The Lonely Warrior again. That seems to be my role in life, Wat. Solitude has some advantages, but they don't include bodily comfort."

Walter was studying him with a steady sinking of the heart. He looked like an old man. His face was lined above a bristling tow-colored beard. Unhappiness rode his shoulder, and a sickness of spirit was manifested in the uneasy glitter of his eyes.

"I shall return tomorrow," promised Walter, in a deeply contrite tone. "Tell me all the things you need and I'll see to it that you have them."

"All the things I need? It would make a long list, Wat. And a word of caution. Don't come back at once. It might be noticed if you came this way again too soon. The bloodhounds would take up the scent. Wait for a week before you venture here."

Walter nodded. "I'm afraid you're right."

"As to what I need, two things most of all: Salt and soap! Soap, Wat! How little we think of it when we live normal lives, but how important it becomes when it is lacking!" He held up his hands, which were roughly grimed with black. "I dream of soap and the fine luxury of a bath. How welcome those pudding-faced Chinese girls would be now if they brought plenty of soap and fine, clean towels! I promise you I would tear off my clothes without any shame at all."

"And what besides salt and soap?"

"Sugar!" cried Tristram eagerly. "I drool at the chops when I think of the taste of something sweet. And a needle and thread and some bits of cloth. Look at me! I am a human colander, I am so full of holes. And a flint and a sharp knife. A whetstone, perhaps? Ah, there are so many things I need! Some candles and—and—do you suppose you could bring me some marchpane? I dream all the time of crunching down those tender sticks."

"Not so fast! I must get all these things fixed in my mind."

Tristram laughed. "Don't take me too seriously. I know you can't come back up the Clough with loaded sumpter mules."

"I intend to find ways of getting you everything you want. Is there anything else?"

"A hundred things more, I am afraid. Some new bowstrings most particularly. A fresh supply of arrows. Some oil to keep the bow in proper trim. A calendar would be most useful. I have lost all track of time." Tristram paused. "How demanding I must sound! I know, Wat, you can't furnish a palace for me up here on the Clough."

"I shall do my best." Walter dropped a hand on his friend's shoulder. "There is something I can do that's much more important. I am going to see to it that you get safely out of the country again. You can't stay here much longer like a hunted wild beast."

Tristram shook his head with instant determination. "I have no intention of leaving England. I have no stomach for foreign lands, Wat. The outlandish gabble they speak is beyond me, and I would be as alone as I am here in the woods. I know I can never hope to live again as a law-abiding citizen, but I am English, and here I shall stay until I die!"

"Listen to me, Tris. Things are going to change. I can smuggle you out safely and in time, I am sure, with the right kind of influence, a pardon can be obtained for you. God knows what will happen to you if you stay here alone much longer!"

Tristram looked up at the sun, which was sinking behind the snow-covered walls. He shook his head again.

"It goes deeper with me than I have said, old friend. The new laws will be of little good to common men. I doubt if the slavery in which they exist can be abolished without a rising in force of the peasantry.

It is coming, Wat! The yeomen of England will rise and demand that they be given the right to live like men, free men! It is coming as sure as that the sun will soon sink back of those rocks. It may not be in our time, but—it is coming! God hasten the day!" His face had changed, and a strong light burned in his sunken eyes. "I think of little else as I lie up there in my cave; and now I am beginning to see that I can play my part in it, even though I never dare venture far from Scaunder Clough. If I run away, I will soon be forgotten. But if I stay here, refusing to be driven from the soil I love, the memory of me will remain with them. When the time draws on for the common men of England to demand their rights, they will recall what I have done, and it may serve to strengthen their resolution!"

The stoop had gone out of his shoulders. He looked at Walter with a pride that took no count of the bitter kind of life he must face.

"No, Wat!" he cried. "Here I stay. If they catch me and hang me up on the gallows tree, so much the better. Then I *will* be remembered as one who died in a just cause!"

He leaned then against the rough rock surface of the Witch and relaxed into a smile. "I am delivering an oration like a sophister at Oxford. But—I mean every word I have said. And now, what news do you bring me? Wat, has there been any word of Maryam?"

"None. What communication is possible between two worlds so far apart?"

"Poor little Taffy! You might as well face the truth. It's not likely you will ever hear of her again." He paused and studied Walter's face carefully. "You must become reconciled to it, Wat, and marry the Lady Engaine. It's the proper and natural thing; and I can see that it's inevitable. It would bring our poor people much relief, old friend, for I know you would be an easy master to them."

"I can't look that far into the future yet," said Walter.

"There is one thing I want you to know: I did not loose the arrow that killed your brother. Not that I had any scruples. He had to die for all the things he had done. But as it happened, one of the others had his arrow ready, and it found its mark. We were hiding in the woods, and I saw you plainly when you rode up. The same man, having had his taste of blood, was all for making a finish of the family. But I stayed his arm. As to what happened after that, you know more than I do."

"Engaine has full sway now. She is making such amends as are in her power."

"I have heard that things are better." Tristram turned to Walter and dropped a hand on his shoulder. It was rough and chapped, and all the nails were broken and black. "Don't look so unhappy, Wat. I live well enough. I have plenty to eat, and my cave is warm. I have no complaints. Come, smile at me." He was smiling himself in the old, friendly way. "You can do something else for me. Turn those gems I left with you into gold and see to the distribution of it. My father is old and needs very little, but I would like him to have enough to see him easily to the end of his days. My brother's widow and the boy too; see that they get their share of whatever is brought. Perhaps a coin could be spared for a poor old fellow in Cencaster named Handy. He went to the Crusades and came back a broken hulk; and now he lives on scraps that he struggles for with the dogs of the town. I would like to think I had done something to ease his lot. And there's old Dame Gurdy who was a gossip of my mother's and who needs help badly. Do what you can for them, Wat."

"I swear that none of them will ever be in want. It will be done in your name."

The sun had fallen below the rim of the towering wall above, and the shape of things in the gorge had become more unreal and unnatural.

"You should be on your way," said Tristram. "We must say no farewells. You will be back soon, I most earnestly pray. The sight of you has put new life in me and bolstered my courage for the dark hours I spend in my cave." He smiled eagerly. "Wat, I would like a pet of some kind. A dog wouldn't do; his barking might cause suspicions. Could you find me a cat, think you? A female. A tom would be too much abroad, but a tabby might find herself a mate and fill my home with friendly kittens. It would indeed be a boon."

Some distance down the path, Walter turned and looked back. Tristram had not moved. They waved to each other and then stood still, watching intently in the fading light.

It was not only the hunted cave dweller that Walter saw. As he stood there, with a disinclination to leave that held him until he could no longer make out the tall form of his friend, he was seeing also the self-effacing student who led the clerks of Oxford in a bold rescue, the cheerful companion of his long travels, the courageous archer who taught the Mongolian bowmen a lesson. In place of the lined cheeks and unkempt beard, he saw a face that was calm and unselfish, and eyes that were friendly and cheerful and true.

"Must this be the end of five years of friendship?" he asked himself, as he began to stumble back toward the cover of Bramway Spinney.

He could not put away the fear that he would never see Tristram again.

3

There was a marked change in the attitude of Simeon Bautrie when he issued forth from his stone cubicle. He squinted obsequiously at Walter and said: "Welcome, sir. Our lady and mistress will be glad to hear of your arrival."

That Engaine was very glad was the purport of a message brought with gratifying promptness by a dark-eyed maid who spoke with a foreign lisp. The maid rolled her eyes at the tall visitor and said her mistress was at the moment in the hands of her dressers, but she was seeing they made haste as she hoped for a talk with him before supper. There would be a goodly company at supper, the girl added with a nod and smile. A cousin of the countess was a guest in the castle, and there was as well a great gentleman from France who played on a cither and sang most beguilingly. Things had changed very much, and it was always gay in the Great Hall these days.

He was escorted by a page in black and gold livery to a room in the main tower, where he changed his clothes, and then to an apartment in the immediate vicinity of the Great Hall. A fire burned on the hearth, and the Tartar hangings were drawn so tightly over the windows that no drafts could detract from the comfort. A hospitable wine jar, crowned with oak leaves, stood on a table, with a circle of cups ready for use. Water spouted in a high, gurgling arch from a silver laver.

The only discordant note was the fact of another occupant. Ninian was pacing up and down moodily, hands clasped behind his back, eyes bent on the tips of his shoes. They were of the kind known as crakows, and the toes turned up so extremely that they were bound to his knees with silken cords. He turned when the door opened, and a look of dismay settled on his sallow countenance.

"Bastard!" he exclaimed. "You here?"

Walter grinned as he responded, "You seem pleased to see me, Ninian."

"Then my looks belie my feelings," declared the son of the border marcher. "I would as soon see the devil himself in my cousin's house as you. I have been hearing reports of you, Bastard. It's said you make claims to be a great traveler, even that you have been all the way to Cathay. I believe nothing of the kind." In a tone of the most intense exasperation, he demanded, "What are you doing here?"

"Paying my respects to a neighbor."

"A neighbor! There is rank presumption in your use of the word. It sits ill on my stomach." Ninian scowled. "I hear that by some hedge-creeping connivance you have succeeded in riving lands from the holding of Tressling. Under the circumstances it is hard to believe you capable of such effrontery as to show yourself in the home of the gracious lady you have robbed."

Walter did not respond at once. With an amused smile he studied the aggrieved expression of his old comrade of Butterbump Hall.

"Are you married, Ninian?"

"No."

"But you aim to be soon?"

Ninian stopped his pacing. He looked suspiciously at Walter and then gave a short nod. "I expect to be married soon."

"To your fair cousin, no doubt?" Walter's smile grew into a full laugh. "That will account for this great indignation you feel over the return of the lands to their rightful owner. You consider that your rosy expectations have been dealt a foul blow, my good Ninian. Will it add to your discontent if I say that I regard the recovery of the lands of Gurnie as a matter of small personal importance? Not," he added, "that I do not appreciate the generosity of your fair cousin in not opposing the royal decree."

A look of alarm spread over Ninian's face. "You say that Engaine did not oppose it? That is a lie, Bastard! It assumes a cordiality between you which I refuse to credit."

Walter laughed again. "I suppose I should challenge you to mortal combat for the use of that word, my bold ex-clerk. But I have small regard for the laws of chivalry, and I feel more disposed to bend you over my knee and belabor you like a naughty little schoolboy."

Ninian moved to a discreet distance, from which he surveyed his companion with a hostile eye. Walter had donned his Venetian finery for the occasion, and the richness of it clearly was an added offense in the eyes of the smoldering aspirant to the shoes of the late earl.

"You are a very gay-looking bird, Bastard," muttered the latter. "I have heard of these new styles in dress. It's said they will soon be worn

at court." He ventured nearer and felt Walter's thigh with an unbeliev-
ing thumb and forefinger. "Gog's wounds, they are real! I thought your
chausses must be padded to show such a well-rounded leg."

"Men of spare shanks," said Walter, with an appraising glance at the
far from impressive legs which showed under Ninian's long tunic, "always suspect padding in men of more robust build."

Engaine entered the room at this moment with a smile which gave
place at once to a frown. The smile had been for Walter, the scowl was
exclusively for the benefit of Ninian. The period of mourning was not
over, but as most widows married again within the year it was not surprising to find her in bright colors. She was dressed in a tightly laced
kirtle of green with an overjacket of royal blue which fitted faithfully
and lovingly the slender line of her waist before sloping out to portray
with equal fidelity the roundness of her hips. In the front of the green
barbette in her hair was a sapphire of most unusual size.

She swept into the room with such regal haste that the boy page following her had to step lively not to lose his hold on her long shimmering train.

"Has my cousin been making himself disagreeable, Walter?" she
asked. Then she added, "As usual?"

"Ninian was always a disagreeable fellow. If he has changed, I have
yet to see evidence of it."

Engaine faced her suitor imperiously. "I did not expect to find you
here," she said. "I will esteem it a favor if you will withdraw."

"I have no intention of withdrawing, fair cousin," said Ninian indignantly. "Am I to infer that Walter of Gurnie is a more welcome guest
than I? Perhaps I should have been prepared for this. It has always
rankled in my mind, Engaine, that you sought sanctuary at Gurnie."

"It may have been," declared Walter, "that the Lady Engaine could
not be sure she would be received elsewhere, through fear of her husband's power."

"On the other hand," said Ninian, "it may have been there was an attraction at Gurnie. There has been much talk, fair cousin."

"Talk!" Engaine faced him with a sudden glint in her eye. "You will
explain what you mean, and at once!"

"Surely you knew something of it. There has been much talk, Engaine. You need not frown at me; I had no part in spreading it. If the
proof had not been forthcoming at once that the killing of Edmond was
the work of peasants, it might have been very difficult for Walter of
Gurnie to prove his innocence."

Engaine looked at Walter, and the expression in her eyes said unmistakably, "He has gone too far this time." When she answered, however, it was in a restrained tone. "I am conscious of my obligations as a hostess, Cousin Ninian, even if you seem to have no regard for the limitations imposed on a guest. But there will be no more talk of this kind, if you please."

A gong sounded faintly from the distance. Engaine turned to Walter. "I had hoped for a few words in private, but now we shall have to wait until after supper. Your arm, fair guest."

Ninian scowled at being thus passed over. As he fell into line behind the boy page, he muttered, "Things are coming to a strange pass when lackland adventurers are honored above men of honest birth."

"What an ill-natured gossip he is!" whispered Engaine, who seemed to have recovered her high spirits. Her hand pressed very lightly on his arm. "Who knows, Walter, he may yet find himself with a real reason for his disagreeable moods."

Walter had never seen the Great Hall, and he looked about him with the greatest interest as he escorted her down the dozen stone steps leading to it. Its length he estimated at eighty feet, its width at half of that. In the center of one wall was the large recessed window from which the Norman woman and her guests had watched the feeding of the hungry children, and there was a smaller one at the far end. The dark stone walls, which he had heard were twelve feet thick, ran to such a height that the detail of the beams could not be made out in the upper gloom that the candles failed to dissipate. It would have been a cold and bare chamber had it not been for oak paneling to a height of nine feet, an innovation of Earl Rauf's; and paid for, no doubt, out of the ample inheritance of his wife. There was a platform at one end on which the minstrels sat. They were tuning up their harps and pipes when Engaine appeared at the top of the steps on the arm of her humble guest, and they quickly struck up a lively air. Walter saw her smile proudly. It was clear she relished this grandeur in which she moved as the chatelaine of Bulaire.

"Will Edmond's mother be with us for supper?" he asked in an anxious whisper.

Engaine shook her head. "You will be spared that. She seldom leaves her room now, and I am frank to say it pleases me that she doesn't."

In spite of the splendor of the setting and the richness and variety of the dishes served, the meal proved a dull one. Walter, perforce, sat at the very end of the dais and so had little chance to participate in the conversation. This was no hardship, for it ran on topics which interested him not at all and was monopolized spaciously by Guibert de Bezières, the troubadour from France. This great man, whose face bore an absurd resemblance to that of a horse and who oozed an offensive pride, seldom permitted the talk to stray from the accomplishments of the fast-diminishing and now little considered troubadours of the continent. When the meal was over, he produced his cither and proceeded to play the *sirventes* he himself had composed, singing the words in a nasal and affected voice. Walter thought the airs commonplace and the lines so stilted in sentiment as to be an affront to the intelligence, and he was amazed to note the deep respect on all other faces at the board. Even Engaine, who had her favorite hawk behind her on a high perch and devoted much time to seeing that he was well fed, seemed to be attentive.

"It is clear," he thought, "they consider this braying clown to represent all that is fine and great in life."

He contented himself with watching the company, his gaze resting most often on the animated face of his hostess and on the glum features of Ninian. The latter quaffed cup after cup of wine and was soon far sunk in a maudlin gloom.

As it was his purpose to ride home to Gurnie that night, he took the first opportunity of bidding Engaine good night. The company was beginning to break up, and so she was free to go part of the way with him.

"I am happy you came," she said, as they climbed the steps, her boy page close on her heels. "A short visit, Walter, and one long overdue."

"I came to thank you," he answered, "for your more than generous attitude in the matter of the land."

She gave him a quick side glance. "That," she said, "was a chance to repay a very deep obligation. The land belonged to your grandfather by every right. I always regretted the selfish grasp my father kept on it."

"You never let me see how you felt about it."

"There were many things I never let you see, Walter." A moment of silence followed. "Will you return very soon, when there will be fewer guests and less distraction? We have many things to say."

"I will come most gladly."

She seemed to hesitate. "You must know that I am a very inquisitive person and that I am always concerned about my friends. I have heard of no move on your part toward the—the breaking of what must now be a most inconvenient bond to you. Is it because you have found the cost would be greater than the state of your purse allows?"

"My grandfather is concerned about the cost, but he is very firm in his belief that I should set about it at once in spite of that. I have done nothing, though I must be honest and say that the cost has not been the reason."

She bent a reproachful look on him. "What, then, holds you back? It seems to me, Walter, you are being very absurd."

He answered with a sigh. "I suppose I am. I should begin to think of the future."

"If it had been the cost——" she said slowly. "At the moment I am rather hard pressed. I have not been able to find the money that Edmond and his mother amassed so carefully."

"His mother won't tell you where it is?"

"She says it is hers." He could feel her arm stiffen. "She is more than half out of her mind, but she has sense enough left to keep the secret. I sometimes wish I dared turn her over to the gentle attentions of Jack Daldy!"

"But, surely, the money belongs by right to your son."

"Some of it belongs to me. I have had a thorough search made of the castle, but it has been of no use. It is not in her room; I have made sure of that." Engaine allowed her anger to subside. "In spite of that I am in a position to help you. You made a very generous offer when it seemed I would need help, and that emboldens me to say that now I would be happy to do anything I can."

"I thank you most gratefully, but it will not be necessary."

They had reached the entrance to the gatehouse, and he could see the spiked frame of the portcullis suspended above them. Her step became slower.

"You are most deliberate, Walter. I suppose it's your Saxon blood. But it compels me to make an admission. It is not my intent to remain a widow long. The domain of Bulaire needs a firmer hand than mine; and, if I must speak the whole truth, I am not suited to a solitary life." She dropped his arm and stepped back. "Ninian is not my only suitor. Don't be too deliberate. You might live to regret it; and, by the same token, so might I."

4

Walter hummed to himself "The Two Sisters of Binnorie" as he tied up the bundle. He was feeling in a more hopeful frame of mind. The bundle would be rather conspicuously large, but there was satisfaction in the knowledge that he had obtained everything Tristram needed, even the calendar for which he had traded the sacrist at St. Tenenan's Priory a substantial stock of newly made paper. Long before daybreak he would be on his way, and there would be no curious eyes to sight the bundle and wonder what it contained.

No, there was one omission after all. This would call for some explanation. On the chance that Tristram might not be there when he arrived, he opened the bundle and wrote on a sheet of paper in which the calendar was wrapped.

You will find everything here but the cat. We have one mangy old specimen in the scullery, but I must find you a younger and more likable pet than our old Skeek. The next time I come, a handsome and sleek lady, with sharp claws and a contented purr as well as romantic notions in the family line, will make the trip with me.

What think you of this fine sheet? The paper yard is a hive of industry these days, and now we have real proofs to show that we actually did get to Cathay. Does that please you, thou very idiot?

It had been a hard day, and he thought longingly of the need for sleep before starting out in the dark for Scaunder Clough. One duty must be performed first, however: he must pay his evening visit to his grandfather. The master of Gurnie had not stirred from his room for a week past.

When he entered the small bedroom, a feeble hand was raised in a gesture of surrender.

"I give in to you," said the old man. "There is no longer any strength in me to hear more of your wild theories. Have it your way, Walter. Give the knaves everything you think their hearts desire."

"I had no intention of discussing these matters," said Walter. "I came to ask how you are feeling."

The master of Gurnie shook his head slowly. "I cannot rest, my boy, because of all my pains and discomforts. If I lie on my back, my head is taken with a dizziness; but if I turn on my side, the weight of my head causes my ears to ache, and when I wake they are stiff and sore. I cannot abide to stay in one position for long, but it hurts me abominably to make a change. I sleep so little, Walter, and my head is filled with the most curious fancies." He added in a tone of hopeless misery: "I am at odds with my body. There are times when I long to be free of it!"

"It is this cold weather, Grandfather. When the snow is gone and the sun warms up, you must take a ride over the old domain. It will drive your ills away to see how broad the pastures are and how thick the woodlands have become."

The old man sighed. "I may never have the strength for it. As you know, I have not set foot on the land since it was taken away from me by Old King Harry, and I have longed so to feast my eyes on the fine, fat acres and know they are mine again. But it—it is all very dim now. I don't seem to care as much about it."

After a moment of silence, Walter said: "I have followed one of your suggestions, Grandfather. The sheets are being made a little smaller, and yet the greedy sacrists pay the full price without a word of protest."

The old man did not answer. Walter realized then that he was very sick indeed.

Wilderkin stopped him in the dark passage and whispered in his ear, "Someone to see you near the paper yard, master."

Walter was startled. Visitors never came after darkness fell unless they were belated travelers who had lost their way, and in that event they applied for lodging at the postern. Could it be Tristram?

"I could not see his face, but I knew the voice," said the seneschal. "It's the old tavernkeeper of Little Tamitt."

Walter made his way to the paper yard, fully prepared for the worst of news. A cautious "Here!" directed him to a clump of trees at one side. Camus Harry had flattened himself against a trunk, and he did not move when Walter stopped beside him.

"I had to let ye know," whispered the old Crusader. "Tristram Griffen is dead!"

"Dead!" Walter did not know he had cried the word aloud until a hand reached out in the darkness and gripped him roughly by the wrist.

"Easy! Do ye want to rouse the whole household? I'm in danger enough as it is. Yes, he's dead, our brave Tris. The best o' the lot of us, he wur!"

It was several moments before Walter asked in a strained whisper, "How did it happen?"

"I felt concern for the stubborn fellow, and I visited the Clough this morning. I found him in his cave. He had been dead for—for some time."

Walter was finding it almost impossible to hold his feelings in check. "I knew it was coming," he said, with a sob. "Something told me when I saw him a week ago. Tris, Tris! What am I to do now!"

"There's nothing ye can do but keep a still tongue in yer head. It's over and done with. The fine lad is gone; and all the regrets we can babble won't bring him back."

"What caused it, Harry?"

"I think he had a fall. He had crawled to his cave." Camus Harry's voice conveyed the suggestion of a shudder. "A damp, cold hole it wur! He was a staunch 'un to endure so much for a matter o' principle. I tried my best to make him join us, but he wouldn't give in. And yet, when I found him there, I knew he had the right o' it. He went to his Maker with a clear conscience, Tristram Griffen did. It'll be different with me when my time comes!"

Walter was leaning against one of the trees for the support it gave him. Words came slowly. "I was planning to leave before daylight and take him the things he needed most."

"Ye should a-done it afore this. He needed things bad, I can tell ye."

"He warned me not to come sooner. Not," cried Walter, in a fury of self-condemnation, "that I can take any comfort from that!"

"Perhaps it wur all for the best." Camus Harry sighed deeply. "But it goes sore against the grain to see him took in his prime. We will be needing men like Tristram Griffen."

"Is there—anything I can do now?"

"There's nought ye can do. I must go now. There's twenty full mile I must make on shanks his mare afore morning."

"What—what did you do with the body?"

"I wrapped him up in his cloak and covered him with earth and stones. I piled 'em high so the wild things couldn't get at him. He'll rest there well enough till we can find a more decent grave for him. It may mean some'at to ye that he'd traced a word in the ashes. Surg—surg— it wur something like that."

"*Surgite!*" cried Walter.

"Aye," said Camus Harry. "I think that wur it."

The Oxford rallying cry! After a tense moment, Walter said in a low whisper, "I know now what was in his mind when he died. He was thinking of a day that is coming. Perhaps also he was dwelling on the past and—and taking some comfort from it!"

"I'm away now, Walter of Gurnie. Ye'll not likely see me again."

"It was more than kind of you, Harry, to come so far to let me know!"

"Ye wur the best o' friends. I could do no else."

Camus Harry left his post by the tree and made off into the darkness. Before Walter could rouse himself to return to the house, the shadow of the old tavernkeeper came gliding back to his side.

"That bundle ye spoke of," he whispered. "I could make good use o' the things myself. Would ye think o' tossing it out to me over the palisade?"

"Follow after me to the house. I'll bring the bundle out to you."

"We do well enough. But it's a hard life, Walter of Gurnie, and a bare 'un. Would there be sugar in the lot?"

"Yes, there's sugar. Tris asked for it especially." The grief that Walter had been holding inside himself could no longer be restrained. He cried out: "Tris, Tris! So this has to be the end of it! Everything has gone wrong." He gulped determinedly and, when he spoke again, it was in a lower tone. "We were together for five years. No man ever had a better friend."

"Better days are coming," said Camus Harry. "Make no mistake on that. If only he had lived to bear a hand!"

CHAPTER XVII

Marseilles

WHEN THE NEW BIREME had picked its way through the gap in the chain stretched across the Gargata and had sailed into the harbor of Marseilles, with the Winged Lion floating in the breeze and the ship band playing triumphantly, Maryam was again certain that at last she had reached her haven. The busy town clustering around the landlocked harbor bore a closer resemblance to the city of Walter's description than had Venice. The people had whiter skins, and many of them had blond hair and beards and, even, blue eyes.

It was well that the end of the long journey had been reached, she said to herself. Her strength would not have been equal to more travel. Since leaving Venice she had seldom been able to summon the resolution to leave her cabin. Hope long postponed had taken its toll, even more than the fatigue and the intensity of the heat. It had been a long and slow trip, for the bireme had touched at all ports up the coast of Italy, and two vicious storms had held them inactive for weeks. The one consolation she had was that the sea air had restored her son's health. He was growing fast now and was finding the use of his tongue. Back from jaunts around the decks with the faithful Mahmoud, he would chatter to her about all the things he had seen.

But again it did not take her long to know that she had been mistaken. Everyone she stopped with her eternal query, "London?" pointed inland and to the north, with the spacious wave of arm, moreover, which indicated that the distance was great. London, then, could only be reached by another land journey. Remembering the terrible months they had spent on the blistering trails between Aden and Alexandria, her heart sank. Would her strength carry her through another such?

She obtained two rooms in an inn between La Tourette and the Carreria portus. Marseilles was the very core of the pilgrim traffic to the East, and this particular inn was filled with bronzed and bearded homecomers as well as the eager neophytes who were starting out for the Holy Land. The owner, strange to relate, was an honest man; a hunched-over morsel of skin and bone, convinced that he, Pierre Marchus, was a vicar of the Heavenly Father in the care of these fanatical travelers. He took infinite pains to see that they were registered and numbered and that the cards they received for their outward passage allowed them their full deck space of seven *pans* by two and a half and that they had not paid too much. He made it his concern that the homecomers were not overcharged for the stout sandals they needed for the long tramps ahead of them. He fended off the commercial harpies who tried to get from them the relics and other valuables they had brought back.

One glance at the weary party of three was all that Pierre Marchus needed to convince him that they had been directed his way by the Hand of Providence.

His first care was to find some means of communication. After various futile ventures, he produced a merchant who had a smattering of Greek at his command. The merchant listened to Maryam's story with many skeptical shakes of the head.

"London," he said, "lies far to the north. It is a city of small merit and no charm. Madame would find it little to her taste."

"My husband is there," she protested.

She had discarded her veil now that the East was so far back of her, and the merchant studied the thin pointed face under her wide-spaced eyes with attentive care.

"Husbands are easy to get. Madame could find another husband, or a generous protector, without going so far as this unhealthy city of London."

Maryam made no response to this.

"I have seen many thousands of the English in my time," asserted the merchant. "It is my opinion they do not make good husbands. Their country, moreover, has nothing to recommend it to a lady of good taste and uncertain health."

"I have a small son who has never seen his father, and it is my earnest desire to reach London while I still have enough strength."

The merchant lost interest then and reported to Pierre Marchus that the thin woman had a madness in her which made her insist on going to London. It was incomprehensible, but there it was.

Pierre nodded his head understandingly. "It is clear she is a good woman," he said, "and as such not to be appreciated by the likes of you, monsieur the leather merchant. I must arrange to send her north with the first party."

But she did not set out with the first party. She had contracted a fever on board ship, and it soon appeared certain that she would set forth instead on a much longer journey, one moreover that men, in spite of their deep faith, knew little about. It was fortunate that she had fallen into the hands of an honest man. The worthy Pierre saw to it that she had every care, even though he had no expectation that she would live to repay him.

2

Maryam's illness was a long and disordered blackness in which she lived over and over again the whole of the more than three years of incessant travel. Most particularly her sick mind was filled with the days at Amboyna, where her son had been born. The aromatic odors which had greeted them when they reached that port of the spice trade had always been associated thereafter with uncertainty and a wild fear and pain so great as to be almost unbearable. As she tossed and moaned on her couch in the little Marseilles inn, she was going through it all again: the hurried removal from the ship, the hunt for a place where the child could be born, the kindly look in the yellow face of the Chinese woman who took her in charge. The Chinese woman had been full of talk, and the dreams echoed with the clack of her tongue, which, of course, had been beyond understanding, the cackle of triumph when she held up the healthy man child before the pain-dimmed eyes of the mother. The woman had insisted on doing curious things, and all these were magnified and distorted in the fevered mind. Maryam had visions of huge basins in which yellow hands stirred gifts, and of collected articles, all as large as the pillars in the Great Interior Palace, in the midst of which her small son was placed in the belief that the first one on which his eyes lighted would show what manner of man he was destined to become. All the people in her dreams were gigantic in size, many times taller even than Bird Who Feathers His Nest Lu Chung, and their faces were vague and she could not be sure whether they meant well or ill.

Gradually the fantastic dreams cleared away, and there were intervals when she knew that she lay on a narrow couch in a room with cool iron shutters. She was conscious of forms that came and went: Mahmoud, who rolled his eyes at her in an intensity of anxiety, and a small man with a hooked nose and the kindest of eyes. She was so weak that she had no will to stir as much as a finger, and her mind was capable of no more than a flutter of anxiety as to the well-being of her son. She watched the warm sunlight filtering through the shutters and was sure that at last she had come to a gentle and hospitable land.

In one of these intervals she became aware of a sound which never stopped. It was faint and seemed far away, and at first she paid no attention. Gradually, however, the meaning of it forced itself on her consciousness. It was a sound of weeping, and she discovered it was her son who was responsible for it. There was no urgency in the sound, no suggestion of physical pain or terror. It was instead a monotone of hopeless grief which went on and on without any stop. She forced herself to sit up, although the effort caused the carved iron shutters to whirl around her with a sickening velocity.

She was alarmed now. Something had happened to upset the boy most seriously. Was he developing an illness himself that he cried so steadily? She must find out at once. Sliding from the bed to the floor, she began to crawl, with an effort that was almost completely of the will.

Reaching the door, she looked into the other room. The walls were dancing around her now, and it was difficult to see anything clearly. She was finally able to make out the figure of the boy, kneeling on the floor. He still wore the coat she had made for him from the Robe of Sixteen Summers, although he had completely outgrown it, and its shabbiness made even more pathetic the task with which he was concerned. Weeping softly, he was bending over the inert body of the dog Chi and endeavoring with a fan to brush away the flies which swarmed about it.

"Walter!" she whispered, weakly.

The boy turned his tear-stained face. "Modda!" he burst out in a sudden excess of grief. "See! Chi sick too."

Maryam realized that Chi's sickness was of the past. The tiny tan body was already rigid, and a glaze had settled over the round brown eyes.

"Don't take it so hard, little son," she said. "Come to mother."

"No, no!" he cried, continuing to swing the fan back and forth. "Chi sick. Chi needs Walter."

She managed somehow to draw herself up to a sitting position. The strain was so great that she was unable to speak for several moments. In the meantime the boy had begun to sob harder than ever, as though a realization of the truth had come to him.

"Chi is dead," said Maryam in a whisper. "You must be brave about it, my son. Little dogs do not live long. I will get you another dog, a very large dog, my Walter. One so large you will be able to ride on his back like an elephant. Come, don't cry any more."

The boy looked around at the mention of a big new dog, but this respite from grief was a brief one. The tears began to fall again, and he returned to his hopeless fanning.

"Poor little boy!" she said to herself.

The sharp pang she had felt on realizing that Chi was dead made her realize how intensely her son was feeling the loss of his pet. He had seemed to grow more attached to the dog with each day. He carried him wherever he went and talked to him in a language all his own which seemed nevertheless to have some coherence, for many strange words recurred all the time. He even insisted on combing out the long tan coat (not too successfully, it must be said) and saying, "Chi must look nice. Chi must look very nice." Maryam often heard him whispering to the dog when they were curled up together in bed.

"My lonely little son!" she whispered. "Why should this happen now? Why could he not have kept his pet until he—until he gets to London and can live like other little boys?"

She heard Mahmoud come shuffling into the room at this point. It was well that he did, for her small store of strength was completely exhausted. She suddenly crumpled up on the floor.

It was some time later when she became conscious again. She was weaker than ever, as was to be expected, and it took a long time for her to gather her senses sufficiently to see and hear what was going on. She realized then that much time had passed. The sun no longer shone on the windows, and the shutters had been opened to admit more air. The room seemed to be filled with people. Mahmoud was there, and the friendly innkeeper, and the leather merchant. She made out after a time that there was still another man, a very large man in the gray robe of a pilgrim above which she saw a huge, round face. At first she was inclined to think it was a sunflower she saw; for the pilgrim's face in reality was as round as the head of that autumn visitor, and a reddish beard stuck out around his chin in a way to foster the resemblance. Her son was sitting solemnly in one corner. He was no longer crying, but the eyes he kept fixed on her face were still unhappy.

She heard a rumbling voice issuing from the full lips of the stranger. He was speaking in French, and so she had no way of knowing what he was saying.

"I tell you, it was a disgrace," he declared. "They were packed on the ship from stem to stern. Seven *pans* for each of them, as the law provides? They will not have half of that. Not many of them will live to see the Holy Land. And," he cried, with new vehemence, "as many more were left standing on the dock with their cards of passage in their hands."

"It is always the way," sighed Pierre. "We try to save them from being robbed. But these sea captains! They are no better than pirates."

"I have been to Jerusalem twice," went on the pilgrim. "I have seen things both times that would make your blood congeal in your veins. They die like flies, the poor, weak fellows. Ah well, they seek salvation, and it may be that the more they suffer, the surer they can be that the sacred portals will swing wide open for them. Perhaps it is the will of God that they suffer this way." He hunched his gray robe comfortably about his massive shoulders. "How content I shall be to set eyes again on the cliffs at Dover. My wanderings will be over."

"You are English," said the innkeeper, "and that is why I asked you to come. This very sick woman desires to go to London. She may never be able to go herself, but the child must be sent home to his English father. I thought you might be persuaded to wait until we know what the Lord has decided in her case. I would rest more easily in my mind if you took her with you, or if it is not to be that way, the boy alone." He paused to draw a sigh. "I have never ventured to see the Sepulcher, and it is only in small matters such as this that I, Pierre Marchus, can hope to win grace."

The word "English" registered on Maryam's mind. She said to herself, "This pilgrim is from London, and so perhaps he will help us." She motioned Mahmoud over beside her couch. When he obeyed, she indicated with a weak gesture that he was to open the hem of her tunic, which lay across the foot of the bed. His exploring fingers found there no more than one very small pearl, the last of her carefully conserved resources.

"Please," she said to the leather merchant, "this is all I have. Will it be enough to take my son and our servant as far as London?"

The merchant held the pearl on his palm and studied it with a shrewd eye. Then, after explaining what she had said, he passed it to the inn-keeper.

"We must see that an honest price is obtained for it," said Pierre Marchus, with a trace of doubt in his tone. "If we do that, there may be enough for the three of them. But it will have to be stretched very fine."

"The Lord will provide," said the pilgrim.

The merchant explained and she allowed herself a sigh of relief. She had been watching the face of the pilgrim, and it seemed to her that she could read in it great kindness and a willingness to help.

"Tell them," she whispered, "that I do not expect to go myself. I—I am very much weaker. It does not matter about me, but my son must be taken to his father. His father is a tall man, and he belongs to a very great family. His name is Walter of Gurnie. He does not live in Lon-don, but I cannot tell you anything more about him. Ask the good pil-grim to see that my son gets safely to London."

She felt herself slipping back into unconsciousness. "It will be for the best," she thought. "My Walter will not have a wife who knows noth-ing about his kind of life and who would be a great trouble to him. Perhaps he—he has already come to see this and is content with things as they are. My son can now be raised like any other English boy. Soon he won't even remember about me. I have tried so hard to find my Wal-ter, but—it is better this way."

CHAPTER XVIII

Leeds Castle

FOR THREE HOURS the conversation had continued without break or in-terruption, and rarely in that time had the serious eyes of the King left Walter's face. He had asked many questions.

The royal interest had centered chiefly in the story of the war and the results of it, but he had insisted as well on hearing all about Maryam and the marriage. "Never, on my honor, have I heard a more romantic tale," he declared at the finish. "Nothing in Tancred or Arthur de Bretagne can equal it. The Queen must hear your story, just as you have told it to me. It's too bad the ending cannot be a happy one, for my *chérie reine* is all for the union of loving hearts in everlasting amity. Still and all, as the lady is so far away, it is perhaps fortunate that the tie is susceptible of such easy snipping."

"The separation, my liege, has caused me much distress of mind."

"But it is final, and you will get over it." The King nodded his head. "My advice is to find yourself another wife, one of full English blood. So promising a sire can well be expected to raise many fine sons and daughters. I would not want to issue a merchet writ against you for obduracy in singleness." The royal memory cast back to the story which concerned the high state of the visit to Kinsai. He slapped his long and muscular thigh and laughed heartily. "The two birds of golden plumage! A rare story, Walter of Gurnie, and one most difficult to believe if so many proofs had not been forthcoming. This, for one." He indicated the emerald ring which Walter had presented to him immediately on being introduced, and which now reposed on a velvet cushion embroidered with the cross fleury between martlets or. "It clearly is of Eastern workmanship. But I refer more particularly to the mass of authentic detail you have supplied. I have listened most attentively, expecting to find some flaw in your tale of wonder, to catch you in slips. On my honor, there have been none such. Your story fits together with the closeness of a suit of Sicilian mail."

"I have not invented a single detail, my liege."

"Of that I am well convinced."

They sat in the private hall of Leeds Castle, the most beautiful of all the royal residences. It was, nevertheless, a simple apartment, most plainly furnished in oak and with nothing to indicate that royalty dined here save the arms of England above the hearth and the five-shelved cupboard with a spicery on top like a triple-tiered tower. The walls were painted a cheerful green and were without hangings of any kind, so that sunlight poured generously in through the lancet windows. The chairs and table were monastically plain.

The apparel of the King was of a matching simplicity, a sleeveless surcote of plain saye cloth which reached to his knees and displayed the red cross of the Crusades on the breast, and gray hose which fitted his remarkably long legs without a wrinkle. His shoes were of soft gray felt and lacked decoration. The sole concession to grandeur was a topaz of unusual size which hung on a chain around his neck.

"The point which caught me most in the telling," went on the sovereign, "was the use of the iron tubes which belched fire against the Chinese fleet. A mighty arm in battle, surely!"

There were several men of the royal household grouped about them. One, a young courtier whose tunic of crimson samite made him seem very gay in comparison with the plainly dressed monarch, shook his lank black locks at this point.

"May I say, my liege lord and king," he interrupted, "that I own to grave doubts on the score of these fabulous instruments? Were they not dragons our doughty traveler saw? It is well known that the land of Cathay is full of dragons which consume whole cities with the fire they spit forth."

Some of the others nodded in agreement. The King looked at Walter with a silent command to supply the answer. The latter took up the challenge with readiness.

"England is no different from Cathay except in customs and ways of living and in the color of our skins," he said. "Has anyone met a dragon on the road to Cheringe? Dragons exist only in the imagination of the tellers of stories. But," he cried, vigorously, "I saw the *Hua-P'ao's* with my own eyes! I saw the Chinese ships go up in flames. I studied the tubes carefully, and I can explain how they are made. I only hope the Mongolians do not bring them against us when Bayan of the Hundred Eyes has finished with the Manji country."

The same doubtful member of the party expressed his dissent again with a loud laugh. "This heathen general, of whom you appear to think so well, seems to be sure it will be as easy to conquer Europe as to play a game of pitch-farthing or bob-apple. He will sing a different tune when he has tasted the steel of chivalry."

"You are a great dotterel, Hal," said the King impatiently. "I, for one, do not underestimate the might of the Mongolians. They gave the brave knights of Europe a bad beating when they swarmed into Poland and Hungary under their wise Sabutai. I have seen them in action, and it is only too certain that they know the art of war." Then he added with a shake of the head: "But I see small need to anticipate an early attack. From what we have heard today, the Manji country is a vast one and very rich. It will take years to pacify it and set its new government to running. By the time that is done, the appetite for conquest may not run so strongly in the veins of the Mongols. There is nothing to quench martial ardor like the enjoyment of the fruits of victory."

"My liege," said Walter, "I wanted to say that there is a great Englishman who knows the ingredients of the strange powder which spouts death and destruction. I heard him tell of his discovery of it in a classroom in Oxford before I set out for Cathay."

The King looked disturbed. "Do you mean Friar Bacon? I have heard of his activities at Oxford. The reports of him are far from favorable."

"He is the wisest man in all the world!" cried Walter. "He predicted many of the strange things I saw in Cathay. Give him support in what he is trying to do, and he will change the whole face of life!"

"And you think it would be a good thing to change the whole face of life?"

Walter looked the King steadily in the eye. "Yes, my liege," he said. "The life that men live today needs change very badly."

"Friar Bacon is a dabbler in black magic," interposed one of the company.

King Edward shifted uneasily in his chair. "Rumors have reached my ears. The friar stood well with the old pope, but our new Holy Father regards him with grave disfavor. It is because of that he has been imprisoned."

"But he is an English subject," protested Walter. "A word from you and the Franciscans will release him. This truly great man must not be kept any longer in a dark cell. Make it possible for him to return to England, sire, and he will work miracles which will add splendor to your name."

"It is not as simple as you think, Walter of Gurnie. Members of holy orders are subject to the authority of their own superiors. They take umbrage at any hint of state interference, and they can create a pestilential lot of trouble when they are crossed. Do you know that your advocacy of Friar Bacon might place you in danger of excommunication?"

"I only know," declared Walter, "that the one clear white light in the world is in danger of being extinguished."

The King frowned in silence for several moments. "You have all the fire of a zealot in you. Well, I shall give some thought to it. It is possible something can be done for Friar Bacon."

A servant entered through the buttery hatch with a large flagon of malvoisie. The King waved him aside, but the members of his suite were not equally abstemious. They accepted replenishment of their tankards, and as they sipped their wine they continued to watch with the closest interest. Sensing their lack of cordiality to the turn the talk had taken, the King got to his feet. He drew Walter aside into a window embrasure.

"I need not tell you that we live in an age which resents all suggestion of change," he said in a low tone. "Not one of these head-shaking officers of mine has aught but disapproval of the new laws I am enacting. In their hearts they think ill of me, even though they smile to my face and give me honeyed answers." His voice dropped to a whisper. "You have put new thoughts in my head, my bold venturer into unknown worlds. Changes must be made slowly; and you must not expect miracles. But I am disposed to look more closely into the possibilities of the future."

From where they stood they looked straight down a wall of rock to the waters of a small lake which served as moat. On the far side stretched the green wooded hills of Kent against the light of the late afternoon sun. It was a perfect setting for this lovely home that Edward had recently presented to his queen.

"England is a land of great beauty," said the King in a musing voice. Walter had noticed that he spoke English with a slightly foreign accent, but there could be no doubt of the sincerity of his attachment to this country his Norman forebears had conquered and had ruled so sternly. "I have lived much abroad, too much as I see now; but always when I return to this green isle I think how bountiful God was when He fashioned it. There is only one thing wrong with England, Walter of Gurnie, and the answer to that can be found in the attitude of these gently-born caynards guzzling their mulled wine back there. I trow, I shall find a way to shake them out of their apathy and selfishness."

After a long pause, during which the eyes of the King continued to study the wooded land across the strip of water, he turned back.

"And now I must say that I have had unfavorable reports of you as well. You thought ill of me before you set out on your travels. You spurned the idea of entering my service."

Walter hesitated. "I thought a great injustice had been done me," he said finally. "The bar sinister is lightly regarded by most men, but my lack of an honest name has always been to me, my liege, like the flick of a lash on raw flesh. I was young, and I—I resented being handed over, body and soul, like a villein with an iron plate around my neck."

"You were outspoken about it." The young king was studying him intently. "How are your feelings on that score now?"

"I am sure, my liege, that you are the real English king we have needed so badly. The rash things I said rest heavily on my conscience, for I know how wrong I was. I should be happy of a chance to show how much I have changed."

"You shall have the chance." The King nodded his head approvingly. "I shall need men about me of your stamp, men who are not afraid to undertake new and bold ventures. I am strong for the laws of chivalry, and yet I must tell you that what you are doing now, this making of paper, may prove of more value in my realm than all the deeds of knightly emprise these fellows dream of performing. As for the lack of an honest name which seems to concern you so deeply, there is a remedy for that."

He turned and called, "Hal, my sword!"

The young courtier took the royal sword from where it lay on a table by the hearth and brought it to the King.

"Kneel down, Walter of Gurnie," said Edward.

Walter obeyed in such a turmoil of emotion that his knees struck sharply on the stone floor. This could mean only one thing, and yet he could not bring himself to believe it was happening to him. The possibility of such a reward had never entered his head. Was this a dream, he asked himself?

It was not a dream. In a daze of happiness he felt the light tap of the sword on his shoulder and heard the voice of the King say: "You have proven yourself a man of high courage and, which I esteem in equal degree, of vision and purpose. I gladly dub thee knight. Rise, Sir Walter Fitzrauf!"

2

He had a name of his own at last! No longer was he Walter, the bastard of Gurnie, the recipient of slights and the butt of every idle tongue; he was Sir Walter Fitzrauf, knighted by the hand of the King himself and pledged to the service of that enlightened monarch. True, the newly acquired prefix was Norman, but it was one of the words that general usage was merging into the common language, and he doubted if even his grandfather, had he been alive, would have caviled at it.

Walter left Gloriette, as the small section of the castle was called where the King and Queen had their private rooms, and walked across the drawbridge to the main part. He was in such a mood of exultation that he had no eyes for the beauty which surrounded him.

There was no escaping it, however, when he set foot on the green sod of the outer island. Surrounded by a wall of *enceinte* with a battlemented top and five stout bastion towers, this space was called the inner bailey. This seemed a misnomer, for the general effect was of a spacious garden with level lawns and many fine shrubs and trees. Already the servants were raising torches in tall iron sockets against the imminence of dusk and setting out movable tables, of the kind known as dormant, in readiness for the evening meal. The fine fall weather had brought the court down from London in full force, and the dining chamber in Gloriette was much too small to accommodate such large numbers. Supper was to be served outside.

The bailey was crowded with men in rich cloaks and their ladies in all the gayest of colors. A hum of chatter filled Walter's ears as he stepped down from the drawbridge, and he roused himself from his pleasant reverie to look about him with new interest. "This is the court of England," he thought, "and, strange as it may be, I belong to it."

He strolled across the grass, and unconsciously his stride took on more assurance, and perhaps he held his head a little high. He could look every man in the face, without any of his old feeling of being set apart. It was both pleasant and stimulating, and he found himself reveling in this new sense of equality. He paced the length of the gardens and was starting back when a voice hailed him.

"May it please you, my lord——"

It was Engaine's dark-eyed maid. She dropped a curtsy and said, "My lady would like to speak with you."

"Where is she?"

"If my lord will deign to follow, I will show the way."

Engaine had an apartment in one of the bastion towers, of the same size as the room assigned to him but quite different from it in every other respect. She had the happy faculty of transforming her surroundings quickly and making them seem a part of herself. There was no suggestion here of dark stone walls and the bareness of sheer utility. There were bright hangings and a multiplicity of small articles which had turned the chamber into a pleasant feminine bower. He was conscious at once of an enticing perfume on the air.

Engaine was sitting near a corner window with the light showing glints in her hair under its gold net. A blue gorget was wound around her neck, with vivacious bows at each side, and over this her eyes sparkled at him in welcome.

"I have been waiting for you for a long time," she said reproachfully. "I heard you arrived early this afternoon, but I must say you have kept yourself in the most complete seclusion. Where have you been?"

"In audience with the King." He was fairly bursting with his news, but he decided to hold it back and thus savor a little longer the pleasure of the surprise.

"Please sit down, Walter. I have things to tell you."

The maid had ensconced herself in a corner near the door, for the sake of propriety, no doubt, and the only other chair was covered with some article of obviously intimate feminine use. He looked at it doubtfully.

"I fear it is one of my plackards," laughed Engaine. "Blanche, you slovenly girl, remove it at once.

"But," she went on, when the maid had whisked the petticoat away and Walter had seated himself, "it is full four hours since you came. Have you been with the King all that time?"

Walter nodded. "Every minute of it. I had much to tell, and he seemed interested in my story."

"Well," said Engaine, dropping him a curtsy of mock humility, "you have been most highly honored indeed. His King's Grace must have been placed under a spell by your eloquence, O great traveler!"

"We talked of nothing else. He was the most attentive auditor I have yet had. Some time, perchance, you will care to hear more about Cathay. Your concern has been disappointingly small, I am compelled to say."

Engaine smiled. "I seem to remember that I showed a—shall we say a *sharp* interest?—in *one* phase of your travels, my good Walter. And you, I can also recall, were rather loath to tell me everything I desired to know."

Walter shifted his position uneasily. "The King's interest was in matters of warfare and the details of Eastern rule," he said.

"And in that I have no interest at all." She leaned forward in her chair. "What talk there has been about you! Everyone has been anxious for a glimpse of the man who went to the ends of the earth. Those who saw you arrive spread the most glowing reports of your appearance, and all the ladies of the court are agog over the very tall and handsome stranger. I shall have to be very firm to save for myself any share of your attentions."

Knowing that she had something to tell him, Walter still held back his own news. His mind was so filled with it that he had to drag his mind away from its flights of pleasant speculation when she spoke.

"The gold has been found," she whispered, "and the coffers of Bulaire are filled to overflowing."

"I was beginning to think that the hidden hoard was apocryphal. Where did you find it?"

"Did I tell you that Edmond's mother refused to have the bier moved from the chapel? It never occurred to anyone to disturb it when we were searching so carefully. But there it was all the time, in a sack of canvas." She smiled radiantly. "What a pair of misers they had been! I am rich, rich! Or at least my little son is; which comes to very much the same thing, for I shall control the purse strings for a long time. Some of it had come from Tressling, and so I have a right to consider a part of it mine."

"I judge," said Walter, "that you have already made plans."

Engaine leaned forward in her chair and nodded eagerly. "I am ambitious," she said. "I want to see Lessford one of the great houses of England. When my son grows up, he must be as powerful as the earls of Gloucester and Hereford and Arundel are today. You agree, I trust, that it is a laudable aim?"

"The policy of the King is to reduce the power of the barons, not to augment it."

She swept that aside with a regal gesture. "I am not ignorant of such matters, and I doubt if the King can do much to curb us. There have always been strong nobles, and I am sure there always will be.

"There must be a house in London," she went on. "To live so continuously at Bulaire, as we were compelled to do by Edmond's parsimony, is no longer wise. One must be seen at court." She was talking with renewed eagerness, but in a low enough voice to keep what she was saying from the ears of the girl. "The money could not be applied to a better purpose than the purchase or building of a house. Naturally it must be on the Thames and as near Durham House as possible. There must be gardens running down to the river."

Walter was not in accord with her ideas as to the future, but he could see no reason why she should not do as she wished. She was well suited to the life of the court, and she would be happier in her town house than at Bulaire. The future would take care of itself, or rather the King would set the pattern of it.

"There must be a water gate with marble steps and a barge, a large one with a very gay cover. It is so pleasant to ply up and down the river with trumpeters in front and a rowing crew in full livery! You will be thinking, I am sure," she said, looking at him with sudden suspicion, "that I am a spendthrift and a rattlebrain. But it is all for a purpose, Walter. I am not a great spender, and I don't think I am overfrivolous. Show plays such a large part in the power of a baron. As I said before, I am very ambitious."

"And now," he said, when a pause indicated that her flow of confidences had reached an end, "I have something to tell *you*."

She leaned over the back of her chair to throw the window hangings further back. "It is getting dark. But not so dark that I can't see the glow in your eye, Walter. I know it is something important you have to tell me. Come, I am most impatient."

"I have a name at last, Engaine, and I am wondering if you will like the sound of it. Sir Walter Fitzrauf!"

"Sir Walter Fitzrauf!" Her eyes lighted up as she repeated it. "You have been made a knight? So soon, Walter! It is indeed the best of news. I am so happy about it I could weep!"

"The King knighted me after our talk. Since then my feet have scarce touched the ground. There are moments still when my mind refuses to believe in my great good fortune."

They were both leaning forward now, their heads close together.

"This means you will enter the King's service?" She had fallen into a thoughtful mood. "Perhaps you will be the one to win the power I have been dreaming of. His King's Grace must have been greatly taken with you, Walter. Will you live permanently at court?"

He shook his head. "No, there has been no suggestion of that. I have work to do at Gurnie."

"But surely you will give all that up now. It is so—so unknightly. I don't like to think of you as a maker of paper."

"The King considers what I am doing as most important. Under no circumstances will I give that up. I am sure that soon paper will be made all over England."

"Then let others do it, Walter."

A pause ensued. It was growing dark in the room. Walter drew his chair closer to hers.

"I can begin to plan for the future now," he said. "I did not feel free to think of anything until I had an honest name."

Engaine called to the maid, "Blanche, it is very dark. Some candles at once."

When the girl had left the room, she asked: "Have you none made as yet? Have you nothing to tell me?" She shook her head with a touch of exasperation. Then she laid both hands on his shoulders. "Kiss me, you great dolt!" she whispered.

3

The next morning Walter was summoned to Gloriette for a further audience. It was nine o'clock, the hour of tierce, when he arrived, and he wondered at the activity of the palace servants. They were taking down all the hangings and tapestries and packing them away in standards. Glancing into the chapel, he saw that the stained glass had already been removed from the lancet windows and was being covered with straw in special cases to await the next arrival of the royal owners. The court, quite clearly, was preparing to move on.

The King sat in front of the hearth, and Queen Eleanor was beside him, their chairs so very close together that they reminded Walter of the lovebirds Maryam had kept in Kinsai. The devotion of the King was talked of all over England, constancy being a rare thing with monarchs of that, or any other, age; but observing the fair wide brow and sweet eyes of the Queen, it was not hard to understand. She was lovely, although her beauty was to be found mostly in a gentleness of charm. Her neck was bare (her one vanity, for it was slender and white), and she wore her hair loose on her shoulders. Her features were delicately chiseled, her movements graceful and infinitely engaging.

Documents were heaped up on the table in front of the King, and he was regarding them with a dismal eye when Walter entered. The Queen, however, was eating breakfast, and with such lack of ceremony that the visitor was amazed. No servants were in the room, although the attentive head of a maid could be seen behind the opened hatch. The meal consisted of a plate of chops and a glass of milk, and the Queen was eating with great daintiness, employing a most curious-looking four-pronged instrument. This, Walter was to learn later, was called a fork, and it was one of the innovations she had brought with her from Spain. The table was laid with articles of quite regal costliness: benison cups of silver white, beautifully chased, and salts of the same metal, and a handsome hanaper filled with drinking vessels and plates.

The King pushed the documents to one side and called to an official who stood in a corner: "Away with them, my good spigurnel. I have more congenial matters now to engage my attention."

The official gathered up the documents into his arms and withdrew. The King then gave Walter a courteous inclination of the head. "Forgive me this early summons," he said. "We journey on today, as you have already heard, no doubt. It will be said we are continuing our royal processional; but to be truthful, it is necessity which takes us away from this most pleasant home. We stay in one place until all the food has been consumed, and then we move on. I have no domain capable of feeding my hungry court for more than a fortnight." He turned to the Queen. "This is Sir Walter Fitzrauf, the great traveler of whom you have been hearing such remarkable reports."

Queen Eleanor smiled and held out her hand for Walter to kiss. "I esteem it a pleasure to meet a man of such daring and enterprise," she said. She spoke Norman French, but with a soft accent which made the language of the court sound even more pleasantly on the ear. To the King she added: "My little Estelle pointed Sir Walter out to me last evening. I had a good look at him then, I confess. You and I, my lord and king, have also been to the East, and on that account I felt a special interest. But I was not alone in it. I saw how often the eyes of everyone turned in his direction."

The King motioned to a near-by chair. "Stand not on ceremony," he said to Walter. "In fact, stand not at all. We have little liking, my *chérie reine* and I, for the tiresome bowing and shuffling which we must endure so much."

When Walter had hesitantly placed himself in the chair indicated, the ruler proceeded at once to the point of the summons. "I have been inquiring about your great Roger Bacon and getting a perplexing variety of answers. It seems to be generally believed that he is leagued with the devil, and my sober bishops pull long faces and say he is in very bad odor at Rome. May I whisper in your ear that this is not altogether against him? Also I have heard mention of certain methods of teaching he uses which seem to have good sense. It is said that he can produce thunder and destruction from hazel twigs, which must be the burning powder of which you spoke yesterday.

"I am of a mind to agree with you on the whole," he went on. "Such a bold and adventurous mind should not be shackled in darkness. For your ear alone, I have this to say: I shall make some approaches and see if his release can be brought about."

"My liege, I can find no words to express my gratitude and my relief," said Walter fervently. "I have seen Roger Bacon twice only, and yet I am strongly convinced of his greatness. It will be hard to curb my impatience for the day when I can tell him of the things I observed in Cathay."

The King laughed. "Then you will suffer in your impatience for a long period," he said. "The passing of letters across the seas takes an infinity of time. It may be a matter of years. But you may rest assured that your wonder-working friar will emerge in due course from the durance in which he is now held."

Queen Eleanor had finished her breakfast. She dipped her hands, which were small and white, in a water laver and then dried them carefully. The King watched her with a tender smile.

Then he squared around suddenly. "Your part of the country has been causing me much concern," he said to Walter. "The villeins have shown a rebellious spirit. Not that they are to be blamed entirely. The house of Bulaire has not recognized the King's justice but has seemed determined to set up laws of its own. This," he cried, "cannot be tolerated any longer!"

"All right-thinking men have been hoping you would intervene, my liege."

Edward gave him a shrewd glance of appraisal. "A strong hand is needed at Bulaire to restore order and justice. It is much to be desired that the countess will wed again. I have been hearing things, Sir Walter. I am glad of this opportunity to say that I see great advantages in a match between you and the Lady Engaine."

"Edward!" said the Queen, in her gently modulated voice.

"Yes, my sweeting?" The King's voice carried the merest hint of a consciousness of guilt.

"You made me a promise, my fair lord."

"I am not forgetting it, *chérie reine.*"

"I know you have not forgotten." She had picked up an embroidery frame, and her fingers were now busy with needle and yarn. "But is it possible you are a little hasty in voicing an approval which might be construed as a command?"

"The matter lies not in my hands. The lady, being a widow, is free to make her own choice. I am sure, my heart, that you agree with me on the advantages of such a match. You think well of the countess."

"She is very beautiful," answered the Queen quietly.

Edward waited for her to continue. When she added no further comment, he asked, "Is that all you are going to say?"

The Queen seemed to have become completely absorbed in her task. She held the frame up to the light and studied the partly worked pattern. "It is a lovely design," she said thoughtfully. "But I am afraid I see certain faults in it. They will be very difficult to correct." Then she glanced contritely at her royal spouse. "Forgive me, fair lord. You asked a question?"

Edward gave vent to a laugh with a grumbling undertone. "The Queen of England is incurably romantic," he said to Walter. "She was much taken with what I was able to tell her of your marriage to the girl of the East. I promised her she would hear the whole story from your own lips."

"I may have been mistaken, my lord and husband, but it was my understanding I would hear this very romantic story before there was any discussion of—of other matters." The Queen smiled at Walter over the embroidery frame with which her fingers were again busily engaged. "I should like to hear it very much. Are we likely to have a better opportunity than the present?"

Edward settled back in his chair and spread out his long legs. He said, in a resigned tone, "You might as well get on with it, Sir Walter."

It required much prompting on the part of the royal consort to elicit the whole story. Walter's tongue stumbled at the start, but with the aid of her questions he found himself telling of Maryam's escape from the slave train, of the long time she played the part of a servant in his tent, and finally of the curious turn of events which had thrown them together again. He was reluctant to speak of their life in the Abode of Everlasting Felicity, but his royal inquisitor would permit of no scamping. She continued to ply him with verbal promptings which brought out the pattern of their days in the imperial palace and made clear how happy and devoted they had been.

The frame had fallen into the Queen's lap. She was watching him with the deepest absorption.

"Was she so very beautiful?"

"Yes, liege lady. She was smaller, perhaps, than most English women. Her hair was very dark, but she had blue eyes, a heritage from her father."

"I need not ask you about her qualities of heart. Her courage and her steadfastness of spirit have spoken for themselves. I have found it truly a most charming and romantic story." She gave the King a quick side glance. "You agree with me, fair lord?"

Edward nodded without any great show of enthusiasm. The Queen then propounded the question which, clearly, had been on the tip of her tongue from the start.

"If a miracle should bring this Maryam of yours to England, what then?"

"She is my wife, liege lady."

"You would consider yourself bound to her? You would have no thought of seeking a release from the bond in order to make another match? A more advantageous match?"

Before Walter could reply, the King sat up in his chair again and said in an aggrieved tone: "You are an overzealous advocate, my sweeting. How resolutely you have set about the spoiling of my plans!"

"But, Edward, I had reservations about these plans of yours." The

Queen had resumed her work. "I have read the answer to my question in our young knight's eyes."

"It is in your mind that I should have begun at the other end of things. Well, Eleanor, I might as well tell him now."

"Yes, Edward."

There was something in the King's manner which suggested a schoolboy detected in a fault. Nevertheless he reached over and patted her arm with a loving hand. "How firmly you believe in the sanctity of the wedding tie, my Eleanor! Still you may be right; you so often are. I shall now strive to make amends for my headlong approach."

He got to his feet and walked over to Walter with long strides. "A very odd story has come to my ears. A courier arrived from London last night with these papers and brought the story with him. It is probably of no consequence, a mere coincidence, but—well, you should know of it. My fair spouse is sure it means——" He paused to give the Queen a smile. "But I shall tell you the story first. For the past three days a woman has been seen continuously on the streets of London. She walks up and down, calling a man's name. Apparently she can speak no word that our good burghers understand. All London is full of talk about it, and crowds of idle fellows have taken to following her about."

Walter had sprung to his feet in turn. The words of the Queen were racing through his mind: "If a miracle should bring this Maryam of yours to England . . ." Could it be that the miracle had happened? Had Maryam found her way to London in search of him? It seemed utterly impossible, and yet a wild hope was tugging at his heartstrings.

"My liege lord," he stammered, "does it appear that she has come from the East?"

"It is believed so."

"And the name she calls?"

"It can in truth be no more than a coincidence, though my fair spouse is only too eager to think otherwise. The name she cries is 'Walter.'"

All sense of courtly etiquette deserting him, Walter cried in an exultant voice: "Then it is Maryam! I am sure of it! The miracle has come to pass. God and St. Aidan, it is true!"

The Queen nodded her head and gave him a smile which almost matched his in elation. "I am certain of it also. Your Maryam is in London and seeking you."

The King was still unwilling to share their conviction. "By the Rood," he said, "there are many hundreds of men in London named Walter, and women with good reason for finding them. I very much fear we have roused hopes in you which will lead to nothing but disappoint ment. Still it may be wise to get to the bottom of it. It is an interruption to a plan that I have very much at heart; but now that I have had time for consideration, I shall be well content if it is your wife from the East. It would make the necessary measures quicker and easier."

"Edward, Edward!" said the Queen, shaking her head at him. "Have you lost all belief in the permanence of true love? Come, put his mind at rest. Tell him the rest so he can be sure."

"The rest? There is nothing more to tell, save that the woman is always accompanied by a black servant."

"Now I can indeed be sure!" said Walter. "The black servant can be none other than our faithful Mahmoud who accompanied us all the way from Antioch to Kinsai."

Queen Eleanor looked first at the King and then at Walter. Her eyes were shining mistily. "There is to be a happy ending to the story after all. I suspect, fair lord, that your plans have indeed suffered an interruption. One that will bring them to nought."

Edward shook his head slowly from side to side. "I am King of England," he said. "And yet what a demonstration this has been of the way my authority can be disregarded! I begin to fear I am a henpecked man." He started to laugh then and dropped an arm over Walter's shoulder. "The matter has been taken out of my hands, it seems. Still I have some shreds of power left. You have my permission to leave for London at once."

"At once!" said the Queen urgently. Then she proceeded to show that doubt on one point lingered in her mind. "Tarry not to speak to— to anyone."

CHAPTER XIX

The Sign of the Merrytotter

THE YELLOW DRAGON was a down-at-heels inn within a stone's throw of the Tower. Attracted by the name, Walter left his lathered horse in the care of a groom and sought the landlord within.

"Aye, master," affirmed the publican, in response to his urgent questioning. "The woman passed here not more as two hours agone. She wur shouting 'Will! Will!' at top o' lungs and she went on to St. Nic'las Shambles."

Walter's heart sank at these words, but he took fresh courage when a clamor of denials drowned out the landlord. The speakers were all sure it was "Walter" she cried, except one dullard, who stank of the tannery and who stood out stubbornly for "Alf'ud." They disagreed also as to the course she had taken. One said she had last been seen near the Eye Bourne close to Westminster. A second was sure she had stopped at Frere Pye Gardens, a third was clamorously positive she had crossed London Bridge and disappeared in the maze back of Bermondsey Cross.

He paced the streets feverishly for two hours, asking questions of everyone he met, until finally the fall of darkness made further search hopeless. He then made his way through deserted roads to the Sign of the Merrytotter.

Conand's Elspie met him at the door. In all the times he had visited the house he had never come face to face with this unfailing producer of grandchildren. Once he had heard her fleeing his approach by way of the outside stairway in a panic of diffidence, and on another occasion he had caught a glimpse of her back disappearing through a door. Trapped by his unexpected arrival, her broad face went white. She emitted a loud "A-a-ah!" of consternation and then turned and ran to the back of the house.

It was Anne, now quite leggy and more sure of herself than ever, who did the honors. She dropped a curtsy and said in even tones: "I hope you will not laugh at my mother, my lord. Grandfather says no one must laugh at her even if she is such a goose. Did you want my grandfather?"

"Yes, Anne. I must see him as soon as possible. It is most urgent."

"But my grandfather has gone out. I don't know when he will come back, my lord. He has gone in search of a woman who cries in the streets. She must be a funny woman, my lord, as funny as my mother."

Walter felt a slight sense of relief. "Your grandfather knows the city so well he is certain to find her," he said to the small girl. "I shall see you receive a present for being the one to tell me."

The child's eyes opened wide at this. "A ribbon for my hair?" she asked.

He began to pace about the room, his intensity of mood making it impossible to relax even in view of the very good possibility that Joseph would be successful in his quest. He was realizing as never before how large London was, how many dark streets it contained and how many retreats it offered for visitors of limited means. Perhaps Joseph would fail after all. As he walked up and down, a prey to his forebodings, he heard the child prattling about the red ribbon she was to receive and the new cloak her grandfather would have to get for her to go with it.

He thought of starting out again and crying "Maryam!" from one end of London to the other, but decided it would be wiser to wait until Joseph returned. If Maryam had been found, he must not be away when she reached the house.

When he heard Joseph's voice at the door, he rushed forward, crying, "Have you found her?"

Joseph shook his head. "No, my lord Walter. But set your mind at rest, I will find her tomorrow. Bright and early I will bring her to ye."

"Tomorrow may be too late!" cried Walter. "Anything might happen to her in the meantime."

The look of concern deepened on Joseph's honest face. "There is nought we can do tonight," he said. "Every honest house in town is closed up and barred. We could shout ourselves hoarse and no 'un would pay us any heed." He added, in a more reassuring tone: "I sent my stout Toby off to Gurnie today, my lord. He was to bring ye on at once to Lunnon. I am well convinced it is your lady. I had been away, and it was not till this morning I saw her. Great dotterel that I am, I gave no serious thought to it until she had vanished. It wur only then I put two and two together. She is not tall and she has blue eyes. A big heathen, with the blackest skin I ever set eyes on, wur with her."

Walter's state of mind was such that any shadow of doubt could disturb him. "Mahmoud is not big," he said, with a shake of the head.

"It's more as three years since ye've seen him. Don't the heathen grow same as Christians?" Joseph nodded with complete confidence now. "We'll find her tomorrow. All my stout lads are to stop work for the day, and I'll give each one a district. They know their Lunnon, and they'll run her down as sure as hunting dogs after a nye of pheasants."

Walter began to pace the room again in a mood which refused all proffers of comfort.

"I can't believe it yet, Joseph," he said. "Have you any idea of the distance from Cathay? You could go from London to Gurnie a hundred times and still be no more than halfway. My brave Maryam! If she has really accomplished this miracle, it has been because our Father sent His angels down to help her on her way!"

"It is said as she shows signs o' weariness. Her voice was fresh when she first started, but now it's getting weak. Crowds has took to following her about, and they're not as friendly now as at first. A baker says the heathen stole a loaf o' bread from him."

Walter's apprehensions were getting greater all the time. "She will be completely at the end of her resources. Joseph, I know I shall go crazy with this delay! Where is she tonight? Hungry, cold, tired! Sleeping in some uncomfortable hole! I won't be able to sleep for thinking of her." He shook his head despondently as he thought about the story of the stolen loaf. "They must be in dire want if Mahmoud is back at his old tricks."

"There is a round of cold beef in the house, my lord. Things'll look better on a full stummick."

"*They* may have no supper tonight!" cried Walter. "I would not be able to swallow a bite. Joseph, promise me we will make an early start."

"My stout lads'll be off the leash by the hour o' prime," said the ex-squire.

Walter found a room in a tavern close at hand. The common room was filled, and the noise that rose from it made the possibility of sleep still more remote. The moon had come out, and he sat at his window, looking with somber eyes over the huddled rooftops.

London by day was a cheerful place, but by night it took on a sinister aspect. In his troubled state of mind he imagined that the moon just above him was seeking out the dangers which lurked in black alleys and secluded courts, the secrets hidden behind the crow-stepped gables of the shuttered houses, the evil that stalked, hand on ready knife, in the streets; and, perhaps, trying to give warning of them. It was maddening to think that Maryam was alone in this city of fear and menace.

Once he started, thinking he had heard a cry of "Walter" in the street below. He threw open the sash and leaned out, holding his breath in eagerness. It became clear at once, however, that it was only some belated roisterer piping a drunken greeting to another prowler in the dark. "Twelf' clock, and if all's well I'm the Pope o' Rome!" came the answer, with a loud laugh.

"It may be as hard to find her here as in Kinsai," he said to himself. "Maryam, if it is indeed you, where are you? What unhappy thoughts are in your mind? Have you given up hope after all these weary days?"

He closed the windows and lay down on his lumpy and far from fresh bed. As he had expected, he did not sleep a wink that night.

2

It was late the next afternoon when little Anne, who had stationed herself in an upper window, cried out in an excited treble: "I hear my grandfather's voice. He is very pleased, for he is talking fast."

After fruitless hours spent in the heart of the city, hours of frantic questioning and listening to suggestions and running down rumors about Maryam's whereabouts which proved to be wrong in all cases, Walter had returned to the Sign of the Merrytotter to see if anything had been heard from the other searchers. He did not pause to question the child, but was out of the house in a trice.

His eyes lighted first on the triumphant figure of Joseph in the van of a procession nearly half a block long. The ex-squire was tossing his hat in the air as he walked, like a minstrel or troubadour in advance of an army returning from battle, and his face was wreathed with smiles. Towering inches above him was one of his grandsons, and immediately after them stalked a figure in a soiled burnoose, which flapped against his black shanks, and a turban concealing a large part of his face. This ebony apparition was leading a small boy by the hand. Next in line, and walking with a perceptible limp, was a woman in white. She was closely surrounded by curious townspeople, and at first Walter could not catch more than a momentary glimpse of her face. The line of her cheek stirred memories. He could not be sure if it was his imagination or not, but his heart began to pound. She was turning her head in all directions with an expectancy that refused to be daunted, and, perhaps by force of habit, she called once in a weary voice, "Walter!" It was not his imagination this time; it was the voice he had heard so often in a garden in Kinsai, strained and weak now but with the same sweet timbre! All doubt left him. With a sudden and overwhelming realization that the miracle had come to pass, he cried, "Maryam!" and began to force his way frantically through the knots of people who had gathered to watch the strange procession pass.

Joseph saw him and called out, "There's no manner o' doubt about it, my lord Walter, it's yer lady." If Walter heard, he made no answer. He was keeping his eyes fixed on the slender, drooping figure as he worked his way forward, the blood pounding exultantly in his veins. There! He had caught a full glimpse of her face. It was thin and pale, and her eyes seemed larger. He laughed aloud in the infinite relief of complete recognition.

"Maryam!" he cried again.

She stopped and looked about her with raised head in suddenly revived hope. Then she saw him. For a moment she remained perfectly still, as though unable yet to believe her eyes. Her face took on an ecstatic look then, and, dropping a small bundle she was carrying, she began to run toward him.

"Walter! Walter! At last I have found you!"

Her strength was exhausted when they met, and it was a limp burden that he gathered up in his arms. He was so filled with delight that he wanted to shout out in praise of the divine dispensation which had brought them together again. The next instant, however, he realized that her head had fallen motionless on his shoulder.

"Make way!" he shouted, urgently. "Out of my road! The lady is ill."

He heard a familiar voice close at hand, babbling, "Masser! Masser!" and, in spite of his desperate hurry to reach the house, he looked back over his shoulder into a broadly grinning black face.

"Mahmoud!" he said. "So you found me after all, my fine, faithful fellow!"

"Yes, masser. Long way we come."

Then Walter discovered that it was difficult to move. A weight had attached itself to one of his legs. With considerable effort, he managed to turn his head and look down. A small boy had wrapped one arm and both legs about him and was pounding at him furiously with the other arm.

"Mahmoud!" he called, in some perplexity. "I seem to be in difficulties here. Pull me free of this angry young fellow."

Mahmoud forced the boy to break his hold and then hoisted him up, still struggling and weeping, to his shoulder.

"Masser boy," he said, grinning broadly. "He afraid you carry his mother off."

"His mother!" Walter turned a look of utter amazement on the servant. "Mahmoud, what do you mean? It cannot be——"

Mahmoud nodded, and his grin spread clear across his face. "Yes, masser. Big surprise. Son of family, this. Fine boy, masser. Nearly three year."

Walter found himself incapable of motion. He stared again at the servant and then at his son who was struggling to get down from his high perch; for the purpose, clearly, of going again to his mother's assistance.

"He is my son!" he said to himself. "It is hard enough to believe my wife has been restored to me. But this! This passes belief!"

"Yer lady has fainted," said the voice of Joseph at his shoulder. "Ye should get her inside at once."

Walter looked down at the head resting against his arm. Maryam's eyes were closed, and her lashes looked very long and dark against the pallor of her thin cheeks. He could not be sure she was breathing, and a wave of fear swept over him that she might still be taken away from him. Stretching out his free arm, he began to battle a way through the clustering onlookers.

"She is very ill, Joseph," he said, his anxiety crowding everything else from his mind, even the unexpected existence of a three-year-old son. "How light she is! I can carry her so easily that I—I begin to fear the worst."

Joseph, who was helping to clear a path for them, looked back with a reassuring smile. "Good food and plenty o' rest is all she needs," he said cheerfully. "Conand's Elspie will have a pot o' soup on the fire. It'll bring her around fast."

"God grant you are right!"

They reached the door under the swaying sign, and Walter paused for a moment to look back.

"I am told that is my son," he said, in a voice so full of awe that it was very little above a whisper. "I am not yet sure I can believe it. This must all be a dream." His voice broke. "A wonderful dream, Joseph."

"There was no need for me to be told, my lord," declared the ex-squire. "One glance at that fine fellow and I knew him for yer son. He's the living image o' ye and my lord Rauf; though I swear I can see a look o' my old comrade, Wat Stander, about him too. And what a high spirit! How he did pitch into ye!"

Conand's Elspie emerged from her seclusion to take charge. She placed Maryam on one of the huge beds in a back room and forced a sip of strong wine between her lips. Then she began to chafe the thin wrists, whispering in solicitous tones: "There, poor wee lamb! You are so pretty, so very pretty, my lady!" While engaged in these ministrations, she kept her head lowered, being particularly careful not to allow herself the presumption of catching Walter's eye.

The latter stood beside the bed and watched the still form of his wife with such apprehension that Joseph finally demanded that he also drink some of the wine. Walter did so, but without letting his gaze wander for as much as a second.

"Do you think she will be all right, Joseph?"

"Of course, my lord. See, there's color in her cheeks already."

True enough, the patient's breathing had become steadier, and the faintest suggestion of color could be seen in her cheeks. Walter sat down on the side of the bed and lifted one of her hands. It was no longer cold. He glanced at Joseph and nodded happily.

There was a weak flutter of the eyelashes, and her eyes opened slowly. They remained fixed on Walter's face with an expression that told him she was trying to believe this was not a part of the darkness and confusion from which she was emerging.

"Walter," she whispered. "You are really there? It was not a dream, then?"

"It is not a dream, my Maryam," he said, bending over and taking her other hand. "You are home at last, beloved! It took me a long time also to believe it was anything but a dream." He paused and leaned closer. "How are you feeling now?"

"Better, Walter."

Joseph interrupted to say, "I think my lady needs food."

Maryam tried to protest when Conand's Elspie brought in a bowl of soup and held out a spoonful of it to her. Walter said that she must try it and placed an arm behind her shoulders to raise her higher. She allowed her head to rest on his arm in perfect content to have once more its protection and support. Her eyes smiled up at him tremulously.

"It will do you good, Taffy," he said. He allowed his arm to tighten about the frail shoulders. "Come, try a little of it."

Maryam was loath to take her eyes away, but she complied after a moment. The warmth of the soup proved grateful, and she sighed and said: "You are right, Walter. It is very good."

He took over the feeding then, making a loving ceremony of each motion of his arm. After several mouthfuls, however, she shook her head. "That is enough, I think. I will finish it later."

Walter let her sink back on the pillow but did not remove his arm. Bending over until his lips touched her ear, he whispered: "I am so happy, and yet I can't say any of the things I want you to hear."

"There will be time—later—to hear them." It was such an effort to speak that she said nothing more and let her eyes convey something of what she herself was leaving unsaid.

"I have missed you so terribly," he went on after several moments. "I did not know what to do. The whole world was between us."

She nodded slowly. "I know, Walter. You—you couldn't have found me. I had to find you." She paused for more breath. "It would have been —so much easier if you had taught me more than those two words I knew."

"Walter and London. You seem to have made good use of them, my dear one."

She did not say anything more for a long time. Then, "They brought me all the way to England, my Walter."

"I will not cease to marvel at it as long as I live."

"I thought—near the end—that I would never finish it. I was very sick, and I had given up hope. But the God you had told me so much about gave me the strength. And so I came."

Conand's Elspie brought in bowls of soup for the boy and Mahmoud, who fell to work with every evidence of appreciation and enjoyment. The newly united lovers knew this only from the sound, for their eyes still refused to part. They were having an emotional feast of their own; for long moments they would gaze at each other with a deep intensity, then they would smile and nod and smile again, and finally, as though rounding out a cycle, they would find themselves simultaneously in the act of blinking hard to hold back the tears of a great happiness.

Finally Maryam motioned to him to bend his head down close to hers. "I think," she whispered, "that now you should go and speak to your son."

Walter got up and crossed the room. He looked down at the boy, who had finished his soup and was sitting quietly on the floor.

"What is your name?" he asked, speaking in Greek.

"I am Walter."

"Walter? Of course! I would have been very much disappointed if it had been anything else. You are the third Walter, and we hope there will be many more of them, in a direct line, all Walters of Gurnie. Have you any other names?"

The boy shook his head as though puzzled at the question. "I am Walter," he said.

"Then we must see to it that you have others when you are baptized. Alfgar for my grandfather, and Edward for our great king, and Rauf for your own grandfather. Walter Alfgar Edward Rauf Fitzrauf. Now that will indeed be a fine name for a small boy!"

After a moment of silence, the proud father asked, "Would you like to go over and speak to your mother, my son?"

The boy nodded quickly. Walter picked him up and tossed him high in the air. The boy smiled, for the first time, and kicked his heels, which clearly was a sign that he had decided he was going to like this tall stranger after all.

When the pair of them were seated on the side of the bed, Walter holding his son on his knee, Maryam smiled at them with an impartiality of love. "I hope you like the gift I brought you," she said.

"He is a splendid fellow, our small son. What a great fighter he is going to be! Just like his two grandfathers. My mind is full of plans for him already. And for us, Maryam."

She smiled again and said, with a faint show of her old spirit: "What a very long way I had to come in search of honorable runaway husband!"

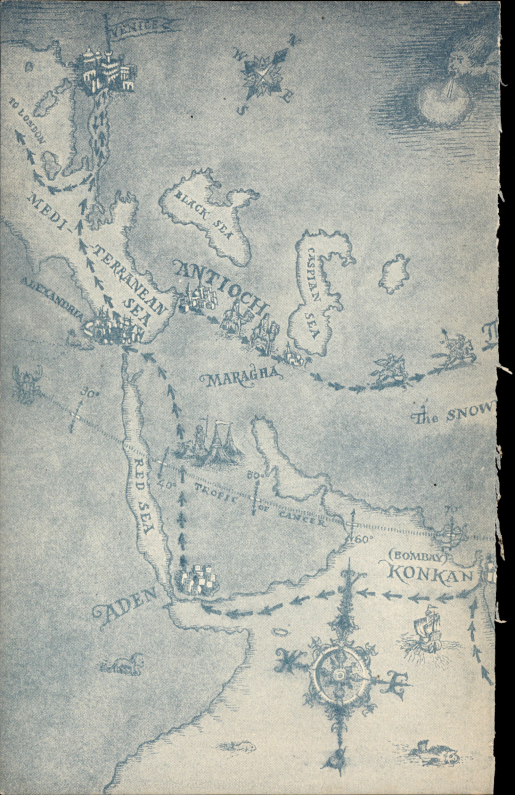